# ONE *Killer* NIGHT

# OTHER TITLES BY TRILINA PUCCI

## Romantic Comedies

*Tangled in Tinsel*

*Knot so Lucky*

*Three Ways to Mend a Broken Heart*

## Prep School Romance

*Filthy Little Pretties*

*Vicious Little Snakes*

*The Scandalous Series*

## Forbidden Love Dark Romance

*Just like Heaven*

*Sinning like Hell*

*The Star-Crossed Series*

Dark Mafia Books

*Truth*

*Worship*

*Depraved*

TRILINA PUCCI

This is a work of fiction. Names, characters, organizations, places, events, and incidents are either products of the author's imagination or are used fictitiously. Otherwise, any resemblance to actual persons, living or dead, is purely coincidental.



Published by Montlake, Seattle
www.apub.com



EU product safety contact:
Amazon Media EU S. à r.l.
38, avenue John F. Kennedy, L-1855 Luxembourg
amazonpublishing-gpsr@amazon.com

ISBN-13: 9781662531811 (paperback)
ISBN-13: 9781662531828 (digital)

Cover design by Caroline Teagle Johnson
Cover image: © Anton Porkin, © appleuzr, © Designer, © Dimitris66, © greyj / Getty; © Paper Wings, © A_KUDR, © Anna_leni / Shutterstock

Printed in the United States of America

*For Grandma.*
*Thank you for expecting me to shoot for the stars. I hope I made you proud.*

Dear reader,

The location for this book is heavily inspired by one of my favorite cities in the world, Boston, and then whimsically entangled with my second-favorite town, Stars Hollow. So, if you're looking for correct GPS directions in your romance, you will be sorely disappointed. You'll also be disappointed if you think there's a calendar where all these dates align. It's fiction, we're leaning in. Now, let the fun begin.

# Playlist

*Murder on the Dancefloor—Sophie Ellis-Bextor*

*Black Hole Sun—Soundgarden*

*Should I Stay or Should I Go—The Clash*

*These Dreams—Heart*

*Psycho Killer—Talking Heads*

*Late Night Talking—Harry Styles*

*Juke Box Hero—Foreigner*

*Not Like Us—Kendrick Lamar*

*I Love You, Please Don't Hate Me—Sam Fischer*

*Crazy on You—Heart*

*The Summoning—Sleep Token*

# PROLOGUE

Running. That's all there was.

That, and the sound of broken tree limbs that bounced off the forest walls mixing with the cries still falling from her lips.

Her heart thudded, strumming a frantic rhythm of absolute fear as she ran with four boys. They tore past the trees, marking up their hands and looking over their shoulders, until they emerged into the camp's clearing. A fork in the road.

"Where do we go? What do we do?" the girl said breathlessly, her voice still laden with her crying.

"Fuck. Fuck. Fuck. We're gonna die here," one of the boys rushed out, running his hands through his hair as they stood in a group.

"Shut up. We're not dying," another said.

She felt one of them hold her hand, and it made her wipe her eyes trying to make the river stop flowing, but it wouldn't.

"We have to find a place to hide. Somewhere he won't think to look," the tallest of the boys said.

"What are you talking about? He's gonna find us . . . You saw what he did. He sliced Mikey's throat open . . . He choked on his own blood."

The nervous boy panicked again. She couldn't stop panicking either. Not after what she'd seen. Her eyes closed as sobs began to wrack her body. The image of flesh opening and blood spilling out imprisoned her senses.

She swore the smell of blood still stank with every intake of breath.

"We have to split up," one of them barked. "That's our best chance." Her eyes popped open as that boy walked backward away from the group, shaking his head and shrugging. "If he kills one of you, then that buys me time to get away. I'm sorry. It's every man for themselves."

"No," she whispered, meaning for it to be louder, but it was too late—he was already running toward the mess hall.

The wind blew, but that's not what made their heads turn in every direction. *He* was coming for them, and he'd do to them what he'd done to the one they'd left behind.

She felt her hand being squeezed before blue eyes connected with hers. "I'll protect you. We'll stay together. Everything's going to be okay."

She nodded, but a wicked crack of a tree branch turned their heads again, and the four of them knew *he* was here.

"Oh my god," she whispered to herself.

They'd be picked off one by one.

"Go, go, go," the tall boy urged the one holding her hand. She tugged it so she could make her move. "Hide at the boathouse."

Her body trembled, as if it knew they would die tonight, but they were running again—until every hair on her body stood and her skin prickled, their feet skidding to a stop.

A bloodcurdling scream was the only sound to pierce the heavens as death occupied the face caught in front of them. His body sank slowly to the ground as his last breath foreshadowed their future. A monster stood before them, wiping his knife over his sleeve.

"There's no running from me."

# Chapter One

## Goldie

***Present day, Halloween***

"Wait. What the heck are you? I can't tell."

My sister, Evie, smiles as she wiggles a bloody severed finger at me through FaceTime. It's doubtful she can see my returning smile through the minuscule mesh cutout in my blow-up costume, but that doesn't stop me.

"What it looks like." I tilt my floppy, oversize head while awkwardly trying to prop my phone against a can of hair spray on a rack in the middle of the Walgreens, before I back up, making a swish, swish, swish sound. "I'm a large theropod. Also known as the OG of predators." I spin my tiny arms around quickly before holding them open like I'm saying "Ta-da."

"I'm a muthafuggin' T. rex."

"Nuhhhoooo. You're such a nerd. But you even have little claws." She laughs. "That's amazing."

"Who needs a sexy cat costume when you can have a little fan inside to keep your booty cool. It's the twenty-first century. Comfort over cute all day, every day."

My laughter joins hers before she claps her hands together, trying to get us back on track. We tend to veer in every conversation we have.

"Okay, focus. I need as much blood as they have. Buy it all. I can't believe I ran out. Uh, gawd, Golds, I really want to make a good impression on these guys. New kid knocks it out of the park and all. Ya know?"

I'm nodding, but I don't think my big dino head is moving, so I blurt out, "Yeah, Eves, I get it, and I got you. What are big sisters for? Plus, you're the most creative special effects wizard in the city of Boston. That company is lucky to have you. Stop worrying. You've already got the job."

"You're right. As usual. Also, I'll pay you back tonight, so get as much as you can."

"Evie. I've been out of work for two days—it's not desperate times just yet. I can swing some Walgreens blood."

As her lips part to respond, her eyebrows shoot up, too, like she's had a brand-new thought, before she suddenly disappears from the screen, yelling.

"Goldie. Oh my god. You have to see the head. After I drained it, it turned out so good. Literally, epic. I'm so glad I chopped it off."

I chuckle under my breath, looking around the shelves for the fake blood, because if anyone were to overhear this, they'd probably call the cops. I'm suddenly imagining me, as a dinosaur, explaining that my sister made a fake dead body and then decided to use it for her company's annual Halloween party.

She's dressing as Wednesday, holding Uncle Fester's head; there's even a light bulb in his mouth. It's diabolical.

The sound of things falling in her apartment draws my eyes just as her butt comes back into the frame.

"Ooh, I'm excited to see your headless uncle," I joke, but before she says anything, the gruesome creation's dead eyes are staring back at me.

Holy cheese and crackers. Wait, did I gasp?

My head whips to the side, blood instantly draining from my face.

Oh god. No . . . It wasn't me.

Two of the most precious senior citizens—I'm talking about real Disney movie *Up* characters—are gaping at me wide eyed, ashen and horrified. The little cardigan-wearing husband's holding a bag of candy, probably for trick-or-treaters, as his eyes volley between the phone screen and me.

My mouth falls open, but nothing comes out. Not even the laugh that's stuck in my throat as I shake my head and jazz-hand my claws, but I'm pretty sure it looks like I'm about to attack because now they're backing up slowly, the wife's aged hand clutching her husband's forearm.

Jesus, Mary, and Joseph.

"Oh gosh, no, no, no . . . It's not what you think. We don't even have an uncle . . . It's just a nickname my sister had for the body . . ."

I'm stumbling over my words, rambling a hundred miles an hour, embarrassed and on-brand awkward while shuffling toward them, my tiny arms waving in front of me.

The old man drops the candy on the floor as he makes the sign of a cross over himself.

"Oh god," I rush out, intertwined with laughter, before righting myself back to serious. "No. I didn't mean—"

Evie cuts in loudly, "Sheesh. I miss the old guy. Good ole Unc. Too bad he had to go, but that's what happens when you do bad things. Like buy the mini Snickers instead of the full size. Amirite?"

She makes a slicing motion across her throat, along with an evil laugh, and all three of us look down at the candy on the floor . . . minis.

I'll kill her.

Or, more likely, go to jail for murder since Pop-Pop and Mimi are as white as ghosts. For a hot second, as we stand in the most awkward silence, I think there's a chance they might actually yell for help.

Sweet little Betty White finally looks at her husband as if to say, *Let's get out of here. These girls are unhinged.*

And you know what? Fair.

But I try to fix things anyway. I raise my voice to their backs as they turn, swinging my tiny arm back and forth between the phone and myself. "She's lying and a horrible person. But not like murderer horrible. Just regular awful . . . We didn't kill anyone. I swear. It's fake."

My sister's cackling as I flop my blown-up dome down and cover my face with my three claws before I hiss "What is wrong with you?" as I look back at the screen. "They looked like they wanted to call the cops. What would I have done? Run? I'm pretty sure the cops would've been able to hear me at least halfway down the block. Either that or the friction from this suit would've set me on fire."

Evie's hands muffle her giggling, but she still manages to get an eye roll out of me.

"Come on. I'm supposed to ignore the opportunity for comedic gold? The bit presented itself. It was my obligation to accept it." I reach for the zipper of my costume to free my head as she adds, "But no more super-fun distractions. Just hurry, 'kay? I need bluuhd."

"Yes, psycho," I breathe out. "I'm on it. I will haul dino ass the whole five blocks."

She hangs up as my shoulders shake. I clear my throat quietly while, out of my periphery, I notice someone new coming around the aisle, but I'm already mid-swish-swish back to my phone. But I don't get a look at whoever's approaching because as I reach out, my polyester claws make me clumsy, and my big blown-up fingers knock my phone sideways, plummeting it straight off the shelf.

"Noooooo—"

I'm squealing my plea to the phone gods as it dives toward the floor in what feels like a dramatic slow-motion reenactment of "fuck around and find out."

Gah, why didn't I take my hand out of the costume?

To drive that point home, the piercing smack against the floor forces my eyes closed and my soul into deep cracked-screen pain.

I grunt as I bend over, not caring about who's watching.

Which is exactly the opposite of what the Lord intended for this costume because the head grows taller and pops back over my real one. Since I'm not zipped, my face lands somewhere around the neck, leaving me in the dark while I try and swipe the floor with my teeny freaking arms.

"Dammit," I grit out, swishing louder and louder, not reaching anything, just grabbing at air like a jackass, looking a lot like Chris Farley in *Tommy Boy* when he put the coat on that was too small.

"I hate you," I groan, talking to the costume while trying to move myself to a better position. But because my life brand has suddenly become "hot mess," my tail hits a shelf, knocking a bunch of stuff onto the floor.

"No wonder I went extinct," I mutter before I jerk back up with a heavy whoosh of a breath. My dino head flops halfway off before I'm soul-shatteringly arrested.

Frozen.

Like cemented in place.

Oh. My. God.

Standing tall enough to force my chin up is a drool-worthy neck tattoo attached to the first and hopefully last hallucination I'll ever have because if I'm dying, he's definitely heaven. My lips part and then shut before repeating the process as my lashes flutter a bit too fast, maybe to keep time with how my heart rate just picked up.

A pair of sapphire eyes so boldly accessorized by the dreamiest olive skin stare back at me. Not to mention a jawline that makes me want to see him get angry, just so I can watch it tic. He runs his hand through effortlessly sexy charcoal black bed head hair before he smirks.

This man cannot be real. Except it kind of feels like I've seen him before.

"Damon?" I whisper, my thoughts tumbling out faster than my mouth can stop them.

Oh my god . . . I just said that aloud. I called him the *Vampire Diaries* guy's name.

Before I can enter into evidence a defense plea of mentally unfit, his voice washes over me, deep and rich, like the embodiment of luxury—or velvet—or something else that feels insanely sexy.

"No . . . Noah, but I do have a brother named Stefan."

My eyes pop open. "You do?"

He scrapes his teeth over his bottom lip, letting it glide out slowly before shaking his head no.

I have to curl my pout in over my teeth to hide my embarrassment, still feeling the burn in my cheeks, as he bends to swipe my phone off the floor.

Jesus, he's the hottest guy I've ever seen in my whole life. And I'm dressed like a flipping dinosaur. Amazing.

My hands work quickly and of their own accord, shoving the costume off my head and smoothing my errant hair because I'm not thinking, at least not with my brain. No, that's malfunctioning as I swallow hard, watching him straighten to his six-foot, I'd-have-your-babies height.

His eyes glimmer with amusement as I swallow down my dignity.

But still, we stand in silence, the Walgreens store playlist becoming our meet-cute score as our eyes stay indecently locked, just staring at each other, me on bated breath.

One blink. Two. Three.

Is that "These Dreams," by Heart? What in the eighties is going on here? Maybe I am actually hallucinating, and the universe is trying to clue me in.

He tilts his head, his blue eyes seductively shy, like a modern-day James Dean, dropping them away before meeting mine again. "Good news. It's not broken."

"Not broken is definitely good . . . great, even—"

I exhale quietly, trying to regain my cool, but his eyes stay locked on me, making me feel like when I was thirteen and saw Jesse McCartney for the first time.

That was my sexual awakening. Now, I'm thirty and wide awake. So, so awake. Insomnia-level awake.

He bites the inside of his lip, right at the corner, with just his canines, before he extends my phone and hits me with a full-watt smile.

And RIP to any common sense I had for my personal safety.

If this man wanted me to come see the kitten in his basement, I'd turn off my location and follow him there. Right now. Good god, he's gorgeous.

I reach to take it from his palm, but his eyes dart to my hand.

"Three fingers were problematic before, so maybe . . ." He trails off.

"Huh?" I look at my hand, realizing I'm still wearing the costume thing over it. "Oh yeah. You saw that? Awesome."

With an embarrassed huff of a laugh, I hurriedly tug off the hand covering with my teeth, shove the fabric back out of my mouth using my tongue, and let it fall to the ground.

But he catches it. Fuck. Why was that so hot?

I need to get it together. I'm acting like I've never seen a living man . . . albeit the most beautiful one ever to exist. *Still, stop it, Goldie.*

"Are you gonna make me do this all night?" he whispers conspiratorially, leaning in toward me and giving me my first dose of goose bumps. "I mean, I'm free, but . . ."

My nervous smile seems to cut him off because he stops talking and smiles back.

"No . . ." I reach out and take back my phone and costume piece, hoping for flirtatious and not weird. "Thank you . . . Noah, not Damon."

"My pleasure . . ." He pauses, sliding a hand over his jaw before hooking it around the back of his neck. His eyebrows rise, and I realize he's pausing slash asking for my name.

"Goldie," I rush out, uncaring if I seem too eager.

"Goldie . . ." he repeats to himself like he's trying it on for size. "I like that. So then, I guess it's my pleasure, Goldie."

He likes my name, so much so that he's said it twice. I'm cooked.

I grin, feeling my cheeks burn, our eyes still deliciously locked on each other like there's no choice in the matter.

You know in books when they say the air crackles between two characters? Well, we're a fucking bowl of cereal. Snap, crackle, and poppin' everywhere and all over the place.

*Ask me for my number, ask me for my number.*

Noah lifts his chin like he's going to say something, making my pulse stall, sprint, and stutter. His lips part as he reaches for his back pocket, his eyes still burning into mine with a glint of amusement or bewilderment. I can't tell.

All I know is that they're like two crystal-blue lakes that feel deep and inviting.

God, this eye contact is so intense that I should consider purchasing a pregnancy test along with my sister's blood. Oh shit. Evie!

"Crap. My sister! She needs blood."

"Where?" he rushes out, looking over his shoulder, but I'm already spinning back toward the shelf, a bit more flustered than when I started this journey.

I look back over my shoulder apologetically while simultaneously grabbing all the tubes of fake blood. Instantly, I realize I don't have a basket, so I just start shoving them down the neck of my costume, letting them fall all the way to my legs.

Screw it, I'll sort it out at the counter.

"Sorry. Not here. At her apartment. I was on a time crunch because of the decapitated head. From the dead body she made . . ."

The smile on his face hasn't left as he nods, even as he dives his hands into his front pockets and says, "Relatable. Um, soooo . . . okay." He points at my now-bulging dinosaur ankles. "I guess I'll leave you to your prehistoric shoplifting. It was nice meeting you."

No. Damn. I was doing the flirting thing so well. I'm mid-grab when very unqualified words tumble out because I can't let the guy let me get away. But what I'm doing, I don't know. This is cool-girl territory. I typically belong to a different region.

Fuck it. I've already almost killed an old couple from shock, embarrassed myself plenty in front of the hottest man alive, and I'll probably end up on YouTube, branded as a furry getting arrested for theft.

I literally have nothing to lose. I need to shoot my Jurassic shot.

I drop the last tube down the front of me and spin toward him.

"Hey, there's this party if you wanna come . . . I mean, you did say you're free. And I owe you for helping me out and all. Even though we're complete strangers, serendipitously meeting in aisle nine of Walgreens."

The look on his face is either wholly captivated by my charm or scared for his life, so I add, "Plus, you're already wearing a costume."

Neither of us even tries to hide our smiles as his eyes drop to his front because Noah is, in fact, wearing a jacket, jeans, and a T-shirt.

"We're in aisle twelve," he muses before rocking back on his heels. "You're a strange girl—"

On any other day, I might be insulted, but he says it like it makes him more curious about me. And I'll take it.

"—and honestly, it's fitting that something unexpected would happen to me tonight."

I shrug coyly, biting my lip. "So, I guess it's fate, then."

His Adam's apple bobs as he reaches into his back pocket again, pulls out his phone, and hands it over. I. Am. A legend.

"Put your number in?"

I can't stop the cyclone of butterflies in my stomach as I stare at the screen, typing in my information before I return his phone. He taps it against his palm, his face mirroring what I'm feeling before he reads what I've entered.

"Rexy . . . ? Didn't want to go with your name, huh?"

"Figured I'd cover my tracks just in case I got predatory later."

He laughs before quietly sucking in a breath through his teeth, his eyes dropping over my costume. Noah gives a small headshake before he turns and speaks over his shoulder.

"Have fun, Goldie. Don't get arrested." He holds up his phone. "I'll text you once I walk away—you know, so I seem cool and aloof."

I swish-swish back a few steps, my legs heavier because of all the bloody tubes inside my costume. But as I watch him walk away, I can't help myself, and I check out his ass. *Nice.*

The smile on my face grows because just as my eyes pop up, he glances back again, so I raise a claw, giving him a small wave, trying to act nonchalant and not like a perv.

"Yeah. I mean . . . I won't hold my breath because I'm also aloof and cool. So, like, cool, whatever."

Right on cue, I step on the stuff I knocked down earlier with my tail, tripping over my own feet before regaining my ground.

My hand slaps over my mouth to hide my giggle, and I smartly stand in place, watching him leave the whole rest of the way down the aisle until he turns the corner, out of sight.

Holy. Shit.

I can't help myself. My hands hit my knees as I give a little celebratory dino twerk because I freaking hate Halloween, always have, but tonight might just be the best night of my life. I barely get that thought out before the ding hits.

With zero regard for cool protocol, I scramble to look so fast that there's a decent chance I just gave myself whiplash. But it's my sister, which makes me scowl. Still, I refocus and hustle to the counter.

**Evie:** Are you on your way because your location says no

**Me:** Shush. I'm busy. I just met a

guy. Like a HOT guy

**Evie:** What!!!!! Did you get his number? If you say no, I'll make sure to add chicken shit to your headstone when you die.

In answer to her question, my phone dings again with an unknown number, and a smile bursts out over my face. I shake my leg faster, scooping everything up off the floor to get rung up quickly.

I swing my head around, looking for him. But he's nowhere to be seen, so I prop my foot up on the counter and motion with my eyebrows for the checker to grab the last of the tubes peeking out from my ankle as I swipe open the message.

**555-565-8596:** I have a problem . . .

I should play it cool. My fingers fly over the keys.

**Me:** You're intimidated by my wingspan?

**555-565-8596:**
Obviously. But I'm thinking I need a costume for tonight . . . seeing as nobody's supposed to know I'm a vamp. This is Damon, btw.

That's exactly how he's going into my phone.

**Me:** Well, Mr. Salvatore. You've always been a problem solver.
I believe in you. Just don't cover your face. I like that part. See you in an hour—550 Harrison St.

I hear him laugh from somewhere in the store, making me crane my neck to try and spot him one last time.

I'm smiling ear to flipping ear until I hear, "That'll be $114.56."

What the fuck!

My head darts up as my foot hits the ground. That's highway robbery. But I pay using my phone and grab my bag. Pausing in the doorway, I look up into the theft mirror that's on the ceiling. Noah's staring back at me.

He lifts his phone, so I look at mine, not having heard the alert.

**Damon:** Are you stalking me?

**Me:** Nothing ventured, nothing gained, right?

**Damon:** See ya soon, weirdo.

This time, I do play it cool, breezing out like I'm the main character in a movie starring whatever actress fits that bill, and finally text my sister back.

**Me:** Add another plus one for your party. I've got a hot date.

# Chapter Two

## Noah

What the hell did I come in here for? My eyes search the shelves in front of me, not really focused on anything because I can't even remember why I'm at this damn store.

That girl knocked me on my ass. All, maybe, five foot six of her.

I'm literally standing here, mentally turning in circles while smiling like a loon.

A forceful whoosh of air bursts between my lips as I clasp my hands behind my head, forcing my T-shirt just up above my belt buckle. I can't help myself and clock the ceiling mirrors in the front of the store again, knowing she's gone. Because damn. I'm rocked.

I can't say I've ever been picked up in a Walgreens by a girl in a dinosaur costume, possibly shoplifting fake blood. This is a first. And it's either the most incredible origin story or the coolest party opener I'll carry with me throughout my days.

Before I can lose myself to too much thought, my phone rings, forcing me to refocus back into the real world.

It's my buddy Chase.

"What's up?"

I wipe a hand over my mouth to try and make my smile go away.

"Dude. Where are you? The candy's officially gone—" Candy. I snap my fingers before grabbing an oversize bag of full-length Snickers. "—and these kids out here are acting like the cast of *The Sopranos*. I just got shaken down for the change in my pocket by some little hustler dressed like a blue dog. Remind me never to agree to hang with you on Halloween again. Next year, I'm going to a dive bar with girls dressed like sexy cats."

"Shut up," I laugh as I walk to the checkout. "I've got some more, but there's a change of plans. I'm dropping it off because I got something to do. You're on your own for the night."

A chorus of high-pitched voices rings out on the other end: "Trick or treat."

But before Chase answers me, he grumbles, "Beat it, we're out."

"Dude," I toss out with a laugh as I hand the clerk the money for the candy.

But Chase keeps ignoring me because whatever three-foot-tall costumed gang standing on my front porch protests, "Aww, come on, it's still early. This house sucks."

There's shuffling, maybe the sound of paper, before Chase snaps, "Here, Capone. Read a magazine, ya little teamster. Save the teeth you have left."

The sound of the door on my house shutting has me laughing harder as the night air hits me. I'm only two blocks from my place, but I'm not sure he'll survive until I get there.

"Why do people have kids?" he says before pivoting back to what I said. "And what are you talkin' about? You invited me. I'm not babysitting your house, surrounded by these hoodlums. They're probably gonna egg it anyway."

I turn the corner as four tiny vampires run by, making me lift the bag so I don't accidentally hit them with it.

"I met a girl."

"Where?"

I shake my head over his lack of common sense.

"At Walgreens."

He scoffs. "The only women at Walgreens at nine p.m. on Halloween are gram-grams and crackheads."

"Well, she definitely wasn't either."

"Oh shit. How hot? Come on, details. She have a nice ass?"

"You're disgusting. Stop it. You can't talk about women that way."

I cross the street, jogging a bit to let a car hurry and turn.

Chase draws out his words. "Throw a guy a bone. Between the two of us, you're the handsome one. I have to live vicariously through your dating life. Last week, this gorgeous, leggy blonde told me I looked like someone who made their own cheese. What does that even mean?"

I chuckle. "You do make your own cheese."

"I'm a chef, Noah."

Now I'm really laughing.

"Listen, yes, she was gorgeous. But I have no idea what her ass looked like because I didn't look . . . Also, she was in a blow-up dinosaur costume."

I see my house a few doors away, and Chase is bravely walking back out onto my porch. A group of kids ascends. I hang up on him, pocketing my phone before tearing the bag open.

He points at me. "He's got your loot, ya feral animals."

I grin, filling little pumpkin buckets with candy bars before I walk up my stairs.

Chase steals a candy bar, rips the package open, immediately takes a bite, and talks with his mouth full.

"Bro, hot girls wear nurse's outfits. And cats, as previously stated. Even princess costumes with those garters. Gahhh, fuck me," he moans, his eyes rolling back. "Those are the best. What they don't wear is dinosaurs. She's a total red flag. That girl reads books and is probably up on current affairs. And those girls definitely don't make out in the bathrooms of dirty bars."

He's literally hopeless. There's a reason—maybe several—why he never gets a date.

"You're depraved. You know that, right?"

He follows me inside the house as I toss the candy on a table by my front door. Anticipating the sarcasm I know is dying to spill out of him, I beat him to the punch. "The one thing I know in life is 'hot' is easy to achieve. 'Interesting,' though . . . Well, that's way harder. And man, was she interesting."

Chase flops down on my couch, kicking his feet up on the ottoman.

"So, you're dissing your best friend for some interesting girl you just met . . . at a place where I buy my athlete's foot powder."

"You're a fucking hater. And yes, I am." I look over my shoulder, a thought bubbling before tumbling out. "I need a costume, though."

"Wait, it's a party. And I can't go?"

"Yes, it is. And no, you can't."

He shrugs, finishing off his candy bar.

"Well then, that should be easy. Put on a sheet and go as a ghost since that's what you're doing to the bro-hood."

I laugh. But honestly, not a bad idea.

An hour and a half later, my matte-black Indian Scout growls to a stop as I park in front of a warehouse. A large and fairly nondescript one, set against the pitch-black darkness, with no other vehicles in sight.

What the hell?

I look around because I've never been to this side of town, mainly because it's industrial, just a bunch of warehouses by the docks.

A clang comes from the distance but dies out just as fast, forcing my head to swing over my shoulder. My eyes take in nothing, only darkness.

I wait for the sound to happen again, but I'm only met with silence.

Quiet is always eerie. The way it hangs in wait, almost taunting me, making my pulse the only thing I hear. I check the address on my phone before looking up at the steel building again and taking off my helmet.

Yeah, this isn't ominous. I get invited to a random-ass party by a random girl, only to arrive at the beginning of a horror movie.

This may be the worst impulse I've ever acted on because currently, the vibe is a lot like *Well, he really got himself killed* and less like *We never saw it coming.*

I mean . . . Female serial killers are a thing. A shiver grazes my muscles. Jesus, I've got to stop thinking like this.

My phone dings with a text, reading my mind.

> **Chase:** Yo . . .
> just me casually
> stalking my best
> friend's location.
> This is a terrible
> idea. RIP or run,
> dude. Also, I ate the
> rest of the pizza in
> your fridge.

I shake my head as I dismount my bike, looking up and down the deserted street again. A streetlight flickers in the distance like a siren calling my attention, so I squint into the darkness, trying to see clearly, still coming up empty for any sign of life. If this is a party, where is everyone?

What's wrong with me? What's she going to do . . . steal my liver?

I pocket my phone before I reach inside the leather satchel attached to my motorcycle and pull out Chase's creation—a spare bedsheet with flowers on it turned Casper.

Here goes nothing.

I make my way toward the door, still glancing toward a couple of spotlighted spaces along the dark, gravelly road. Movement catches my eyes, so I stare down to my left, locking on a crow perched on a bobbing cable wire strung between two poles. It's staring back at me.

"Watch it, buddy. You almost got your ass beat," I call out, entertaining myself.

In my defense, I think all men are suspicious by nature. We're always on guard. Or maybe it's just me mixed with . . .

God, I hate this night. This street isn't helping, though.

Truthfully, Halloween always fucks me up. Ironically, the sheet over my shoulder isn't my actual costume. Tonight, my real disguise is "normal guy."

This year, though, I'm determined to enjoy the change of course from guy who dreads Halloween to the guy who's met the most interesting girl.

Lost in my thoughts, I walk closer to the building, only a single door in view, and use my helmet to knock. But when nobody answers, I lean in, pressing my ear to it. Is that music? I swear I can hear the faintest sound. So, I bang again, harder.

With a jerk, it suddenly swings open, making a scraping sound like it needs to be oiled. I step back so it doesn't hit me as music bounds out, wafting into the air around me.

Ha. There is a party. My liver lives another day.

A giant man wearing a yellow T-shirt labeled **Thrills Event Staff** looks me up and down, mostly down because he's got to be almost seven feet tall.

"Entrance is at the front."

"Oh shit, my bad. I parked here by mistake . . ." I say with weaponized incompetence, looking over my shoulder and hoping he doesn't make me go around.

He looks annoyed but takes a clipboard from another yellow-T-shirt-wearing guy who's passing by and grunts out his words.

"Name."

Fuck yeah.

"Noah . . . Adler." Why did I add that? She doesn't even know my last name.

The Jolly Green Giant shakes his head. "First problem is you're not wearing a costume." He looks up from the clipboard. "Second, there's nobody on the list with that name."

I smirk because, somehow, I knew this might happen.

She really is the most interesting girl.

I hold out my helmet, my forehead wrinkling for him to do me a solid. He does with a sigh, making me grin as I drape the sheet over my head, adjusting the homemade eyeholes.

"First problem solved." I gingerly take back my helmet, adding, "Try Damon Salvatore."

He looks down for a beat, then steps out of my way, holding the door open. "Have a spooky time, sir."

I'm laughing to myself as I step over the threshold. Because I feel like there's no other kind of time to be had. This night keeps getting better and better.

Three steps inside the party, the music kicks up as a band introduces themselves. An electric guitar strums a familiar rhythm before everyone onstage begins jumping to "Psycho Killer," by the Talking Heads. But I'm undeterred as I search the room, looking for a cute little T. rex and coming up short.

However, what I am getting at great lengths are seriously elaborate costumes. There's prosthetic after prosthetic and fabricated gore everywhere. Damn. One person after another draws my attention with pieces so intricate they could easily be in movies.

Who the hell are these people? And what kind of party is this? The moment I think it, I spot a neon sign by the entrance that says **Mass FX—Bringing the Magic to Reel Life.**

Oh shit. Okay, that makes sense. She works for a special effects company. That's cool. Or maybe her sister does, since she said she was taking the fake blood to her for the dead body.

If I ever find her, I'll ask.

I keep making my way through the crowd, eyes back on the prize.

A woman with fish scales all over her face blurts out "Boo" as I pass by, so I chuckle and lift my hands, waving them to play along.

Peopling isn't usually my thing. Neither are parties. But tonight, I'm the definition of *If he wants to, he will.*

I went from debating whether or not I was about to be killed to knocking on an unnumbered, unlabeled warehouse door for a girl whose last name I don't even know. At a party I wasn't even originally invited to.

But there's something about a girl who makes "hot mess" look intriguing.

A bunch of *Star Trek*–looking aliens walk by as I crane my head to look past them. Where is she?

I'm about to pull my phone out to text her instead of trying to be cool and just happen upon her when a high-pitched screech, something like a dying owl would make, comes from my left, forcing my attention around.

There's a guy in white face paint dressed as the bad dude in *Hellraiser*. He's looming over some girl at the bar while the people surrounding them laugh.

He must've scared her.

As if to give proof of that, she presses her hands to her chest like she's trying to jump-start her heart. I grin, but it almost immediately starts to fade as auburn curls fall in front of her face. Wait a minute. My eyes narrow as she puts a hand on her knee, presumably to catch her breath.

I'm already moving in their direction as she stands up, laughing along.

My eyes stay locked on her, and the grin that faded on my face from before suddenly finds its way back into place.

*Hey, I know you . . .*

Goldie sweeps her long, spirally curls over her shoulder, smacking the chest of the guy who just frightened her.

Damn, I almost didn't catch that it was her because she's not in her costume anymore. Instead, she has on one of those one-piece legging / tank top thingies in olive green and is wearing black Nike Court Royale 2 high-tops. It's smoking hot.

Helplessly and without permission from my brain, my eyes drift over her frame, over each curve and bend as she moves, speaking animatedly while using her hands. I'm indulgently taking her in, lingering in some places but only glancing at others so I can still call myself a gentleman.

Never mind, I am a perv. I can now confirm her ass is better than nice.

I don't know what most guys like; all I know is what she's got is what I want.

I'm closing in on her, trying to think of a good opening line, beginning to get distracted by my nerves.

I should've just texted her. Dammit.

She's still talking to the nails-in-the-face guy when I sidle up to the bar, put my helmet on top, and eavesdrop, trying to buy myself some more time.

"Is that the third time I've gotten you tonight?" he says.

She huffs playfully. "Yes. And I think the third time's the charm. So now you're done."

He laughs, rubbing her arm. "Come on, Goldie. How is someone afraid of their own shadow at a Halloween party?"

She laughs and grabs her drink, accidentally brushing my ghost arm.

"Sorry," she politely breathes my way, giving me an opening to interrupt her being flirted with.

*It's okay, buddy. I don't blame you. I'm here to do the same.* Before he steals any more of my time, I pounce, letting my voice carry.

"Don't be. Goldie, right? Hold on a minute. Did you do something different? You're almost unrecognizable."

Goldie looks over her shoulder for a second before a smirk blossoms. She nibbles her lip, completely turning my way as I continue.

Ever so boldly, I take her hand, bringing her fingertips close to my ghosty eyehole.

"Are the claws different?" I raise her arm above her head, spinning her halfway around. "Or maybe it's the tail . . ." She giggles as I bring her back around, this time stretching her arm out. "I got it. You got an arm-lengthening surgery since a couple hours ago?"

She shakes her head, delivering her comeback with diabolical sincerity while our fingertips still touch as I drop our hands between us.

"No, silly, I did a middle part in my hair instead of side . . ."

She pulls her hand away to touch her chest as her eyes grow wide before she sucks in a sudden, dramatic gasp. "But you look pale as a ghost." She presses her palm to my covered forehead. "Are you sick? Maybe even deathly ill?"

We stand there, staring at each other, me smiling even though she can't see it.

Then we laugh.

And it's kind of magical. Damn, I really want to get to know this girl.

Pinhead steps up next to Goldie, reminding both of us that he's still here. He's armed with a furrowed brow as he looks directly at me.

"Hey, who's your friend, Goldie?"

*Okay, time to scram, buddy.* But he keeps going as he reaches to shake my hand.

"I'm Scott. I own the company."

Ooo, big flex. My eyes stay locked on hers as I extend my hand to him and answer.

"I'm her boo."

She laughs, and I like it. It's the kind of laugh someone has when they're comfortable in their own skin. The dude shakes my hand before packing up his dignity and bowing out.

"Well, you two enjoy the night." He looks to Goldie, who's locked on me. "I'll see you around? Maybe another scare before the party's over?"

Goldie gives him a nod, still smiling at me, and barely whispers "Sure" as he leaves.

This is wild. Our chemistry is crazy. I'm so attracted to her that it feels illegal. I glance over at Scott as he's leaving, but she draws me back.

"He's my sister's boss."

So, this is her sister's job.

I tilt my ghost head, looking back at her. Goldie downs what's in her glass and places it back on the counter.

"Buy me a drink?"

I immediately raise my hand to the bartender, noticing a sign that says **OPEN BAR.**

I've been set up.

"Okay, but I gotta warn you. Carrying a wallet in the afterlife is tricky. So, you can only get what's free."

She giggles again. Man, I'm going to do all my best stand-up and steal from every Netflix comedy special I've ever seen to keep that sound coming.

"Tonic with two limes, please," she orders.

I add mine along with hers. "Same."

She looks surprised that I'd drink the same drink she does, but instead of questioning anything, we just keep glancing at each other, neither of us knowing what to say.

"What happened to the dino getup?" I toss out, wanting to take the damn sheet off.

"I decided to go with the after-dark version. This is sexy Rexy." I smile as she rolls her eyes, adorably so. "Just kidding. It unfortunately fell victim to a concrete wall about three blocks into my walk . . . Between that and asteroids, I figured it was time to give in to natural selection."

For a second, I totally picture her in a deflated T. rex costume, walking down Main, and it makes me chuckle.

Her fingers tap the bar as, I swear, the music gets even louder. She must feel the same because she steps in closer to me, our arms brushing.

"You know, I half expected you wouldn't come."

She takes her drink as it's offered.

"Why?"

I take mine as she shrugs, and it's shy. Which, ironically, seems like it would be on brand for her. I don't know what to say, so I hard pivot to another topic.

"So, how long has your sister been doing this?"

She takes a sip. "Her whole life, but she's finally getting paid now."

"Cool. What have you been doing your whole life?"

She touches the end of her hair so delicately I'm not sure she knows she's doing it. But I can't stop noticing.

"My whole life? How much time you got?"

All night. All week. Whatever works.

She smiles wistfully. "I'm a hopeful writer who's working on working as a florist. I have an interview next week."

That's the best description of unemployment I've ever heard. She should definitely stick to writing.

I nod. "Basically, the next great American novelist feeling uninspired, relying on a little beauty in the meantime."

"Something like that." There's another long pause as we both face forward. Even the awkward parts are making me smile. Maybe I'm grateful for the sheet after all.

Goldie's voice carries up to me again. "What do you do? Other than haunt people and turn into a boy for first kisses in spooky mansions."

I can't help but chuckle because her television and movie references are set to expert mode.

"Graphic design. I mostly make a lot of boring corporate logos, but eventually, I'd love to create sneakers."

I wait for her to make a joke about me being a forever twelve-year-old, like most people do.

But instead, her hand touches my shoulder. "No way. That's so cool. I love it, and now I know who to ask for a custom pair on my birthday."

She's a cream-and-white leather Converse high-top with stars, flowers, and book quotes wound up the back.

"When's your birthday?"

Goldie only smiles before rubbing her lips together, coating a sheen of wetness into a shine. I nod, understanding, lifting my drink.

"Guess I'll have to stick around to find out."

The coy look she gives me makes me blow out a gentle exhale.

I start to take a drink to cool off, but I hit fabric, blocked. I laugh, watching her eyes light up with humor.

We forgot a mouth hole.

As if she hears my thoughts, Goldie grabs a straw from the bar, then raises her hand to my face and gently tugs the sheet until one of my eyeholes is lined up with my mouth.

I feel the straw touch my lips, so I take a long sip.

"You weren't supposed to cover your face," she teases, so I give it back as good as I'm getting it.

"And you were supposed to be a dinosaur. Looks like we're both liars."

With a huff, she tugs my sheet all the way down, exposing me. "Bold choice with the flowers."

"I'm in touch with my feminine side."

I don't know what comes over me, but I blurt out my next words as I run a hand through my hair. "Do you want to get out of here?"

She smiles. I keep going.

"Maybe go somewhere we can hear each other better? I wanna know you . . ."

She's shaking her head before answering, but when she does, I'm toast.

"Are we walking or driving?"

# Chapter Three

## Goldie

I can't believe I'm doing this. I almost laugh to myself over the unpredictability of tonight. But instead, I shift my head to the side, resting it on the broadness of Noah's shoulder as I tighten my arms around his waist and watch the world whip by.

I've never been on the back of a motorcycle, let alone had a spontaneous first date like this, but I swear there's just something about this night that screams *Do it for the plot*.

Although, I did manage to keep some of my marbles and introduced Noah to Evie before we left. That way, if I go missing, she can give an accurate sketch to the police. Especially since I'm positive she paid attention when they met.

*"So, you're the aisle nine hottie. Nice."*

*My eyes grow wide as I glare at her. She doesn't care, mouthing "He's hot" as she stands like a cartoon villain, stroking Uncle Fester's head.*

*"Noah," he offers coolly.*

*"Evie," she replies just as the light bulb flickers from Fester's mouth.*

*"And it was aisle twelve . . ." Noah shoots back playfully, but then he furrows his brow. "Don't do me dirty, Wednesday. Should I be worried? Does she do this often?"*

*"Yes, she does. Tons," Evie dramatizes. "A real convenience store black widow, that one. Be careful, you might not wake up in the morning. Before you, there was an elderly couple she tried to scare to death."*

*I gently tug his arm, desperate to end my embarrassment, but he stays in place and looks down at me with a shrug and a wink.*

*"Eh, I'll take my chances."*

*I sigh and finally interrupt.*

*"Okay, bye. That's all you get. We're leaving now."*

*Evie kisses my cheek before Noah pats Fester's head and chuckles again. "Really great work" is all he gets out before I drag him away.*

The feel of Noah's hand covering mine pulls me from the fresh memory, making me smile again for the thousandth time. He's been doing that the whole ride—all ten minutes of it—checking in to make sure I'm okay.

And as much as it's reassuring and thoughtful, it also makes me feel like the blush on my cheeks may stay crimson even after we stop the ride.

The moment we made it out of the party, it was like we were both infused and bubbling with flirtatious, excited energy. We tripped over our words as we tried to figure out what to do and where to go, then orbited each other, so close we even almost stumbled as he tried to pull out his spare helmet for me to wear.

It was cute. He was cute. He *is* cute.

Jesus, I just met this guy a few hours ago, and all I want to do is hang out with him all night. Which is so weird and extremely unlike me. I'm not a risk taker—that's my sister, which means nothing, considering I'm adopted, so it's not like the trait skipped a generation.

If anything, I guess maybe a little bit of her bravery's been nurtured into me because the moment he started walking away in that store, I felt compelled to . . . I don't know . . . I guess I just totally get those nineties movies like *Before Sunrise*, where two strangers meet and connect in some kind of bizarre chemical way and have to hang out.

He feels like someone I shouldn't miss out on.

So now, I'm on the back of his bike, rolling into somewhere unknown with goofy enthusiasm plastered on my face, secretly wishing I could explore his abs by accident and definitely on purpose without getting caught because holding on to him, forced to take in his delicious cologne, is the sweetest torture.

The man smells like cedarwood and vanilla, mixed with sleepy, lustful thoughts and a dash of unregretted bad decisions. I'll take it in bulk, please and thank you.

Noah slows to a stop at a light, so I begrudgingly separate my body from his, leaving my hands politely on his waist, just over his jacket. Because while my thoughts may be in the gutter, that doesn't mean I have to act like it.

His shiny black helmet turns in profile.

"Scary or fun?" he calls out.

"Fun," I say back, a little breathless.

His gloved hand lands over mine. "Wanna go fast? There's no sign of life down this road."

My heart ticks up a notch, but I nod quickly.

He reaches back, taking my other hand, and slides them both back under his jacket across his stomach to secure me in place. My chest presses to his back.

Thank god my sister had a hoodie in her car because I'm pretty sure he'd know just how much I liked what he was doing if he could see all the goose bumps up my arms right now.

"Hold on tight, killer," he yells.

I do, wrapped heavenly around his sturdy frame as he takes off. The squeal that bursts from my chest is drowned out by the growling engine and suffocated by his back because I immediately hide my face. I can feel him laughing as the revving grows even louder.

The wind licks my cheeks, even as they stay hidden, making me mold to him even harder as my thighs tense. Oh my god, this is wild and recklessly fast. Holy shit.

Because I can't not, I peek, seeing the trees reduced to a blur.

Whoa. The feeling is exhilarating, making my breath stutter before I gasp. Because the moment Noah slows down, my stomach does a little flip. I laugh, not even realizing how excited I am until I feel my chest heaving against his taut muscles.

"That was incredible," I blurt out, loosening my grip on him as my head falls back, and I shout to the sky, "You're crazy!"

He just squeezes my hands, securing them to his stomach and keeping them warm as I look over his shoulder, seeing twinkling lights ahead from the little square that makes up the center of one of my favorite neighborhoods in Boston, Beacon Hill.

"Is this where we're going?" I say, but he doesn't hear me.

Sometimes my sister and I just walk around admiring all the brownstones and history. It always feels like a scene from *St. Elmo's Fire*, like I should be wearing a cream crew neck sweater as fall leaves drift down around my feet, decorating the sidewalks in burnt orange. Beacon Hill is November, the number twenty-four, and all things cinnamon. I love it.

Currently, however, there's a large barricade prohibiting entry onto the street we're riding toward, which makes sense because people are everywhere, walking every which way with kids dressed as superheroes and witches, laughing and enjoying the night. This neighborhood is infamous for stuff like this.

"Are you trying to get to the park over by . . . or the bars off Cambridge?"

He doesn't answer again.

Although we're going slow, Noah doesn't seem to be looking for parking. Which is weird because the park is a far walk from here, and so are the bars. Plus, we should've gone down . . . All the independent thoughts I'm having start to finally hang out and get acquainted as the realization hits me, accompanied by him pulling into a driveway.

Hold up. Did he bring me back to his house?

When he told me to trust him because he knew the perfect place, I thought we were going somewhere people go before they get down to business. Oh, this ruins him.

This is why I don't do stuff like this. No way am I going inside. Inside is where the bed is. And there's no way I'm sleeping with this dude. I barely know him. Why are guys like this—gross. Tonight just went from magical to murked.

See, this is why I need to go back to boycotting dating—because the men in this city are only for the streets. Sluttiest of sluts, all of them.

As soon as the bike shuts off, I let go of his overused abs and hike my leg over his sexy bait bike.

"Hey, so—" is all I get out because he speaks at the same time.

"I hope you don't mind. My buddy Chase said I could use his driveway. This is his house." He hitches his finger over his shoulder before taking off his helmet and looking at me shyly. "He's barhopping, maybe, probably . . . Either way, I thought we could walk around the neighborhood. I don't know, it's pretty cool here, and the decorations are top tier. And that's from someone who hates Halloween. Plus, most of the neighbors give out spiked and nonspiked cider, since I'm thinking you don't drink. And the Alcott house, the *Little Women* writer, is around here somewhere . . ." He bites his lip with a small headshake, suddenly looking unsure as I stare back in awe. "Now that I'm saying it out loud, I guess it's not really date material, but I just figured there'd be tons of people around because girls have that 'stranger danger' thing to worry about. Although you did jump on the back of my bike pretty easily." I raise my brows, but he just smiles. "Anyway, we'd be able to hear each other, unlike a bar or something . . . I mean, we can do something else if you hate it—"

He's perfect. Literally perfect. I take it all back, which only further proves that there must be something horrifically wrong with him.

I narrow my eyes, now even more smitten and humbled.

"Are you a serial killer?"

He shakes his head. "No, but I know someone who knew a guy."

A burst of unladylike laughter explodes outward, immediately snuffed out because I bite my bottom lip.

Noah walks around the bike, setting his own helmet on his seat before he brings both his hands to my borrowed one.

"So, what do you think . . . You wanna loiter with me?"

He unbuttons the strap and gives it a tug, freeing me, before bringing his hand back to brush the hoodie off my head. I must look a mess, but I don't care because I have a crush.

A butterfly-inducing kind of crush that might make me write his name with little hearts in my journal as if I'm not thirty years old. Honestly, if I had a shirtless picture of him in poster size, I might be convinced to put it on my wall.

I giggle to myself over my silly girl thoughts before I sigh and answer him.

"I have conditions."

He takes a step back, and my feet want to follow.

"Name 'em."

How is he so cool with just two words?

"You have to promise to steal me the first bag of Skittles you see."

He secures our helmets and smirks. "Taking candy from a baby . . . I'm game. But you said 'conditions,' plural."

A light breeze blows a strand of my hair over my lips, so I sweep it away as I walk toward him. Stopping in front to look up past the patterned tattoos and the chiseled jaw directly into his eyes, I uncharacteristically say the exact thought in my head.

"You're right. It was plural . . . It has to be unforgettable."

He searches my eyes. "What does? Tonight or the theft?"

I shake my head. "The kiss you give me at the end."

Without a thought or an answer, Noah grins and takes my hand, leading me around the barricade into our very first date. And I swear I'm already hoping it won't be the last.

Half an hour later, we've been weaving our way around, talking about everything and nothing. Mostly how we share a side-eye attitude toward Halloween.

He shifts his body to avoid some little kid dressed as Chucky.

"Like I said, I'm here for fall, but all the gory stuff isn't for me. Everyone wants to pretend to be a killer. Real life is scary enough."

I pop the last of my Skittles into my mouth.

"Agreed, but like, a little witchy vibe is fun sometimes. I'll rock out to some *Practical Magic*, but I'm calling it with anything truly scary. I'm too fragile."

"Oh, I believe you."

He smiles, dramatically wincing as he touches his shoulder because a few houses back, as a giant skeleton came to life, I nearly climbed him like a tree.

"Whatever," I grumble as he winks. "That thing was horrifying."

I'm suddenly hit with a shiver since I'm not exactly dressed for the weather.

"Here," he offers, shrugging off his jacket.

I shake my head, but Noah's already putting it over my shoulders, letting me slide my arms in and drown in it.

"What about you? You're only wearing a T-shirt."

He's adjusting it on me, and it takes everything I've got not to dip my face and inhale until it's burned into my nose forever. As weird as it sounds, it's literally the most reasonable response to his scent.

He shrugs and slides his hands into his front pockets, which makes his already-defined biceps look even bigger. But I don't just notice that. My eyes are glued to the snake that's tatted around his left arm.

"I run hot. I'll be fine."

*Yeah, you do.*

He looks at me, then looks away again.

*Wait, I didn't say that thought aloud, did I? No? Did I?*

My eyes grow owllike for a few seconds of worry as I stare forward before I pivot and try to rebreak the ice.

"So, where are you originally from? Because I don't hear an accent. And I don't meet a lot of guys here who don't have one."

"Stop meeting a lot of guys," he teases.

Oof, he's too good at this. Because everything he says is grin producing, as well as addictive. But I maintain my cool as he continues.

"I'm from a nowhereville little fishing town between here and Maine."

"So, New Hampshire," I say flatly.

He smiles, not looking at me, and points to a house with giant spiders all over the front.

"Eww, I'd never sleep," I laugh, stepping in closer to him. "I hate spiders."

"Even the cute ones?"

He says it without any recognition of the insanity laced within that statement.

I do a double take and stare at him. "There isn't any such thing."

"Excuse you. Tarantulas are adorable. All furry-legged."

As he says it, his fingers crawl up my neck under my hair, making me squirm and squeal as I inadvertently curl my body closer to his.

"Stop," I fake whine before shaking my arms like I have the heebie-jeebies and shoving his immovable shoulder, making him chuckle. "What's your animal hard pass?"

"Cats."

"So, it's a no for pussy, check." His mouth drops open, and I laugh. "Sorry, dirty jokes . . . too soon? Am I cut?"

"I might like you even more."

The way he looks at me makes me nervous, so I try to refocus.

"Nobody dislikes cats. You're making that up."

"I don't dislike them. I hate them. Real disdain."

I gasp, stopping in my place as he does, too, just in time for him to double down, crossing his arms.

"They're superior, condescending, and disloyal. I refuse to house and feed something just to be judged by it."

My smile tries to stay suppressed but fails as we start walking again. "Wow, who hurt you."

He nods in full acknowledgment, cracking one of those sexy smirks again.

"Her name was Princess Peach. She shit in my shoes and left me to live with my neighbor. I still have the heartbreak and the laser toy I got her."

We share a matched laugh before he takes my hand again, guiding me around a group of teenagers stopped in the middle of the street, comparing their loot.

I look at him at the same time he looks at me.

"Your turn," he prods, rocking his side into mine. "Where are you from originally?"

"Oh man, questions like this are so loaded because I don't really know . . ."

He looks at me, puzzled, as I keep explaining. "I'm adopted, so I'm working with very little info. All I know is that I came to live with the great Camilla and Stephen Monroe when I was twelve hours old."

"Twelve hours old?"

I nod. "Well, kind of. I was left at a police station in Portland, Oregon, without a birth certificate or anything. It was by the grace of god that my mom and dad even saw me. They just happened to be at the station, filing a report about a stolen bike, and my mother found me in a bag by the door. She heard me, actually. She swears it was the only time I ever cried as a baby . . . as if I was calling her name. It took them almost a year to actually adopt me, but I guess it was meant to be. I came here for college and never left."

Silence spreads out between us before he chuckles. "Wow . . . that's something. But nothing I wouldn't expect from the most interesting girl I've ever met. And I have to say I'm glad you told me because I've been trying to figure out how you and your sister were born to the same people. You don't exactly look alike. At all."

I can't help but laugh because my sister is a gorgeous biracial treasure created by our Black father and Spanish mother, with naturally bronzed features that perfectly complement her warm brown melanin complexion. And we couldn't look more different.

"Yeah, she's a bio kid and a perfect blend of our parents. Evie was my single five-year-old's wish written to Santa trying to manifest a baby sister. But we do get asked why I look like the national spokesperson for Irish airlines a ton. Which sometimes sucks because, unlike Evie, I'll never know who I favor."

Noah runs his fingers through his hair. "Have you ever thought of doing those genetic testing things? The ones that can link you to relatives?"

I nod. "Yeah, my mom even bought me one once. But . . . I don't know. It's stupid because I *wish* that I knew more, but I kinda don't want to know either. I just want my sister to be my sister and my mom and dad to be my mom and dad . . . no extras or little asterisks next to their names. I guess I'd rather live in my current version of life and keep wondering if my eyes are only this pretty because they're a mixture of people I'll never know."

Noah frowns and stops me as his eyes scan my face.

"Nah, as someone who's only known you for five seconds, I can't imagine you looking like anyone but you. Some people are meant to stand out as independent creations." His finger feathers over my cheekbone. "I guarantee nobody's ever had freckles on their cheeks exactly like this."

*Noah's kind.*

And he just called me "pretty." In the slyest way.

My lips part, but nothing comes out, so I opt to tug him toward a cider stand, suddenly feeling more flushed under his stare.

"Your turn. Tell me about you . . . sisters, brothers? Are you close with your parents? Give me the dirty details now that you know my life's story."

He doesn't let go of my hand as he pulls out his wallet, holding it out to me so we can work together to grab some cash for the drinks.

"There's nothing to tell," he fills in. "I'm an only child from a boring town, and now I'm here, trying to make the most of my life. Now is the most interesting part."

I raise my brows. Okay, onion, make me peel those layers.

"And your parents? Are they still in New Hampshire? Do you see them often?"

It's impossible to miss how he straightens a bit and rolls his shoulders back, avoiding my eyes as he pockets his wallet before accepting his drink.

"I never met my dad, and my mom never talked about him. I lost her a few years back in a car accident."

"Oh shit. I'm sorry, Noah."

He smiles forgivingly at me. "No, don't be. It's fine. I'm good. It's just not the razzle-dazzle I was going for to leave you impressed and awed by me."

I take a sip, strolling next to him as our hands lightly swing.

"Okay then," I breathe out, peeking up at him. "Redo. Impress and awe me. But be forewarned: I'm a tough judge, much like Princess Peach."

He chortles. It's cute.

"Oh man. Okay, no pressure. Let's see . . ." I can feel his eyes on my profile before he says, "I can juggle fire."

My face whips to his. "Shut up. Do it right now."

"I thought you'd at least fake apathy. You were supposed to make me work for it. Damn, Princess would be so disappointed."

I spin my body toward him with faux incredulity on my face. "Cats usually are though, right? You know what, forget the razzle-dazzle. We're rapid-firing. Getting all the bullshit first-date talk out of the way."

"Are we on a date?" he tosses back sarcastically.

I narrow my eyes and ignore him because he's already nodding his agreement to my rapid fire.

I point to myself. "Thirty. And a Scorpio."

"Thirty-one, and I don't have a clue, but my birthday's July first."

Ooo, he's a Cancer. It's criminal how compatible that makes us.

He tilts his head, his fingers absentmindedly sliding up and down in between mine. "My turn? I don't have any social media."

"Stop love bombing me."

He laughs, and it mesmerizes me for the millionth time.

"Favorite color?" I shoot out.

"Red . . ."

He lifts our joined hands to the end of my hair as he adds, "And yours?"

"Sapphire."

He blinks, then takes over. "Favorite flower?"

"Baby's breath . . . you?"

"Chives."

I smile as his eyes drop to my lips, lingering and making me stall for a second.

"Favorite food," I say, slower this time, as he locks his eyes back to mine.

He grins before answering. "A Belle Isle lobster roll."

"Same," I whisper.

Whoo. Whatever's happening is making the world feel like it's shrinking around us, locking us in a bubble. People surround us, but they're oblivious to the spin we've seemingly found ourselves in. The round and round of two people with the kind of chemistry that leads to one-night stands where you break things as you make your way into the house because the kiss can't stop.

Except I'm not sleeping with him, so we're just going to have to stay trapped right here. Which, honestly, isn't too bad.

We stand deliriously locked on each other until I forget if there's a question on deck, so I throw out another for good measure.

"Favorite time of day?"

"Twilight . . ." I say first, but he just stares into my eyes.

So I raise my brows, waiting for him, and repeat my answer, quieter this time.

The sides of our mouths both pull as he nods, not at all answering the question. "Yeah, Team Edward for sure."

"No," I laugh, touching his chest with my free hand. "I was asking what time of day you love, not about the movie."

"Can I kiss you now?"

My heart stops as he lets go of my hand. But I don't get to speak because he's already bending down as I nod.

Our lips fuse together in the middle of the cobblestone street, like a sigh of relief halting any thoughts, blurring out the world into frayed edges as the first touch of his mouth lingers, then melts deeper into the kind of kiss where I can't tell whose breath is whose.

It's romantic, not crude. He's purposeful, not aggressive. It's perfect.

Noah takes his time, teasing his tongue against mine before drawing back, letting the slickness of our lips slowly glide over each other's. He's not just kissing me with his mouth, either, but with his fingertips peppering along my jaw before he cradles it.

My body arches flush against his, my hand tangling, balled up in his shirt. I'm holding on for dear life because I'd said "unforgettable." And if the measure is whether or not I remember my name, well, I don't. So, he's lived up.

He pulls away, his warm breath still igniting my lips as he stays close enough to kiss me again.

"That was my best shot. But I'll keep trying if it didn't make the cut."

"Maybe once more for good meas—" I whisper back.

He cuts me off as he dives back in, leaving me even more breathless than before. My head's spinning as he whispers, "Better?"

I nod, almost unable to speak. "Yeah. You should take your jacket back. I feel sweaty."

He grins before pulling away-away, forcing me to unhand his shirt and open my eyes. Good god, my legs feel weak.

"Fuck," he draws out, swallowing hard enough that his Adam's apple bobs as he takes another step back. "Can I see you tomorrow?"

I look down at my watch, scraping my teeth over my bottom lip over and over. "Tomorrow is almost today. So, I guess you tell me."

"Cool," he says on an exhale and a pregnant pause before blurting out, "Wanna hang out with me for another sixish hours and watch my favorite time of day?"

*Sunrise. His favorite time is sunrise.*

"Yeah, I don't really have any plans until Wednesday, sooo . . ."

It's Saturday.

Noah takes my hand again, and somehow, we turn away from each other to meander back down the street, the silliest of grins plastered on our faces.

"Most interesting girl I've ever met," he says under his breath before sipping his cider.

I nod. "Yeah, it's definitely been one killer night . . . Now, let's go find something to set on fire so I can watch you juggle."

His laughter fills the sky as he drapes an arm over my shoulder and pulls me in close.

Cedarwood and vanilla. Delicious.

I take it back. I think Halloween is starting to grow on me.

# Chapter Four

***Camp Weonoke—years prior***

"Hey, you're the new girl, right?"

The pretty blonde smiled shyly, mainly because the boy talking to her was cute. Not because she was friendly. By nature, she was suspicious of handsome, tanned boys who talked to her. She'd be naive not to be. They typically had an agenda.

But that was the exact reason her parents had forced her to come to Camp Weonoke as a camp counselor.

Socialization, they'd said. *Bullshit,* she'd said in her mind, then rolled over in battle.

"I'm Davis." He held out his hand, but she didn't shake it, making him grin as he continued. "This is my fourth year as a counselor. First year as *head.* I know you're new to this chaos, so if you need anything, let me know. That's pretty much my job."

His smile was stacked full of perfectly lined teeth. She nodded and picked up more of the supplies she'd been tasked with bringing back to the mess hall. But when the last of the paper napkins in her arms wobbled, he jumped forward.

Their bodies were closer together, almost uncomfortably so. Almost.

He secured the stack for her, and she noticed he smelled like money. Like the Polo aftershave so popular with boys like him.

"Seriously, don't be shy," he pressed. "We're going to be stuck together for the next two months. It could be fun."

He looked at her like there was more to his meaning, and she contemplated whether she liked that.

"Okay, well, I'll leave you to it." The bright-eyed, megawatt-smile boy shrugged shyly before he turned away.

When he glanced back and waved goodbye, he dropped his clipboard and stumbled, embarrassed. It cracked his beautiful facade and made her giggle. That was when she decided she would trust him.

"Sonny," she said with the full breadth of her silky voice.

Her name hung between them as he stared into her eyes and righted himself while he hugged the clipboard against his chest.

"It's nice to meet you, Sonny."

He made a goofy gesture toward the sky as if he equated her name to the good weather.

It was silly, but he was cute, so she acted like she'd never had that happen before.

"See ya around." He looked nervous again as he gave her a little salute.

She smiled, bigger this time. The boy walked away, and for the first time, she wasn't so mad that she'd been banished from home. Maybe camp would be exactly what she needed. A summer she'd never forget.

# Chapter Five

## Noah

***November***

"Jesus Christ," I shout, startled, almost dropping the towel from around my waist. "What the hell are you doing here, dude?"

Chase stares back at me incredulously as he holds open the door of my refrigerator.

"You gave me a key."

"That's not an answer," I bark, gripping my towel in one hand and shaking my hair out with my other. "I could've killed you."

Chase gulps back the bottle of water he just took out of my fridge, ending with a deep, thirst-quenched exhale before answering me.

"With what? Your dick? Relax, the security guys are at my place, finally installing the new cameras, since some hoodlums tried to break in on Halloween. You're lucky your bike wasn't stolen. Anyway, I figured I'd come over early—"

When I stare back blankly, he places the bottle down. "Early because we're going to that art show thing . . . the one the brunette invited us to last month . . . you know . . . with the big—"

His hand is hovered over his chest as I hold up mine, stopping him.

"Dude, I told you I wasn't going. I'm not talking to other girls anymore."

His whole face distorts as if I've just spoken gibberish.

"I didn't think you were serious. Noah," he groans. "If you tell me you're dissing for the 'other plans' you've been out with like a hundred times this month, I'll lose it."

I smirk, crossing my arms and leaning against the counter as I shrug. "Technically, it's only been three weeks."

Chase laughs a few times, punctuating each huff. "I could've filed a missing persons report for the first week alone." He lifts his hand to his head like he's searching for someone as he looks around. "Noah . . . are you out there? Come home, Daddy misses you."

I chuckle. "Come on. I'm into her. Can you blame me? The night we met was . . . Fuck, it lasted the whole night into the next day. She's—"

"This 'whole night into the next day,'" he mocks all singsongy, interrupting me and making me laugh again.

"Stop being so dramatic. If you worked on your personality, maybe women wouldn't be so repulsed, and you'd get to second base. And stop hating on me for having a girlfriend."

Silence, and then his voice fills the room.

"Girlfriend?"

I wince. Dammit.

"This isn't real life." He throws a dish towel at me, but I duck, laughing. "I'm living in a simulation. She had better be the best sex of your life because you're doing it for both of us now. No wingman means I'm in my priest era."

I raise my brows, and he holds up a finger. "Nope. Eat whatever you're about to say. I heard what I said. Point is—"

"Nothing," I gripe before tossing the towel back, connecting with his face. "There is no point. And don't talk about sex and Goldie, ever. Plus, I don't know if you're aware, but women do this really cool thing called speaking. It's nice."

"So is getting ass."

"You're disgusting."

Chase stares at me, his eyes growing wider by the second. "You haven't fucked yet, have you?"

"Enough," I groan, lifting my hands, but he laughs. "She wants to take it slow, and I respect it."

"Does she even know she's your girlfriend? Or is this like when I was thirteen and named all my children with Megan Fox after watching *Transformers*?"

Why am I friends with him? I can't remember.

"This is not at all like that. And no . . . I haven't technically had the conversation with her, but that's what tonight's for."

Chase crosses his arms, looking smug.

"Fine," he says flatly. "If this is happening, then I get to meet her. To approve. And since you screwed me for hot guy fall. What are the three of us doing tonight?"

I scoff and make my way back out of the kitchen toward my bedroom.

"Very funny. Hell no. I'm taking her to dinner and a movie. Alone."

Shit. I said the "dinner" part out loud. I stop and turn to face my occasionally lovable but mostly jackass friend.

"Dinner and a movie?" he accuses, his eyes locked on mine, making it hard to keep a straight face.

I nod, but he repeats himself . . . heavy emphasis on the first word.

"*Dinner* and a movie."

Fuck.

Chase clears his throat, placing his palms on my kitchen island.

"Where are you having dinner, Noah?"

I feign ignorance. "I don't know. I let her choose. Some Italian joint."

He repeats my last words slowly before smacking the marble. "You mean to tell me that you've met her sister twice now, and I'm still a secret?"

*Met* is an overexaggeration. She said hello to me as she left Goldie's apartment while we were enjoying our favorite food. But there's the truth, and then there's Chase's truth.

I interlace my fingers on the back of my head. "You do realize that me and you aren't in an actual relationship, right, whack job? Plus, I want her to like me."

"I'm your best friend. There's no you without me. And may I remind you, since you clearly hit your head today, that I'm the owner of a Michelin-starred restaurant." He scowls, making himself look like Robert De Niro. "The amount of disrespect right now is on par with *The Godfather*."

"You never got the star."

He tosses his arms in the air. "I always knew it was you, Freddy!"

I'm laughing as he jabs his finger at me, making his way to the door. "I'll see you and the home-wrecker tonight at eight. But I'm only making dessert for her. We'll see who she likes better once I feed her."

I wave him off, only saying, "It was Fredo, not Freddy, wacko," because he's certifiable. Grabbing my phone, I text Goldie, chuckling to myself because I need to change her name in my phone.

**Me:** Change of plans. We're going to a friend's restaurant.

**Rexy:** Is this the infamous Chase I've heard so much about?

**Me:** Yes. But promise me something?

**Rexy:** Maybe . . .

**Me:** Still like me after.

**Rexy:** You assume I like you now. Bold choice.

What is it with me and collecting smart-asses? God help me, these two are going to love each other.

Goldie's smiling sweetly as her eyes shine brightly, reflected above the dim candlelight on the table. Her tongue darts out over her bottom lip, hoping for more of the elaborate concoction that graced our dinner table, as she speaks to the chef standing before us, coincidentally my best friend.

"The food was incredible. I wish I'd eaten less just so I'd have leftovers. You're so talented."

It's like watching a puppy get scratched in all their favorite spots, rolling right over. He literally doesn't know what to do with his hands, and I think he's blushing.

"I'll cook for you anytime." He hitches his thumb at me. "This one never appreciates me."

She eyes me humorously as I roll my eyes. I admit it, he wins. She likes him more for sure, but after the bluefish he served us tonight, I can't blame her. And if the fish hadn't worked, he also followed through and only sent out dessert for her. Prick. But the way she squealed and clapped her hands made me more smitten and him more enamored.

She sighs. "Well then, it's Noah's loss. I'll always appreciate you."

"Shit," he rushes out before looking at me. "Why'd she have to go and be so great . . . Now I feel bad that I poisoned your girlfriend's food so she'd give you back."

*Oh fuck.*

My heart hits my throat as I stare back at him. Chase knows what he said, too, because he's trying not to smile and to play it cool as his gaze shifts back to Goldie.

She bites her bottom lip, her eyes connecting with mine, but she says nothing. I'm going to hold him under in the dirty dishwater for this. The grin on my face won't go away as I run my hands through my hair before dropping my eyes to the table momentarily until she says, "Ehh, I think I'll keep him . . . since I seem to have survived."

Chase clears his throat, but I just keep staring at Goldie, completely unable to look away from those green eyes. Damn, I'm spun in that web.

"Well, since I've been foiled, you can make it up by setting me up with your sister."

My head immediately starts shaking as I wave a hand in front of him, laughing as I speak.

"Absolutely not. No way. Do not set this shit show up with your sister." I lean in closer across the table, taking her hand. "He's not even house-trained. I'm pretty sure he drinks out of the toilet."

Chase scoffs. "It's a bidet, you fucking heathen."

More laughter spills out of her. I knew she'd love him from the moment the first of many inappropriate things was said.

She smiles at me again, and I give one back, but I swear the only thought I'm capable of makes me want to kiss her.

Goldie is a beautifully dangerous creature. The kind that makes men believe in all the shit they've sworn off. Like girlfriends and commitment and that maybe someone like her could like someone like me.

A couple passes, eliciting a nod from Chase as they sing his praises, and he eats it up before bringing his attention back to us. But during the diversion, I take the opportunity to steal a fleeting second, a moment to take in the normalcy of a place in time when a girl I like meets my best friend. It's so ordinary and perfect.

Can I have this? *Not if she really knew you.*

Chase's voice interjects like cold water over my thoughts as I inconspicuously breathe through the tightness nestled in my chest.

"So, what's the big after-plan? Now that meeting me's set the bar so high?"

She shakes her head, searching my eyes. "I think a movie, but maybe a walk first?"

I nod and let go of her hand, ready to wrap this shit up, until Chase puts the bill down in front of me.

"I'm not paying that. You made us come tonight."

I stand, and he chuckles.

"You dick. It's my number for her sister."

"Why is it on a piece of paper?"

"I'm making a grand gesture." He looks at Goldie, who's standing too. "You might want to rethink this guy. Trust me, ask him about the last girl he brought here and how well that turned out . . ." He coughs like he's trying to cover what he's saying. "She left him for me."

"Complete fabrication," I instantly shoot back, looking at her with a wrinkled forehead. "I've never brought another woman here, let alone rolled the dice subjecting someone to him." I shift back to the humor in my best friend's face. "If this woman stops talking to me, I'm going to burn your place down."

Goldie's laughing at us again as I shove the paper with his number back at him. He faces her, ignoring me as I walk around the table. He takes her hand and kisses the top in dramatic fashion before talking more shit.

"Listen, go easy on Noah. I might be lying, but I'm trying to help because he's ugly, and girls never like him. Not everyone can have my personality." She grins wider at his baloney. "Knock me a little kiss right here," he says, turning his cheek to her.

She does, and he makes a point of overexaggeratedly biting his lips like he's enjoying it. My hands find her waist, turning her away before I lead her far from my degenerate friend.

"It was nice meeting you, Goldie."

"You too, Chase," she calls out before I grab our coats at the front, hearing him at our backs.

"Feel free to exaggerate my good looks when you talk to your sister. 617-374—"

I can't help but laugh as I push through the door. The moment we get outside, I can feel her staring at me.

"What?" I breathe, turning my head to look at her.

*Man, she's pretty.*

"Nothing. You two are great together. How long have you been dating?"

My shoulders shake with amusement.

"No, but seriously, you two seem like family. How long have you known each other?"

I slip my hand into hers as we stroll down the sidewalk. Opening up isn't easy for me, but my life in Boston is the exception to that. It's the here and the now. And that's the part I like.

"It feels like I've known him forever. Like we grew up together, but I met him out front of my junior college. He was drunk, in only his underwear, out on the lawn. Campus security was trying to figure out what to do with him. He lied elaborately and told them he knew me." I laugh, remembering. "I was just passing by, but he was convincing. Or maybe they didn't want the hassle, so they let him go. We've been best friends ever since."

She seems entertained, wrapping her other palm around my bicep, and our hands stay joined. "Was he in school with you?"

"No, he was an unpredictable rock star in culinary school. His family has money. They're from Wellesley, which is how I eventually got into Boston College. A good word from someone who has the school of business named after them helped get me to the top of the pile. I think it was their way of saying thanks for keeping Chase on the straight and narrow. Little did they know, I've always been kind of a hell-raiser."

She chuckles as some guys pass. "Were you a bad kid?"

Before she can try and coax an answer from me, a voice booms from behind us.

"Hey, man . . . hey"—my eyes are on hers until I feel an insistent hand on my shoulder, stopping me—"I know you. How've you been?"

I turn, Goldie letting go as I tuck her behind me. Some guy in a Mets jacket smiles back at me, but I look around, confused. "Sorry, man, we've never met. You've got the wrong guy."

He shakes his head, slightly slurring when he speaks. "No, it's me, Peter . . . Ronnie's cousin. You're, umm . . ." He snaps his fingers. "Davis, right?"

Goldie's face presses against my shoulder, and I can feel her smile. "He's a Noah, not a Davis."

The dude frowns, his eyes locked with mine as he works out whatever thought he's having. But my eyes go to the hand still on my shoulder, and he takes it away.

"Wow. I could've sworn . . . my apologies." He gives us a salute before adding, "You look so much like a friend of my cousin's. I used to visit him every summer in Darkwater Bay until I was, like, sixteen for the sailing regatta. I live in New York now."

Goldie giggles quietly, whispering up behind my back, "And that's his whole life story."

I shrug, smiling. "Yeah, what can I say? It's like the lady said, I'm Noah."

He nods and gives us an embarrassed wave, then apologizes again before stumbling back to rejoin his friends, and we continue our stroll. I only glance back once.

"That was weird," she breathes out before grinning wider, turning her body toward mine as she teases, "Okay, come clean. Are you running from the law and you haven't told me . . . *Davis*?" She emphasizes the name, making me laugh. "And what happened in Darkwater Bay? Don't make me call the FBI. A girl has a right to know who her boyfriend is."

"Very funny," I laugh and spin her around into the shadows of a convenient alley, her body trapped between me and the brick. I look down, my hand on the wall beside her.

"Boyfriend, huh? You sure?" Our eyes stay connected, the silence growing before she bites her lip. I smirk. "Because I am."

She nods. "Me too."

"Then I guess I should come clean. I'm an upstanding citizen originally from Hempstead. But I do have one confession—"

Her eyes are locked on mine as her chin juts up in a challenge.

"I'd really like to kiss the fuck outta my girlfriend."

"So what's stopping you?"

*Damn.* I'm on her in an instant. The feel of her mouth on mine makes me want to lose my mind. This kiss isn't like our first, slow and savoring. No, we're already messy and fevered, armed with an urgency.

A need.

My fingers thrust between the strands of her hair as her own curl into my waist before they greedily ascend up my back. It makes me hum my approval because her body molds to mine as she does it.

We're rough breaths and teasing tongues doing something we shouldn't.

I nip at the tender flesh of her bottom lip, almost shuddering as she whines. The sound tastes as potent as my desire feels. My other hand engulfs her neck as my thumb runs up and down her throat.

Fuck, I want her. Under me, on top of me. All over.

I've never wanted to hear a woman moan my name more in my life. My heart's beating out of my chest as we kiss and kiss, losing ourselves in the moment, the whole world growing more and more hazy.

I pull back, feeling too wild. Needing to control myself, but not really wanting to, only hearing her ragged breath as our lips remain hovered.

She swallows, and even in the shadow, I can see the flush on her skin.

*I want to kiss her again.*

Goldie must be thinking the same thing because she lifts her chin and gives me a singular chaste peck before repeating it over and over, until she's forcing her bottom lip between mine, coaxing me back to her.

"Fuck me," I whisper, giving in.

I can't stop myself. I'm back for more, tasting her tongue and feeling its warmth against my own. Her arms crowd between us but only to raise her fingers to my jaw, cradling my face, as we fuse together, sealed so tight that it's unseemly.

We're raw, unadulterated lust. Two kids in an alley about to do the kind of shit reserved for dark rooms. But now that the Pandora's box of sex-filled energy is open, we're slaves to the consequences.

She wraps her arms around my neck, and my thoughts go from kissing her lips to kissing every damn piece of her. To laying her open and fucking her until we're sweaty and spent, breathless and sated.

I tear my mouth away, my head dizzy, mind afloat.

We're near panting as I smile down at her, pushing against the wall to create a sanctity of space between us.

"You're a killer . . . a black widow, for sure. Go on, kiss me to death."

She tries to laugh, but it's airy and woven between short exhales. Her fingers lift to her swollen lips, wiping the shine away as she shyly turns her head toward the street. I bite my lip before dipping my head to kiss her jawline softly.

*What is it about her? She's fucking mouthwatering.*

"Oh my god," she whispers.

"Mm-hmm," I hum, lost in the softness of her skin.

"No," she quietly laughs. "We have an audience."

My lips begrudgingly leave her as my head whips up, my narrowed eyes following her line of sight to a group of people crossing the street. They're laughing, all their heads taking turns to look back over their shoulders in our direction.

I smile and feel Goldie's embarrassment as she hides her face in my chest before she whispers to me, so I cover the back of her head with one hand, shielding her with my arm.

Whatever she says vibrates through my shirt, and I wish I could say I hear her, but I don't. Because my eyes are still locked in place.

Across the street, about twenty yards past the people, is a silhouette. One just outside the spotlight of a streetlamp. An unmoving statue.

Watching.

The smile I'm wearing slowly fades until it's gone because my blood runs cold.

A car passes, its tires echoing off the tension I feel, but the statue moves only to tilt their head.

It's unnerving when you can feel someone looking at you, like ice down the spine. I've said it before: Men are always on guard. But it's not men. It's me.

And I don't know if it's my simmering paranoia or if I'm truly feeling what I'm feeling. But rage, palpable and thick, winds itself closer, dredging along the cracked asphalt, aimed directly at us. My eyes narrow, piercing the space, my pulse jumping up a notch as adrenaline begins coursing through my veins.

Maybe it's fight or flight? *No, it's always fight.*

As if to prove myself right, my jaw tenses, and I take a firm step toward the outside of the alley, but Goldie holds me in place, kissing my chest from the outside of my shirt, her cool hands beginning to roam my stomach just underneath it. It makes me blink a few times rapidly, before I let out a harsh breath as my abs contract under her touch.

Moreover, it serves to break my momentum and makes me glance down at her.

"Hey, we should get out of here," she purrs, oblivious to my reaction.

"Not until . . ." I begin to say, looking back across the street, but it's empty.

Like a hallucination sent to sabotage what's real and right in front of me. I volley between her and the street only twice, with Goldie winning the war.

*Focus on the now, Noah.*

"Not until what?" she prods as I look back to her, a deep V forming between my eyebrows.

But I shake it off and smile. "Not until you promise you won't regret becoming my girlfriend. You know, now that you've met the puppy."

She pushes me away and begins walking backward out of the alley, dragging me along by my shirt.

"Well, that's an easy answer, but why don't you ask me again in the morning."

# Chapter Six

## Goldie

Noah's back hits the door with enough force to knock the wind out of him, but he's completely unfazed as he cradles my face, our mouths doing their level best to exhaust us.

We haven't stopped kissing since his bike pulled into his driveway. It was like the universe rang the sexy-time dinner bell and we were starved.

"Sorry," I say, floating between excited laughter and lustful impatience as we bump faces awkwardly when he tries to reach behind him to open his front door.

"Keys," he mumbles against my lips, urging me to help him.

We're fumbling and shoving our hands into all his pockets, trying to get his damn door open, completely out of breath from our refusal to stop kissing.

But we just can't stop.

"Oh my god," I groan as he grabs the back of my neck, keys forgotten, only lips remembered. "Just bust it open."

My plea is accompanied by the sound of his key sliding into the lock.

*Thank god.*

Noah spins me as the door opens, backing me up into his house before kicking the door shut behind him. I don't know whose clothes come off first, but we're immediately clawing at each other.

Our jackets thud as they hit the floor. My bottom presses to the top of the couch as we toe off our shoes. And my purse is flung onto the couch as his belt's whipped off with a snap.

He chuckles as my shoulders jump, and I do the same into his lips.

We're feral. But a week in your thirties once you've met someone is like dog years, so a month is tantamount to starvation.

We kiss sloppily, pulling away and diving back in as we make our way through the living room. I only risk breaking it to look down, trying to find the right buttons on my shirt to start with, but as I lift my eyes, Noah's mid-drag, his shirt sliding over his head.

Sweet Jesus. My mouth goes dry.

His hair's messy and possibly even more sexy than it was before, and his eyes are shining even bluer. I've spent weeks wondering what he'd look like when we got *here*, and it's exceeding all my expectations.

I'm walking backward, not knowing if I'm about to run into anything, as I stay fixated on every groove of his abs and defined muscle on his chest. The tattoos that start on his neck are deliciously painted down over his chest and his arms, even covering his twelve-pack. In fact, they go all the way down over the V on his lower stomach, disappearing beneath the tops of his jeans. It's like a gorgeous sheet of armor, forcing me to stare at the precision by which he's been sculpted.

He unbuttons his jeans with one hand before unzipping and shoving them down his muscular thighs, stepping out.

"You're beautiful," I say, feeling even more breathless as I reach the last button on my shirt, letting it fall.

He's stalking toward me, faster than each of my steps, his jaw slack and his gaze boring into mine.

"Bed, floor, or counter."

He delivers those three words with an indecent amount of gravel in his voice, and I shiver, forgetting everything I was doing, half blinking and feeling heady, unable to answer.

Noah closes the distance, snaking out his hand and removing mine from my waistband gently. His words feel less so.

"Uh-uh. Get off. That's for me."

His fingertips tickle my skin slowly before he curls them just inside the top of my jeans, jerking me forward. I gasp, then smile, biting my bottom lip as he tugs me closer with a hiss sucked in between his teeth, his eyes landing on the swells of my breasts. They're still half hidden by black lace. I'm mesmerized by his tongue, staring as it darts out, swiping the most seductive path across his bottom lip before he draws it between his teeth and lets it glide out slowly.

The room suddenly feels quieter, the desperation we felt earlier replaced with his intention: Noah wants to savor this.

His voice lowers to that quiet, sexy baritone I've come to wish for when we're on FaceTime late at night.

"I haven't slept with anyone in over six months. I'm good to go. Ask and I'll show you the results."

"Okay . . . yeah, no. Me either . . . or me too . . ." All my words are jumbled and impossibly affected by him, so I giggle before correcting myself. "What I mean is that I'm good to go too. And I haven't slept with anyone in forever."

The top button of my jeans pops, making my shoulders tense in surprise before goose bumps bloom over my soft tummy. Noah's staring down at me, the ghost of a smirk on his face as his fingers pinch the zipper. And then, almost sadistically, he slowly lowers it.

The rip of the metal fills the space, crackling like the energy dancing between us.

"Are you on the pill?"

I never thought in a million years that someone could make those particular five words sound so inviting and sexy. Words won't come out of my mouth because my pulse is pounding everywhere. And I mean everywhere.

Noah's hands lift from the front of my jeans to my hips, his palms sliding over my skin before he tucks his fingers inside my jeans, guiding them off my body. His eyes never leave mine as he does it.

My chest rises and falls quickly as he dips his middle fingers under my thong, dragging those down too.

"Goldie . . ."

The way he pauses after my name makes me close my eyes so I can concentrate on every sexy syllable about to come out next.

"Killer, if you let me, I'd like to die inside you tonight. Bare. Because all I can think about is how I want your cum all over my cock." He kisses my mouth just as I feel the air hit my exposed center. My eyes spring open, fixed to his as he fucks me with only words. "Would you like that, baby? My bare cock inside your cunt?"

My eyes follow him, watching as he lowers himself to the floor along with my clothes, kneeling in front of me. He lifts his chin to look at me, and it's so striking in the moonlit room that there's only one answer to give.

"So much yes . . ." I swallow. "And yeah, I'm on the pill."

My eyes flutter back as I feel the warmth of his breath tickling, then cooling the wetness shining over the soft tuft of hair on my pussy.

"Fuck, that's sexy," he whispers.

Noah's face plunges forward as he palms my round ass, running his tongue over my clit like we're sharing a kiss. I suck in a harsh breath, instinctually gripping his hair and holding his head as I'm gorgeously assaulted. My stomach contracts as he eats me, forcing me to hunch over a little, unable to control myself.

"Oh god. Fuck."

He switches to kissing me gently, growling as he does, his tongue laving over my clit and around it, devouring the evidence of my lust. Holy hell, this man knows how to eat. It's like he's sharing what he does to my mouth with my pussy.

Noah doesn't just want to fuck me. He wants to leave his mark in every way.

And it's working. The bar has been reset.

"Noah, I don't think I can take it. It's too much," I pant, my legs barely able to keep me up.

He hums, enjoying me, making me buckle. But instead of falling, I'm held up as his arm wraps around my hips, keeping me in place. He swirls pressured figure eights, manipulating and flicking my swelling clit before sucking, then letting it go with a pop as he tears his face away to stare up at me.

I shudder, mid-groan, and my hands fall to his cheeks as broken heaves of breath leave my lungs.

"You're too good at that."

"Not my fault you taste so fucking good on my tongue."

To prove the point, he licks the light sheen of my lust coating his lips, and it's the hottest thing I've ever seen.

"Step out," he directs, motioning his head to my pants pooled at my feet.

I obey as his palms run up and down my waist while burning kisses into my stomach. *Is this too early to call it as the best sex I've ever had?*

Noah stands, and my eyes provocatively drop to the bulge protruding from his boxer briefs. The entire imprint of his impressive length shows, and apparently, the energy Noah gives off is honest. He has a very big dick.

*Nope. Not too early.*

All I can think is that I want to feel him. Everywhere.

His shoulders draw in as he runs his hand up and down the outside of his underwear over his shaft, letting out a sexy grunt, eyes closed for a moment like he's desperate for a little release. Some friction to relieve the same white-hot need I feel too.

"You never answered my first question," he levels, his gaze blazing back to mine as his hands find my waist.

*Question?*

I'm led backward again, this time at Noah's pace. First, through the kitchen, his head motioning to the counter before he raises his eyebrows, then says, "Or," looking down at the floor. We don't stop, still moving backward, turning down a hallway before one of his hands lets go of my waist and slaps the door of his bedroom open.

"Or?"

*. . . bed, floor, or counter.*

"All three," I rush out.

I'm immediately lifted as our mouths seal together with abandon. Wet, rough kisses lead the charge as he carries me to the bed. The moment I hit the soft mattress, my legs never unhooking from around his waist, I grind my core against his rigid length and let out a moan at the same time.

His large hands slide up my forearms, roughly gripping my wrists, holding them in place above my head as his lips leave mine, beginning an assault on my jaw, leading down to the crook of my neck.

"Noah . . . that feels so good."

He grinds into me again as my legs squeeze tighter. The friction between our bodies makes my thoughts fuzzy. I feel him bite my neck before he gently runs his tongue over the spot and sucks.

I gasp, arching against his heavy body, writhing under his touch. Because he's somehow pressing all the right buttons. Buttons I didn't even know I had. I've never been the kind of girl who sleeps with a guy for the first time and lets him give me a hickey. But somehow, with Noah, I'd let him mark up my whole body in anticipation of the pleasure I know he'll give me.

"Tell me to stop and I'll stop," he groans, sucking a new spot harder this time, drawing my skin into his mouth.

There's no denying that mark.

"Mm-hmm," I moan. "Don't. Don't stop."

I feel him smile against my flesh before he lifts his head.

"Good, because I'm just getting started."

He's still holding me down as he snatches my lace bra over my breast with his teeth, exposing me before sucking my pert nipple. I hiss, enjoying the jolt of pleasure. The way his tongue circles the pebbled bud before his mouth kisses the soft flesh surrounding it, sucking and biting, draws porn-worthy moans from my chest.

"Oh god, yes."

He switches sides, uncupping me in the same fashion before his tongue darts out, licking between my breasts up to my throat and peppering it with open-mouthed kisses.

I grind my core against his length again, and he rocks into me too. It's heavenly. He moves from my mouth, kissing my cheeks over to the soft spot under my ear. God, Noah's determined to make out with my whole body. I'm sure of it.

I tug my wrists, feeling the weight of his insistence to keep me there. My voice is husky, thick with my desire.

"I want to touch you," I rasp, trying again. "Let me . . ."

His mouth melds to mine as he lets me go before, in a flash, he rolls us over. My legs unlock so that I'm straddling him, looking down at the gorgeous creature whose hands are instantly roaming my stomach.

I reach around myself, unfastening my bra and slipping it off.

"I've never felt anything so soft," he muses, cupping my tit, his thumb brushing over my nipple.

He pushes off the bed so that we're basically face-to-face. "I can't stop touching you." His palm reverently presses to my breastbone, between my cleavage, as my chest rises and falls. "Can I do it all night?"

He looks at me shyly, dropping his eyes to my tits before meeting mine again.

I nod as I bring my fingertips to his shoulders, feathering them over his skin, tracing the pictures and designs, and smiling as his breath stutters.

"Yes. All night. Because I haven't stopped wondering what you'd feel like since the night you kissed me."

Without a word, Noah's eyes lock on mine as he takes one of my hands and lewdly runs the flat of his tongue over my palm before dragging it down his chest, forcing my hand against his skin as it moves farther down his stomach until my breath catches. Because he's slid my hand inside his boxer briefs and around himself.

He swallows hard. "What do I feel like, Goldie?"

He's warm and thick in my hand. And his skin is smooth, but I can feel the protruding veins around his hard cock, rigid in my hand.

"Like a good time," I answer slyly, grinning as he exhales sharply when I close my hand tighter around his hard length.

I circle my hand, sliding it upward before gently pushing down, feeling his hips involuntarily jerking under my careful stroking.

"Fuck. That feels . . ." is all he manages as I tease his cock, giving him just enough relief without the promise of an orgasm.

He groans, grabbing the back of my neck and jerking me into a kiss, but I don't stop touching him.

Noah's other hand roams my body, kneading my breasts before his fingertips caress my collarbone as we kiss, our lips swollen. We're alight. On fire. The heat between us gathers and multiplies with every touch.

I start to rock, my body in tune with what I'm providing him.

"Fuck me," I whisper once, then twice, our lips so close I'm breathing air into his lungs.

"Lift," he growls into my mouth before I take my hand off his cock.

He bites my lip, then sucks the pain away, smirking at me.

He pulls his cock from his underwear, clumsily shoving the briefs down far enough to give him room before the slick precum on his dick rims my entrance.

I'm on my knees, clutching his shoulders, staring down as he teases himself through my wetness, rubbing his desire over my clit and back to where I beg him to be.

"Please," I breathe out, wishing I could swallow him inside of me.

"Not yet. I want to fuck every part of you with every part of me first."

I moan, trying to lower myself onto him, but he holds my waist, whispering into my skin.

"You don't want my tongue—"

It flattens at the base of my neck, drawing up my throat and over my chin until diving into my mouth. But too quickly, he pulls away.

"Or my teeth—"

The hand that was on my waist presses to my chest and pushes me back before he bites my nipple with just enough pressure that I gasp.

"And I haven't even used my fingers—"

A deep inhale fills my lungs as he parts my labia, spreading me open before running his fingers up either side of my swollen hood, igniting all the sensitive nerves.

My body melts into him, taking everything he gives as he brings his fingers together and rubs my bud in slow, decadent circles. I rock my hips, teased not only by the slow, rhythmic motion of his fingers playing with me but also his cock readied at my opening, pressing ever so slightly.

Each time I move, I feel the head of his cock barely brush my hungry entrance over and over as he works my body as if he's known it his whole life.

"You keep making that sound." He groans threateningly. "Fuck me, you're so sexy."

I don't even know what sound I'm making because all I can concentrate on is the feel of him stroking himself underneath me as his fingers pick up the pace, playing with me.

Jesus, the depravity of him jerking off at my entrance almost makes me come on the spot.

"I want you inside me, Noah. Please . . ."

My head falls back, exposing my throat for him to kiss. And he does, hard and desperate.

I'm lost to this feeling. Needing him. Wanting him to fuck me until I can't speak again. I feel like I'm going to explode.

"Noah," I almost say on a deep, breathy exhale because my body's beginning to build.

But it's all I get out because Noah can't take it anymore either. He thrusts himself inside me, pulling me down so hard it feels like all the air is knocked out of me.

"Fuck," he bellows.

Our bodies are sealed tight. My arms wrap around his neck as we hold still, both rocked by the sensation engulfing us.

I feel his chest rising and falling, my own matching, each of us unable to move because I've never felt bliss like this. The tightness of my stretched cunt over his hard length pulsating inside me because we're so fucking turned on that we may not make it past this one moment.

His warm breath on my neck slows just before he starts to move, rocking me backward as he ever so slightly pulls out, then pushes back in.

"So. Fucking. Good."

I kiss him slowly, my pussy contracting as I try and meet his pace, but he rolls us again so that he's back on top, his palms pressed on the bed to protect me from his full weight.

He pulls out and thrusts back in, his pelvis pressing tightly to mine. It hurts just the right amount good dick should. It'll make me sore enough to leave me with a reminder I was very well fucked.

My hand grips his ass, urging him for more as he begins slowly, without any rush, letting the muscle between his groin and belly button brush my clit each time.

I moan, eyes closing, spreading my legs wider and lifting with each thrust, wanting more of everything.

"Look at me." His palm comes to rest at the base of my throat as we stare at each other in hedonistic pleasure.

My mouth falls open, matching his, my eyes fluttering back with each draw of his cock.

"I want to hear you call my name. Say it for the neighbors to hear." He grins, picking up the pace.

I draw my leg up over his hip, giving him an even deeper angle, and watch his jaw tense as he takes complete advantage and hits my G-spot.

Fuck. This feels so good.

Noah's cock glides in and out, making the sides of his ass indent under my hand.

"You want to come, baby? Tell me . . ."

His voice should be illegal because I'd do anything he wanted right now.

"Yes . . . I want it . . . please . . ."

His breath grows heavier, the hand around my throat tightening a bit.

"Do you need to use your fingers?"

I nod rapidly before his face nestles into the crook of my neck, and he reaches to take my hand off his chest, sliding it between us. One set of my fingers finds my bud as the other stays gripped to his defined ass cheek.

"Fuck yourself with me."

I swallow under his palm, the motion thick in my throat because it's so dry. I start to rub, but Noah grabs my hand, again saying "Get it wetter" before sliding two of my fingers inside me, along with his cock.

"Oh god," I groan gutturally before they're pulled out and put back on my clit.

Sex, sweat, and all the sounds that go along are ripe in the air, conducting our symphony of lust. He grabs the back of my leg, pounding inside me, still stretching me as he looks down between our bodies, watching me roll my fingers over my clit.

"Fuck, you just got wetter," he groans before kissing the hell out of me.

We fuck with no words. Just grunts and moans. His hands are in my hair now, pulling the strands as he hammers inside me like he's possessed. The faster he goes, the faster I do, too, reduced to the basest instincts, chasing the sweet relief we both need. I contract from the inside, tightening around his cock, rubbing the walls of my pussy all over him.

"That's it, baby. Let me feel you. Let me make this tight pussy cry."

I slap the bed, gripping the comforter because I can feel it happening. My legs tighten around him unevenly as my orgasm builds, pooling in my stomach, making my clit throb and feel numb.

He all but forces the air from my lungs, fucking me faster and faster with decadent ruthlessness as my fingers move in desperation.

"Come for me. Do it," he growls out. "Let me fuck you into bliss."

"Yes, yes, yes, yes . . . fuck me . . ."

My body's tensing so hard, wanting it, needing it, until all I can see is searing, white-hot light behind squeezed-closed eyes.

I come so hard that I scream, my back arched, bucking off the bed as my legs open mercilessly wide, and my hands sting from the force of my grip on the blanket.

"Noah."

"Oh fuck. You're so tight . . ."

Noah's voice is so strained I can barely make out his words as he hammers into me, over and over, gripping my leg hard enough I'm sure it'll leave a mark.

"You have the sweetest goddamn cunt," he whispers to himself, lifting his body off mine before throwing my leg over me to fuck me sideways.

His large hand grips my hip as I lie breathless, panting, barely able to control the shaking in my body as I stare up. He's solid, tensed muscle from jaw to stomach as he locks eyes with me.

"Again," he demands, rolling his hips impossibly hard and fast as a trickle of sweat bleeds over the sheen on his body.

"I can't," I whine, my body already beginning to prove me wrong.

The look on his face is determined and almost menacing as he narrows his eyes. The urgency he's fucking me with is unrelenting as his thumb slides between my ass cheeks and presses the taboo spot.

I gasp, immediately rocked by another spasmed, quieter orgasm ripping through me.

His guttural growl bellows and echoes throughout the room as he stills, almost grinding his teeth as his abs pulse before he exhales harshly and falls behind me.

"That was . . . incredible," I whisper before licking my dry lips.

His arm wraps around my waist before he drags me closer, making me squeal as his smile blooms against my back.

"Gimme like thirty minutes, and we'll do it again."

I giggle. "Can't forget the 'ors.'"

Noah nuzzles my neck, peppering kisses behind my ear.

"Looks like a sun," he whispers, making me smile because he's found my birthmark.

"It's how I got my name. My mom said she just knew I was destined to be a Goldie with a birthmark like that." I feel him smile against my skin again. "How'd you get your name? Lemme guess, a love of animals and water?"

He chuckles, nipping at my skin, making me wiggle around to face him with my arms squeezed in between us.

I lift my finger to trace the black-and-white outline of the wings that peek over his shoulder. The tattoo spans the whole top of his back, and the delicate tips of the feathers end on his neck. It's hot as hell.

"What made you get this one?" He licks his lips as he smirks at me but says nothing. I swallow, trying not to blush, opting to bite my bottom lip instead.

"It was for the Sarah McLachlan song. For all the adopted pets."

I giggle. "Liar."

He winks as my finger lands on another tattoo, an intimidating-looking skull close to his throat. I raise my brows.

"Let me guess . . . You were a really big fan of the TV show *Bones*."

He's still silent, just smiling. But the way he's looking at me tells me he's enjoying this little game as much as I am.

"Are you going to tell me about any of them?" I flirt quietly, my finger drifting over another.

His voice is gravelly as he closes his eyes, enjoying my touch. "How about you choose your favorite, and I tell you about that one."

I grin, scooting away just enough to wave my hand over the whole front of his body. "This one."

He laughs before tucking his hand between me and the mattress and flips me over. I shriek as my back is pulled to his front again and his arms wrap around me in a deliciously tight hug.

"No more Q and A. I want to enjoy the best sex I've ever had before we take a catnap because then it's counters." *Called it.*

The moment he squeezes me tight, all I can seem to think is: *Is it weird to send Walgreens a thank-you card?*

Because I'd really like to say, *Thanks for being open on Halloween so that I could be a dino patron and meet the potential man of my dreams.*

# Chapter Seven

## Noah

My bedroom's drenched in darkness as my eyes spring open, my pulse racing like I just ran the hundred in the Olympics. Only the sound of my heart thuds in my ears. Holy shit. I blink rapidly, scrambling internally for my bearings, not unable to move but still heavy with fear.

*Fuck.* There's sweat on my brow. I lift a hand to my forehead, slicking my hair away, before I try and swallow, but the sting of my nightmare seems to still be leaving its mark because my throat's aching from strain.

I was trying to shout in my sleep.

*Breathe, Noah. Just breathe. You're home. In Boston. Focus on the now.*

I don't remember what I was dreaming about, but it doesn't matter. The aftereffect is always the same. Damn, I haven't had something like this happen to me in a long while. They used to happen a lot when I first left home, but it's been months since I can remember feeling like this.

I let out a quiet exhale, trying to pin down what triggered it. But the reasonable part of my brain finally wakes up. *Or maybe just stop being a fucking head case?*

As if the universe knows to throw me a bone to pull me from my fucked-up mind, a soft sigh catches my dark, swirling thoughts, grounding them instantly as I turn my head and lay eyes on her. *Goldie.*

She's snuggled up to me, head rested on my arm. Her rich, thick locks are strewn out over my bicep. So peaceful and . . . beautiful. My mind drifts away from the hairs on the back of my neck, still standing on end, and firmly to the memory of her straddling me.

And the way her body moved in response to everything I did made me half wonder in the moment if I'd have to say the thing no man wants to excuse—*I swear this never happens to me . . . I always last longer.*

The blanket falls as she moves, exposing a peek of her nipple.

So fucking gorgeous and soft and supple.

*Like velvet.*

I stare back up at the ceiling, having heard the words in my head like the old barbershop dude in *Coming to America*. My mind clears as I half smirk and refocus on the present.

Swallowing again, this time with more ease, I glance back at her, hoping to soak in some more calm and maybe another pervy look.

She's so blissful. I want that.

*Did I lock the front door?*

The thought seems random, but it's not.

It's funny how peace triggers chaos. But I guess that's the best description of life because one never veers too far away from the other. Unexpected bedfellows of sorts. So, I guess if she's peace, then I'm admittedly chaos.

My eyes search the darkness. I'm still wondering . . . *When we came in, we were going at it . . . did I remember . . .*

Ever so gently, I draw my arm from under Goldie because there's no point in second-guessing myself or debating from under warm sheets. I know, from experience, that the only thing that will quell the paranoia or ease my worry is to just fucking check.

She smiles in her sleep the moment I'm free, mumbling something I can't quite make out. It makes me grin. And I swear my fingers act of their own accord, brushing an errant strand of hair from her eyes.

*How is someone so cute when they sleep?*

Easing off the bed, I look around the floor for my boxer briefs, noticing the time on my clock we apparently knocked off the nightstand. It's lying on top of my underwear. I shake my head and tug them on before heading out of my room.

As I quietly shut my bedroom door behind me, I'm encased in more darkness. None of the lights are on. But we didn't bother earlier, too busy stripping each other down in the moonlight, like a pair of horny teenagers trying to bone before her parents came home. Now, though, it's as if someone's stolen the moon.

Thankfully, my eyes have adjusted as I navigate the long straight shot through my kitchen into the living room. At least that's what I think before I trip over my discarded shoes, then hers.

"Goddammit," I huff, kicking the shit out of the way, walking off my stubbed toe.

With one hand running through my hair, my other reaches for the door handle, twisting it, even though I know it's an automatic lock, before I check the dead bolt.

*Unlocked.* The click to secure it is as loud as my irritation.

Grinding my jaw, I draw back the curtain from my window to inspect the street, searching up and down the quiet. It's exactly what 2:00 a.m. should feel like on a Friday night—empty and sleepy. Everyone's either still partying, passed out, or grown up.

There's nobody. But I still can't shake the faint worry of *somebody.*

A car alarm sounds, making my head whip in its direction, but it's cut off just as quickly.

"Fuck," I whisper to myself, hating that I can't make my mind stop.

*Go back to bed, and it'll stop.* I let the curtain close and shake my arms out. *We do still have the counter and the floor to accomplish.*

The tension in my shoulders dissipates slowly, easing off as I inhale. I'm turning around to head back to the gorgeous woman in my bed, and as I do, my eyes drop down to the floor. I've left the curtains open just enough that the streetlights created a streak over the carpet, exposing the large, dingy brown envelope peeking out from under the couch.

I narrow on it, my jaw tensing.

When I kicked the shoes out of the way, I must have shoved one under and hit it. I glance toward the hall that leads to my bedroom before I bend and drag it out.

Unable to stop myself, I tug at the rigid string wrapped around the button that holds it all closed, unwinding it before I open it and reach inside, sliding out the first thing I touch.

The worn newspaper clipping is barely readable save the headline as I stare down, feeling the familiar hollowness in my chest as my heart picks up pace.

Massacre Leaves Broken Hearts in Small Town

I glance toward the hallway again before choosing another.

Body Never Found

Adrenaline floods my system in waves. I'm shivering but not cold. I glare at the thin paper between my fingers, fixated on those three words: *Body Never Found.*

My skin tingles like I'm wired. Like every nerve ending in my body's sparking at the same time, my jaw instantly sore with the power with which I grind my teeth.

The only sound in the room is my breath, heavier and more audible as my chest rises and falls faster and faster.

I'm helpless to stop it. Helpless against the anger inside me. To the rage that bubbles right under the surface, waiting to be unleashed.

The world around me begins to disassociate, like the blurred edges of a fire, until suddenly, all the air evaporates from my lungs, a back draft of consciousness sucking out all the oxygen before an explosion of realization.

My head snaps to the right.

The crisp feeling of cold slices across my cheek first, like a slap that wakes me up. I can't feel the paper I'm holding as my eyes narrow into tunnel vision directly on the thing that's wrong.

The back door. It's open.

A breeze billows in, making the hinges squeak, disturbing the silence as the wood frame sways.

Shadows tucked in corners of the room dance in my periphery, like taunting demons, but all I can process is the fucking moonlight that's illuminating the kitchen island.

Everything inside me stills, all that I'm feeling transforming into unnerving calm. Because there are only two options: Someone's in my house. Or they just left.

I shove the papers back inside the folder, then squat and hide them again, never taking my eyes off the door.

As I stand, slowly and quietly, my hands ball into fists, and corded muscles in my back flex. But my feet are already moving as I search the space like a predator, stalking toward the back door.

Passing the hallway leading to my bedroom, I double-check that it's still closed before the quiet sound of a whetted blade punctuates the space as I swiftly and expertly slip a butcher knife from the block.

I sneak behind the door, not making a sound, the only line of sight the crack in the door between the frame and the hinges. I lift my chin as I strain for a better look, the heavy steel knife dangling in my hand brushing my skin, but I'm glued in place. I don't even swallow, twisting the glinting metal around and around, trying to stay hidden in the shadow.

The silence stretches out longer and longer as I listen.

Leaves rake over the porch, crawling over each other, grating the quiet, and wind chimes from the neighbor's house softly play, alerting anyone who's listening that the night's awake.

But I only hear the footsteps that grow closer.

There's shuffling and the knock of a chair from the porch as another breeze sways the door harder, but I touch the handle, controlling it.

Seconds tick by like an old wall clock. Tick, tick, tick. But still, I don't move. Like the man who watched us tonight. I'm still. Waiting.

The whining in the wood gives away weight on the threshold, so I fling the door open and draw back the knife, aimed to the gut.

But a screaming meow erupts, along with a bloodcurdling cry. *Fuck.*

"God flucking! Shiv!"

A streak of calico launches at me, bouncing off my bare chest as Goldie's arms flail toward the night sky. I immediately tuck the butcher knife behind me as I step away from the doorjamb. Bile rises to my throat.

She's wide eyed, half spun around herself as she stands in one of my T-shirts.

"What the hell are you doing out here?" I shout, feeling panicked, motioning with my head over my shoulder. "You were sleeping. I didn't know . . ."

*Fuck. Fuck. Fuck.*

She laughs. I frown.

*She's laughing? She's fine. It's fine.*

Goldie puts her hand on her chest like she did when that guy at her sister's party scared her, completely oblivious to the cold metal in my hand.

"Apparently, getting the shit scared out of me. I couldn't even cuss correctly. What the hell, Noah?"

*Pull it together.*

"Me?" I try and smile, swallowing hard, finally feeling my pulse again. "You're sneaking around like a creeper. I could've killed you with my bare hands."

She chuckles again like I'm joking. The knife twitches, nicking my thigh.

I eat the pain, keeping my mouth shut as she walks back inside.

"Well, Jason Bourne, your ex was making a ruckus outside your window. Which doesn't open, by the way. You should fix that."

She passes me into the kitchen, still breathing hard. I shift, keeping what I'm hiding hidden before closing and locking the door. My head's still swirling, trying to process, finding success with each second.

"Anyway, I figured she was yours, so I snuck outside to introduce myself. You know, kitty to kitty. Didn't want her sneaking in to shit in my shoe." She chuckles at her own dirty joke. "I thought you heard me while you were spying on your neighbors from the window."

"I didn't see or hear you." *This is why you don't bring women home, Noah.*

The urge to double-check that what's under the couch is still hidden scratches at my mind, but I keep my eyes trained on her.

She shrugs. "Huh, must've been the car alarm."

I'm smiling with as much sincerity as I can muster, but it's fake because I'm still teetering on the edge.

"Yeah, it was nothing."

I follow Goldie around the kitchen island, then quietly slide the knife back into where it belongs when she turns away from me. My face lifts to hers as she opens the fridge, lighting up the room.

"Why are you up, anyway?" She looks over her shoulder to my fingers, still on the tip of the knife's handle. I let go, leaning against the counter nonchalantly.

"Midnight snack," I lie while she hands me a water before she gets her own.

I twist the top. But then she smiles, and the magic of it makes me remember our previous plans.

It restarts my focus, letting me be Noah again.

She bites her lip. "I could eat . . . if you're offering."

I smirk, letting my eyes drift over her, knowing I'm going to turn my white lie into the truth. Until an annoying meow between my feet drags my attention away.

"No way, troublemaker," I groan, discarding my water. "You had your chance to be my one and only. Out—you've been replaced."

I stand to walk past Goldie, back to the door, enjoying the sound of her laugh as she protests, "No, let her stay. I just went to all the trouble to smuggle her in. Plus, we're friends now. And it's cold out."

I shake my head, but my eyes lock to hers just as her fingers skim my chest. "It looks like I'm her only friend, though. She got you here and somehow on the back of your leg too. There's blood."

My eyes drop to my chest, seeing the reddening scratches, knowing exactly what got the back of my thigh.

I grin. "In fairness, you threw her at me."

Her eyes gleam, her smirk teasing. "In my defense, anything's a weapon when someone sneaks up on you."

"I live here," I say flatly, grabbing her waist and making her squeal as I plop her down on top of the counter.

"Yeah, well . . . I . . ." Whatever retort she was hoping to sassify doesn't make it off the tip of her tongue.

I raise my brows. "Done trying to win? 'Cause I'm suddenly starving."

The smile on her face is bright enough to light the room, even though the goddamn fridge is still open. Fuck it, that's one door that can stay that way.

We're fixed on each other wordlessly before I start bunching my shirt up over her hips. She audibly inhales, licking her lips when I expose the fact that she's not wearing underwear.

"I couldn't find them," she whispers.

"Good."

I take a step back, my fingertips skimming over her knees as I admire my meal.

"What do I get for a snack?" Her voice is the embodiment of sex.

"I'll make you a grilled cheese when I'm done."

I slide my hands up the inside of her thighs before gripping them and jerk her to the edge of the counter. She shrieks, her palms smacking the counter before I dip my shoulder, flinging her directly over it.

"What are you doing?" she squeals, laughing, her hands hitting my lower back.

"Job security, killer."

# Chapter Eight

## Goldie

***December***

"A dunk tank?"

I say it mostly to myself, but Noah nods. "Yeah, and I plan to spend every cent I have in my wallet right here."

Our heads turn at the same time, our eyes locking, a shit-eating grin on his face as he adds, "It's for a good cause."

When Noah invited me to the "little Christmas market" thing Chase was participating in, I never anticipated arriving at the set of a *Gilmore Girls* winter festival.

Besides the ball pit dunk tank that said best friend is currently fighting for his life in, every carnival ride a person could imagine litters the wintry park square, surrounded by stark trees strung up in lights. Rows of quaint vendors are sprinkled over cobblestone streets, selling trinkets and jewelry, adorned with cute hand-drawn signs that read **A PORTION OF THE PROCEEDS GO TO FEEDING AMERICA.**

All set in the neighborhood next to our first date.

I shake my head as we move up in the long line we're standing in for a chance to dunk Chase. Which I can't help but notice is made up mostly of women. *My money's on his exes.*

"I can't believe I've never heard of this event . . ." I pause to smile, only because Noah's hand slips into mine. "How have I lived here, for . . . like, ever and been missing out on this?"

Noah grins down at me.

"Because it started this year, that's how." My forehead wrinkles with curiosity as he continues. "Chase was doing some chef guy meeting with a bunch of other restaurant owners in the area, and I guess the conversation led to the local food banks and Christmas, so they decided to raise some money." He shrugs. "I just put them in touch with Feeding America because I did some pro bono work for their website."

*"Just put them in touch" . . . shrug . . . "pro bono work" . . . shrug . . .*

Jesus, this man's a master class in humility and sex appeal. My stomach does that little flip it's been doing more and more over the last few weeks.

Which is dangerous because everyone always says to date someone who likes you more than you like them, but unless Noah's totally obsessed with me the way Bill Nye likes science, I'm fucked.

I think I started falling for him the night we met. And now I've found myself doing that thing girls do who are down bad. I find ways to bring him up in every conversation, making my sister hate me. I also go about my days at my new job pretending that I'm not daydreaming about him.

Except I am. A lot.

Worse yet, he's spent almost every night at my house since the first time we rang that dinner bell. The urge to let him leave a toothbrush behind feels seriously intrusive.

This crush is crushing me into a lovesick fool.

I'm still staring up at him, lost in thought. But I can't help it because he's fine as hell and pretending not to notice me. It's cute.

Noah lazily tilts his head before narrowing his eyes on me.

"You're such a little stalker." He leans down closer. "Wanna sneak in my window later and do dirty things?"

I grin harder. He kisses me.

A quiet, breathy laugh leaves me before I pull away, teasing, "Your windows are all nailed shut. How exactly would I do that? You know what, scratch that. It's no fun if you know I'm coming."

So gently that it makes me shiver, his thick fingers find their place right around my throat as his eyes fix on mine.

"Killer, I always know."

I swallow because that felt dirty before I'm kissed for the second time.

As his hand lowers, I'm struck by a thought. Something I've come to realize about Noah is that he's a man of few words, but the ones he chooses always hit the mark.

I sigh as I open my eyes, still stuck in a bubble.

He lifts our joined hands, brushing his thumb over my cheek, where I know I'm blushing, but damn if he doesn't always make me. People cheer from next to us, reminding me we're not alone, so I clear my throat, hoping to pull myself out of my Noah haze.

Thankfully, I'm saved by the ding . . . the ding of my phone.

We both step away to a more respectable distance, smiling sillily, as I let go of his hand to see who's texting me, already knowing it's my sister.

> **Evie:** I'm here. Just parked. I stole a spot in front of some news vans. 😈

And this is why she should be labeled "Evil," not "Evie," in my phone. She's a demon.

I chuckle and look up at Noah. "My sister said there's news vans. That's great, right?"

He nods, glancing over his shoulder but saying nothing before shoving his hands into his pockets.

**Me:** Hurry up.
We're in the middle
at the dunk tank.

**Evie:** Ten four.

Noah's voice nabs my attention, pulling my face up to his.

"Does she know you're setting her up?"

My mouth falls open, and I pretend to be shocked over such an accusation, even though Noah's onto me.

I've hung out with Noah and his bestie more than a handful of times now, and each time, I'm more and more convinced Chase is perfect for my sister. But that's stayed my little secret, especially since when they first met, it didn't exactly go swimmingly.

Evie's an acquired taste . . . although Chase's refusal to dine on her every word wasn't the problem.

"I'm not setting her up . . . I would never. How dare you accuse me of such nonsense. I'm just not *not* setting her up."

He shakes his head as we step forward in line again. "You're just gonna throw them together again and see what happens?"

"Exactly."

"You know who else famously did that? The Romans. You didn't bring any lions, did you?"

I laugh, rolling my eyes. "Hear me out . . . Evie's like a hot guy in a girl's body—allergic to commitment, immune to being love bombed, and food is her love language. And Chase is, well, the ultimate sarcastic dudebro chef. They're the same person. They just need a little nudge. It's a perfect match."

"Or a potential bloodbath." He winks.

I shove at his chest, but Noah catches my hand there, lowering his voice so only I can hear. "Let's make a deal. If they hate each other—"

"Which they won't," I interject, but he ignores me, continuing.

"—and *she* eats *him* alive again, you're staying up late with the baby to dry his tears."

I scoff and shift sideways so my body faces him as I wrap my arms around his waist.

"Oh, ye of little faith," I tease up to his profile. "This could be the meet-cute to their happily ever after. And twenty years from now, we'll all sit around at dinner, laughing about how I set-not-set them up."

*Oh no . . . words go back in my mouth.*

My eyes bug out for a second, thankful he's not looking at me. Until he does, so I whip my face sideways, staring at nothing, my lips folded under my teeth.

Holy shit. *Did I just forecast us into our future life together?* I long-hauled us all the way to fifty.

I'm chewing the inside of my cheek when his voice hits my ears, and I feel the tickle of his five o'clock shadow.

"I bet you're fucking hot at fifty. You think I have a beard?"

Fuck it. I let the smile on my face bloom as my eyes meet his, and I shrug coyly before I lift the tips of my fingers to his chin.

"I hope so. They do it for me, ya know."

Noah immediately laughs, deep and rich. *Yeah, I'm not falling. I've fallen.*

"Oh yeah," he sexily rumbles down. I can hear the grin all over it. "Maybe I'll grow one out now? But whaddya gonna give me if I do?"

Before I say anything else, my phone dings, and I begrudgingly extricate myself from him again.

**Evie:** All black.
Really? So slutty.
Tell him put that
bde away when
he's around me.

It's kind of disrespectful.

**Me:** No but how
did I get so lucky?
He's like a Golden
Retriever in a
Doberman dis-
guise.

**Evie:** I mean, not to
be incestuous but
your boyfriend's
hot.

"Tell Evie I said thanks."

My face swings to his, my eyes bugging out because we've been caught, but he's smiling at a sweet teenage girl behind a table lined with orange balls. Apparently in the midst of my texting, we've made it to the front of the line.

He hands her a hundred-dollar bill before grinning back at me.

I chuckle. "So rude. Didn't your mother ever teach you not to read other people's texts."

He winks. "Luckily I have a girlfriend who doesn't keep any secrets."

"Or do I?" I tease, only for him to let out a little growl as he reaches to tickle me.

I'm giggling just as I hear my sister's voice behind me.

"Dunk the chef? Really?" she laughs. "And with balls that look like tomatoes. That's next level. Who's the unlucky victim?"

*Oh shit.*

I spin around, realizing she hasn't put it together yet.

"Where have you been?" I rush out, immediately hugging her like she's been away at war.

"Hey," she greets Noah, who just says "Spartacus" under his breath before she pushes me off her.

But not before I strategically turn her away from seeing my secret. Now Noah and I can see Chase, but her back is to him. This suddenly feels like a bad idea.

Evie scrunches her nose before her lips purse, sarcasm readied. "Golds, why does your face look like that? Did you eat spicy food again?"

"Shut up," I groan, and glance over her head, trying to figure out how to introduce this spontaneous yet completely planned setup. "I need to talk to you about something . . ."

Her frown lines form before her voice rises nervously. "Shit. Mom told you. That's why you're so weird right now." She lifts a hand. "It wasn't really my fault, but I do feel bad."

My brows lift, and I don't even have to look at Noah to know what Evie just said has piqued his interest too. The best part about little sisters is they always confess their crimes before they're even up for interrogation.

"Uh, told me what . . . ?" I lean in toward her, watching her swallow the realization that she's fucked up.

"Shit." She winces and I nod, motioning with my hand for more.

The background sound of girls cheering for the chef to be dunked makes me smile but doesn't distract me from my sister. I know she's going to try to escape from this conversation like Houdini out of handcuffs. It's not happening.

"Nope. Out with it, right now, or I'll—"

Evie's hand flies over my mouth to stifle the rest. "Fine. Remember that guy I hooked up with last week? From the café we went to. The kind of ugly one but he had those gorgeous blue eyes. Super gangly, but funny. He was like a bunch of trade-offs."

I squint, moving her hand as I try to remember him from the roster she has.

My head tilts thoughtfully. "Yes?"

"Leather jacket with 'The Smiths' spray-painted on it, and you said, 'Great band,' and he said—"

"'It's my last name,'" I finish, nodding. "Yeah, I remember him."

Noah chuckles as he grabs my back pocket to guide me closer to him before his arms wrap around me. I let my chin rest on his forearms.

Evie fake chews her thumbnail. "Well, he won't see me anymore because he almost died in front of your place."

My eyebrows shoot up as my eyes almost pop out of my head. "What! My place? How?"

Noah's body is firm behind me, tensed, as Evie looks sheepish.

"So you're going to be mad . . . I went by to return your new black boots—"

"I didn't loan you my boots," I cut in.

She bites her bottom lip and shrugs. "Yeah, that's the 'You're gonna be mad' part . . . I took them without asking. You were at work late, so I made him wait outside for me and—" My mouth falls open as I suck in a shocked breath as she continues. "Apparently, he was sitting on your stoop, and someone hit him with a crowbar and took his wallet."

"Jesus, is he okay?"

"Yeah." She scowls as if I'm the problem. "I wouldn't be telling you like this if he'd actually almost died or had been disfigured. I'm not a monster. Although, blaming me and never talking to me again seemed a tad bit overdramatic and frankly unchivalrous."

"Evie," I admonish, but she shrugs, grinning. "Noah, weigh in . . . Am I wrong?"

He says nothing as I frown, thinking about how often he's left my apartment in the wee hours, before I look up at him. His eyes meet mine, and he kisses my forehead.

"You're staying with me tonight. And tomorrow."

I nod as Evie pushes her braids over her shoulder. "That's probably a good idea. Crime is getting out of control in this city." She turns in the direction I don't want her to go, but I'm not really paying attention. "You should put an extra dead bolt on the door. Maybe get one of those lipstick Tasers?"

"Yeah, agreed," I say, still kind of freaked out, but before I can finish my thought, Evie gasps, jerking me back into the present.

Because the sound is less shock and more like she's been set on fire. Her head swivels around slowly, her eyes locking to mine.

"What. The actual. Fuck . . ."

My sister's throwing daggers at me. And she's hitting me right between the eyes. Everything we were just talking about disappears from my mind because the jig is up. Noah releases me and we look at each other, his "bloodbath" prediction sinking in. I don't want to admit the truth as my shoulders hit my ears.

Chase's voice carries to us. "No way. Do not give that man any balls. He's lived this long without them. What's a few more minutes until my shift is up?"

He's noticed Noah, but some people are still lingering in front of Evie and me.

"I can't believe you're trying to set me up with this jackass again." Evie narrows her eyes. "I'm telling Dad you did this to me."

Noah rubs his jaw sympathetically, whispering "You're in so much trouble" as my shoulders start bouncing.

*I so am.*

"No," I say, completely unconvincing. "It's just friends hanging out. Why would I do that?" I huff a few empty laughs. "I mean . . . you're . . . no . . . come on."

But it's too late. Our cover is beginning to walk away, and I can see on her face that she doesn't believe a word I'm saying. The shit is officially about to hit the fan.

Noah walks up toward the throwing line, taking a fake tomato out of the bucket and tossing it in the air as Chase squirms in the seat, looking for a way out.

"I will not go gentle into this good pit—"

Noah laughs. "Now you're adapting Dylan Thomas. I didn't know you could read. What are you scared of? There's no water, just balls . . ."

It's hilarious that the water's been substituted, but it's December in Boston; hypothermia is real. That and shrinkage could level a man for life.

"These things are dirty," Chase bellows, pointing to the ball pit he's hovering above. "I don't think they've cleaned it since borrowing it from whatever day care was available. *Toddlers* touched this parasitic plastic. Do you understand that? You can't dunk me. It's against bro code . . ."

Noah keeps smirking as Chase begs. I would smile, too, but I'm busy pretending my sister isn't burning a hole through my face.

Her voice drops low and sinister. "I will pay you back for this. You won't see it coming, and it will be apocalyptic."

I squeeze my eyes shut because she's a lot of things, but a liar isn't one. I'm so screwed. Reminder to self: Take away her key.

In contrast to her quiet threat, Chase is still yelling. "They're basically cave dwellers who play in their own shit. That's the fate you're damning me to?"

My hand covers my mouth, hiding my laugh, but maybe the motion is what nabs his attention because the next thing I know, Chase is throwing himself forward, gripping the edge of the tank. He looks back and forth between Evie and me, stopping on her with almost literal hearts in his eyes before he spreads his arms wide.

"My earthly goddess. We meet again."

Evie bristles, her head drawing back. She absolutely hates him. Noah throws his arm over my shoulder as I hide my face in his chest for a second, already laughing too hard.

But it's short-lived because her eyes whip to ours, vengeful, as Noah says "Jesus" under his breath.

Noah was right. This is definitely Colosseum-level matchmaking. Except Evie's the lion, and I've sent Chase to his death.

My sister pushes past us, looking at me first.

"You are fired as my sister. Move over," she barks at Noah, taking the tomato out of his bucket before locking eyes with Chase. "Cheers to necrotized fasciitis."

Chase gets halfway out with "I think I love you—" as her arm rockets the tomato straight into the center of the target.

Chase yelps, balls fly, and my sister lets out a "Whoo."

"Four years of high school softball," I offer to Noah's whispered "*Damn.*"

He leans down close to my ear. "I guess we'll just have to have two Christmases for the rest of our lives. The grandkids are gonna be so mad."

I grin. He's never letting that one go.

But before I can say anything, Evie's already spinning back around, making us stand straighter as she throws her long, knotless boho braids over her shoulder.

"I'm finding food. Do not invite that man to Friendsmas, or I will go no contact."

Without another word, she cuts between Noah and me, forcing us apart but leaving us to do the only thing we can—laugh.

Especially as Chase blows spit balls away from his face and calls out after her.

"Baby . . . come back. I vote this is how we tell the kids I met their mother."

# Chapter Nine

## Noah

We've been from one end of this festival to the other, proof of that being the cutest pink tint on the end of Goldie's cold nose. Not that the cold has slowed her down any. I've never witnessed someone so invested in homemade bath bombs.

Truth be told, I didn't actually know what they were until she gave me a lengthy explanation about the importance of self-care. I swear I was interested; I only laughed because Chase equated baths to dirty body soup.

The thought makes me chuckle to myself again as I watch her browse a rack of bracelets with her sister.

"All right," Chase breathes out as he comes to stand next to me, holding a bag with a goldfish inside. "This shindig's ending in thirty, so . . ."

My eyes fix to the fish. "Where did you get that?"

His forehead wrinkles like I'm the weird one for asking.

"I . . . won it. Little-known fact about me, Noah: A water gun in a clown's mouth is my Olympic gold. Nobody's better."

Right as he says it, two elementary school–age girls walk by and side-eye him, to which he raises his voice.

"I'm especially not losing to cheaters who let their parents help them aim. Not today, playas."

I shake my head, staring at his profile. "Stop talking. For the love of god. Please."

Goldie shivers as she approaches, also eyeing the fish but choosing not to address it. Which makes me smile as I reach out, for the millionth time today, and pull her body close to mine, enjoying the heat that melts between us. It's not just the feeling that I like, it's the security of having her within arm's reach. Especially after Evie's news today.

I didn't like it. I may never let her leave my house.

"What's next?" I say to her upturned face. "The event's ending in about thirty minutes."

"Ferris wheel?" Chase throws out, staring at Evie, who pretends to vomit.

Goldie shakes her head. "Too cold."

"Cannolis?" Evie tosses out as Chase grins with a dirty joke written all over his face, making her scowl again. "Don't speak, cretin."

He pretends to lock his lips and put the key in his pocket.

Goldie sighs, still staring up at me, so I whisper, "My place? Just the two of us . . ."

She nods, biting her bottom lip before snuggling closer. God, I might keep her. The scent of her hair wafts upward, making me dizzy on her as I lean down for a kiss, but Chase claps his hands together, interrupting the moment.

"House of Mirrors?" He shifts between all of us excitedly, sloshing his fish. "We have to . . . It's a staple of a carnival, like gamja hot dogs and cotton candy."

"I do love a Korean corn dog," Goldie says as she looks up at me, buying into his unknowing cockblock.

But Evie's face is deadpanned as she stares at Chase. "How are you the most unrelatable relatable person I've ever met? It's astonishing."

He grins and hands her his fish. "His name is Knievie. Like Evel Knievel, but Evie—"

"Yeah," she cuts in, shaking her head. "I got it."

She groans as she walks past him and takes the damn fish before grabbing Goldie with her other hand, dragging her away from me. "You're going in with me."

Goldie mouths "Sorry" over her shoulder as she's whisked away a few steps ahead, making my eyes shift to Chase, who just winks at me. "Rome wasn't built in a day, baby."

"JC, I fear you'll be stabbed to death before you get a single stone up."

He looks at me, fully confused. "What? Who's JC? Are we talking the great JC Chasez of NSYNC? Because he built that empire on the voice of an angel—"

He's still running his mouth as I tune him out and shove my chilly hands inside my jeans pockets as we follow behind the girls, with only the hint of a smile on my face as I watch Goldie laugh with her sister.

She's so beautiful. I just want to stare at her all day . . . Damn, I like the fuck out of this girl.

I knew that before this moment, but today's really driving the point home. This has been one of the best days I've had since I moved here. And that's because of her. Which is a problem.

At the time when we first met, I was happy to follow her lead. Respect her boundaries. Mainly because I'm not a piece of shit.

But now, I feel like the girl from that doctor show where she's all *Pick me, love me.* Especially since those five little words she said earlier keep clanging around in my head like they're in a mosh pit: *And twenty years from now.*

I knew she was joking. And that's the aforementioned problem—I can't stop thinking about how I liked the sound of it. I'm falling hard for this girl, and there's no part of me that thinks she isn't feeling something more too. That much was obvious with the slip of her tongue. How much more, though, seems like muddy waters I'm too chicken to dip a toe in.

Fuck. I'm acting like a thirty-one-year-old middle schooler.

Pretty girls really do reduce men to boys.

My brows draw together as I watch her ass sway in front of me, but it's not enough to hypnotize me away from my thoughts.

"Noah. Are you coming?"

Goldie's voice carries over to me, and I suddenly realize that I've been standing in place, silently reasoning with myself.

"Yeah." I grin, running my hand through my hair.

Chase gives me a look, like *What's wrong with you?* But I shake my head, closing the distance to my girl.

I smile to myself, relishing the sound of that . . . "my girl." Because that's what she is, all mine.

When I reach her, she slides her hands into my jacket pockets.

"A penny for your thoughts."

I shake my head. *Chickenshit.*

"A quarter?" She winks.

I give her the same response. She smiles brighter.

"Fine," she huffs. "Keep your secrets."

"A kiss," I counter.

She pulls her hands from my jacket, resting them on my chest before raising to her tiptoes as I lean down.

Our mouths touch softly before they begin to press together with more insistence, as if one taste couldn't be enough. It can't be. The fullness of her lip dips between mine just as my hand lifts, cradling her face to deepen our kiss.

Fuck, kissing her is next level.

Goldie's soft moan drifts between us, and her body sinks into mine. It's like a siren's call, becoming my only focus. But still, I kiss her with absolutely no rush, taking my fucking time.

Our heads tilt, tongues starting to tease and dance as my fingers slide back into her hair. She moans again into my mouth, making my grip tighten.

Every sound and every taste that comes from this woman makes me want to devour her more, to do shit to her nobody else should see.

Her fingers curl around the fabric of my jacket, holding me close as we teeter toward lewd.

Fuck it. I don't care.

I'm going to kiss the fuck out of my girl. And who's going to stop me?

Both my hands are in her hair now as I hold her face to mine, kissing her like she's the air I need to breathe. Our mouths are sealed, tongues swirling, and all I can think in this moment is how I can't make myself end it.

"And it seems there's not just charity in the air. Love is too."

The voice in the distance slowly begins to seep in, growing louder until everything registers at once—the sound of Chase's and Evie's commentary, the laughs and cheers from the rides, and the news reporter.

It all hits me at once. Like a brick shattering our perfect bubble, reducing every ounce of heat I'm feeling to ice.

Goldie's breathless as I jerk away, immediately turning my back to the cameras, pulling her in front of me.

"Shit. Sorry," I mumble, blinking too fast, trying to keep my grin in place.

She's laughing. "We keep doing that . . . making a show of it." She smiles up at me. "Maybe this is our moment. Now we can piggyback off this fame to a million-dollar OnlyFans."

I swallow, hoping she thinks my heart's beating fast because of her.

It is . . . *it was.*

I walk her backward toward the House of Mirrors entrance and away from the news crew as she tucks her hands under my jacket, closer to my body.

"Oh my god, you're so cold you're shivering," she says sweetly.

*Be fucking chill. Say something.*

What I can't say is *I'm not cold. Adrenaline and panic are the same. They spike quickly and drop off just as fast.*

I clear my throat. "The only people making seven figures are selling feet pics. And these dawgs are shy. So, we'll just have to be poor and happy."

I glance over my shoulder, seeing that the crew have stopped filming and are packing up, so I look back at her. This time, my smile feels more genuine.

She dramatically rolls her eyes. "Who said we were using *your* feet? We're trying to make money."

More people file in behind us, and just like that, we're back to being lost in a crowd. All the tension in my shoulders sloughs off as I throw myself back into this conversation.

"No way. I'm taping your shoes to your feet. There will be no feet pics."

She chuckles, still rolling with the joke. "God, you're such a tyrant. Fine, but I'm only agreeing because I like you so much."

I stare down at her, half a smirk on my face. There must still be a little adrenaline running through my veins, making me brave, because I go all in.

"How much?"

Her brows rise. "What?"

I start playing with a piece of her hair.

"How *much* do you like me? You said, 'so much.' So, I wanna know how much is so much."

I can feel her grip on my shirt tighten. "Well, what's my scale?"

The familiar crackling between us starts firing like an electrical box. We're just staring at each other, half smiles on our faces, silently urging the next question.

"One is I'm your boyfriend. Ten is –"

Only the sound of my heart is in my fucking ears as I stare at her mouth, scared to say the rest. Goldie blinks those big doe eyes up at me while nibbling on her bottom lip.

But just as I start to finish my sentence, Evie's voice cuts in. "It's our turn."

Goldie's spun around and pulled through the doors into the maze of mirrors, leaving me standing by myself.

"Fuck," I rush out, snapping my face to the guy at the door who's holding his arm in front. "Let me in."

"Sorry, man, only a few at a time. You and your friend have to wait."

I look behind me at Chase, who's too busy staring down at his phone to pay attention.

"Come on," I press. "I was having a moment with a girl. Don't do me dirty."

The guy looks behind me at Chase. "Hey, you good going with the next group so your friend can find his true love?"

I don't even get to hear what that smart-ass says because the minute the dude lifts his arm, I tear inside.

Which is decidedly the wrong move because I almost run directly into a mirror and break my nose.

"Shit," I snap, jerking back to save my face and waiting for a moment to gain my bearings.

My head whips side to side, but everywhere I look, there's me. Over and over with nothing but darkness surrounding me. Goldie's laugh in the distance makes me smile as I extend my arms, letting my hands feel out the space.

I feel one mirror, then two, before I find the right pocket so I can slip into the next spot.

"Killer, where you at?" I yell, hearing her laugh again.

I'm slowly making my way through the space, feeling around so I don't maim myself, chuckling as I do. Chase is excommunicated for thinking this up.

I turn into a new clearing before circling around to get my bearings, but see myself for miles until, bam, I spot her.

I spin, thinking she's behind me, but she's gone. So, I spin again, and she's there.

"What the hell?" I whisper.

She smiles, but it's not at me. It's not at anyone.

My head whips around, trying to figure out how I'm seeing her, but just like that, she's gone again.

"Hey," I laugh, stepping forward too quickly and hitting the wall. *Shit. I'll be unconscious before I ever get her answer.*

I'm reaching out, feeling my way slowly, as something in my periphery grabs my attention, so I turn my head, expecting my girlfriend, but as I do, my face drops.

Because I see Goldie, but I also see . . . *wait* . . . I blink hard, giving my head a small shake because what I thought I saw isn't there anymore. It's just Goldie.

What the fuck? I swear to god, I saw . . . *Get your head together, Noah. This is because of the cameras and shit. You're spooked.*

My mouth's slightly agape as I try and gain my bearings again, feeling my way through the maze of mirrors. But my heart keeps speeding up. It won't stop, gaining speed each time I get a wisp of her before she disappears again.

*Chill, Noah.*

The hair on the back of my neck starts standing on end, pricked up around goose bumps. My eyes land on her with each twist and turn I make.

She's there, and then she isn't.

There. And not.

My head whips right. *What was that?*

I'm not sure if I said that out loud as I swallow, rubbing my jaw, as a streak of her snatches my attention left. I reach out instinctively, catching a sliver of dark shadow off to the side.

But then it's gone.

I feel my chest rising and falling quickly as I move with urgency, tapping the space around me to get through faster. To get to her.

What the fuck is wrong with me? I'm losing it.

No matter how fast I weave through the maze, it feels like I'm too many steps behind her. Each time I round a corner or slip through two spaces, she's there, then gone.

And so are the flashes of a black boot. Then a navy jacket. A balled fist.

A man. Following her.

I'm gritting my teeth, a deep-set V forming between my eyebrows as I turn left, suddenly in the middle of a larger space, every direction of my reflection prismed.

"Goldie."

Her image appears in small diamonds next to mine as I spin around, trying to figure out a way to get to her, until I'm frozen in place.

Because next to Goldie's image is *him*. The same silhouette from the alley.

I shake my head, trying to make him disappear again. But he doesn't. He's unmoving, watching her as she multiplies and divides for me in the mirror.

"Hey," I say, almost too frozen to speak before repeating myself with more force this time. "Hey."

The stranger tilts his head sideways. Just enough to tell me he heard me but not enough for me to see his face. His jaw tenses before he moves, disappearing.

*Fuck. No, no, no, no.*

I'm slipping and bumping into wall after wall, trying to get to her as my pulse races. I feel panicked, glimpsing Goldie laughing, her hair flying around as she makes her way through the maze. Because he's there. Behind her. Then next to her . . . Is he next to her? I don't know. I can't tell.

"Goldie," I yell.

Her head turns in the prism, a hundred of her looking right at me. She smiles.

I start to yell to her again, but as fast as I see her, she's gone, and as I step forward, the man appears in the same way.

He reaches inside his jacket before the glint of silver arrests my entire soul and lets a monster inside me take over.

It feels like I'm blacking out as I make my way through the mirrors, completely lost in a haze of fury and fear. I move faster and faster, my breath shuddered, mouth opened.

The only thought in my mind: *Kill.*

A red exit sign feels like an explosion, or maybe that's just the force I use to bust through the door. The dark hallway's lit by the real world on the other side, but I'd see her anywhere. I charge forward, my vision drowning in rage, eyes fixed on the shadow of Goldie against the wall.

*Kill.*

The motherfucker standing over her turns his head just as I grind out my words.

"Get your fucking hands off my girlfriend."

He takes a step back but doesn't say a word. Because he can't. I've wrapped my hand around his throat, pinning him next to her.

I pull her behind me, tightening my grip, staring into his eyes.

"Why'd you follow her through the maze? What the fuck was in your hand?"

He's sputtering, slapping at my wrist, but I don't give a shit. I press harder, feeling the force of the pressure all the way up my arm.

I glance back at her. "Did he hurt you?"

She shakes her head quickly, eyes wide, while trying to pull my free arm as Evie and Chase come running.

"Noah. Dude," Chase yells. "What are you doing? You're choking him." His hand taps my veiny forearm rapidly. "Let him go, buddy."

I'm heaving breaths, shaking my head, blinking so fast that everything around me feels like a movie slowed down to the frames.

*He had a knife. He was following her. Kill him.*

"Please, Noah." *Goldie?*

With my free hand, I frantically reach up, feeling around the inside of his jacket until a sharp crack echoes off the concrete, forcing my eyes to drop.

A silver cell phone lies shattered at my feet.

"Fuck. He's gonna kill him." Chase's voice is closer now and louder. "Let him go, Noah. You made your point."

I nod a few times, trying to process. *It wasn't a knife . . . It was a cell phone?*

She's okay. It's okay.

In an instant, I drop my hand and step away, scared of myself. The guy folds over, hands on his knees, sucking in long heaves of breath.

"I'm calling the cops," he rasps over his scratched throat. "You're a fucking psycho."

Goldie slides her hand into mine, yelling back, "Call them, and I'll tell them how you were harassing me."

I feel murderous all over again and start to lunge at him again, but Chase pushes his hand on my chest to stop me.

"Whoa, whoa, whoa."

The asshole stands up and scowls at us. "Telling you your tits were nice isn't harassment. It's a compliment."

"Fuck you. And I bet forcing me against the wall is normal too. You're a pervert," she shouts back.

"Why the fuck were you following her?" I bellow, pointing a finger at him, still restrained by Chase.

He scoffs, rubbing his neck. "What the hell are you talking about? I never followed her. I work here."

"Not anymore," Evie snaps.

Chase is eyeing the guy down just like me as he volleys between us.

"Get the fuck out of here before I choke you again," I grit out.

He mumbles "Fuck this" under his breath as he stumbles away, but all I can focus on is Goldie.

She wraps her arms around my body, but I don't even realize I'm hugging her back until I look down.

"Thank you. You're my hero," she whispers, and I notice her eyes are shining.

"Are you okay?" My fingers brush her jaw.

She nods. "I am. Thanks to you."

I say nothing, our eyes fixed as the thought in my head settles into my bones. I would've killed him if he'd hurt her.

"I'll never let anyone hurt you. You're precious to me . . . Goldie, I—" I pause because the way she's looking up at me is knocking the wind out of me.

Holy shit. I am incapable of not falling deeply in love with this girl. I couldn't stop this if I wanted to. I wouldn't even walk away for self-preservation.

Her hands curl around my jacket as her voice stays intimately quiet. "Hey, you never finished what you were saying before . . . One is you're my boyfriend, ten is . . ."

My tongue darts out over my lips, ready to say the words. "Ten is you're falling for me too."

Those words hang between us as she stares up into my eyes. We're locked in, neither of us making a move to stop what's happening.

"Ten," she whispers quickly and somehow not.

Her burgeoning smile matches mine inch for inch as it all sinks in, but when it does, I cradle her face as I pull my baby into a kiss.

But as much as I want to lose myself like before, this one's short-lived because our children begin making a scene.

Evie starts fake vomiting as Chase slow claps next to her.

I hate them.

I shift my face to theirs. "If you two are done, I'd like to kiss my girlfriend and take her back to my place."

"It's better than jail," Evie teases as we all make our way off the goddamn attraction.

Chase pats my shoulder, already rebounding from what just happened.

"Mazel, guys. Listen, before you go, though, put in a good word for me with . . ." He motions over his shoulder to Evie.

"I can hear you," Evie rushes out, making me grin.

I look back at my girl and kiss her again, uncaring of the world around us as we melt into our bubble and let the soundtrack, which is set to a score only two people destined to go from hate to madly in love could create, play loudly in the background.

*"You know I'd choke someone for you."*

*"You make me want to aspirate the vomit produced in my mouth every time you speak."*

*"If you go, I go . . . Let's Romeo and Juliet this bitch."*

*"We just witnessed harassment. Are you that slow of a learner?"*

*"Cuff me, baby."*

# Chapter Ten

## Noah

Sweat trickles down Goldie's smooth back as my fingers draw a line between her shoulder blades until my hand wraps around the nape of her neck, holding her in place as I fuck her from behind.

"Fuck, killer. You feel so good."

She's breathless, face down, her bottom lifted as she grips the sheets. It's gorgeous.

I thrust inside, stretching her with a steady, torturous rhythm. I'm hitting her G-spot each time my thick length bottoms out, sealing the front of my pelvis against the softness of her ass.

"Please," she moans. "Noah, I want to come."

My voice is guttural and raw. "Not yet." I grip her hip as she tries to circle it. "Uh-uh. I said we're fucking longer."

I know it's sensation overload. We've been at it for long enough to feel like two live wires. Every inch of her skin is so sensitive to my touch that she can't stop writhing, her body begging for her release.

The sound of her breath huffs out each time my body rolls my cock in and out of her welcoming warmth. She contracts herself around me each time, cradling my shaft inside her, rubbing our flesh torturously.

"Noah," she whines, "oh god."

She snakes a hand between her legs, touching herself, gasping as her body ignites, but I pull out to the tip, making her suck in a breath over the loss.

My deep, gravelly baritone rips out of me as I grip her hair harder, forcing her chin to the mattress. "You want to come so bad . . . Don't cheat, ask me nicely, killer."

A smile lifts the corners of her lips before she licks her dry lips.

"May I come . . . please." Her voice strained and needy.

I smirk. "What my baby wants, my baby gets."

The instant I let her go, I pound into her, fucking her so hard her body jostles against the bed. Goldie's mouth falls open as shuddered cries escape. But I hold her prisoner, in place, barely able to catch my own breath as everything inside begins tightening.

All the mangled, garbled words fall from our mouths like rain from the sky, pooling around us like a symphony of sex as we climb higher and higher. Bodies contracted. Eyes squeezed shut. One of her fists is balled in the sheets, the other hand rubbing herself in all the right places.

"Noah!" she screams long and hard into the bed, convulsing. Coming.

My thick cock draws out, dredging my cum from the softness of her cunt before hammering it back inside. She's cresting over her bliss as my fingers dig into her hip.

The sound of my voice spills over her, gutted and full of the edge she's come to crave. "Oh fuck. Baby. Fuck, fuck, fuck . . ."

I still, jaw tense, stomach hollow before filling her with my lust. My body gives growing slack, more and more, until I'm folded over hers and we're both a puddle of entangled, sated bliss.

"Stay the night," I whisper, pressing a kiss to her shoulder.

She nods, her voice barely working. "'Kay."

The warmth of Goldie's bare back melts into me as we spoon, my discarded blanket still caught between our legs.

"Let's never leave this bed," I say between peppering kisses to her salty skin.

I can hear the smile riding on the hum of her laugh before she wiggles, scooching around to look at me. Her elbow rests on my shoulder as she weaves her fingers through my messy hair.

"Actually, I was just thinking you should come over for dinner."

I scowl. "I thought we were staying here."

"I don't mean tonight."

"You should be dinner," I whisper before kissing her neck. "And dessert."

She squirms when I get to a ticklish spot, so I hold her close. But she pulls my face to hers using my hair.

"How about next Wednesday?" She's being persistent.

My fingertips run down the curves of her naked body, knowing exactly where this conversation is heading, so I take a detour.

"Wait. A. Minute," I say dramatically. "We're not eating for a week? You're just gonna stay here and let me fuck us to death? I like it."

She chuckles before pressing a soft kiss to my lips. "Will you be serious? I really want you to come over for New Year's Eve."

I groan, my palm engulfing her hip as I push her away, extricating myself to sit with my back to her.

"Killer, I don't know . . . We talked about this. Chase expects me to come to the restaurant. I'm sure your parents just want to see you, since they flew all the way in for Christmas."

When I look over my shoulder, Goldie is sitting back on her haunches, pulling my T-shirt over her pert breasts.

"Noah," she says so sweetly it makes me mad at myself. "My parents are dying to meet you. *That's* why they flew all the way in. I talk about you all the time. Why don't you want to? Do you feel like we're moving too fast? Are you wanting to slow down?"

*God, no.*

"No, Goldie—" I start, but she touches my shoulder, cutting me off, before I feel her chin rest on it.

"Is this because you're an onion?"

"An onion?" I chuckle, using the blanket to cover myself as I shift to look at her. "What does that mean?"

Goldie grins, playing with a strand of her hair.

"It means you have layers, Noah Adler. And they all need peeling. You're always so quick with a head nod to answer any question. Or a dreamy stare that makes everyone forget what they even asked. You're definitely a man of few words. Which means getting to all the good stuff takes time . . . and work. So, I think, just maybe, a 'meet the Monroes' is making you feel a little too vulnerable?"

"Ooo," I grunt, putting my hand over my heart, hating and loving that this is her opinion.

After all, true happiness is being seen . . . *That is, unless you're trying to hide.*

I smirk, reaching for her waist. "First off, onions make people cry and give them indigestion. I demand a new vegetable before this conversation goes any further."

She bites her bottom lip, trying not to fall for my charm. *Good luck, killer. I'm laying it on thick.*

"Onion," I scoff, grinning and instantly captivated as I watch her mouth work into a pursed seduction before she frowns like she's deep in thought. But when I open my mouth to speak again, her finger presses to it so she can take the floor.

"Artichoke," she says resolutely.

I can only raise my eyebrows, urging her to elaborate because she won't let me breathe.

"Because it's layered, good for you . . . and the heart's the best part."

The way she's looking at me—a little unsure with an equal measure of hopeful—makes my chest want to cave in.

Goldie gives a little shrug. "Does that get me to the second thing you were going to say? Because you said, 'First off.'"

I circle her wrist and drag it away from my mouth as we stare at each other until I break the silence. Finally, being serious.

"Killer, I'm not scared of your parents asking me questions. Even though I hate talking about myself. And it's not that I don't *want* to meet them . . ."

"So then why won't you come?" she rushes out.

But I have to look away from her because sometimes she makes me feel so exposed that I'm not sure I can say what I need to.

"Because you scare the shit out of me, Goldie. You make me want shit I didn't think I could have."

My eyes lift to her frown. She's not understanding, so I reach up and cradle her face. "They mean so much to you. And I guess I haven't made it obvious enough, but you mean so much to me already. I'm falling for you every day, more and more. So, if I fuck this up . . ."

She throws her arms around my neck, knocking us back down on the bed as she rushes out her words. "You won't. I promise."

Her hair is wild, draped down around us as her eyes stay locked to mine.

"Say you'll come. Make it my belated Christmas miracle."

The smile always hiding in wait when I'm around her comes into view. Who the hell am I kidding? There's no reality where I say no to her. Even if it turns me into a liar.

"Okay. Okay," I gripe, pretending to be exasperated. "I'll come"—my hand slips between her legs—"but only after you do . . . twice."

"Stop being so nervous."

"Easy for you to say. They already like you."

Goldie stares up at me in the hallway just inside her door, her bright-green eyes lit with humor as I let out a long, audible exhale and adjust my shirt collar, feeling like I'm suffocating.

She grins, running her hands over my ribs and around my back, hugging me.

"Relax. You're going to do great. I thought you said you felt better after your talk with Chase yesterday?"

I rest my chin on her head.

"It was more like 'Desperate times happily accepts desperate measures.'"

She laughs, but I grimace thinking back on his advice while telling her about it.

*"Noah, listen to me. To secure the bag—the bag being G—you have to win the dad over."*

*"Please don't refer to my girlfriend as 'the bag.' That's just . . . no . . . immediately stop."*

*"Don't be such a Chad," he throws out with way too much middle schoolgirl sass before he postures like he's done something cool. "Taylor Swift says that. My niece told me. She calls me 'guncle'—it means 'greatest uncle.'"*

*My head falls back as I rub my hands down my cheeks. This was the worst idea I've ever had. Why would I ask him for advice?*

*"That's not what that means."*

*"Okay, Chad . . . Anyway, back to my point. Because you look like a professional de-virginizer, you're gonna have to make him love you."*

*My head snaps back up. "What the fuck are you talking about? What's wrong with the way I look?"*

*He takes one of the cookies I bought to take to Goldie's, then smells it, looking like he's been poisoned. "Did you make these? Are you trying to kill them?" It's tossed back into the container. "I'll make a dessert for you. Stop with the cry for help."*

*"It's from the grocery store, asshole. Can you stay on point? What's wrong with how I look?"*

*He chuckles. "An unaware king, how cliché. What I mean is if I were her dad, I'd hide my wife. You're like every woman's wet dream with the motorcycle, the blue eyes, and the tattoos. You know what . . . Maybe flirt with the mom?"*

*"Chase. This isn't helping. I want them to like me."*

*"Okay . . . sorry, I veered. I'm locked in now—you just gotta get on his level. It's easy."*

*He does a mic drop motion with his hand.*

*I wish I could drop him . . . from a bridge.*

*"And I do that how?"*

*He laughs like I'm clueless. "Dads love to talk about three things." He starts counting them out on his fingers. "Barbecue. Lawn care. And the price of gas. You can't go wrong. Just wind him up and sit back. Trust me. He'll love you."*

*I run my hand through my hair, feeling sicker by the minute. "Chase . . . they live in a condo in downtown Portland and drive an electric car."*

*His mouth pulls at both sides with an uh-oh look, but then he snaps his fingers and points at me.*

*"You still got barbecue, dude."*

"Uh, so," she interrupts, "my dad's vegan."

I shake my head, trying to run from the memory.

"I'm so fucked."

"I'm telling you, they're going to love you," she breathes out, lifting to her tiptoes to kiss my chin. "Just remember the stuff I told you."

I'm nodding like I'm getting a pep talk before a big game. "Your mom's part of a rose club; her favorites are the cabbage ones. And she hates Joanne for winning best garden because she uses store-bought chemicals. Your dad builds model cars and occasionally likes to run half marathons. They just got back from Paris, where your mom discovered she was suddenly late-in-life lactose intolerant."

"Yes, but don't mention I told you that she hotboxed everyone with her ass in a packed elevator all the way up to the top of the Eiffel Tower."

I grin. "That one goes to my grave. And should've gone to yours . . . You're a terrible daughter."

"Shh." Goldie smooths the only necktie I own down my chest. "This is an especially nice touch, Adler."

"You think? I thought it said 'respectable'"—I wink at her—"and not 'I do dirty things to your daughter.'"

She chuckles, picking up where I left off. "Absolutely. Who doesn't like a suitor in a tie? It's a universal green flag. See, you're already *nailing* the job as my parents' fave."

My hands land on her hips as I walk her backward toward the wall behind her.

"Am I nailing it? I guess I should spend tonight really hammering it home."

Her hands lie flat against my chest as I cage her in. She licks her red-lipsticked pout before her voice gets raspy.

"You know, I'd be happy to arrange a good pounding . . . of information . . . tonight."

Fuck. Her eyes, and those lips. I'm a goner. We're lost in our flirtation. Faces inching closer because we're about to kiss until Evie's disgust fills the room.

"Eww. You're not even whispering . . . and/or clever. Both are rude to subject me to."

Goldie presses her lips together, trying not to laugh, as I release her from the cage I had her in.

"Sorry," Goldie offers insincerely, still smiling at me.

Before any one of us can make a joke, there's a knock at the door, making Goldie and I swing our heads in that direction. Evie walks between us, leaving only me standing in possible panic before Goldie and I look back at each other.

"They could hate me. Even with the tie."

Goldie's hand slips inside mine. "Won't happen. You've got this. They'll love you . . ." Her lips pull into a soft smile, but she suddenly looks nervous before she adds, "Because I do, Noah. I love you."

The wind is knocked out of me as I stare back into her eyes.

*She loves me.*

My lips part as I begin smiling back at her, but her finger covers them as she shakes her beautiful head. "No." A small, huffed laugh escapes her like she's giddy. "Don't say anything. Find a better moment. Knock me off my feet."

Neither of us says another word as we turn at the same time to face the door like two lovesick fools, but Evie winks back at us with her hand resting on the doorknob.

"I may have told Mom that most of Noah's tattoos were inked in prison . . . That's for trying to set me up with the STD. Twice. Happy New Year, guys."

*Fuck me.*

"You remind me of your mom," I say quietly as I adjust myself on the couch so my body's facing hers a little bit more.

Goldie does the same. I reach up and tuck her hair behind her ear, letting my knuckles brush over her birthmark. Man, she's beautiful in this light, with the fire going.

What am I talking about? She's beautiful always.

"Noah, I don't know if you know this," she deadpans, "but I'm adopted."

"You're such a smart-ass."

She says nothing, just takes a sip of her wine with a sly grin, and I get a little more lost in her and this moment as the conversation flows around us.

I inhale, dragging my bottom lip between my teeth before begrudgingly turning my attention back to the room.

Evie and her dad are going head-to-head in Scrabble as their mom keeps reminding them to keep it clean.

"'Twat,'" Evie blurts out. "That's eleven points."

Their mom scoffs, but Goldie's father, Stephen, kisses her cheek. "It means 'incompetent man' or 'fool,' honey."

"Oh, I know what it means, and right now, you're the epitome of it."

The room laughs, including Goldie, who's smiling wider. It's like a scene from a movie. Something semi-wholesome and heartwarming. And nothing I've ever experienced.

I motion my chin toward her mom. "What I was saying is that you remind me of her because you're both dry and witty. And you make people feel warm around you. You're like cozy people."

Goldie plays with the button just under my collar, staring up from under those long lashes.

"Am I your blankie?" She swipes her tongue over her bottom lip, collecting a drop of red wine.

I chuckle. "Something like that."

Glancing up to make sure nobody's looking, I lean in and whisper in her ear, "Now that I've passed meet-the-parents, do I get to do dirty shit to their daughter?"

She shivers. "Maybe . . ."

"Why maybe?" I protest, pulling back and staring into her eyes.

She shrugs, and it's all the foreshadowing I need to know she's flirting with me.

"Because they were so easy on you. I was kind of hoping they'd believe my sister and put you on the stand. Really grill ya. Peel back the oni—"

I raise my brows, and she changes her direction. "Artichoke."

"Thank you." I quietly clear my throat as she mouths, "You're welcome."

"But I wonder if Camilla and Stephen know what a bully their daughter is. I should take my present back now that you've outed your true self."

She feigns surprise. "'Camilla and Stephen'? Really?"

I nod with audacious confidence. "Yeah, we're best friends now. Duh. I've seen all the Facebook albums."

She laughs, and I memorize it. Her palm touches my chest.

"Yeah, I'm sorry about that. Mom really loves those roses. And don't you dare threaten to take away my beautiful journal. How else will I record one of my many genius thoughts that will eventually lead to my literary greatness?"

I chuckle quietly. "So humble."

Her tongue runs just over her canine tooth as she grins with a small shoulder pop. Damn, when she flirts like this, it drives me wild.

"Baby, that's nothing I've ever aspired to be."

Before I can ask if her aspirations align with my dirty thoughts, her dad disrupts the moment.

"Noah, I don't know if my daughter told you, but I have this rule . . ."

Oh shit. I suddenly feel like I've been caught in my underwear half out her bedroom window.

"No, sir. What's that?"

Goldie laughs because I'm back to "sir" just as Evie throws her hands up, griping over their dad's Scrabble word.

"'Caziques.' That's three hundred and ninety-two points," he says with a grin before turning his attention back to me.

"As I was saying. We started this tradition back when the girls would come home to us every school break. They were notorious for bringing home friends."

I teasingly cut my eyes at Goldie when he says "friends," grinning when she elbows my ribs.

Stephen chuckles, winking at her as he continues. "We asked they share what traditions are dear to them, whether it's prayer or a dish they love. We like to incorporate small acts to make people feel at home. I'm a firm believer that family is a choice you make"—his gaze moves to Goldie, and there's so much love—"so anyone under a Monroe roof becomes ours. So, tell us. How can we make you family tonight?"

My lips part, but nothing comes out. Because, damn. I feel like I've been sucker punched. That's nothing I expected him to say, and I feel unprepared to answer.

Not even a lie springs to mind quick enough.

I search the space, not really focused on anything as my brows draw together. I can feel their eyes on me, but all I can do is swallow and look down at my hands. I don't go back there . . . to my past. To my memories. All I have of myself is now, but I can't say that.

"Dad," Goldie rushes out, shaking her head, silently admonishing him. "Too sensitive. You know his mom—"

I kiss the top of her hand, cutting her off. "It's okay. Seriously."

Stephen frowns. "I'm sorry, Noah. That was inconsiderate of me. It's just I read once that people who lose someone never get the opportunity to speak about them because others always assume they don't want to, and I was trying—"

I shake my head, stopping him as Camilla puts her hand on his shoulder. The way they're both looking at me, I don't know how to describe it . . . I think I just wish my mom were here to see it.

"No. No, it's okay. Thank you. It's kind of you to ask," I say, genuinely meaning it. "There's this part of me who wishes I could talk about her all the time. I loved her."

I pause, saying all the rest in my head.

*But if I do, everything around me dies like flowers without the sun. I don't get to be Noah anymore, and I've worked too hard to go back to a roomful of locks.*

"Grief is such a bastard," Camilla offers, and I nod. "Someone once wrote that it takes more than just the people we love. Sometimes our memories become so painful we lose the time we lived with them as well."

I blink, feeling the truth of that statement almost viscerally. "Who wrote that?"

"My daughter." Camilla nods to Goldie.

I look down at my girl, feeling way too fucking seen. She really has a way of doing that to me.

"What was your mom's name?" Goldie says sweetly. "You've never told me."

For a second, I almost speak it like I haven't forgotten how. But then I blink, and the moment's gone.

"Mary . . . her name was Mary."

Goldie smiles, and it was worth the lie. I turn my attention over to her father.

"My mom loved holidays, but she was a complicated woman, so we didn't have much in the way of tradition. A lot of love, just not a lot of festivity. Although, there was one thing we did. Tonight . . . on New Year's Eve, right at the stroke of midnight, we'd yell a word to try and be the first person to say it in that year. It was silly, but for a kid it was special. I'd spend hours trying to think of the one word nobody else would say."

"I love that," Camilla breathes out, clapping her hands together once. "May we do that?"

I swallow hard, my throat thick as I nod and smile. "Yeah, of course."

"Then it's settled. For Mary," she adds, lifting her glass as everyone follows.

Goldie lays her head on my chest, laughing as her sister immediately begins arguing about which word she's claiming. But I'm lost in my thoughts.

It's really fucking hard to process getting everything you ever wanted. And that's what this is . . . everything I've ever wanted. I close my eyes for a fleeting second, and the memory is just as long, but the feeling doesn't leave even after I open them.

Mom would've loved this.

*"Noah, no. What are you doing?"*

*My chubby little fingers stay working, trying to unlock the next lock on the door as I press higher on my tiptoes on the chair. But my mom wraps her arm around my waist and plucks me off.*

*"What have I told you? You can never unlock the doors. They keep us safe."*

*I blink up at her, tears starting to brim my six-year-old eyes as she grips my arm.*

*"But . . . but . . ."*

*"No 'buts' and no exceptions." She looks so mad. My lip quivers.*

*"But Mommy, how will Santa get inside? We don't have a chimney. And everyone at school says he comes through the chimney."*

*She lets out a sigh and crouches down so we're on the same level, rubbing my small shoulders.*

*"Noah. There are monsters in the world. Scary monsters. And if you unlock that door, they will come and get us, baby. Promise Mommy you'll never unlock the doors again."*

*Tears spring from my eyes, but before she can grab me, I run. I run as fast as I can to my room and throw myself onto my bed, face down.*

*"Santa won't come. He'll never come. I hate those stupid locks."*

*I feel her hand on my back, rubbing small circles. "Hey . . . hey, now. Don't say bad words. There's no need to cry, little love. You didn't let me finish. Your friends are wrong. They've never heard of the magic of Santa."*

*I sniffle, still face down but listening.*

*"He doesn't need a chimney. That's just a story. He can turn himself into sparkle and dust to get through the cracks."*

*"Nuh-uh," I mumble.*

*"Yes huh," she pushes back. "I even have proof." I lift my head as she continues. "I happen to know that for the best little boys and girls, he leaves a present out early."*

*My eyes grow wide while I listen on bated breath as I sit up. She winks at me. I try and do it back, both my eyes closing.*

*"I bet if you checked your stocking . . ." she says, drying my eyes with her fingers.*

*That's all it takes for me to scramble off the bed and tear into our small living room, right to the long green secondhand stocking I got from a yard sale last year.*

*I reach inside, feeling my heart almost explode as I smile from ear to ear.*

*"I got one. I got one."*

*My mom's standing in the door, watching me with that sad look on her face that never goes away.*

*"See, baby? There's magic all around. And one day, maybe you'll even be free of those locks and live a beautiful life."*

Everyone's on their feet in Goldie's living room with hats on their heads and party horns in their hands, yelling at the television as the ball in Times Square gets lower and lower. *Ten. Nine. Eight. Seven.*

Goldie's hand finds mine, her smile wide as she looks up at me. I feel like I could die today, and nothing would beat this moment. *Six. Five.*

Everything I want to say to her begins to bubble to the surface, and I can't even count as I look down at her, feeling my chest rise and fall faster. *Four. Three.*

I turn and face her. *Two.* My hands cradle her face. *One.*

"Happy New Year!" rings out, along with everyone's silly words: *Pewter. Arachnoid. Moist.* Everyone groans as they look at Evie, but I pull Goldie's face to mine, our lips almost touching.

"Noah," she says quietly, making my name her word, but I say the only thing I can't hold in anymore.

"Goldie . . . I love you too."

# Chapter Eleven

***Camp Weonoke—years prior***

"Somebody could hear us."

Davis's hands roamed over Sonny's chest as the two hid behind an unused shed.

"Nobody will hear us. Now, will ya just kiss me again? I haven't stopped thinking about you all day."

She laughed before he sealed his lips to hers. He'd done that since the day they met—made her laugh. It was a dangerous weapon. One he now used to get her to agree to things she shouldn't.

But all those "shouldn'ts" always felt too good to deny. Something she'd never admitted because he seemed to like it when he talked her into things.

*It's the chase,* she thought. *Boys like the girls who seem like a challenge.*

"Your lip gloss tastes good."

His compliments felt the same. It was the other reason she'd let him "talk" her into over-the-shirt action. Davis wanted her, and everyone else wanted Davis.

It was the first time someone had chosen her.

His hand slipped up her shirt, this time slowly, as if it were asking permission. She let it get to the underside of her breast before she said his name and pushed his hand away.

"Sonny," he rushed out with a huff, then stepped back. "Everyone else is doing way more. We're eighteen and in the middle of nowhere. Why not?"

She looked into his eyes, wondering if he'd love her. His face softened as he reached for a lock of her long hair.

"Come on. You can't blame me for wanting you. You're beautiful and easy to talk to."

Davis stepped closer to her again, this time armed with a devilish grin.

"And you're my girlfriend, so it's natural."

She smiled. She was his girlfriend. Davis had never said those words to her. Maybe he would love her.

But when he put his hand back on her waist, she held his wrist again.

"Those are just words, Davis."

She wanted action. Proof of his love.

"Fine," he huffed, then whipped out a pocketknife.

Her eyes grew as wide as his smile. He walked away. She followed him to a tree, where the sharp blade cut and sliced through the wood and sap until what was left made her feel warm inside.

"There. 'Davis and Sonny, forever.'"

This time when he turned her around and pressed her back to that tree, she didn't stop him. And when his hand tucked under her shirt, she didn't push it down.

But what was most surprising was that she didn't even stop him when the other boy, the one who stared at her all the time but never spoke, watched them from the tree line.

To mine,

I saw you. But you know that.

He's too good for you. But you know that too.

—Yours

# Chapter Twelve

## Noah

***April***

"Hey, did I tell you my boss submitted my work to that shoe company I love? They're scouting for new website designers."

I say it nonchalantly, but Goldie's head pops up, her eyes open wide.

"Noah. That's amazing. Are you nervous?"

I wasn't before, but why am I suddenly now? My heart beats funny, almost like it skips a beat, as I peer down my nose at her, thinking about my future. We're lying on my living room couch, whatever we were watching long forgotten as the rain beats down outside.

It's a perfect day. Me and my girl, doing nothing.

From where she's lying on her stomach, Goldie reaches over me for another marker. They're strewn out over the coffee table.

I smirk as she uncaps it with her teeth.

"Not really," I finally answer. "Should I be?"

"Yeah," she says excitedly. "What if they love your work so much, they're like, 'We have to steal him away to design shoes for us.' That's your dream."

"Sneakers," I correct playfully. "And that's not happening. But I like your imagination."

She rolls her eyes and tilts her head, hyperfocused on what she's doing—which is coloring in my tattoos.

It's her favorite thing to do . . . get me shirtless and decorate me even more. Currently, she's bringing the skull on my rib cage to life. I squirm as the swipe tickles.

"Imagination is sustenance for dreamers *and* fools," she whispers before looking up at me. "Which one we are depends on our choice."

I smile as she gently blows on her artwork.

"Who said that?"

"Me."

I grin, clasping my hands behind my head as I stare at the ceiling. "Then I suppose today I'm a dreamer."

She bites her bottom lip, but instead of kissing her I keep talking.

"You know, you're really good with words. Have you ever thought about—"

"Shussha ya mouth," she teases, interrupting me. "I'll have you know I wrote something." It's my turn to look surprised, but she ignores me, coloring while she speaks. "A piece for that magazine I told you about a few months ago."

I sit up quickly, forcing her back onto her haunches as she groans because she's colored outside the lines.

"Noah . . ." she gripes.

But I push. "Can I read it?"

She shakes her head, then puts the lid back on the marker before tossing it back on the table.

"No. No way. I can't . . ."

Her eyes won't meet mine, and I hate it.

"Hey . . ." She looks off to the side, so I use my fingers to guide her chin back. "Come on. Why not? The whole world will get to once they publish it. This is huge."

Goldie's eyes squeeze shut. "*If* they publish it." When she reopens them, they look greener and more nervous as she shrugs. "It's just easier to get rejected when nobody else knows."

"I'm not nobody," I complain as charmingly as I can before I take her face in my hands, feeling her lean into them. "To quote this mad hottie I love, 'dreamer or fool'?"

She scrunches her nose, pretending she's miserable, but I know better. Even Princess knows better because she jumps up, purring and rubbing her face all over Goldie.

I close the distance and kiss my girl gently, brushing her hair away.

"I love you, killer. Let me do this with you. You don't have to do this stuff alone. Plus, I've never known anyone that could make me feel half the things I've felt with only a few words."

She groans but keeps her eyes on mine. "You're biased."

"So? Doesn't mean I'm wrong."

Since I've known Goldie, writing's always been something that's private to her. She never talks about it, and I don't pry. But I've watched her throw away countless ideas in the trash, write daydreams down in her journal, and stare at her computer screen before slamming it shut, mumbling to herself that goals are overrated.

I've watched her process for six months, and if she's finally broken through whatever wall she's been on the other side of, I'd like to be there to celebrate with her too.

Goldie blinks up at me, and there's a rawness in her expression as she blows out a heavy breath.

"If you hate it—lie."

"Done," I rush out, letting her go as she uses my body to get off the couch.

My chin lifts as I watch her walk before I rub my hands together, making her laugh.

Goldie rummages through her giant bag before pulling out some folded papers. She looks over her shoulder at me before she walks back, holding them out while chewing the inside of her cheek. We're smiling at each other as I stand, take them, and unfold them before looking down at the title:

History's Overrated, Unless You Live in the World or You're an Adopted Kid at a Routine Doctor's Visit: How the Absence of My Past Mapped Out My Future

I lift my head, my eyes connecting with hers. "You wrote about being adopted?"

She nods cautiously like she's still debating whether or not to let me read it. "The thing is, one night, I started thinking about the first night we met. And how you asked if I'd ever looked into my history. Like, tried to find my birth parents—"

Without thinking, I reach for her hand, remembering how we walked around.

"—and honestly, I started thinking about how so many times in my life, I've run in the opposite direction from my past or prebirth."

She chuckles quietly, and I do, too, before I cut in: "It makes sense, though. Your family's pretty incredible."

"Exactly," she rushes out, squeezing my hand. "I was so lucky that it felt greedy to harbor ideas of some loving reunion with the people who couldn't keep me. Plus, how would that actually feel if that's what happened—I reunited with people who could tell me things about myself . . . stuff my parents never knew. Would it ruin what I have? Leave that little asterisk next to their name despite how open they are to it? It always seemed like a risk too big to take."

Her eyes start to glisten as I search them. She'll never know how deeply I understand the last part of what she's said. Or that she's become the thing I'm not willing to risk.

Goldie lets go of my hand, running hers over her hair.

"Sorry, I'm dumping all over you. You should just read it, and I'll shut up."

She doesn't need to tell me that there's so much more she wants to say. It's in the way her eyes search the space in front of her without really looking at anything and how she's already picking at her nail polish.

"Hey." I shake my head. "No. Talk to me. You don't tell your sister this stuff, and I know you don't talk to your parents about it. I'm your person, Goldie. It's Noah plus Goldie forever, right?"

She frowns, glancing up at me, and then it all spills out.

"Fuck. I think what I didn't realize is that once Pandora's box is open, there's no closing it. Once I started questioning things about myself, I couldn't unquestion them. Where I get the color of my eyes . . . whether freckles run in my family . . . who gave me the longer second toe . . . who else is allergic to pineapple. All those questions were just hanging out in the back of my mind, eventually joining forces to remind me I didn't truly know who I was."

I reach for her, my hand finding her waist.

"But you do know who you are," I push back. "You're the most self-aware person I've ever known. What came before you doesn't make or change who you are now."

Even as I say it, I have to wonder if it's more for me or for her.

Goldie's eyes lock to mine before she steps in closer, letting me hug her. Because I need what I just said to be what we both believe.

"No, Noah, that's not totally true." Her chin drags upward, bringing her eyes to mine as I look down. "Sure, I know how I like my coffee or how my love of flowers definitely comes from my mother. But I've been writing and writing all these years, trying to be the next great whatever, and I always get the same critique: 'Your writing doesn't connect with the voice.' And what all those rejections really mean is that I have impeccable technical abilities but nothing to say—"

I start to interrupt, but she puts her hand on my chest. "—and that's because I pretend I don't have history. That pot of a thousand ingredients who all cooked to make me who I am. Only having an origin with my family isn't enough. Noah, we're a collection of stories and history passed on *between* nurture and nature—"

I feel numb.

"—and I only have the 'nurture' part because I've always run away from the reality. So, I wrote about feeling disconnected. And how that void is also a piece of who I am. Which I think is rare but relatable. But I guess you'll tell me," she chuckles. "Because no one's ever really seen me until you."

I do see her. But I wonder if that seems as dangerous to her as it does to me. I'm not sure I can trust myself to speak right now. To not spill all my deep, dark secrets at her feet so I can give her what she's gifted me.

The truth.

Instead, I press the papers to my chest with reverence and kiss her. I kiss her until I feel my legs under me again.

"Thank you for letting me read this," I whisper into her lips.

She lets out a whoosh of breath before letting the moment fade out to a lighter vibe.

"Okay, enough of all the serious shit. Go read fast because I'll be over here dying of anticipation just as quickly."

I chuckle, following her lead, before deciding to do something I've been holding off for later. I'm not sure why, but it just feels right to give her my present since that's what reading this feels like.

"Hold on. I've got something for you too. Stay here."

Her eyes grow wide as I wink and walk past her in a flash, heading into my bedroom. When I come out a few seconds later empty handed, her brows raise.

"You got me air. Thanks, breathing has always been my favorite thing."

I reach out to tickle her as I stop in front of her. "Smart-ass. Listen." I hold up her article. "I'd like to read without you hovering, so go open the box on the bed."

"Yay, presents."

She bounces and claps at the same time, like the cutest fucking thing in the world. Wait until she sees what I got her.

I scratch the back of my neck. "You might hate it, so . . ."

A kiss is pressed to my cheek before she walks quickly, but my eyes follow her, watching, before I whip back to the words on the paper.

I slide a hand over the cover page before I open it and dive in.

I'm two paragraphs in when I hear, "Who wraps a present with duct tape? It's diabolical." I smile, continuing. When I turn the page, she yells, "Noah. A box inside another box. Seriously?"

I chuckle, still focused on what I'm reading because she was right. I am biased. I think every word of this article is perfection.

It's so honest and raw. And that's fucking me up a little bit because if Goldie not knowing her birth parents feels like a void she needs to fill, if she needs to know her past, then how does she keep loving a guy who's erased his?

My eyes have swept the last paragraph, devouring every word, just as I hear her scream. I'm folding the papers back in half as her excited face stares back at me from the kitchen with my note in one hand and a new key chain in the other.

Her fingernails tap the wall like her emotions are ready to explode.

"You first," I say.

She can't even contain herself, running to me before I catch her with one arm as she jumps and wraps her legs around my waist.

"Yes," she rushes out. "Let's move in together."

She's breathless as I grab the back of her head, going in for a kiss until her hands press to my chest.

"No, no . . . you next."

I laugh because I'd almost forgotten.

"It's genius. Entertaining and funny. Emotional and really relatable. It sounds like you. They'd be fucking idiots not to publish you."

I mean every word.

She kisses me, and I don't know if it's the sublimity of this moment coaxing out my memories, but as I open my eyes and we stare at each other, something sad sits on the fringes. Something I've run from for a long time that seems to still be chasing my future.

*"Hey, can I talk to you?"*

*Lily pulls me next to a bank of lockers.*

*"Yeah, what's up?"*

*"I can't go to homecoming with you."*

*"What do you mean? It's not for a month. You can't suddenly have other plans."*

*"My dad said no."*

*"Because you're going with me?"*

*She nods. "I'm sorry . . . It's because your mom, and . . . well, because, ya know?"*

*I don't say anything back because there's nothing to say. Why did I even ask her? I knew better. This town hates me and wishes I was never born. That'll never change.*

*As Lily walks away, I look up at all the eyes in the hallway glancing in my direction. All of them staring at me like the psycho they think I am.*

*Maybe there is something wrong with me.*

*Everyone always says some people are just born bad. I turn away from the gawking and slam my shitty locker door, feeling a sting. When I look down at my palm, the skin slowly turns from pink to red, blood rising to the surface.*

The first cuts always hurt the most, *I think before wiping my hand over the metal door and walking away.*

# Chapter Thirteen

## Goldie

***June***

"Hey, what's up?" I say, answering my sister's FaceTime before something catches my attention. "Hold on, is that an alien behind you?"

Evie laughs. "Yeah . . . his name's Trevor."

A green, bug-eyed creature stares at me from behind her, looking like something from an old episode of a show our parents watched—*The X Files*. Her office is the strangest place. It's exactly what you'd picture a mad scientist's lair to look like.

"Trevor, huh?"

She nods like it's the most natural choice of name without elaborating. It's so like her.

"Cool, well, what's up?" I chuckle.

She's tinkering with something, her feet on her desk as she speaks.

"Mom told me to tell you . . ." She pauses, suddenly more focused on the screen. "Are you at home?"

We're too much alike to not actually be blood related. I shake my head.

"No. I'm packing up Noah's kitchen. He already did most of his stuff himself, but I offered to help since he had to work. What did Mom want to tell me via messenger?"

She finger guns me. "That she officially told Joanne—the bitch-face, dirty-rose-growing gardener—the hell off."

I set the brown packing paper down, my mouth falling open as I squint in thought. "She didn't say 'bitch face,' though . . ."

Evie grins, amused with herself. "Nah, that part was me. But they did have a very rousing, albeit polite, passive-aggressive exchange that was punctuated by silence and long sighs."

"Stop. I can almost picture it."

I laugh, resuming my work, and reach for another glass to wrap.

Evie wags her perfectly manicured brows before taking a drink of her soda. "So when's the big move-in date with the father of my future nieces?"

I sigh, still smiling. "Would you quit? Thankfully, this Friday. Between my lease and his, it was a pain. But it turned out to be perfect because now we have the whole weekend to get settled in."

She rolls her eyes with the perfect amount of jealousy. "Yeah, and to check out your new, amazing neighborhood." I wiggle my shoulders in a little dance of celebration as she complains. "*You're* such a bitch face that your hot boyfriend snagged a place in Beacon Hill."

"You can always come visit. You know who else lives in the neighborhood? The giver of that fish next to Trevor."

She holds up a screwdriver from the many tools on her desk. "Don't ruin this moment . . . Just let me have it. I was just picturing myself lying on your comfy couch. And if you mention Ruth Bader again, I'll seek revenge."

I chuckle again before looking down at the box of dishes. She and Chase are never going to get along.

Evie mumbles as she turns in her chair, blocking the view. "What kind of name is Knievie, anyway? She's clearly a *she*. He's a moron."

"While I'd love to know how you know the sex of the fish, I gotta go. I want to finish this before Noah gets home."

She leans into the camera. "Wait, wait . . . last thing. Have you heard anything about the article yet?"

It took me about a month after I submitted it to tell my family about what I'd written. And just like I expected, they've been understanding and the best hype squad. My dad even has me mostly convinced to hire someone to look into my birth.

But I worry that when someone wants to hide, they usually stay hidden. Still, it feels too empowering not to try.

"Not a word," I whine. "And it's excruciating."

I dramatically drop my head onto my forearms on the counter. I'm still pouting with my face hidden as I hear her in the background.

"It's going to happen. I believe. Keep me updated. I mean, if you have time between your wifely duties."

My head snaps up to her goofy smile. "Shut it."

I press the end button with gusto without saying goodbye. Because she's insufferable. She's lucky I love her.

I slide my phone into the back pocket of my jean shorts as my music kicks back on, blasting in my ears. "'Wifely duties.' Is she serious?" I say to myself before humming along to the Chappell Roan song in my ears.

On the upside, I will repay her teasing with a healthy dose of sister karma when she falls in love. The thought makes me smile as I look back at the empty cabinet, debating what to do next. I suddenly remember that I left a water glass on his nightstand last night, so I spin, patting my hand on the counter to the rhythm in my ears as I head toward Noah's room.

But the moment I enter, the lights dim, except they weren't on. I look around, noticing dark shadows cast over the walls. The afternoon suddenly feels like evening.

My eyes dart to the window, which is now framing angry, deep-gray and purple skies outside. Whatever's kicked up is arriving in a hurry, because the curtains start billowing and whipping around at the bottom.

"Shit," I whisper before running to close it.

In the two seconds it takes for me to get there, the rain's already pouring like a seam has torn and all the water's bursting from heaven. I grip the wood frame, flecks of white paint chipping off the old wood, just as thunder booms.

"Jesus," I breathe out, having to use a lot of force to shove the pane closed, but not before whips of water hit my face. "I should've left the nail in."

I told Noah there was something wrong with that window. Makes sense why someone had tried to permanently close it. More thunder clicks just as I remember that the small window above the kitchen sink is open too. So I spin, heading out in a hurry as I wipe the rain from my cheeks.

But as I turn the corner, I scream, a loud guttural implosion of shock and fear. The AirPods in my ears fall, bouncing to the floor as my hand darts out in front of me to protect myself.

A man stands like a statue in the doorway, eclipsing the view behind him, partially shadowed as water drips from his T-shirt onto his work boots.

My chest heaves as his almost-black eyes stare back at mine. And it's terrifying. Because they're dead, no life behind them. Even the way he blinks is methodical.

"Hi. Why are you in my house?" I say cautiously, but he doesn't answer.

Or react.

Chills explode over my body as my heart pounds like it's trying to escape. Silence permeates the space between us, louder than the faint chorus of music still playing on the ground.

His presence feels like a blanket of fear, and it's suffocating. The thunder claps in the sky, making my shoulders jump. But not his.

"Sorry," he says quietly, almost monotone. "Didn't mean to scare you. The door was open," he offers coolly, motioning to it. "And your cat was outside."

He lifts Princess Peach from beside him, kissing her head. *What the fuck.*

I draw my brows together, wishing he'd let her go. Because no, my door wasn't open, and my cat wasn't outside. She never leaves the house now.

Everything inside of me is in panic mode.

There's a man in Noah's doorway. And I'm alone.

He's lying, and there's no way I could fight him off.

Fuck. I can feel my chest rising and falling faster as I take a slow step backward, the pressure on the ball of my foot sinking to my heel. But his eyes jump to my feet as his head tilts, his large hand roughly stroking the cat. I freeze.

*Can I make it out the back door?* I just need to stay calm. Play it cool.

A small, forced smile peeks out on my face, making the heavy breaths through my nose loud enough for me to hear.

"Thanks for bringing her back," I rush out, pointing to the floor. "You can just put her down there."

"It was probably unlocked," he says, not letting go of the cat. I frown, confused and really freaked out. "Your door . . ." he adds as if reading my mind. "These old houses do that . . . open easy. If you don't lock them, a good gust of wind will swing it right open."

I want to be relieved, but there's something off about this guy. Still, I nod, trying to feign nonchalance.

"Okay, yeah. Good tip. I'll make sure to pay attention to the locks better."

My pulse is throbbing, beating so fast I can feel it on my neck.

He takes a small step inside, making the metal threshold creak under the weight of his foot. I blink faster.

*Stop him. Now. He can't come in!*

"I just cleaned the floors," I rush out loudly.

His eyes bore into mine, all the shadows from his face removed, giving me a better look at him. He has deep pox scars all over his gaunt cheeks and an angular jaw, like someone who could've been handsome once, but life got to him.

"Sorry," I whisper. "I didn't mean to be rude. It's just . . ."

Anything else I was going to say is lost because fight or flight is kicking in, and I think I'm a "scared in place."

His voice is so level, as if he's detached or void of emotion.

"You really should be more careful. You never know what could happen to the things you love."

As he says it, Princess meows hoarsely, and too quietly, like he's squeezing her. My lips curl under my teeth as I try not to cry or run because all I want to do is make sure she's okay.

I reach into my back pocket, hand around my phone, trying to remember how many times to press the side buttons to call for emergency.

Goddammit. I should've paid better attention to everything. Not just the phone instructions but to Noah as well. He's so adamant about locking the doors and windows. I didn't listen. I don't even remember if I locked the door behind me when I came in.

The wind howls outside, and he turns his head, so I take the opportunity to take another few steps backward, repeating myself from before. "Hey, thanks again. Really. You can just set her down."

But he doesn't. He hums a quiet laugh, making my blood feel ice cold.

His eyes shift back to mine slowly before they narrow, and he holds her out to me—by the scruff of her neck.

"Come get her . . ."

The taunt makes me shiver, and a small, broken cry stutters from her. Because his grip on the back of her neck is so harsh her fangs are bared as she hangs limp.

"Wouldn't want to get your floors wet," he adds with an uneasy, treacherous smirk.

My eyes grow wide. *Oh my god.* The steps I just took backward are regained out of protective instinct until my mind catches up, and I stop short.

*What do I do? What the fuck do I do?*

"Of course, yeah." I clear my throat, searching the room but not sure what I'm even looking for, before I grab a T-shirt off the couch and slowly walk step by frightening step toward him.

The sound of rain becomes louder the closer I get, and my eyelids flutter as the sky lights up behind him with lightning.

I open the shirt and extend my arms, feeling every hair prick on the back of my neck. "Come 'ere, baby," I say, but when I reach her, she suddenly hisses, scratching and fighting, bucking her body and nabbing at his arm with her claws.

"Fuck," he grunts, throwing her to the ground, and I dive.

My hands fly out to try to catch her, but she's already on her feet, scratching the floor as she runs to Noah's room. My knee hits the ground and I gasp, feeling the sting, then catch myself from face-planting as my hand hits the floor.

The cry about to fall from my lips stays wedged in my throat as my breath seeps out like water around pebbles, stuck in my lungs because his hand is on my elbow.

The stranger in my door has got ahold of me. And his grip is too tight to be friendly.

I can't move or scream, paralyzed by fear as he brings his other hand closer to my face. *Do something. Fight. Run.*

But all I can manage is to squeeze my eyes closed and try to shakily inch my head away as his rough fingers brush my hair over my ear, grazing my birthmark.

"You really should be more careful. Wouldn't want to ugly such a pretty face."

My fear finally snaps into flight, and I push against the floor, scrambling back to stand. I grab the door to force him to let go of my elbow. It sways, but no more than that because his boot's still butting across the threshold, stopping it.

"I'm fine. See?" I begin to ramble, to buy time before he tries to kill me. "Thank you. But you should probably get going before the rain gets worse. Wouldn't want two potential fatalities on my conscience. Again, thank you for getting my boyfriend's cat. He's on his way home, but I could call him and tell him what you did?"

I'm aiming for easy and braver than I feel as I pull my phone out and dial Noah, hoping it'll scare him away. But I can hear the shaking in my voice and see it in my hands.

The ringing echoes around us through the speaker as I hold my phone there for him to see.

*Please answer.*

It rings again as he stands there, his eyes locked on mine.

*Noah, fucking answer.*

My heart picks up to an even faster pace as it goes a third time.

But before Noah's voicemail comes on, the stranger darts out and ends the call, letting his scarred hand linger for a second.

The longest second of my life as I never let my eyes drop from his.

*Please fucking leave. Please, god, make him go away.*

And like an answered prayer, he slides the tip of his steel-toe boot back across the line but holds me with his words.

"No need for more thanks. You already told me everything I need to hear, Goldie."

*Goldie . . . how did he know?*

He raises his hand to his chest slowly, tapping it with his finger, making me look down at my shirt. Fuck. I'm wearing an old tee my sister got me with my name stitched on it.

I blink three times quickly and frown as my hand slides down the door, lining up with the dead bolt, ready to lock it the instant I close the door.

"You make sure to lock your door," he says with a half smile, his eyes dropping to where I'm secretly touching the cold steel on the other side. He takes another step backward. "There are monsters out."

All he gets is a nod before I shut it and lock it—all the locks—and then rush to the kitchen window and the back door too.

"Fuck," I breathe out, turning on the sink and drinking straight from my cupped hand. I hear a meow.

Princess is on her back, rubbing herself over the floor, unfazed and unharmed.

"You know what?" I hiss at her, glancing out the window to ensure he's gone. "Noah was right. You're problematic. And if you had a shoe, I'd shit in it right now."

I sneak to the front door and peer through the peephole—he's already across the street—before I turn around and let out a relieved breath. My attention turns to my feet as Princess weaves between them, headbutting me. I pick her up just as my phone dings.

**Damon:** Hey—sorry I can't pick up. I'm in the meeting. Everything okay?

I want to type *No, I was possibly almost massacred*, but I look toward the door again. The guy's gone, and I don't want to worry him when I know he's at work. Things are going so good for him, and I don't want him cutting out just because I never listen to reasonable advice.

**Me:** All good. Just miss you and I'm ready to blow this joint.

*I'll tell him later.*

I lift Princess so we're little eyes to big eyes as I say, "How about you don't almost get me killed anymore since I'm the one who buys you the expensive cat food." She meows again, and I scowl, adding, "Also, let's keep this between us. I have a feeling our boyfriend would be really pissed off if I told him I never locked the door and almost got us skinned and worn by some psycho."

# Chapter Fourteen

## Noah

I grin, staring at the flat-screen in front of the conference room. Work isn't just dragging by; it's also towing my fucking patience with it. Because the keys to the new place are burning a hole in my pocket.

Fridays are supposed to be fun. People even label them that way, but this one feels like a tech-nerd last supper—we're all gathered in the dark around a twenty-person table, watching a PowerPoint presentation that I'm pretty sure is boring me to death.

I just need to listen and be an adult for forty more minutes before I can call my girlfriend and turn back into a fool in love.

Fuck it. I sneak my phone under the table and type out a text to her.

**Me:** Well, sad news . . . I'm in the longest meeting to ever exist. In fact, we may never see each other again so we should probably say our good-byes now.

**Rexy:** Don't even joke like that. But at the very least send a courier with the keys first. Beacon Hill awaits.

**Me:** You only loved me for the location. I knew it. This hurts my feelings.

**Rexy:** Damn, now I feel bad because I actually only love you for your heart 🍆. But let me make it up to you. NSFW coming your way.

The grin on my face keeps spreading as I volley between the PowerPoint and the phone in my lap. This meeting just became completely worthwhile. But as soon as the picture populates, I huff a not-so-quiet laugh because Princess is staring back at me.

**Rexy:** Hey, don't
show anyone my
pussy, okay?

My tongue darts out over my bottom lip as I think of something creative to text back until I hear a voice from the front. "Noah? Did you have a thought?" It forces my head up to a waiting set of eyes.

*None I can share.*

"Nope. Sorry, my throat's just dry." I rub my Adam's apple for good measure.

Tech nerd number one goes back to his presentation about the use of the newest application that's supposed to revolutionize the business, but my head stays in the gutter as I type back.

**Me:** Don't worry,
your kitty's safe
with me. I will say
it's a little hairy,
but who am I to
nitpick.

**Rexy:** Want me to
shave her bald?

I laugh again, picturing a hairless house cat, and this time the entire table looks at me. *Shit.* Since my smile isn't going anywhere, I go ahead and stand, motioning to the door before excusing myself and clear my throat a few more fake-ass times. But thank god for conference room shades—nobody'll know I'm lying since my phone's already to my ear as I call her.

"Picture's not enough? You needed the voice too?" she answers.

I'm stalking toward my office, grinning from ear to ear. "Joke's on you. I just got fired from getting a hard-on thinking about you and the kitty I like most, except now people think I jerk off to PowerPoints."

She gasps, faking shock. "Wait, that's not a thing? Well, now I feel awkward."

Her amusement joins mine as I close my office door behind me.

"When are you coming to get me? I want to move in already," she whines.

I grab my backpack and shove my water bottle inside. "Listen, killer. I'm not even planning on sitting at my desk. I'm packing my shit and leaving." *Thanks to this terrible dry throat that must be a sickness coming on.* "I'm coming for my baby, so she better be ready."

"I'm ready," she squeals. "Love you."

"I love you too," I say as the call disconnects and my boss walks in.

He's staring at me from the doorway behind black-rimmed glasses, wearing another signature turtleneck. It doesn't matter how hot or humid the weather gets; the man always wears a turtleneck.

He's like a broker but cooler version of Steve Jobs.

"Hey, before your fake tuberculosis settles in and you jet to that cute little nurse waiting, will you grab those files for the Knox/DeLuca project for Nike? I want to give them a once-over."

Fuck. I look over my shoulder and nod. "Absolutely."

I like my boss. He's an older, no-bullshit kind of guy who doesn't care what the hell anyone does as long as the work gets done. He's also always been a big fan of mine.

As he turns to leave, he pauses and grabs the doorjamb. "By the way, your work really impressed the people over there at Nike. They like your eye. I have a feeling I'm going to have to match a future offer, or I'm gonna lose ya to the West Coast. Either way, I just want to go on record as saying I'm proud of you, kid."

My mouth falls open as he walks out, a half smile wavering between full-on shock and *Holy shit.* I don't even know how to process the possibility of what he just said.

Nike wants me . . . to design for them. *What the fuck.*

My thoughts feel disconnected, as if I can't finish a sentence in my head before another happens. Goddamn. My mouth finally closes before opening again. Is this real life?

I reach for my phone to call my girl but stop short, still processing, because Goldie said this would happen.

*"What if they love your work so much, they're like, 'We have to steal him away to design shoes for us.' That's your . . ."*

Dream. My fucking dream.

I let out a breath as I slowly sit in my chair, a laugh brimming. This is happening. It's fucking happening . . . the job, the girl, the life.

I run my hands through my hair before it all finally settles in, and I explode, boxing the air in celebration, swinging my arms out in front of me so hard it makes my chair spin sideways. I have to smack my hands down just to stop myself.

"Fuck yeah," I breathe out, drumming a little on the desk. I'm breathless, my head falling back as I stare at the ceiling before I whip it back up. "Shit, what was I doing?"

I look around the room, totally thrown off before laughing to myself as I remember, so I lean over and pull open the bottom drawer of my desk.

It slides out gently, making all the files sway, and I root around, a smile still plastered on my face. I walk my fingers past project after project, my mind still whirling over all the possibilities I'll be offered, not really paying attention to what I'm doing.

*Will I have to move? Would she go with me?*

The last thought hits me like a brick, drawing a deep V between my brows as I accidentally flip past what I'm looking for and land on what I've been hiding.

It's as if my touch recognizes the worn paper, because my eyes are instantly drawn to the brown envelope bending under my finger. I swallow hard, all my happiness dulled and all thoughts quieted.

Any peace I felt before is doused by the chaos of life. *Those two fucking unexpected bedfellows.*

I slowly slide it from its spot, glancing up at my door to double-check that nobody's coming in. I'd brought it from home when Goldie began sleeping over more often. I couldn't risk her finding it or the questions she'd ask when she did.

That first night we were together was too close for comfort.

My eyes close for just a second, helping me steady myself before I lay it on my desk and stare down at the weathered material. There are fingerprint oil–stained marks scattered around the top, soaked in over time from my skin because I've opened this envelope too many times to count. But here I am anyway.

My jaw tenses as I unwind the fraying string that holds it closed before I upend it. The familiar news articles scatter across my desk before I reach for the first one.

Dark Days in Darkwater

I close my eyes for a moment before taking a deep breath and pull the rest of the headlines closer. Reading each one and lingering.

Massacre Leaves Broken Hearts in Small Town
Body Never Found
Lone Survivor Drops off the Grid

My office chair creaks as I lean back, staring at the history, before I reach back inside for the notes—four of them written on yellowed papers that have served to define my whole life. I hate these notes.

But like a fucking sadist, I start pulling them out anyway . . . then stop. My eyes fix on the colored paper just peeking out as my jaw works.

"Why am I doing this?" I whisper to myself, but I don't have an answer.

For so long, I've lived trapped in this fucking folder along with these articles and letters. But since meeting Goldie, everything's changed. The impossible feels real and right within my reach. When am I going to trust that I can live the life I deserve?

I almost hear that last part of my thoughts in my mom's voice.

Without warning, the memory of the cops standing at the door makes my throat tight.

*Police lights swirl around the sky, bleeding into the small windowpanes. I turn over my shoulder and eye two cop cars parked in front of our house.*

*Everything after I stand feels like it's happening to someone else—my soda missing the table, tumbling to the floor . . . me walking to the door as another officer shakes his head as he comes up the path.*

*It's all lagging as I try and focus on my breath, but I only hear it inside my head. I swing open the door, the knocking registering after the fact, my eyes volleying between them.*

*The older of the two takes his hat off, pressing it to his chest.*

*"Son, we're so sorry to be here . . . We did everything we could to save her . . ."*

My chest feels like it's caving in as I shake my head quickly to pull myself from that place—the one I don't want to live in anymore.

Because I don't have to. I can leave this now. I can just be Noah and Goldie.

"Focus on the here and now," I breathe out, past the sadness, because there's no point in looking backward.

My mother lived her life looking at the past, but I'm free.

I'm here doing exactly what she wanted for me. Living the life she couldn't give me. Not with her always having a reason to look over her shoulder and a hammer waiting to drop.

"It's time," I say, taking one last deep breath and finally letting it all go—my past, the worry, and the goddamn burden of it all. "Be done with it."

I lift my head and stare into the middle space as the chaos stops feeling like it'll always win out. Goldie, and this life . . . Nothing beats this peace.

As I leave the office, I make two stops, one to see my boss and the other at the dumpsters out back. And this time, I don't regret tossing the folder. That's the thing about starting over—you can't look back.

# Chapter Fifteen

## Goldie

Noah drops the last of the moving boxes by the front door, then wipes his brow with the bottom of his T-shirt, exposing that perfectly chiseled stomach of his.

*Damn, my man is fine.*

"We already got some mail." He motions to an envelope on top of the box and grins as I objectify him from our new kitchen before stripping himself of the shirt altogether, reading me too well. "Is that what you want?"

"Oh yeah. Give it to me, baby," I tease back.

That is what I want because honestly, he's legitimately mouthwatering. At least, that's what mine's doing as I watch him become the most effective ad for hiring movers.

It'd be a billion-dollar industry if tatted, shirtless men built like gods showed up to pack your boxes. The number of women who'd move on a weekly basis would be staggering. There really is a missed opportunity for someone to have a business named Dick and a Box, with a motto "All the Richards you need to pack your *comings* and goings."

I smile over my dirty joke, still glancing at him as I open the fridge and pull out a bottle of champagne. I ran out to buy it after he called with his news today.

I've been waiting to open it until after Chase and Evie left. Which was about five minutes ago, when she almost killed him for asking why people win Oscars for special effects. However, the silver lining to the almost-homicide is that now Noah and I can celebrate without our new place getting taped off as a crime scene.

"Hey, you . . . fancy-pants shoe designer," I call from across the open-floor plan, holding up the bottle. "It's time to celebrate."

His head tilts before he looks adorably embarrassed while scratching over the skull taking up real estate on his rib cage. "I haven't even gotten it yet."

He's a rottweiler with a golden retriever heart . . . How did I get so lucky?

I position the thick bottom of the bottle on my tummy before I push the cork with both thumbs, straining my words. "But you're going to."

The pop makes my shoulders jump as I squeal because the champagne bubbles over the bottle, cascading onto the floor and countertop with a flourish.

"Oh my god." I look around for something to help stop it. "I guess we're christening the whole place . . . shit."

Noah weaves around all our shit, grinning as he jogs to me, but as soon as he's close, I think *Fuck it* and shake the bottle, making it erupt all over again as I aim it at him.

"Soak it in, stud. This is your moment."

"Oh, you fucked up," he bellows, putting his hand in front of him before he wraps his other around my waist and lifts me off the ground.

Laughter bounds between us as he plops my ass up onto the counter and settles himself between my legs, the fizzing bottle clunking against the granite.

We're staring at each other, covered in champagne, drops of it making my eyelashes heavy. But no matter the mess, we've got matching grins, and it feels like time's slowed down around us to just Noah and me in a bubble of us, where it's quiet and we're the only two people who exist to have ever been in love.

I lift the bottle and bring two of my fingers to his lips, urging them to part so I can let him take a drink. But he circles my wrist before the flat of his warm tongue laves between the seam of them, licking the champagne off.

*Damn.*

"How's it taste?"

Noah gently steals the bottle and juts his chin for me to put my head back. "Open and find out."

I press my palms against the wet counter, my back arching as I tilt my head back and part my lips. He lifts the almost-empty bottle above my head, and I glance at him before only a drop falls on my tongue.

"I think," he says in his deep gravel, and a smile graces my waiting mouth as he smirks, "that it tastes a lot like champagne"—Noah grabs the front of my shorts and tugs them open—"and not enough like you."

Bubbles spill past my lips, straight past the center of my body to my underwear.

"Oh my god," I squeal, my stomach contracting from the cold, but he grabs the back of my neck and pulls me into a kiss, silencing me.

We're already getting sticky as our bodies crash into each other. My arms wrap around his rib cage as I hook my ankles above his ass.

"Fuck, you taste so sweet," he breathes out, cradling my face roughly.

"I love you," I whisper, tilting my head to deepen our kiss as his hand comes to my throat.

His tongue teases mine as it pushes into my mouth, domineering the moment. I moan, feeling my body sag.

Noah uses his thumb to force my chin up as he licks my neck, dragging the strap of my tank down my shoulder to assault me with his lips there too.

"I fucking love you too, killer."

He hums into my wet skin before leaning over me, engulfing me and forcing me backward. I let go of him, walking my hands back on the counter and lowering my body onto the wet surface, our mouths never parting.

Our lips grow more urgent as the sounds of our breath mingle. I gasp as he breaks away to kiss down my chin to my collarbone, and his deft fingers do the work of unbuttoning my jean shorts.

I drag my arms above my head, tickling my body, ready to be devoured, but when I straighten my arms, the skin sticks, peeling away from where it was bent.

"Wait," I giggle, my head popping up, our eyes connecting. "We're all sticky. Let's do it in the shower."

Noah narrows his eyes, his words taking on a fake grumpy growl as he jerks my shorts and panties off and spreads my legs. "Baby, I'm hungry. Let me eat."

I cover my face, a loud laugh bursting from my chest that's instantly transformed into a deep guttural gasp because Noah's mouth seals over my center, all the warmth of his mouth bleeding onto my sensitive clit.

"Oh my god," I exhale, mouth hung open.

The sensation of his wet mouth mixed with my lust makes my eyes roll back and my back arch off the surface. I moan as his head twists, his tongue teasing me like he did in my mouth. One of my legs bends, brushing the side of his body as I weave my fingers through his hair.

*Fuck.* Noah always manages to touch every button at the same time, making me unravel for him.

Strong arms snake under my thighs, wrapping around my hips like he's giving me a hug as he makes out with my wanting cunt, humming into it and sucking my clit gently.

"You taste so fucking good, killer."

"Noah," I pant, my body writhing more. "Don't stop. Please."

He growls, pressing his face into me, inhaling between the soft hairs on my pussy before he licks in between the crease. I gasp again as he uses his finger to spread me wider, speaking illicit words into existence.

"I want to taste you all over my face."

*Jesus.* How is he so barbaric, loving, and feral all at the same time?

He is the delicious epitome of good fucking sex.

"Oh god," I breathe out as he kisses my cunt again and again.

My chest rises and falls quickly, my fingernails scratching against the island. But Noah holds me firmer, eating me out as if it's his only job in life.

"Fuck. Noah." Mewls spill from my lips and I grip his head harder, rocking myself into him.

His tongue never stops. It's an onslaught of pleasure, licking and teasing, moving faster and faster as my hips roll.

"Oh god."

"Mmmm," he growls, gripping my thighs to keep them spread.

Oh god, it feels like the perfect torture. I want to close them around his head and grind myself against his mouth, but he's keeping me at his mercy.

My palm slaps the counter. "Noah, fuck . . . I'm gonna come. Oh god."

He's growling, eating me, massaging his tongue over my clit as I breathe harder, panting audibly. My moans gather into a choral string of lust until all at once every muscle in my body tenses and I suck in an all-consuming breath and come.

A belly-deep scream rips from my lungs until my breath is wasted and I'm forced to inhale, thrusting my back to the counter as my head pops up.

"Oh god" floats out breathlessly.

Noah kisses my swollen clit gently, his touch growing softer as my body puts itself back together. I lay my head back again, my eyes closing as I feel him move back up my body, peppering it with his lips over and under my top as I shiver.

He pulls the front of my damp tank down, exposing my breast, the nipple hard and pebbled, begging for his mouth. He softly runs his tongue over it, sucking gently before it grows harder, making me whimper with pleasure.

I'm still catching my breath, but my body's heating up all over again as I fall down the lust-filled rabbit hole he's providing.

I open my eyes, hazily locking to his just as he leaves my breast and palms it before he seals his mouth over mine. My weak arms drape over his shoulders as we kiss, slowly and intimately.

Noah runs his hand down my leg, guiding it around his body, never breaking our kiss before he slips his other under my back and lifts me from the kitchen island.

He's holding my rear with one hand, and the other's anchored to the back of my neck as his head tilts, our tongues dancing and swirling.

My long hair tickles his forearms as he carries me around the island, passion and that same kind of lustful desperation we share still exploding between us. I wrap my arms tighter around his neck, feeling him grow between my wrapped legs as I press my breasts against him.

"Noah, I want you," I whisper between kisses, needing him inside me like I need air.

The moment we hit the bedroom, he kicks the door open and heads straight for the bathroom. But he doesn't let me go. It's as if we can't get enough—not of the way our lips are bruised or the way our bodies grind.

My fingers weave through his hair, mussing it up as we grow wilder by the second. He's devouring the moans and whimpers coming from my lips as I hold on to him.

"I want you so bad," I whine into his mouth.

"Down," he grinds out, and my feet hit the tile.

We're broken from each other, his decorated chest heaving as he stares down at me. I blink up, my tongue darting out over the coldness I feel on my bottom lip from losing his against it.

His gaze rakes over my body, only half of me exposed. It's lewd the way he looks at me because I can see every single way he wants to fuck me.

It makes me shiver.

Noah lifts his hand, then hooks his finger inside my tank top between my breasts and pulls me closer to him. I start to lift my arms, but he shakes his head, and instead of pulling it over my head, Noah grips it with both hands.

The sound of ripping makes my head drop back as my body jerks forward with the movement. A smile blooms before I bite my bottom lip, enjoying every second of him shredding the fabric right down the middle.

I'm exposed, goose bumps traveling over my bare stomach, the remnants of champagne still damp on my skin. He bends down and takes my other nipple into his mouth as he guides my top off my shoulders with his fingers.

My knees buckle, but his strong arm wraps around me, and I huff a laugh.

He's too good at this. I may die of pleasure.

"My turn," I whisper, pulling his head up and removing him from my nipple.

I start at his broad shoulders as my fingers trace over the pictures. I move down, my palms skating over his pecs, and perversely listen to the way his breath hitches.

Listening to Noah is the sexiest experience I've ever had.

I step in closer, kissing his chest, before licking his warm skin, flicking his nipple with my tongue.

"Fuck, killer," he groans, and I get wetter.

We're standing next to the shower, so I pull away from him only for a second to turn on the water, letting it get hot before my hands snake between his skin and his basketball shorts.

I have to lift them before I drag them off because his rock-hard cock is in the way.

Noah stares down at me with heated desire as I resume my debauchery and begin kissing down the middle of his chest, around his belly button, and past his abs.

Keeping my hands on his body, I run them over his thighs as I kneel in front of him.

I can hear him breathing, the air forced to and from his lungs. His eyelids are heavy and his jaw slack as he looks down at me.

Teasingly, my fingertips feather past his hips, blazing over his skin and making his stomach contract. The vein that protrudes from his Adonis belt to his dick pulses along with his cock as I lean forward, letting the warmth of my breath tickle over it.

I haven't even drawn him into my mouth, and just the anticipation has his head falling back as he weaves his fingers through my hair.

"You have the most beautiful dick." I smile up at him, closing my hand around it.

"Fuck," he heavily exhales.

I slowly twist my hand down his impressive length and back up, letting my eyes roam his body, watching the way he quivers with each stroke.

Precum beads at the tip, so I roll my hand over it, using the wetness to jerk him off in front of me. God, I wasn't lying when I said he was beautiful.

He's perfectly balanced between length and thickness, with defined veins protruding under his smooth skin, leading to his lickable tip. The moment I think about it, I do it.

I run my tongue over the tip of his cock and under the ridge before taking him into my mouth.

"Oh fuck, baby," Noah moans, but I want him in my mouth so badly that I'm impatient.

I hum around his dick, hollowing my cheeks as I suck and run my palms up his abs.

"Goldie . . . fuck . . . slow down."

I can't. I feel powerful. He's panting, urging my head forward but telling me to slow because he wants to fuck me.

My head bobs as I whimper, feeling my clit throb. I'm sucking with urgency, taking him into my mouth as far as I can go, each time flattening my tongue to the underside of his cock.

I look up, but his eyes are closed as his lips fall open, his breath panting faster and faster.

"I wanna come in your mouth," he says, so strained that it feels pained.

I hum my answer, "Mm-hmm," gripping his waist and letting him move my head faster as he palms the back of my head.

"Oh fuck, that's so good. Your mouth is fucking heaven."

His breath is stuttered as I move, my own body rolling along with the motion, turned on by his pleasure.

"Baby . . . baby . . . baby," he rushes out quickly before he steps back, stealing his cock from my mouth.

My mouth chases him as my body leans forward, but Noah reaches down and cups my underarms, hauling me off the floor to my feet. I'm deposited into the shower, barely able to catch my breath before I'm spun around, my breasts pressed to the steamy glass before I feel his cock at my entrance.

He thrusts inside, raising me to my tiptoes as I scream out in pleasure with his lips at my ear.

"Fuck." We hold still, the sensation overwhelming. "Come with me, killer."

I hear the showerhead being removed before he places it in my hand as clouds of humid air waft around, fogging up the glass even more.

Noah draws out from where my softness is clinched around him before he pushes back in. "Fuck yourself, now. Right now."

I do as I'm told and aim the water at my clit, feeling my stomach immediately tighten. My reaction makes Noah growl as he pistons in and out of me, holding my body tightly to him, his chest pressed to my front.

Another gasp escapes me as I turn my head, my open mouth streaking the glass with a rush of air.

He's fucking me too slowly. It's torturous. He's forcing himself to wait for me to catch up.

"Oh, Noah," I mewl.

He cups my breast roughly with one hand in response. His other intertwines with my fingers and slides my palm up the glass, leaving a streak, until it's above my head.

The feel of his lower stomach rolling into my ass as he fucks my pussy takes my breath away.

"You feel so good. You're so tight," he groans.

I whimper, circling my hips into the pressure that's hitting my clit, as he fucks me harder.

"Noah . . ." I cry as he buries himself inside me, begging him for what he's already doing. "Fuck me. Please, please."

I close my eyes as the need to come with him rises and falls, dragging me up the mountain, inch by salacious inch.

With every thrust I grow closer, moaning and crying, sandwiched between the coolness of the glass and the heat from his body. Noah grunts and grinds behind with his own urgency, thrusting his cock harder before pulling out slowly and teasing my entrance with his rim.

His lips touch my ear, feathering kisses over my birthmark.

"I love you, killer," he says tenderly before pounding inside me again.

"Fuck," I breathe out heavily. My clit pulses as I put the water closer, needing it, wanting to come.

Noah fucks me hard, hammering inside of me, hitting all the right spots and massaging my G-spot each time. I pant as my body contracts and tears fill my eyes because it's overwhelming.

"Don't stop. Please." I can't move or speak. I'm a prisoner to this feeling. It's all consuming. Noah's cock grows tighter as my pussy contracts, and I flex my hand under his against the glass. "Noah . . . I'm . . . I'm . . ."

"Give it to me, killer. All over my cock."

Burning white light explodes behind my closed eyes as I squeeze them shut so hard it almost hurts. My back arches like a cat's as my lips part, and I scream, deep and guttural, feeling Noah chasing his own release until he wraps both his arms around me and bellows.

"Fuck."

My body contracts and jerks against his as I drop the showerhead, and his hard cock pulsates inside me, filling me with his release. But even though we've come, neither of us stops moving. We fuck slowly, his face buried into the crook of my shoulder.

"I love you too," I finally say back, feeling him smile.

No other words are spoken as the showerhead clicks back into place, the water hitting his back serving as the only sound.

Noah carefully turns me around, and I look up at him.

"Let's get you cleaned up and unsticky," he says with a smirk.

I nod as he guides me around and back into the water before he lathers a washcloth and washes my entire body, not missing a single damn spot.

Goddamn, how'd I get so lucky?

## Noah

"Crap, we forgot towels," Goldie says, looking around with a smile.

But I wink. "The last box I brought in. It was labeled 'Bathroom' and not nearly heavy enough to be anything but towels. I'll go."

I rake my hand through my hair quickly, making it spray her before I slip out from the warm shower and cover my dick. She's still chuckling as I leave wet footprints through the bedroom into the main living area and make my way to the front door.

"Hey, do you want this letter I brought in earlier? Because it's for you," I yell, tossing it on the couch before ripping open the box and yanking out a towel.

I don't hear her answer as I dry myself off and wrap it around my waist before grabbing her one too. But as I turn, her voice drifts out from the bedroom.

"Who's it from?"

I swipe it off the couch, walking back as I read. "Price and Page . . ."

"Noah!" she shrieks just as I walk through the bedroom doorway.

My eyes spring open as her wet body comes running for me. She's slipping and sliding on the tile as her hands hit the wall to keep herself on her feet, and it makes me laugh, but I also try to save her.

I only get a step toward her, though, before I'm tackled onto the bed with her straddling me.

"Round two?" I chuckle as she scrambles to get the letter from me. Her wet hair whips my face, forcing my eyes closed as her ass lands on my stomach, then back to my groin, knocking the air out of me twice. "Fuck," I groan-laugh. "Why are you beating me up?"

"Sorry," she mumbles as I blink a few times, waiting for the internal bleeding to begin.

The letter is between her teeth as she hurriedly dries her hands on the towel I'm still holding before removing it from her mouth.

"Noah, it's the magazine . . . It's from them, or more specifically the corporation that owns them." My brows rise as I half pop myself up onto my elbows.

Her grin grows bigger before she bounces on top of me again.

"Easy," I laugh, reaching down between her legs to cover my jewels. "That's gotta last us our whole lives."

She nods, and then a host of emotions play over her face, ending in a frown. Her green eyes lift to mine, staring straight into them.

"What if it says 'No, thanks'?"

As if she's holding a bomb, she places the envelope gently onto my abs while she stares down at it.

"Killer . . ." She glances at me, then back. "Goldie, look at me."

When she does, I'm immediately struck by how beautiful she is—nude *and* emotionally stripped bare. "So what if they do? You're brave enough to be vulnerable, and that's more than most people. Stop being completely unaware of how goddamn amazing that is. Aren't you the one who said, 'Dreamer or fool'?"

"No . . . she sounds like a whacked-out wannabe guru. Plus, there should be a third option—scaredy-cat."

A meow makes us both smile.

"Sounds like that one's taken," I tease.

This time we both look down at my stomach before she slowly reaches out and lifts the letter off me. Goldie lets out a small whoosh between pursed lips, and it makes my heart beat unnaturally fast.

*Come on, let it be a yes. Goddammit, universe, I'm owed, and I'm calling it in for my girl. Give this to her.*

She gives me one more glance, and I wink back before she straightens her shoulders and tears into the envelope, then pulls out the paper. I watch with literal bated breath as her eyes track over the words.

I'm laser focused on her, trying to make out what she's mouthing.

The few seconds it takes her to read the verdict feel like a damn lifetime, and I can't help myself but to press. "Well . . . ?"

I push against the bed to sit, bringing our faces closer as my hands fall to her hips.

"What does it say?"

She bites her lip as she looks up at me, searching my eyes, but her face stays unreadable. But I feel it in my gut. She fucking got it. The sides of my mouth start to pull into a smile.

"Yes?" I guess with every bit of hopeful intention, nodding.

A megawatt smile breaks out on her face, and it's the most beautiful fucking sight I've ever seen. Her head shakes a million miles an hour.

"Yes." The paper shoots up as she raises her hand. "This dreamy fool's fucking published."

# Chapter Sixteen

## Goldie

***July***

"I'm one hundred percent going to get fired if I don't get off this FaceTime."

I lean into the fan on the workroom counter because the regular air conditioner is currently being repaired. My only stroke of luck is that the flower fridges work just fine. Since it's a balmy Boston July, I'm considering shutting myself inside one of them.

"You're the only one there." My sister rolls her eyes. "Are you planning to turn yourself in to HR?"

Noah deadpans for the camera from his desk at work. "She might."

"Hey . . ." I complain before the smile blooms. "Just make it quick."

Evie laughs, then sticks her tongue out and crosses her eyes. "You're so weird about celebrating yourself. This is huge, Go-Go."

I hate when she calls me that because I'll literally give in to anything she asks. It's what she called me when she was a baby. I'm about to say "Fine" when Noah holds up his finger, sitting straighter in his chair.

"Wait. I have to patch him in." Evie shoots him a death glare. "Stop looking at me like that, sister of the woman I love. I promised. Killer, make her stop cursing me through the phone."

I chuckle because this is Evie's karma. I said I didn't want to make a big deal about my article coming out tomorrow, and like the good listener she is, her whole plan to make me go viral was born. And I bet it's as off-putting as the bloody hand she keeps picking up to inspect before adding more red, chunky goop to it.

"Hey," I say to my sister, motioning with my head as a blank box with a C pops up on the screen, ringing Chase. "You might want to send Ruth Bader to her chambers."

Noah smirks as Evie's eyes bug out of her head before she tosses a bloody cloth over the tank and tries to act cool just as Chase joins.

"The whole fam's here." I giggle because my sister acts like she's queasy. But that doesn't stop Chase. He looks at who I assume are Noah and me, saying, "Mom, Dad . . ." but then he adds, "stepsis."

"Stepsis?" she bites likes it's the most offensive thing she's ever heard. "What?"

Noah drops his head, shaking it, as my forehead wrinkles, confused. Until Chase nods.

"Yeah . . . 'step.' It'd be weird if I wanted to fuck my—"

"Okay," Noah cuts in loudly, clapping his hands together. "Behave. Our girl is a published queen, so let's watch our mouths around royalty."

Chase winks into the camera. Evie revs a drill. Noah continues.

"Eves, why don't you tell us why you've gathered the troops. And I would make it quick because one of us has a short time limit." He taps the watch I just bought him for his birthday. "And the other says everything that comes out of his mouth."

I have to cover my mouth because I can't hide my smile. Sometimes I think I should buy her a really big apology present for dropping a much hotter version of the *Superbad* bromance onto her lap.

My sister stands off for a few silent seconds, glaring like she's plotting a murder, before she gives in and lets out a deep exhale.

"Thank you, Noah. And *only* Noah." Chase grins wider. "I've gathered you here today because we have work to do so our literary genius gets the recognition she deserves. As we know, the article comes out tomorrow—"

Clapping and hollering suddenly interrupt her flow as Noah and Chase give me a round of applause, so I do a little bow.

Evie motions her hands for them to settle down with a genuine smile on her face.

"As I was saying, she did the hard work, and now we do our part. We're here to ensure the bigwigs at *Vision and Vibe* buy more articles and maybe even hire her on staff. Then she can stop making subpar flower arrangements and live up to her potential."

I lift a finger, demanding everyone's attention. "Full transparency, that's not how it works. I will not be offered any position, I will absolutely still be gainfully-ish employed at the flower shop. Also . . . excuse you. Subpar? I'm so good at making arrangements."

I'm met with silence before every head in the other three boxes shakes.

*Oh my god.*

Noah smirks. "Killer, not everyone is amazing at everything. And that's okay . . ."

Evie hums an "Mm-hmm" in agreement.

Chase shrugs. "You guys are underplaying it. G, you're fucking awful. I figured you were related to the owner, and that's how you kept the job."

I'm blinking a hundred miles an hour as I stare at them.

"Bullshit." I wag my finger in disbelief. "The audacity you three have. Here's what . . . here's what . . . I'll have you know that I'm so elevated in my craft that it was making Lee, the guy I work with, feel insecure. They had to pull me to the register and let him work alone . . ." The last part of that sentence comes out slower than the beginning because I hear it.

*Oh man.*

Chase starts laughing as I press my lips together, and my eyes grow wide.

"Oh my god," I breathe out, my cheeks turning red. "Noooo . . ."

Noah scrunches his nose and rubs his forehead as Evie looks off to the side.

"You guys. I'm bad. Like really bad, huh?"

"Yes," they say jointly before we all laugh together. I run my hands over my face before I smack them on the counter.

"Okay. Evie's right. We have to put me in demand. Clearly my future is not bright here, even though I'm getting shade."

Chase points at the screen recognizing what I did with that joke before Evie high-fives herself with the bloody hand she's working on.

"Perfect. Now that the world's worst floral assistant is on board, here's the plan—"

Chase raises his hand like a little kid, but she scowls, saying "No" before continuing.

"—Noah, Chase, you two will buy a shit ton of magazines and leave them at all the coolest spots in town. Bonus points if they're open to the article. Me and the 'rents will be commenting everywhere it appears online. And Mom's adding it to every single Facebook group she's in . . ." Evie shakes her head. "Trust me, it's more than you think."

Noah's rubbing his hands together like he's ready to gear up, and it makes me smile. How did I get so lucky? I really like this little life.

Chase grins, leaning in closer to the camera. "Is it weird that I feel like an Avenger on a mission?"

Evie raises her brows. "Yes. But Hulk would *really* smash this project if he gave out a bunch of magazines at his restaurant. Because for some unknown reason, the city loves you."

"Are you kidding me?" he barks in that way we all know prefaces a monologue that Julia Sugarbaker would be proud of.

Noah's brows draw together, his face half amused, because he's wondering, like I am, where this is going. I start to pipe up to tell Chase he doesn't have to put any magazines out just in case that's why he's had a sudden change of attitude. But I don't get anything out because he does an about-face, walking away before spinning back around.

"First of all," he draws out, his hands landing on his hips, "from this point on, all my questions are rhetorical for you." He's speaking to Evie, and, judging by her scowl, she knows it. "And B—"

"That's not how that goes," she cuts in, correcting his grammar, but he holds up a hand to shush her.

"*I* . . . am . . . not . . . Hulk . . ."

Evie cuts him off again. "If you're claiming Captain America, then I'll know I've died and am living in a nightmare. If anyone is Cap, it's Noah. Duh, he's the hot one."

Chase sucks in a deep breath like he's been burned—*he has*—before he comes in close again and the camera jostles because he's picked it up.

"Agreed. The dreamy blue eyes alone default to it," he grits out, instantly making me laugh before I slap my hand over my mouth.

Noah raises a hand like he's saying thanks, but I shake my head and start pointing down at the camera, trying to tell Noah to hang up, but he's riveted. He actually leans back in his chair, eating candy as he watches.

Chase scoffs, looking disgusted. "But *I am* disappointed that the woman who'll have my children one day didn't vibe, Star-Lord."

He grows so serious that I have to mute my phone. I know Noah does, too, because his shoulders are shaking just as hard as mine.

Evie points at the screen with the hand in her hand. "Every conversation with you feels like I'm either *on* or should be *taking* a hallucinogenic."

Chase shrugs. "You make me feel out of this world too."

Her hands fly up—all three of them—before she stares hard into the camera.

"The chemistry between me and the rooftop is palpable. I'm out."

Her call ends. Chase stares at the screen in silence before the slyest smile unfurls.

"Did you guys hear that? She said 'chemistry.'"

Noah unmutes and he's howling laughing, "She also said she was flirting with death."

Before I can say or do anything, the bell in the front room chimes, drawing my eyes. I speak over them.

"Hey, I have a customer. I have to go," I say when I unmute, speaking over Noah's laughter.

They both nod as I end the call and slide my phone into the front pocket of my apron. I'm still grinning to myself as I breeze through the swinging door that separates the front and back.

"Hi. Welcome," I greet, before halting in my place and looking around. "Huh," I say to myself as my brows draw together because there's nobody here.

I stand there for a second, feeling confused, because I definitely heard the bell before walking to the front of the store. Maybe someone just peeked their head in?

But as I look out the window, I don't see anyone. There are plenty of people walking around, just nobody out front of the store.

My brows rise as I shrug before I turn around to go back to doing nothing.

The moment I do, my eyes catch on something sitting on top of the glass case.

It doesn't register at first as I make my way to it, but the closer I get, the more my smile grows.

"Oh my god," I breathe out, hurrying the last few steps before my hand smooths over the glossy cover of tomorrow's issue of *Vision and Vibe*. "No way . . ." I look over my shoulder, talking to myself. "They must've had it couriered."

I smile, remembering how I told the editor what flower shop I worked at during our initial conversations.

This is so cool. I sweep open the cover before scanning the table of contents for my page number, taking a second to stare at the title of my article because it feels so surreal. I bite my lip before my fingers begin paging through.

The smile on my face almost hurts. I can't believe something I wrote has been published for the world to read. How is this my life, because it feels too good to be true.

A breathy laugh leaves me, euphoria sweeping through my veins as I swipe the page a few more times to get to page 129. But as I turn to it, a loose page lifts from the others, crinkling against my finger and making me stop.

What looks like an old newspaper article is tucked between the busy pages surrounding it. "What . . ." I say under my breath before sliding it out and reading the headline.

> Dark Days in Darkwater

I scan it, confused, half reading the first line:

> A dark cloud hangs over this small community after five teens are found dead in what officials believe started as a lovers' quarrel and ended in a massacre.

My brows draw together as I turn it over, looking for some kind of explanation, before I flip through the magazine again, curious if there's more. But I find nothing.

"Weird," I say to myself, rereading the headline. I feel like I've heard of this . . . or maybe the name of the town. *Where have I heard this?*

Before the thought can take root, my phone rings, making my shoulders jump. "Jesus."

"Hi," I say, sunshiny, when I see my mom's name and set the article aside. "Guess what I'm looking at?"

"I don't know, but I just got my orders from the general, so I'm ready for tomorrow. Your sister says this is a foolproof plan for the article to become a virus."

I chuckle, accidentally sweeping what I was looking at onto the floor.

"Viral," I correct her, then hear a ding at the door. It's my coworker back from lunch. "We're not hacking into the government."

Lee looks at me quizzically, but I shake my head, pointing to the back before I take the magazine and my mother to the workroom. I only get two steps before I remember I left the paper on the floor, but Lee's already put it in the trash for me.

"Thanks," I mouth as I disappear.

"Mom," I say when the coast is clear, but she's still talking.

"I keep telling your dad that 'virus' sounded strange, but you never can tell with Evie. Plus, I was half listening. Most of her conversation was a rant about someone named Star-Lord."

I grin, my fingers tapping the magazine, impatient to share my news. "Sounds about right. Guess what I got early?"

"Oh, and that reminds me, your father wanted me to tell you he met a lovely couple at one of his marathons. What do you know, they do birth parent searches. He said they were a real-life *Hart to Hart.*"

"Who? What are you talking about?"

She playfully scoffs. "It was a television show from the eighties his grandma made him watch with her . . . back before smart TVs, when you couldn't binge or buy your way out of commercials."

"Okay, great, whatever . . . Will you listen to my news, please? I'm dying a slow death over here."

She laughs. "Yes. Sorry, go."

I take a deep breath. "I got an early copy. I'm looking at my name in print."

She screams, and I can tell she's jumping up and down. Then, because she's the best mom ever, the crying starts. From both of us.

"I'm so proud of you, Goldie. My little ray of sunshine. This is only the beginning. Everything starts now."

# Chapter Seventeen

***Camp Weonoke—years prior***

The boy swept the room, careful not to hit her feet as she stocked shelves with more baked beans and creamed corn.

*Townie,* she thought to herself. She'd heard the camp director say his name but hadn't remembered it, but most people called him Townie. It seemed cruel, but she wasn't one to rock the boat.

Still, she was curious about him.

Mainly because she knew he watched them. It was his blue eyes she'd seen from the tree line the first time Davis went to second base. And she'd seen him again yesterday, when Davis had made butterflies tickle her stomach while getting to third.

This boy was always watching.

It occurred to her that something so sinister, so disturbing, shouldn't have made her more curious. But she was.

"Why do you watch us?" she said, not looking over her shoulder. "Aren't you scared he'll catch you?"

The sweeping stopped, but he didn't answer until she turned around and their eyes met. *What a beautiful sapphire color,* she thought to herself.

"I don't watch him. Just you."

She wasn't sure why that made her feel weird, and not necessarily in a bad way.

"Why?"

He shrugged. "Because you're interesting."

"Do you even know my name?" she retorted.

He licked his lips, steeling his cold blue eyes deeper into hers. "Do you know mine?"

She fleetingly wondered if what she'd say would embarrass him, but she didn't care if it did. He wasn't like Davis. He didn't have any of the charm or well-natured smiles that came so easily to Davis.

*There is an honesty, though,* she thought.

One that he had but Davis could never possess. Because his honesty wasn't a reflection of his goodness. Oftentimes, well-intentioned people committed the worst crimes because they didn't want to hurt someone. Something told her that wasn't an affliction the townie suffered.

"Is your name Townie?" she offered as coldly as the others said it.

He never bristled or looked away. Instead, he walked toward her. Her heart ticked up a beat, and she felt the stock shelves at her back.

"He doesn't even like you," he said quietly, so focused on her that she wanted to squeeze her eyes closed. It was too intense. "He fucks a new girl every summer. It's his thing, and then he never speaks to them."

The crudeness in the way he spoke made her uncomfortable. Even though that was a truth she'd already considered.

When she met Davis, she'd decided that this summer was for exploration. Which wasn't something typical for her, but the motto of the camp was "Adventure Awaits," so she'd figured, *Why not.*

She knew this wasn't something the townie considered about her, and having one up on him made her feel something new.

"Who says I want him to speak to me after the summer?"

They were standing face-to-face now. And even though she still felt scared, she never showed it, facing him with strong shoulders. Because her response was the truth, which was the only thing she appreciated about this conversation. *Maybe not the only thing,* she thought.

"You don't care to be discarded? So, you're a whore?"

She smirked, feeling much less afraid because it was then she realized he was jealous. And that was less frightening than the idea that he watched them to hurt her.

"And what if I am, Townie? What are you going to do about it? Call me names in the hopes I'll stop my errant ways and choose you?"

He swallowed. She'd hit the right nerve, and she wasn't sure if that elated her to know or brought her relief because now she could find a way to end this conversation.

She decided on the former. He'd confirmed the feeling that was fueling her bravery. She was in control. He liked her.

"I think you should stick to sweeping and stop being weird and creepy. Or I'll tell my boyfriend . . . *before* the end of the summer."

She started past him, but he crossed the broom's handle in front of her, forcing her to take a step back.

"Get off me," she ground out.

He encased her with his body, letting the broom drop to the floor as he whispered in her ear, "*I* could treat you like one if you want . . . like a whore."

He didn't back away, crowding her in the stockroom, and she hadn't realized how large his body was. Her chest rose and fell against his navy blue janitor uniform as their breaths mingled.

His fingers touched her throat, and it sent shivers down her spine.

"I'll scream," she rushed out insincerely.

But he never backed up, his mouth still close to her ear.

"I could hurt you before anyone comes."

She turned her face, not away, but toward his cheek to ensure he heard every word.

"They'll still come. So, make sure you kill me because I will tell them about everything you do to me."

He laughed an empty laugh before he drew back, their eyes connecting.

"You think you're so fucking perfect and that I'm trash. You're too good for me, right? Is that it? Perfect Davis can treat you like a slut, but I'd have to rape you in order to touch your pussy?"

Her breath caught at his lewdness. She should have been disgusted, but it made her feel things she hadn't before.

A slow smirk tipped his crooked mouth.

"You like being spoken to that way. My own virgin whore."

At that, she spat in his face. He only blinked.

His crystal-blue eyes stared back into hers as he gathered the disrespect with his fingers, and then he put it in his mouth—sucking her spit off his own fingers.

She watched him, her breath halted and her thoughts stilled.

He watched her back with hate in his eyes.

But instead of pain or retribution like she feared, he lowered his face to hers and kissed her.

She wasn't sure how long it lasted, but it was enough time that her arms and hands had stopped fighting him off and wrapped around his neck. And his long fingers dug into her lower back, urging her body closer to his.

He broke the kiss and stared down at her.

"Be mine."

Feelings stirred inside her naive body, and she wondered why it didn't feel like this with Davis. There was something about this moment that made her feel powerful and wanted. The townie wouldn't hurt her. That much she knew. But he was still dangerous.

Even though it shouldn't, that excited her.

She'd never understand why she agreed. Maybe because she'd never had boys fight over her. Or because she'd committed herself to adventure.

*Do I want to be a girlfriend?* she thought.

Or maybe it was because Townie was right. Davis would discard her after the summer, because that's precisely what a summer romance is—fleeting.

So why not take advantage of the moment and let the townie kiss her like that again?

"Say it . . ." he said with authority. "Say, 'Billy, I'm yours.'" Then he provided a nudge in the wrong direction. "It can be our little secret."

She wouldn't mean it, and that was no matter. Because Billy felt like a story she'd like to tell one day. He felt like a reckoning.

And she'd always been good at keeping secrets.

Later in her life, she'd realize this was when her story had begun *and* ended.

"Okay, Billy, I'm yours."

To my Emerson,

You let him laugh at me today.

Was it because you thought he knew?

You're right. Men know. I could smell him on you too.

—Your Billy

# Chapter Eighteen

## Goldie

***August***

"Earth to Goldie," my sister chuckles. "Have you heard anything I've said in the last ten minutes?"

*Nope.*

I look over to where she's sitting on my couch, grinning as the delicious memory of Noah kissing me all the way from my toes to my lips the night before he left still lingers.

*"I could dedicate a whole week to this . . ."*

*His lips press to my hip bone before French-kissing a path farther north, blazing a decadent trail to my belly button. I draw in a deep breath as his tongue dips just inside before his teeth playfully nip my soft stomach, making me jump.*

*"I swear to god, I could spend a whole week eating you up, killer . . ."*

*He keeps his slow, torturous pace to the underside of my breast, then against my sternum until lazing at the hollow of my throat.*

*"You know what?" he hums. "I'm gonna fuck you until neither of us knows our names."*

*His nose runs up and over my chin as he breathes me in, inhaling every molecule of my scent before he kisses the hell out of me.*

*Leaving me no choice but to believe every word he's just said.*

"Hello!" Evie bellows next to me, pulling me out of my foxy coma.

"What?" I shrug innocently.

"Good grief, Charlie McHobag. You literally just shivered while staring off into the cosmos." She holds up her hand. "Don't share. If I had to guess from all that blushing, it's something I never want to know about. Spare me the trauma."

I laugh, feeling my cheeks burn as popcorn falls between my sister's fingers before she shovels more of it into her mouth, then points to the glowing television screen. A scream erupts.

"I *said* that you were missing the best part." I look back to the TV as she gets excited. "Oh, look, we have a runner . . . Why do they always run? The minute they run, everyone watching knows death is imminent." Evie rolls her eyes. "See? She's fallen, and she's never getting up. Tragic. Bye-bye, busty camp counselor number two."

My hands dart over my face, hiding me from the gruesome blood and guts as I draw my knees up, sitting on the couch.

I'm never sleeping tonight. Why did I let her pick the movie? Even if it's research for her job, I should have known better. Never let the sister who specializes in gory special effects and can also quote every line from any eighties slasher film be the director of movie night. Ever.

I pull my blanket up under my chin.

"How do you watch this shit and eat? More importantly, why are you forcing me to? I thought we were doing a sleepover, not trauma bonding."

The sleepover was Noah's idea. He hated the idea of me being alone in the apartment without him. And I'm glad he mentioned it because I was already planning the same thing.

Evie laughs. "Forcing you? More like gifting you with this opportunity, you big baby. You realize that this film was the first of its kind. It kicked off careers, started a slasher film movement. It's revolutionary. Plus, it's almost spooky season."

"It's August."

"And that would be the definition of 'almost,'" she fires back. "Would you stop being such a baby? Have you forgotten that I need to immerse myself into the vibes of a slasher camp to really get the essence? This job we landed is literally the peak of my career. And, if I'm being totally honest, this is as much work research as it is pure enjoyment at your expense."

I smile back rudely. "What a sweet, supportive sister you are. I hope you get fired."

She laughs.

According to Evie, last week she scored the job of a lifetime when some guy hired her firm to create a replica of an old, abandoned summer camp and turn it into an interactive scarefest for Halloween. It sounds awful, like heart attacks and lawsuits awful. But she hasn't stopped talking about it, even though I've tuned out every gruesome word.

The sound of crunching bones makes my shoulders jump before I dart to my feet, my back to the television.

"Mmmkay, that's it. I am taking myself to bed and leaving you to geek out on *Bloody Bloody Massacre Part Seven Hundred and Forty-Nine* in all its revolutionariness . . . Clearly, you're a psychopath who works for psychopaths." I hold up a hand as she starts to speak. "I will be locking my door, so the couch is all yours."

Evie chuckles as she digs her hand back into her bowl, but as I turn to walk away, she talks with a mouthful of popcorn.

"It's just corn syrup and shitty special effects. Are you really frightened of a little ole scary movie?"

"Yes," I laugh, looking back at her.

She gives me puppy dog eyes, blinking up adorably. "But I came all the way here to hang out with my big sis."

God, she's the worst.

"No way, I'm not falling for that look. No more movie night. I'll have to watch the Disney Channel to counteract this torture."

She pushes her bottom lip out, and I'm about two seconds from giving in until the sound of a chainsaw buzzes through the screen. *On second thought, I'm out.*

I spin around and walk away while waving. I know I'm chicken. Which, if I think about it, is an ironic comparison because if you've ever encountered one of those furry, feathery monsters, they're fearless and evil.

"Come back," she yells just as popcorn hits my arm. "Loser. You just want to call Noah."

She's saying his name teasingly, almost singing it. My hand hangs idle on my bedroom doorknob before I swing around.

"So? Leave me alone. It'll be a miracle if I sleep now." I wave at the television. "Because of that garbage, it's suddenly completely plausible for a man in a ski mask or some devil child to be hiding behind my door . . . with a butcher knife."

Evie cocks her head before she grins up at me.

"Goldie, come on. Don't be ridiculous." As if on cue, a faint *chu-chu-chu* sounds off in the background. "Nobody's *behind* that door. I mean, if anywhere, they'd be standing directly in the entry when you open it."

"Evie!" My voice bursts from me as I yank my hand from the doorknob like it's been burned and hustle my way back to the couch. I'm walking so fast that I'm swinging my hips like the sassy senior girlies in the park who still wear leg warmers.

The moment I jump to my safety on the sofa, I steal more of the blanket from her . . . and the damn remote.

"I love you," she teases, nudging me with her foot.

She's laughing *at* me, not *with* me.

"Well, I hate you. So if you want to win me back, go get me a water from the fridge."

She stands up, chuckling, as my phone vibrates on the coffee table.

"You're just never leaving the couch again?"

I nod, seeing it's a message from Noah. "Pretty much."

She walks past me before I swipe my phone up.

**Damon:** Hey, just got back to the hotel. Round one of interviews was amazing.
Dinner was lonely. I miss you.

"Where's that bag of candy I brought?" Evie yells from the kitchen.

"In the pantry," I answer as I type back to Noah.

As I glance up, she steps backward into the shadows of the kitchen and says "I'll be right back" with a laugh.

"Evie. Not funny," I say, trying to hide my smile before I turn my attention back to Noah.

**Me:** I miss you more. Especially since I'm being tortured with scary movies.

**Damon:** Yikes. What asshole thought up a sleepover?
You should have a talk with him.

**Me:** That's what I'm saying.

Evie's rummaging around the pantry saying something to me, but I'm only focused on my phone.

**Damon:** The good news is the next time I leave my baby's coming with me.

**Me:** Yes, she is.

**Damon:** I'm serious. I won't go if you don't go. You're stuck with me.

The smile on my face is ridiculously big. Typically, the idea of following a guy across the country seems as cursed as getting each other's names tattooed on various body parts. But we're Noah and Goldie—the rules don't apply.

As terrifying as the thought is, my life just doesn't make sense without him in it. I can't think of anything that could stand between us.

**Me:** So, what I hear you saying is that you want me to move to LA.

**Damon:** Yeah but maybe get your own place so it's not awkward when I have girls over.

I giggle.

**Me:** Hilarious. Going back to the slasher film to get some tips and tricks on how to handle my boyfriend. 🔪🔪

"You are sooo gone over him—"

My eyes dart up, meeting my sister's smiling face. She adds, "I swear you couldn't be more in love if you tried. It's disgusting, and I'm jealous."

The vibration in my hand pulls my attention back as she sits back down and puts a water bottle in front of me.

**Damon:** I love you, killer. PS. tell your sister that if she keeps tormenting you, I'll call Chase to come over.

I chuckle a little too manically, making her look at me for answers as I type back.

**Me:** Speaking of the devil . . . he picked up your bike earlier today. Does he know how to ride it?

**Damon:** Why . . . Do you think I would just give him my motorcycle to impress a girl? 😉

My mouth falls open as my eyes grow wide. *I knew it.*

**Me:** Absolutely. Because that's how a good boyfriend loves his boyfriend.

You two are a bromance for the ages.

"What are you two talking about, because the look on your face has me riveted," Evie says, turning her body to face mine.

I smile at her. "Chase borrowed Noah's motorcycle earlier today, but he rolled it . . . like walked it back four blocks to his house. And I knew something was up, because his new neighbor is some gorgeous runway model, so I'm thinking he's using it as a prop."

She rolls her eyes. "Of course he is. Someone needs to tell Temu *Sons of Anarchy* the only meat women want his delicate touch on is the rib eye kind."

I laugh. "The man does make a mean steak." *Hold on.* "Wait, how do *you* know how good his food is?"

She suspiciously turns away from me, her eyes narrowing in on the TV as she takes the remote and flips through new shows before shrugging too quickly. "Because I eat at restaurants."

My phone sits idle in my hand as I stare at her profile, making her squirm. "But at *his* restaurant? You were that curious about his meat-touching skills, huh?"

Her head whips to mine with a scowl on her face. "It was a group of us. He didn't even know I was there. I wanted Indian, but they wanted Chase . . . I mean, his food. You know what I'm saying. Shut up with that look."

I just keep smiling before I shake my head, typing back to Noah.

**Me:** I'm turning into a pumpkin in about an hour. Call me? I have potential hot goss about

your bestie and
mine.

The bubbles come up and then go away, but no message populates. I frown.

"And another thing," my sister snaps, grabbing my attention. "People can be repulsive in real life and be really good at their jobs. That's common sense, Goldie."

"Okay." I fall sideways still sitting crisscross on the couch as she shoves my shoulder, making me laugh. "I'm not restaurant shaming you. I'm just surprised you didn't tell me."

"Why? Look at how you're acting," she bellows, clearly embarrassed, which makes me laugh harder. *Thou doth protest too much.*

"How am I acting? I'm literally saying nothing. I just think you don't want to admit you may like one thing about him . . ."

She picks up a pillow and hits me with it as I squeal. Tears start to blur my vision because I'm laughing so hard. Until I hear Noah's ringtone.

"Hold on," I rush out, putting a hand up to stop the onslaught of abuse when I see "Damon" scrolling across my phone screen.

"Hey," I answer, partly breathless, still amused by her protests as she sticks her tongue out at me.

But the way he says my name makes my body turn cold. I shoot to my feet, eyes searching but landing on nothing in front of me. "Noah, what's wrong?"

"Baby . . ." Noah inhales deeply. He's stammering, breathless, like he's having a panic attack. My heart stops in my chest as Evie touches my arm.

"Noah, what's happening? Are you okay?"

The moment he gets his voice back, he's speaking a mile a minute. My hand shoots over my mouth as my eyes instantly glisten. "Oh my god. Noah, slow down."

I turn toward my sister, then away, not knowing what to do with myself as I try and make sense of what he's saying, answering back in broken sentences.

"How?" . . . "Okay." . . . "Okay." . . . "I will."

My feet start moving, hands shaking as much as my voice as I run into my bedroom with my sister on my heels. "I'm leaving right now. Noah, I'm on my way. It's gonna be okay. I love you."

Evie's standing in the doorway, her face fixed on me. "What the fuck just happened? What did he say?"

My teary eyes meet hers as I shove my feet into shoes and look around for my wallet.

"It's Chase . . . Evie, he's at Mass General." Her eyes grow owllike. "It was a hit-and-run." My voice breaks at the end as she rushes toward me.

"I'm coming with you," she says, wrapping me in a hug. I nod, still hearing the fear in Noah's voice, breaking me.

*"I'm taking the first flight. I don't know when I can get there, but he can't be alone . . . Golds, Chase got hit on my bike . . . This is my fault." His voice breaks, and I know he's trying not to cry. "My mom died alone. I wasn't there . . . Killer, you two are the only family I have left. This can't happen again. Please, please."*

"Let me get the keys. I'll drive," Evie rushes out, our hug momentary because we dash from the apartment, still in our pajamas, with sneakers on our feet and fear on our faces.

Chase can't die. He just can't. Noah's lost too much in life already.

We race to the car, out of breath and everything a blur.

"Thank you for coming with me," I whisper as we pull into traffic. "Noah sounded so afraid, and I don't know what to do. He said Chase's family is in Europe but that he's the emergency contact, so he has to call and tell them. Jesus, apparently Chase is in surgery right now. I don't know how we're gonna get information." Tears stream down my face. "What if Noah loses him? They're like brothers."

"Listen to me," she barks, stopping hard at a red light and staring into my eyes. "We're not thinking like that. We're fucking manifesting.

Chase doesn't die today." I'm nodding back at her, my chin quivering. "He's the goddamn father of my fish . . . And none of us will ever eat again if he leaves. So, he's living. And don't worry, I'll figure out a way to get us back there to him."

I take a deep breath to stop my tears and face forward as her tires screech, hauling ass again.

"You're right," I whisper to myself. "Chase Beckett, you aren't going anywhere. My future husband needs a best man, and I need a cool uncle for my future babies."

"God, what is taking so long?" my sister huffs as she looks over at the glass door of the visitors' room for the millionth time.

I tuck my hair behind my ears. "I don't know. I just wish they'd give us more information."

We've been at the hospital for hours, and outside of knowing that Chase is still in surgery, we haven't been told anything new. Still, thank god my sister has a flair for a good lie because the only reason we know what we do is because of how convincingly she claimed to be Chase's wife.

*"Mrs. Beckett? I am Dr. Mathison. We're so sorry, a Noah Adler was the emergency contact listed on his phone."*

*"We're newly married," Evie rushes out, folding her arms behind her back and hiding her ring finger.*

*I blink as I glance at my sister, hoping her chest isn't moving as fast as mine, but thankfully, she's standing stoic.* Please let this work, please let this work.

*He nods. "Your husband needed extensive surgery. The accident fractured multiple ribs and dislocated his shoulder. He has a multitude of lacerations on his palms and arms. The good news is that x-rays show no trauma to his spine. But his femur is broken, and he has multiple fractures, as well as ligament and tendon damage to his right hand. They needed immediate surgical intervention—"*

*I gasp as Evie's face swings to mine.*

*"Chase is a chef," Evie says in explanation of our outburst. "He'll need that hand, Doc."*

*"We will do all we can to give him a full recovery." The doctor looks down, avoiding her eyes for a moment, and my heart beats faster. "He has some intracranial swelling along with a small bleed that we're paying close attention to, but right now, we're focused on repairing the hand and leg. We'll keep you updated as soon as we can." He motions to a woman in scrubs standing off to the side. "The nurse will take you to the family waiting room."*

I shiver from the memory as Evie looks at her phone. "What time is Noah landing?"

I shrug. "I don't know. He was on standby for one flight and booked for another. I have crappy service in here, so I don't even know if my texts are going through. But I'm thinking sometime in the next thirty minutes."

Evie blows out a rush of air, her cheeks puffing up, as I pull my long sleeves over my hands and put a foot on the cold hospital chair I'm sitting on.

Hospitals are always so cold. I'm glad she had the wherewithal to grab two hoodies from her car. But why does she have them in her car in the middle of summer? How long have these been there?

Oh god. My thoughts are so scattered. I'm volleying between scared to death and shit that's pointless.

I lay my head on Evie's shoulder, existing in silence, as I check my phone over and over, hoping it will miraculously work, while she picks at her nail polish.

"Noah got ahold of Chase's family, right?"

We talked about this in the car, but I'm pretty sure neither of us remembers the last four and a half hours very clearly, so I just nod.

"They won't be here until later today. Even with a private jet."

"Jesus," she exhales harshly, and I sit up straight. "Can you imagine hearing someone hurt your kid like this? What kind of animal hits someone and leaves them there to die?" She waves her hand before grabbing mine.

I start to agree with her, but I'm silenced because the glass door swings open, drawing both our eyes.

"Mrs. Beckett?" The doctor we spoke to before is back. We instantly stand, our hands gripped as she nods. "He's out of surgery. It all went very well. We expect a full recovery for him. And thankfully, the swelling on the brain has gone down, and the bleed has stopped. He's really lucky he was wearing his helmet. We'll continue to monitor him, but this is the best possible outcome we could've hoped for."

Neither of us speaks, trying to process what he's saying. The doctor smiles, his eyes wrinkling on the sides of his face. "Mrs. Beckett. Your husband is out of the woods, and he is going to be just fine."

A collective sigh of relief whooshes between both of us as we immediately hug. *Holy shit.* The doctor continues, but we stay in the hug.

"He's being moved into a suite. Once he's awake and stable, you'll be able to see him."

"Thank you," Evie says, before looking at me with a smile. "It's good."

"It's good," I echo, smiling back and letting out a long exhale. "Let me text Noah."

Even though I don't know if he's getting them or not, I still have to send it anyway.

**Me:** HE'S OKAY!!!!
Out of surgery.
They said we can
go back once he's
awake. Noah—it's
good.

I drop back into my chair, leaning my head against the wall behind me. "Fuck," I say and turn to look at my sister. "What a night . . ."

"May it never happen again," she tosses out with a chuckle as her shoulders sag in relief.

She's typing furiously on her phone as I just sit and breathe, letting the news sink in. He's okay. God, the alternative was horrifying. I can't even think about how I would've told Noah. Now, if only I could relax, knowing Noah knows that. Evie turns to face me.

"Umm . . . did you hear what the doctor said? That he had the helmet on."

I nod. "I know, thank god. I don't even want to think about what could've happened had he not."

But she narrows her eyes as her smile widens. It's then I can see her signature sarcasm gathering like a storm.

"What? Why are you looking at me like that?" I press, not picking up on what she's trying to telepathically say.

"Goldie . . ." She emphasizes my name like I'm missing something.

"What?" I giggle.

She deadpans. "Listen, I'm only saying this because Chase is okay . . . But he had the helmet *on*."

I feel lost because I'm still not getting it. My brows pull together, so she lays both her hands on my arm gently. "Golds, he doesn't know how to ride the motorcycle. Why the fuck was he wearing the helmet?"

The smile on my face struggles to remain hidden because now I hear what she's saying. She lifts her brows, emphasizing her words. "Are you seeing the *full* picture here? The *Sixteen Candles* of it all?"

I shake my head. "No . . . I mean, yes, but I'm not laughing two minutes after finding out he's okay."

She keeps giving me the same look, and it's making it hard not to break. But then she shrugs. "I bet this is the first time in history being the embodiment of a red flag saved someone's life." Her laughter is way too contagious as she shakes my arm. "Oh my god. He was standing out there, trying to Jake Ryan his Vikki's Secret, and got hit by a fucking car. Oh my god." She screams at the end, doubling over.

And now we're both laughing. It's the kind of maniacal cackle fueled by fear getting doused by relief.

She wipes her eyes. "I'm really happy he's okay because this is the kind of shit you can only laugh at when someone lives. But I need you to promise me that as payment for my diabolical lies tonight, you will never, ever, let him live this down."

I take a breath, rubbing my cheeks because they hurt.

"What's funny is this is going to be Chase's favorite part of the story. He's going to tell it to everyone because it's so on brand. Well, maybe he'll love the fact you pretended to be his wife more."

"I don't know what you're talking about," she blurts out, all her humor suddenly lost. "Especially if someone from billing comes sniffing around."

I chuckle before I look down at my phone again. Still no answer from Noah. I wiggle the phone in my hand.

"Hey, I'm gonna go out in the hall and see if I get more bars. I hate that I can't see if anything's been delivered to him."

"Yeah, okay." Evie yawns, stretching her arms. "I saw a vending machine on the way in. Will you get me some hot chocolate and maybe a snack?"

I give her a thumbs-up as I walk out of the waiting room and into the hallway, staring down at my phone. Some conversation passes, and I glance up toward a couple of hospital staff and smile before I walk a little farther down another hallway, hoping for a real signal.

"Come on, dammit," I whisper to myself, only half noticing two guys in suits before I take another few steps.

But then my head pops back up, doing a double take.

"Oh my god, Noah."

He's standing in the middle of the two suits in a wrinkled black T-shirt, looking exhausted. His eyes instantly meet mine, and whatever's being said to him is ignored as he hurries toward me, wrapping his arms around me and lifting me off the floor. My words are spoken into the crook of his neck.

"When did you get here? Did you get my text? Chase is okay. We just talked to the doctor." I draw my head back, looking at him. "My service has been awful. I didn't know if you were getting any of my messages. I didn't know if you were on the plane—"

"I got all the messages," he cuts in. "You just weren't getting mine. Baby, you were my fucking lifeline. Thank you."

He kisses my cheek over and over before placing me back down on my feet. But my face stays lifted to his as he cradles it.

"Thank you for being here, killer."

Noah's lips meet mine, softly, making my eyes close and my body sink into his. I don't think I've realized how much I needed to see and touch him until this moment.

He draws back, speaking inches from my lips.

"I don't know what I would've done without you."

I'm gripping his wrist, staring up at him. I've never seen Noah like this. He looks stripped bare. Outside of the fact that it looks like he's run his hand through his hair a thousand times. Or that I can tell he hasn't slept because there are dark circles under his eyes. It's the fear inside them that has me feeling like the floor is falling out from underneath me.

For the first time ever since knowing him, Noah looks afraid of something. I can't imagine what he's been through tonight. The fear he must've felt from almost losing his best friend in a similar way his mom died. I want to ask him if he's okay, tell him to talk to me, but we're interrupted.

"Excuse me, we just have a few more questions."

Noah only half turns his head to the stranger. "I'll be right there. Give me a second."

I frown. "What's going on? Who's that?"

"Detectives."

My face brightens. "Did they find the people who did this?"

Noah shakes his head before kissing my forehead gently. "It's nothing you need to worry about, killer. Just some questions for me because my bike was involved, that's all."

I glance at the men's unreadable faces before I take a step back, suddenly hearing my sister's voice, so I turn toward it.

"Hey, there you are." She comes to stand next to me before hugging Noah in greeting. "They just told me I can go back and see him. We all can."

I smile but Noah frowns, hitching a thumb over his shoulder. "You guys go first. I'll catch up in a few minutes. I just have to deal with this." His eyes lock to mine. "Tell him I'm here, please."

I nod. "Yeah, of course." But I hug him once more, not really wanting to let go.

He places his palm over the back of my hair. "Go on. I'll be right there."

My sister gently tugs the back of my hoodie when I don't let him go, so I step back, looking at the detectives again. I don't know why I feel uneasy, but it's just a gut feeling. Or maybe I'm picking up on Noah's mood because all the rawness I saw in his face, not even ten seconds ago, has completely vanished as he turns back toward them.

I frown as I follow the waiting nurse with Evie, glancing over my shoulder as I go.

Noah's standing sideways, arms crossed while he rubs his tensed jaw. Both officers look down at their notebooks before each of them asks him something, but he looks so uncomfortable. His eyes glance up at mine, seeing me watching, before he casually turns his back to me.

"You okay?" my sister whispers, calling my eyes back to hers.

"Yeah." But I glance back at him again. "Do you think he could be in trouble for letting Chase borrow the bike?"

"No. Why? Are you worried?"

The nurse stops and swipes her card in front of a secured door.

I shrug. "I just think it's weird that detectives are here and want to talk to him. He was across the country. How could he even help them?"

I look over my shoulder one last time as we walk through the secure entry, and I watch him until the door closes behind me.

But it's not Noah who's staring back at me. It's the detective with the little notebook. And his eyes don't leave my scowling face until I blink first and walk away.

"You gave us a real scare, man," Noah says as I lean into him.

Chase starts to nod but barely lifts his head, as if it's too heavy, before he plops it back down on the pillow.

"Whoa," Chase groans, still hoarse from the tube that was down his throat. "My whole body hurts. I feel like I got hit by a car . . ."

"You did," Noah offers gently, making Chase scowl, then move his lips around as if he's just discovered them.

"That's not right," Chase draws out, repeating the last syllable of the word a few times. "Cars hit deer and speed bumps."

Noah grins at me, and I chuckle because Chase is so high.

"At least he's feeling no pain," I whisper, rubbing Noah's arm. I look up at him, relieved to see him less stressed.

"You're soooo pretty," Chase slurs, turning his attention to Evie, who's seated in a chair by the door. "How did I convince you to marry me?" He looks at us, trying to whisper but failing. "How did I convince her to marry me? She hates me." His eyes grow wide. "Did she hit me with the car?"

Evie smirks along with a huffed laugh, but the nurse looks over her shoulder nosily.

*Uh-oh.* I make eyes at Evie to say something, because I'm not quite sure how much trouble we could get into since we aided and abetted an entire hospital in violating the HIPAA Act.

"Love is crazy like that, hubby," Evie says, giving me a dirty look. "People do bizarre things in the name of it."

I grin as the nurse moves past us, checking Chase's vitals. His head lolls sideways trying to track her, making his eyes cross for a minute.

"How are we feeling, Mr. Beckett? Any pain?" the gray-haired older woman says, smiling down at him.

"We?" He lifts his shoulders and hands as he wiggles the fingers on only one of them. "How many of me are there?"

The nurse laughs, looking over at Evie. "He's funny. You can sit with him now. I'm done. Tonight should be smooth sailing because of all the pain meds and anesthesia, but he'll be back to normal by tomorrow."

"Amazing. Looking forward to it," my sister offers as Chase tries to hold his arms open for her, his casted one unmoving.

"Come to Papa," he growls, making her wince until the nurse looks, which forces a fake smile from her.

I bury my face in Noah's chest as he covers his laugh with a cough. Evie stands from her chair, glaring at me as she walks to Chase's bedside and sits down slowly. But he's already onto something new.

"Oh fuck, I'm broken?" He's finally noticed his hand. He looks up at Noah and me with puppy dog eyes like he's going to cry. "But I'm a chef, Noah . . ."

"Oh, Chase," I rush out sweetly. "You're going to be okay."

But as I say it, it's already forgotten because he's blowing raspberries with his lips.

Noah looks down at me. "I don't think anything's getting him back down. Why don't you and your sister head back to the house and get some rest. I'll stay here until his family gets here."

I frown because I don't want to leave Noah, but Chase's meandering thoughts make me laugh again as I look over my shoulder.

He's staring at my sister again. "You look like an angel." He gasps. "Am I dying?"

She starts to get up, but he whisper-screams, "Wait, wait . . ."

Evie stares me down. "I am dangerously close to cutting off the drip. Pain can be a really good motivator. Maybe now's the time he focuses on his healing."

"Evie," I admonish, but Noah laughs.

Chase tries to wink, but both eyes close. "Angel . . . just tell me one thing."

Evie drips her gaze to him. "Yes, you should go to sleep."

He points toward the ceiling. "Does he know that I'm *your* food god?" She glances at me as my mouth drops open. "I saw you eating my meat the other night . . . hallelujure."

"Oh my god." I laugh as Evie shoots to her feet in protest. "I literally got outvoted for the restaurant."

Noah's chuckling, too, as Chase's eyes drift shut.

"Do you want to head back?" Noah says down to me. "You could probably use some sleep."

I'm shaking my head, but my body betrays me and yawns.

"Yeah," my sister says. "Because I'm gonna need my strength to get through my impending divorce." She points to Chase, who is awake again and tries to tongue her finger. "This is my good deed for the year. I will not let either of you forget it."

"Noted." Noah disconnects from me and walks around the hospital bed to hug her. "Thank you for being here with my girl and being so quick on your feet."

He lets her go, and she fake punches his shoulder. "I expect a really, really expensive Christmas gift this year."

I grin, wrapping my arms around him from the back.

"I'll do you one better," he teases. "I promise to tell him this was a fever dream. You were never here."

Evie points at him. "And this is why you're my favorite." She tilts her head to where mine is peeking out from under his arm. "Are you coming with me or staying here?"

"I think coming . . ." I peer up at Noah. "But give me a sec."

"Yeah, just meet me at the car."

She turns and heads out the door, yelling over her shoulder, "Night, hubby."

"Have my babies," Chase barely gets out before he drifts back into dreamland again.

Noah pulls me into a hug. The kind you stand in for a few minutes to just decompress. We're wrapped around each other, breathing at the same time as the exhaustion of the day finally starts to hit me.

He exhales and kisses the top of my head before I push to my tiptoes and kiss the bottom of his chin.

"Are you sure you want me to go? I can just go grab you some nonwork clothes and change mine and be right back. Or I can stay—I am in pajamas, so it's convenient."

He sighs. "What the hell would I do without you?"

"Don't worry, you'll never find out." I smile.

"Baby, I'm fine. Promise. Go home and get some rest. I'll let you know if anything changes. Me and the food god are gonna watch game highlights and sleep."

"Okay." I chew the inside of my cheek, still wanting to ask him if he needs to talk. "It's just—hearing how scared you were earlier. And how triggered you were about your mom . . ."

He rubs the back of his neck but says nothing, which says everything.

"And I'm sure the detectives didn't help. Are you really okay? You can talk to me, you know. You don't have to be an artichoke today. We can get right down to the heart."

He cradles my face with one hand. "I swear to you everything's fine. *I* am fine." He swallows before giving me a tight smile and pressing a kiss to my forehead. "Stop worrying. I promise I'm good."

I kiss him one more time, unable to shake my worry because I hate that he isn't talking to me. But I don't push. He'll open up when it's time. And maybe that's not in the hospital where his best friend almost died.

Noah walks over to the chair next to Chase's bed as I head to the door.

"I love you," I say, looking back.

Noah smirks with a wink. "I know and I love you too."

I pull the door open and head to the elevator bank. Evie's probably already to the car by now, so I pull my phone from my hoodie and send her a text.

**Me:** pick me up out front.

The elevator dings, and the sound of the doors sliding open lifts my eyes. But I instantly frown because staring back at me are the two detectives from earlier.

I take a quick step back to give them room to exit. "Sorry."

But neither moves, so I step inside. My brows draw together as I put my back to them, leaning over to press the button for the main floor.

"Have you found any leads yet?" I throw out almost immediately, glancing over my shoulder.

"You're Goldie Monroe, correct?" the one to my right says.

"Yeah." I let my answer sit for a second before I turn slightly to face him. "Are we in trouble for something?"

I shift to look at the detective on my left, who smiles and shakes his head. "No. Should you be?"

What the hell is going on? That same uneasy feeling I had before starts to swirl in my stomach. And it's not because I'm caught off guard. Something is off.

"No . . . I just . . . this seems weird. Why were you asking Noah so many questions earlier? And why are you riding down in an elevator just to talk to me?"

He inhales deeply just as the elevator begins to slow. "If you don't mind me asking, how long have you and your boyfriend been together?"

"What?" I blurt out as the doors open.

The one with the mustache motions his arm for me to exit, so I do, but as soon as I've cleared the crowd getting on, I turn to face both of them.

"How is that relevant to Chase's accident?" I hold up my hand. "And if you could answer just one of my questions before asking me another, that'd be great."

My eyes volley between them, but only Mustache answers. "We just want to know how well you think you know your boyfriend."

*Do they think Noah had something to do with the accident?*

I draw my brows together. "Well enough to know he'd never hurt his friend. He was across the country when this happened. You know that, right?"

The quiet detective shrugs. "And you're one hundred percent sure about that?"

My blood boils. This has to be a joke. I think back to how uncomfortable he looked when they were questioning him. Unbelievable. He's devastated over his friend, and they were accusing him of the crime.

I scoff. "Oh, I see what's happening here. A kid from a prominent wealthy family gets hurt, and you see Noah—all the tattoos, the black clothes—and you assume he's done something terrible. News flash: Those two love each other like brothers. You're barking up the wrong tree. Go do your jobs better and catch the person who actually did this to Chase and stop harassing the ones who love him."

I turn to stalk away, but Mustache Guy lifts his finger. "One more question. Where's your boyfriend from?"

An irritated huff leaves my chest as my eyes meet with him again.

"Hempstead," I snap. "It's in New Hampshire, in case you're unfamiliar."

He chuckles. "Yeah, that's what he said too. I guess I'll just have to check again. It was the weirdest thing. We couldn't find a Noah Adler from Hempstead."

I roll my eyes. "I'd say your inadequacies are your problem. Stop making them ours."

This time, I don't turn around, instead stalking straight to my sister's waiting car.

# Chapter Nineteen

## Noah

***October***

"Stop eating the meringues," Chase barks, but I laugh.

"I can't. That icing tastes like those soft mints you get at fancy hotels."

Every time he pipes a dollop of that tastiness onto the parchment, I swipe at least one and eat it. He exhales roughly and drops the piping bag down on the steel countertop, staring at me as his kitchen staff works around him.

"Noah." He inhales harshly, so done with me. "This is not icing." He waves aggressively in front of the bag that's tempting my taste buds. "It's whipped egg whites and sugar. It's what gives structure to buttercream and macarons."

I look down and chuckle over the way he said "macarons," leaning in on the French accent.

"Have you learned nothing during this friendship?" he barks.

"No." I shrug, completely unapologetic. "It's tasty. That's all I need to know. Why are you wound so tight right now?"

His eyes bug out. "Noah, this is my art . . ."

"Oh my god—" I breathe out, but thankfully, I'm saved from the "this is my art" lecture as one of his sous chefs brings a small plate for him to taste.

"Chef."

Chase snatches it, picks up the spoon laid atop, and closes his eyes as he slurps the broth.

"No," he grinds out. "Do it again. I don't taste that spark." He opens and closes his mouth as he tastes whatever's left over. "Try more basil. And lean in on the feta."

He hands the plate back, not looking at the guy as he shakes out his right hand while griping at me. "As I was saying. This is my art"—*seems I celebrated too soon*—"and it's not every day that I get to make a birthday cake for my favorite future sister-in-law to throw her off the fact that my best friend is going to propose to her."

I laugh, holding up my hands in surrender. "Fair. I won't eat any more buttercream structure."

He points at me, smiling at my phrasing.

We're the only two people in the world who know this secret. That tonight, after I surprise Goldie with her nearest and dearest for her surprise party, I plan to drop to a knee and ask the woman of my dreams to be my wife.

Some pots clang as a fire lights on the burners behind him.

Chase picks the bag up again, making more dollops. "So, is everything set? You got the lanterns? And the shoes?"

I start to answer, nodding, but I grimace as he pauses to open and flex his hand before abandoning the work.

He must follow my gaze because he groans. "Come on, stop looking like that. I'm fine. It just gets stiff, but that'll go away."

I give him a tight smile. "I just feel bad. It was my bike. And you could have died."

He smirks, picking the icing bag up again. "Technically, I was standing on the street, not even on your bike. And your helmet saved my life. Plus, it got me laid. Irinka's really into playing nursemaid."

I laugh. "Ah yes, your new supermodel girlfriend."

"Technically, not my girlfriend. She says what I do is murder . . . 'cause of the meat. We are a tragic story of amazing bed chemistry and shitty food taste—it's a tale as old as time."

"Are you Beauty or the Beast?"

He grins. "Like you have to ask. I look amazing in yellow."

We both laugh as I'm hit with another wave of nerves, probably stoked by what he previously asked. I rub a hand over my face, letting out an audible exhale.

He laughs. "Oh shit. Here comes the fear."

"Yeah," I chuckle. "I'm fucking petrified. I literally dreamed last night that she said no in front of everyone. Just left me standing there."

He scowls, rolling his eyes. "That would never happen. And I know we're men and we don't do feelings, but you two consistently prove to everyone around you that love is real. There's nobody else for either of you. I'm really happy you found her, Noah. You deserve this kind of happiness, man . . ."

We stare at each other, me nodding, both of us silently in the feels of it all until it starts to feel too awkward so he adds, "And fucking 'Go Patriots, Brady,' amirite?"

I smirk. "He's retired, Chase."

He grins. "I was born to make soufflé, not plays on a field, brother."

"Anyway, I gotta go. I have to pick up the shoes from my office, then run by the store to get my ghost and then get home before her. They better have a flower sheet."

He laughs to himself, not looking up, as he puts the finishing touches on her three-tier cake. "I can't believe you're re-creating the first night you met. T. rex and all. She won't know what hit her."

I smile as I stand from my stool. Chase looks up.

"Go down the list one more time. Just to make sure all the i's are dotted and the t's are crossed."

I rub my hands together, feeling the familiar flip happen in my stomach again.

"Okay. Evie's told her that her work's annual Halloween party is tonight, so Goldie thinks we're going to that and celebrating her birthday this weekend. I suggested we go as our old costumes from last year, and she thought it was so cute, so no tipping anyone off there."

"Dude, how fated is it that the girl's birthday is a few days before Halloween?"

"Right?" I raise my brows in agreement as I continue. "You've got the bar and food setup handled."

"Check and check. I am bringing my A-plus-plus game. I got a charcuterie board that'll make the ladies want to offer up some charcoocherie."

"This is why you can only date someone who doesn't speak English."

He shrugs like he doesn't care.

I smile wider. "Speaking of women who hate you, Evie is on twinkle lights and music. At eight p.m., I will walk my girl down the same street we first kissed on, pretending the Uber can't find our street, before we make our way to the park where we watched the sunrise. And after everyone screams 'Surprise,' I will lead her over to a champagne toast and then to open her first gift."

"Cue the shoes," he says, then pops his head up as his sous chef reappears, holding more broth.

"Exactly. A custom pair of cream-and-white leather Converse high-tops with stars, flowers, and the quote 'Dreamers or fools' wound up the back."

Wannabe Gordon Ramsay sous looks at me. "I think you should say, 'Accept this ring, and we'll walk this path together—'"

Chase scoffs, then takes the offered spoon and slurps the soup again before he says, "Do you think that this man would go to the length of re-creating their first date down to the smallest detail, only to bring it all home with 'We'll walk this path together' as he proposes? How dare you."

"Because he got her shoes instead of a ring."

Chase shakes his head like he's disappointed, then motions to the soup. "That's not bad. Good job. But you still have to go be ashamed. Hide your face because that was terrible love advice."

"Sorry," the sous chef offers before Chase points at me.

"Noah, please tell these Neanderthals why you got shoes. Apparently, they need a lesson in love as much as how not to overuse the fucking salt."

I grin and look down at my hands as I remember that first night.

"I got the shoes because the night we met, I took one look at her and knew exactly what I'd create. She inspired me, and I didn't even know her. I've always seen Goldie for exactly who she is. And later that night, when she told me that she wanted me to make her a pair for her birthday, I banked my creation in my memory. Funny part was she wouldn't tell me when her birthday was. She actually said, 'You'll have to stick around and find out.' So, here I am . . . stuck, hoping she will be, too, because I tied the ring to the laces."

There's silence, and it's then I notice all the guys in the kitchen staring at me.

"Do you hear that?" Chase bellows like he's some kind of gladiator. "That," he emphasizes, stabbing his spatula in the air, "that is fucking romance."

Applause erupts, and I laugh harder.

But as it dies down and everyone goes back to work, he leans over the steel counter and whispers, "You're not saying that, right?"

I laugh, rolling my eyes. "No, dick. I'm not."

Chase smirks and throws out some orders as he walks around the island to give me a bear hug.

"Proud of you, dude, and once you're in the family, we can really put the hard press on the future recipient of my will. 'Evie Beckett' has a ring to it."

I smack his face playfully as he fights me off before I put him in a headlock. He still doesn't shut up.

"And if Evie doesn't work out, then when you move to LA, you'll have to hook me up with all that fine Hollywood ass."

He wiggles out, swinging at me, but I dodge it as we both grin. "Well, the upside about women in Hollywood is they're used to guys with terrible personalities."

His face deadpans as he holds up his hands, and I walk backward out of the kitchen, grinning while he yells at me.

"Oh, come on. It's not terrible. It just requires some getting used to."

"I'm pretty sure that's what the doctor says before he gives a rectal exam."

I mouth "Sorry" to the waitstaff as they glance up from setting tables for dinner service.

Chase peeks his head out from the kitchen. "I guess that tracks . . . I do love anal."

"Jesus Christ," I breathe out as the maître d' clears his throat to the giggling staff.

The minute I hit the street, the brisk air feels like a deep breath and a shot of adrenaline, making me wired as my mind races back to the fact that tonight I'll be engaged to Goldie.

*If she says yes.*

*She's going to say yes.*

I reach into my pocket and pull out my phone, noticing a missed call from an unknown number, but I ignore it, opting to text my girl instead.

**Me:** Working should be illegal on your birthday. See you when you're home.

**Rexy:** Amen. It's my firm belief that Monday birthdays should automatically transfer to the nearest Saturday.

**Me:** Agreed. But we're still gonna celebrate you a little tonight at Evie's thing . . . and then again on Saturday.

**Rexy:** Sheesh. It's like you love me or something.

**Me:** Or something was an option? Nobody told me. Great now you've already shared my toothbrush so it's too late.

**Rexy:** Dead to me, Damon.

**Me:** Duh, I'm a vampire.

**Rexy:** 

**Me:** Happy birth-day, baby.

♥♥♥

## Goldie

"You know technically if we're going for a repeat of last year, I should only be wearing the outfit I have on underneath this," I say from next to Noah as we stroll down the sidewalk of our neighborhood.

He nods. "If memory serves, you were actually deflated when I showed up at the party. Should I pop you? Maybe rub your ass against the brick?"

I chuckle. "Nah, let's just rewrite history. It kinda felt like being a little kid trapped in a bounce house someone had unplugged. The fabric is surprisingly heavy."

He smiles as we fall back into a comfortable silence, and I look around. Tonight is so picturesque, something a travel bureau would use to advertise "Visit Boston."

The air is as crisp as a Diet Coke, and the leaves on the ground look almost painted on because of the bright autumnal palette. And even though it's warmer this October than most, it's got that *It rained earlier* feel. And maybe because it's my birthday or because it's almost Halloween, there's magic in the air.

Noah points to a stoop next to us littered with pumpkins and little white ghosts.

"You wanna meet some of my cousins?"

I giggle before looking at a house across the street. It's the one from last year that made me climb Noah out of sheer fear. I hold his hand tighter, not because I'm afraid but because I'm having one of those *I can't believe this is my life* moments.

We're literally right back where we started and so far from the people we were.

It's so bizarre the way life unfolds. A year ago, I was newly unemployed, desperately single, and floundering as I looked for a sign to point me in the right direction.

And I guess I got it in a bright-red neon one hanging above the entrance for a local pharmacy. Because now I'm a cute little inflatable T. rex who's deeply in love with her flower-print boo, living in my dream neighborhood, and finally getting paid to do what I love. Albeit only one article.

How is this my real life? I don't remember manifesting it.

But maybe I did when I boldly invited a stranger to meet me at a party. Then asked him to be my boyfriend months later. Let him become the first person to ever read my work. And trusted his belief in me more than my own fear of failure.

I decided without a conversation that I would move across the world for him and that he would want that too.

Somewhere in this year, I started getting comfortable with the uncomfy parts of life and allowing myself to bloom. I owe that as much to my own bravery as I do to Noah's strength. Because I don't think one could've existed without the other.

In the fine words of Jerry Maguire in the 1996 classic, Noah completes me.

I tilt my head, looking up at him through the mesh cutout of the costume. *One day I'm going to marry you.*

As if he's heard my thoughts, his eyehole cutouts shift to my face. "Huh? Did you say something?"

I breathe out a small laugh. There's definitely a little magic in the air.

"No, but I was going to say I heard back from the adoption investigators looking into my birth parents." I'd been meaning to tell him today but got sidetracked, so now's the perfect distraction from my thoughts. "They might have a lead. I'm meeting with them next week."

He doesn't say anything for a moment. Then he gives his head a shake like he was zoning out.

"Killer, that's amazing. Are you nervous? Happy? It's hard to tell from your resting rex face."

I smile, even if he can't see it. "Actually, I'm excited. It feels so silly to me now that I was always so scared to find out more."

He raises my claw and presses it to his covered mouth before he looks up and down the street, then leads me across the cobblestones. But the moment we're in the middle, he tugs my hand, pulling me to a stop.

"What are you doing? We're gonna get run over," I whisper.

He looks up and down the street again. "It's all clear. Just a flower ghost and his T. rex."

I chuckle, but he doesn't move.

"You know I kissed you right here the night we met."

I grin, and butterflies tickle my stomach because I can still feel that moment so distinctly inside my body. How urgent it felt but also the way he took his time as if we both needed to savor every second.

There was no way I wasn't destined to fall in love with him.

From the outside, there's nothing about this moment that could give away what it feels like. I'm sure we look ridiculous to any passersby. But still, I'm staring up into his sapphire eyes, peeking through those eye cutouts.

And even though my costume is trembling because of the fan, I've never felt more swept off my feet.

"Wanna take the risk and kiss me again?" I breathe out. "But I warn you, my teeth are pretty sharp."

My big dino head wobbles as his shoulders shake.

"Promise you won't bite?" he says, his voice layered in the gravel that hits me in all the right places.

I shrug, flirting like a good dinosaur.

We stand in silence as his hands slowly lift to my blown-up dome, the air crackling with that all-too-familiar chemistry that's always ignited between us.

I'm expecting he'll help it off me so we can kiss, but instead, Noah smashes his covered face into mine, dramatically kissing me the way kids make their dolls make out.

I scream-laugh as he wraps his arms around me. "Noah."

His deep rumble of a laugh rolls off him before I jump ten feet in the air because a horn honks behind us.

"Oh my god."

"Oh shit." Noah laughs as he grabs my claw and pulls me across the street to the safety of the sidewalk, making me swish-swish-swish the whole way while I try and keep up.

"Is it 'romance isn't dead' or 'romance makes you dead'? I can't remember," I say, a bit breathless as he stares down at me.

"You're asking a guy in the afterlife. I carry a bias. But still, sorry about that. Are you okay? I was aiming for a moment, not the ER."

I nod, feeling the head wobble. "Right as rain, but I'd be even better if our ride would find us because then I could be a respectable Rexy and make out in the back of a stranger's car."

"God, I love how classy you are." He fake smooches me again, making me laugh, before taking my hand. "The Uber should be over by the park. I think they're already rerouting, expecting traffic for the lookie-loos who drive up and down to see decorations." He glances down at his phone. "We should try and hurry."

"Is the car close?" He's walking faster, holding my outstretched arm behind him as he pulls me along. I keep yapping. "Because I feel like there's a decent chance that I'll get whatever you call rug burn but for polyester if we keep sprinting for blocks. The inside of my legs are gonna look like Hot Pockets—"

His head turns back over his shoulder. "Hot Pockets?"

"Yeah, like burnt perfection because I might start an electrical fire from the friction." I laugh. "Slow down."

"It's just right around the corner. Pick up the pace. Use your arms."

Between going deaf from the swish-swish-swish and my own heavy breathing, I don't notice the thing right in front of my face.

I'm somehow completely oblivious to the scattered tables of food and drinks set out like a foodie magazine photoshoot. All around, twenty or so people stand in the middle of the park where Noah and I spent our first sunrise together.

But just as my mind catches up to my eyes, I see Evie dressed as the twins from *The Shining*, fake body attached to her and all . . . then Chase, who looks like the Swedish Chef from *The Muppet Show* . . . Lee and the owners of the flower shop, all as witches . . . even some girls from college I never see enough of, looking like the cast of *Mean Girls*.

"Oh my god, is that my parents?" I shriek.

But it's drowned out as everyone screams, "Surprise!"

I gasp, claws covering my mouth as my shoulders jump, and I stutter a blink. Confetti explodes into the sky from little poppers in everyone's hands, and it feels a lot like how my heart's just burst.

My head shoots to Noah's, who's already pulled his costume off and is smiling at me big and wide.

"You planned a surprise party for me?" My voice is too high pitched because I'm bouncing between feeling ecstatic and wanting to cry hysterically.

*Oh my god. He's fucking amazing. He's everything.*

"I did. Happy birthday, killer."

"This is . . . oh my god, Noah."

He's already unzipping me as I start to bounce in place, repeating "Oh my god" over and over before I'm finally freed. I reach for him first, but he kisses me quickly and says, "Go. Everybody's waiting."

So I do. I run like the wind straight for everyone as they cheer before I'm engulfed in a giant group hug.

Nothing could ever top this.

## Noah

Music's playing while Goldie's being passed from person to person, everyone wanting to catch up and relive her surprise.

She stops next to her dad, who seems to say something funny because her laugh fills the air, and it's intoxicating. God, I love her. She really is like her name. This woman shines so bright I feel blinded by her but not by my nerves, because those are out in full force.

I take another sip of my drink, feeling my anxiousness double by the second. All I want is to ask her one tiny question, but that feels like launching a goddamn nuke. Because for the last hour, all I've been thinking about is how I could potentially fuck it all up.

What if I ruin her birthday? Or I say something fucking embarrassing in front of everyone and we never live that down? Every year on her birthday, someone will bring it up. Why would I choose this day?

In hindsight, this is feeling like I should've brought her sister in on the ground floor instead of letting a clown—Chase—lead the circus—me.

*Fuck.*

I take another sip, placing the flute on the bar before I turn around, belly up, and close my eyes for a second, trying to settle my nerves. But it's an ill-advised move because just as I do, Chase whispers in my damn ear.

"It's game time."

"Fuck," I rush out, rubbing my face once and letting out a harsh exhale. "I think your fake mustache touched my ear."

Chase chuckles. "Sorry. My bad . . ." I can feel his eyes on my profile. "Are you good?"

*No . . . yes. No.*

"Yeah . . ." I nod, then take two more deep breaths. "I'm fine . . . I'm ready to do this." My face meets Chase's. "I got this, right? What's the worst that could happen?"

He straightens out the collar of my navy suit jacket, eyeing me cautiously. "Yeah ya do, buddy. You're just gonna go out there, drop to a knee, and commit your life to one woman until death. It's a beautiful thing. Unless she says no."

I know he's kidding, but somehow, my body doesn't get that message because I feel my pulse quicken.

I swallow hard, my mouth suddenly dry, so I clear my throat, pulling at the collar of my shirt. "It feels stifling out here, doesn't it?"

"Out where? Outdoors?"

I nod, not catching on at all because I'm internally panicking. I've never wanted something to be perfect in my life until this moment. Honestly, I think a piece of me never thought I'd get to have this with anyone.

There's so much I never got to experience, and I want it all with her. And that's fucking with my head right now.

I rub a small circle in the middle of my chest.

"I'm feeling a little tight," I say, turning toward the crowd to find her.

Chase sounds like he's talking someone off the ledge.

"Noah . . . buddy. You're supposed to be the chill one. The calm to my storm, okay. If you pass out or have a stroke, I don't remember CPR. I was too busy making eyes at some woman taking the class with me. And forget about the dummy. The mouth is crudely suggestive. Point is, I can't save you . . ."

But I'm ignoring him because I'm staring at my girl, watching her smile and brush her hair over her shoulder. She's fucking spectacular. It doesn't matter how nervous I am. How fucking petrified I am about fucking up. Goldie's my anchor. And there's no goddamn way I'm not asking this woman to marry me. I would rather try and fail than to never shoot that fucking shot.

"I can't do this—" I say as his brows hit his forehead.

But I don't get out the rest because Chase cuts me off with "Noah, this is with love" and smacks me right across the face.

Our eyes instantly connect as I tilt my head. "Whoa . . ."

He gives me a smug look, pointing his finger at my chest. "That's right. I slapped you. And you're welcome. You're my best friend, and I'll always be here to slap the hell out of you because there's no time for hysteria. You gotta get it together. Nobody wants to marry a bitch. Now, you go drop to a knee and stop fucking around."

I'm staring at him, unmoving, completely silent as a smile grows on my face.

"I was going to say, 'I can't do this to myself anymore. I just need to ask her . . . now.'"

"Oh." He frowns, and his mouth falls open before it closes, and he raises his brows again. He takes a deep breath and smooths my lapels. "Well, I can see now I may have rushed the pep talk. Sorry about that."

The smile stays on my face as we both slowly turn, our backs leaned against the bar, eyes on the party as he continues. "I was going for the locker room coach effect. You know, like 'bottom of the ninth' kinda shit. You get my meaning. It was an oversight."

I shrug. "Yeah, I mean, it was premature but good."

"I can work on it," he agrees as he passes a drink to me.

I down it before we both chuckle. Jesus Christ.

"I don't know why I'm freaking out," I say after another beat of humored silence. "She's willing to move across the country for me. Why wouldn't she marry me? Because you're right—she loves me, and I love her. So if she says no—"

Chase cuts me off again, turning to face me. "We burn it all down and fuck her friends."

I shake my head. "No. What the fuck is wrong with you tonight?"

His eyes bug out as he shrugs. "I don't know. I misjudged where that was going . . . sorry . . . I'm still in the locker room. I'm nervous, ya know. You're getting engaged. This is a big moment."

My expression deadpans, and he looks apologetic again. "Sorry, yep . . . I hear it. Continue."

I clear my throat. "If she says no, then it's just not the right time. It's a no for now, but not for forever."

"I like it. Playing the long game . . ." He claps his hands together. "You good now? Are we getting engaged?"

*Now?* This fucker. He's going to tell the story about how he had to slap me back from the brink at my wedding. I can feel it.

"Yeah. We're getting engaged," I say with a smirk and then hold out my hand as I look back at her. "Gimme the box."

Goldie's dad looks my way, giving me an approving wink, and I give him a nod. I called him last week to ask for his blessing. He doesn't know today's the day, but it doesn't matter because he gave it without hesitation.

"Chase . . . the box," I say again, but I'm met with more silence and no action.

*What the fuck?*

My heart starts to beat faster than the mile a minute it's been doing as I slowly turn my head to stare at my best friend.

"Chase," I level. "Give me . . . the box."

His lips part, but nothing comes out. And a hollow feeling takes up space in my chest. I swear there's ringing in my ears. My hand rubs over the same cheek he smacked.

"Where are the shoes?" I ask with the kind of calm that will only be accompanied by rage.

He winces. "I thought you were bringing them."

*I'm gonna kill him.* If I wasn't hysterical before, I might be now . . . But only if "hysteria" is a synonym for "murderous."

"I texted you, saying to get them from my house. You read the text. You gave it a thumbs-up. Are you telling me I don't have a ring?"

He takes a step back. "What I'm telling you—mainly because that vein bulging on your neck looks dangerous and like it needs to be seen by a doctor—is that I just have to run out quickly on an errand, and I'll be right back."

"Motherfucker," I hiss under my breath. "We can't just leave the party, Chase. It'll be obvious something's up."

I throw my hands in the air, but he swats them down just as quickly and shushes me. He speaks through a smile as Goldie looks over at us. "I'm sorry. Calm down. She'll never know. I'm stealthy."

I mimic what he's doing and keep a smile on my face. "She will know because you run a mile in twenty."

His face whips to mine. "Abs are against my religion, Noah. I'm a chef, remember."

I level my gaze on him. "I'm going to stab you with your own fucking knives."

He chuckles. "Dude, just take a shot because you're starting to sweat. Relax. I'll be back before the whiskey stops burning in your chest."

"No," I rush out, grabbing his arm. "I'll go. I need to get my nerves in check. And it'll give me time to go over my speech for the millionth time."

He smirks. "You sure? Is this because you don't trust me now?"

I nod. "Yeah. But also, if I stay, I'll just be in my head and antsy."

Laughter bounds from her college friends as they dance to some remix of a Kendrick Lamar song, drawing our attention.

"Just do me a favor and keep her occupied while I'm gone," I say, starting to leave.

He pats my arm before waiting until I'm far enough away not to swing on him to say, "You're considering 'We'll walk this path together,' aren't you?"

"No," I say back, making my way over to my girl.

*Fuck. I was.*

She's talking to the sweet couple who own the flower shop as I wrap my arms around her from behind, dropping a kiss to her cheek.

"Hey, birthday girl," I whisper down to her.

The couple excuse themselves as Goldie turns in my arms, looking up at me.

"Hi."

"Having fun?"

She pushes to her tiptoes to kiss my chin. "The most fun. It's wild—this guy I'm using for sex threw me a party, but now it's awkward because I think he really loves me."

"Sucker," I say quietly, my eyes locked to hers. "Too bad you're taken."

Goldie repositions her arms by sliding them under my jacket as she shivers. Damn, I thought I'd considered everything when I brought a sweatshirt to go over her jumpsuit, but clearly that's not warm enough.

I let her go, forcing her to do the same as I shrug off my jacket and wrap it around her shoulders.

"What about you?"

"I run hot."

"Yeah ya do." She grins. "Whoa. Déjà vu. That keeps happening tonight. It's almost as if someone planned it that way."

I run a hand over her waist, smirking. "Who, me? Listen, keep my coat warm for me, okay? I have to go back to the apartment for a second. I forgot something."

She smiles. "Is it a present?"

I shrug, playing it cool and teasing the fuck out of her. "Maybe. Like I'd tell you . . . You're terrible with secrets."

"Tell me," she fake whines, pushing her bottom lip out.

But I dart down quickly and suck it into my mouth before kissing her. She melts into me as everything slows to a stop around us.

It's just me and her, kissing in this park. Just like last time.

I pull away, but her eyes stay closed, so I kiss the tip of her nose. "I'll be right back. Trust me, it's worth the seconds we'll be apart."

*Because it'll mean a lifetime together.*

I smile at the same time she does, but all I'm thinking is that I can't stop with the cheeseball lines. This one's not going in the speech, but "We'll walk this path together" still has potential.

"Fine," she grumbles cutely. "But if you're gone more than ten minutes, I may find a new sugar daddy. I can't make any promises. I'm thirty-one and in my prime."

I chuckle, walking backward. "I've been warned."

She bites her bottom lip as I give her a wink before I turn and jog back to our place. But all I can think is how to work being her "forever sugar daddy" into my speech.

# Chapter Twenty

## Goldie

I look over my shoulder into the dark, the view of my neighborhood blurred by all the Halloween lights strung up over trees and railings. Doesn't matter that Noah's already disappeared around the corner to get my birthday gift; I still can't stop smiling about it.

What more could he want to give me tonight? It's been incredible. He is incredible. Not only did he bring everyone together to celebrate me, but he's also re-created our first date along the way, and that's so romantic.

A thought suddenly springs forward, making me smile wider: *Is he going to propose?*

No. *Would he . . .*

I pull his jacket tighter around my shoulders, turning my head to smell his cologne while trying to change the subject with myself before I look up and watch my sister.

She's watching Chase . . . and his new girlfriend.

I hum-laugh. "You know if I didn't know any better . . ."

Her face whips to mine, the brunette wig she's wearing swishing with her, which is disconcerting since the fake body stuck to her side feels like it's staring at me too.

"Finish that sentence and it's red to the rum . . . If you must know, I was actually thinking, '*How* is that happening?' Him having a girlfriend feels like a crime against humanity. Is she doing community service?"

I laugh, bumping shoulders with my coworker, who laughs, too, until that damn thought pops back up in my mind, swirling around and tempting me with giddiness.

*What if he is asking me . . .*

"Hey, Eves. Come with to the bar?"

She nods as I excuse myself from Lee and let her follow me. My cheeks are heating up as I bite my lip and glance at her, trying to hide my smile.

"What is going on with you? Why do you look like you have a secret?"

I open my mouth, then shut it, still grinning as I stop at the bar top. "Has Noah asked you for any favors? Or for any advice lately?"

Her brows draw together like she's confused. "Huh?" she chuckles, looking at me like I've lost it. "What are you talking about?"

I look around, making sure we have privacy, then lower my voice. "Okay, so this is probably far-fetched, but tonight . . . the party with everyone I love."

"Yeah?" She motions to the bartender, pointing at her glass.

I lean in closer. "It's more than that. This whole night is like a re-creation of our first date. The costumes, the park . . . Even the lanterns hanging from the trees are just like the ones last year. And not to mention he stopped me in the street as we were walking here to kiss me in the same spot we first did that."

Her eyes grow wide. "Hold on. Do you think . . . Do you think he's going to propose?"

I shrug, but the grin on my face gives me away. "Maybe? I dunno . . . Am I off base?"

She shakes her head, unable to hide her excitement. "Holy shit."

I shush her before looking around to make sure no one is watching.

"Goldie," she says quieter, with a laugh. "He's going to propose."

"Wait, you know that?" I almost shriek, but she puts her hand over my mouth as the bartender sets the drink in front of her.

She laughs again. "No, I'm agreeing with you."

I move her hand and reach for her drink, taking an overindulgent sip before we both just stand there and smile at each other. My hand presses to my chest as butterflies gather in my stomach.

"I'm so nervous."

She raises her brows. "You want him too, right?"

I nod, making her face go back to normal. "Yes. I do want that . . . maybe more than anything I've ever wanted in my whole life. I'm so freaking in love that it's disgusting."

"Agreed." She shimmies, then clasps her hands together. "Oh my god, now that you've committed to moving across the country to be with him, you'll be doing that as his fiancée."

*Fiancée.* Holy smokes.

I grab her hands, trying to anchor us back down to reality before we float away like the one escapee balloon at a party.

"Okay, we need to reel it back . . . We don't even know if that's what's happening. And if it doesn't, I don't want either of us crying on the way home. So, we'll just play it by ear."

She chuckles and looks down at me holding her hands, and I realize I'm holding the dummy from *The Shining*.

I drop it and laugh before she un-Velcros the creepy thing from her side and props it up against the bar.

"Remind me to take that with me, or I have a feeling Chef-Boy-R-Pervert will steal it." But then she gasps, pulling me right back into the clouds. "Wait a minute . . . That could be why he told me to take you to get manicures yesterday. So that your ring finger would look iconic."

Normally that's not something I would attribute to man-think, but Noah is the cream of the crop. Of course he'd think of that.

My lips part as I stare back at her. "Oh, the way in which I would bribe the universe for this to be tonight's destiny. I mean, I would do unethical and wrong things for this to be true."

My sister laughs that maniacal, partner in crime kind of laugh that we did as kids before getting grounded. Because of that, I glance back over my shoulder again to make sure nobody's onto us.

But as I do I feel a vibration by my ribs. My face drops to the front of Noah's coat before I realize what it is. I smile at my sister as I reach inside.

"He forgot his phone," I say in explanation of what I'm doing.

"Let me answer it," she rushes out as I pull the phone from the pocket, the sound growing louder. "What if it's a jeweler?"

She reaches for it, but I draw it back.

"And why would it be a jeweler? If he's proposing, he's already got the ring. Please stick to your current occupation because Scooby gang is not in the cards."

The call stops but starts again, making me frown as I look at the screen and see an unknown caller.

"Jesus, they're persistent. It's probably a spam call."

My sister looks up thoughtfully. "Didn't he say he was waiting on Nike?"

My mouth forms a small o as I nod, remembering how he talked about expecting a call over drinks when we were with her the other night.

"What's it, like, six p.m. on the West Coast?" I rush out, staring down at the phone. I lift my face to where Noah left from, then look at my sister. "Should I answer it?"

"Yes."

I hit "accept" and put the phone to my ear, just as the crowd starts chanting Chase's name, drawing my eyes.

"Hello, Noah's phone."

The cheers are too loud as he drops to the ground, doing the worm. Evie rolls her eyes as I try and plug my ear so I can hear. "Sorry, hold on. I can't hear you."

I point to an empty cocktail table farther from the bar before I start to walk away, but Evie begins to follow me, so I shake my head.

"Keep holding for two more seconds so I can get somewhere quieter."

Evie crosses her arms and mouths "Spoilsport" before I walk past the table and go just beyond the hanging lanterns in a bank of trees.

"Okay, I can hear you now," I say with a smile.

"Hi." It's a woman. "I'm calling for Noah Adler."

*Oh my god. Is this really about to happen for him?*

"He's away from the phone, but I can take a message." I chuckle at the end, but I'm not met with the same sentiment.

*Oh shit.*

"My name's Kate Green, from the Boston Police Department. I'm calling to notify Mr. Adler that case number 678023346 involving his motorcycle is slated for close. But we're still in need of some form of his identification, since he lost his wallet. If he could bring that by the station tomorrow, that'd be great."

"Oh. Sure. Sorry . . ." *I didn't know he lost his wallet.* My mind takes a minute to process the important part of what she said before I rush out, "Oh my god, did they find the person responsible?"

There's silence, then papers shuffling in the background before her monotone voice fills the speaker again.

"We were unable to locate the owner of the gray Altima that hit Mr. Beckett. The car was left at a junkyard, wiped clean of any prints, and the VIN was stolen." Papers shuffle again. "The only other possible lead we had was a set of prints on the motorcycle, and according to Mr. Beckett, after he was hit, the car sped off. That was also proven by some street-cam footage we obtained."

I shiver and pull Noah's jacket tighter, a thought scaring me. "Are you sure someone didn't try and steal the bike and then maybe decided to take it by force later? I mean . . . he wasn't on the bike when he was hit. Why would someone do that?"

"Damned if I know. But it's unlikely it was premeditated. Crimes like these are opportunity based—that kind of planning only happens on television shows and in books."

My eyes narrow, unhappy with her brush-off, so I press. "You said there were other prints . . . If this is a crime of opportunity, wouldn't we be most likely to know the perpetrator? What was the person's name?"

One of Chase's staff, dressed as a baseball player in a Mets hat, gives me a nod while crumbing the cocktail table I walked past earlier. I'm watching him but not really focused on anything as she answers.

"Davis Keller."

I exhale then wince because a feeling of déjà vu hits, but nothing really comes to mind.

"I don't know," I whisper as I stare out, trying to think back to a time when I'd heard that name. Someone then yells "Hey, hey!" in the background of the phone, and my gaze sweeps back over the blue cursive of the busser's hat.

An unsettling feeling continues to grow, almost as if there's something on the tip of my tongue that I can't quite figure out.

"Sorry," Kate says. "We just brought in some drunks. I'd be surprised if you knew the guy. There's been no hit since juvie."

*Davis Keller, Davis . . . Keller.* Davis.

"Even if the juvie had anything to do with it," she continues, "he's probably long gone by now. They always pull a disappearing act. Off the grid is easy when you come from some nowhere little fishing town . . ."

I have to press the phone to my ear harder to hear because everyone at the party starts cheering as my chest starts to rise and fall faster. But I don't notice it as I repeat what she said, hearing Noah's voice in the back of my mind as I do.

*"I'm from a nowhereville little fishing town between here and Maine."*

I blink as the tiny hairs on the back of my neck prick and goose bumps bloom over my arms. It all draws my attention as a slow buildup of everything imprisoned behind the wall inside my mind suddenly starts to fall, brick by brick. All the unknown intakes of information that have been happening start colluding to wake me up—the Mets hat, the drunk in the background, the phrasing, and the name . . .

They join forces, and three things happen: Noah jogs toward me, holding a box in the air. Our eyes connect.

And a memory hits.

*I smile as I tip my eyes up at Noah's profile, only really thinking about how his friend dropped the word "girlfriend" in front of him, and he didn't even flinch.*

*"Hey, man . . . hey—I know you. How've you been?"*

*I look over my shoulder to see that some guy in a Mets hat is smiling at Noah.*

*Noah's brows draw together in seeming confusion before he has an easy smile. "Sorry, man, we've never met. You've got the wrong guy."*

*The man shakes his head, slightly slurring when he speaks but insistent.*

*"No, it's me, Peter . . . Ronnie's cousin. You're, umm . . ." He snaps his fingers. "Davis, right?"*

"Hey . . ." Noah's out of breath as he stops in front of me, yanking me from my thoughts. "I'm back . . . with your present."

I stare at him, blinking a few times quickly as my lips part, my breath stuttering, but no words come out. I'm so confused by what I just remembered that I don't even register his phone at my side, or that the call's been disconnected.

He's beaming at me, his eyebrows wagging. "Did you miss me?"

*This doesn't make any sense . . . how can he be . . . no . . .*

I feel numb as I nod, trying to smile. Except I can't process everything fast enough. Too many thoughts are happening and bouncing off each other. And they don't make any sense.

I'm not just questioning myself; I'm fighting.

Noah isn't Davis . . . That has to be a coincidence. That's the only reasonable explanation. I know him like I know myself.

He smiles as he dips down to kiss me, but I just let him because the pit in my stomach keeps growing. *Why can't I shake this off?* That guy never even said his last name. There are a thousand people named Davis just in Boston, I'm sure of it.

*But then why are those the prints that were found on the bike.*

Goddammit. Why won't my gut stop gnawing at me like the way I am at the inside of my cheek.

*Just ask him. There's a reasonable explanation.*

"Noah," I whisper, closing my eyes for a beat because it feels weird to ask. "You got a call . . . it was from . . . umm. For your . . ." *ID. She said he lost his wallet.*

I hold out his phone, something in my mind making me not finish the rest of my sentence. He grins and takes it. He's bubbling with excitement over the gift, which he lifts for me to see again.

My smile is weak as my other hand softly touches the bottom of his jacket pocket, cupping my hand around it, like a dare to prove myself wrong. But the fabric doesn't wrinkle under my touch because it's heavy, like it's filled with something bulky.

"Do you want your wallet too?" I say softly, motioning with my head down to his jacket.

"No. Leave it there." He grins.

*He lied.*

Noah puts his hand back out for me to take, his face lit with exuberant happiness. "Tell me about the call later. I want you to open your gift first. I can't wait."

He looks over his shoulder motioning to Chase as I blink slowly. My chest feels shaky, and I can hear my own breath. *He lied.*

I don't understand . . . I don't. Why would he lie? This doesn't make sense. I want to say more, ask more, but my fingers slide into his palm anyway because this is ludicrous. He's Noah . . .

Maybe he found his wallet; maybe he just didn't want the hassle. Why am I questioning him?

*You know him, Goldie, better than anyone.*

But the moment we touch, everything slows and we're in that familiar bubble of him and me, and that's when the truth barrages me.

*I laugh as I'm spun around into the shadows of a convenient alley, my back gently pressed to the wall as he lifts a hand against it, trapping me between him and the brick.*

*The way he's looking down at me makes butterflies explode.*

*"Boyfriend, huh? You sure? . . . Because I am."*

*"Me too."*

*"Then I guess I should come clean. I'm an upstanding citizen originally from Hempstead—"*

The memories are vivid, making each step I take feel heavier than the first because they're hitting like waves. But that's the thing about hindsight—it's twenty-twenty, and that's pretty fucking clear.

*"One more question. Where's your boyfriend from?"*

*"Hempstead," I snap. "It's in New Hampshire, in case you're unfamiliar."*

*"It was the weirdest thing. We couldn't find a Noah Adler from Hempstead."*

The lights grow brighter as we rejoin the party, and he walks me past the tables in the middle of the grass, but my mind is fragmented. I'm confused and scared.

I don't understand what my mind is telling me, but it feels like the moment before a car crash—you can see the destruction coming, but you're powerless to stop it.

He looks at me, those sapphire eyes connecting to mine. The ones that belong to the man I love. But who is that man . . . Is he Noah?

Like a cruel answer, the full memory from before takes hold like a hand around my throat.

*"Hey, man . . . hey—I know you. How've you been?"*

*I look over my shoulder to see that some guy in a Mets hat is smiling at Noah.*

*Noah's brows draw together in seeming confusion before he has an easy smile. "Sorry, man, we've never met. You've got the wrong guy."*

*The man shakes his head, slightly slurring when he speaks but insistent.*

*"No, it's me, Peter . . . Ronnie's cousin. You're, umm . . ." He snaps his fingers. "Davis, right?"*

*I press my face against Noah's shoulder, smiling because this guy is so drunk.*

*"He's a Noah, not a Davis," I say with humor.*

*The dude frowns, his eyes locked with Noah's as he works out whatever thought he's having. But I feel Noah tense under my cheek as his eyes go to the hand still on his shoulder before the guy takes it away.*

*"Wow. I could've sworn . . . my apologies." He gives us a salute before adding, "You look so much like a friend of my cousin's. I used to visit him every summer in Darkwater Bay . . ."*

*Darkwater* . . . I've heard that name somewhere. Where . . . where the fuck have I heard that? My eyes drop to the gift being held out in front of me, feeling my pulse throb as I go numb.

My thoughts are racing. So much so that I'm barely aware of the fact that Noah's said "Open it" while motioning to the gift. I tug the ribbon, feeling a lump grow in my throat.

The bow opens before the fabric floats to the sides of the box, and I reach inside and pull out my gift, feeling sick.

How can he be someone he's not . . . He's Noah.

My Noah—the man who bought out all the flowers in my shop to tell me he loves me. The one who listens when I speak and holds me when I need a soft spot to land. No. This doesn't make sense. I'm wrong. My memories are wrong.

I hear myself exhale as I lift my gift out of the box. Noah's voice calls my eyes.

"The first night we met, you told me you wanted custom shoes for your birthday, but when I asked you when it was, you said I'd have to 'stick around to find out.' Well, I stuck around and made the shoes I designed in my head that night, because I only had to lay my eyes on you once to see you for exactly who you are . . ."

He is the one person who sees me exactly for who I am. *But have you ever seen him?* my mind asks before the last memory cuts directly through my heart.

Dark Days in Darkwater

A dark cloud hangs over this small community as five

> teens are found dead in what officials believe started as a lovers' quarrel and ended in a massacre.

I gasp as if I've been shocked by lightning. Oh my god. *No . . . no. Just ask him. Make him explain.*

"Noah—" I start, but then reality grabs me by the throat. *Who are you. What have you done? I can't trust you. You've lied about everything . . . How can I trust anything you say?*

"Killer, don't cry," he rushes out, cutting me off. "Just let me get this out because I can't hold it in anymore."

Tears cloud my eyes, and my pulse races. I'm blinking fat droplets of sorrow down my face as I only faintly notice the party encircling us. My chest feels so tight I can barely breathe because this can't be real. This can't be happening.

*Did he do something? Did he hurt people? No, no, no, no.* I can't even hold space for that thought or I'll crumble to the ground. Not Noah . . . He's gentle and kind and loving and my everything.

*He lied about who he is.*

He unties something from some shoes . . . the shoes that are in my hands. I don't even know when I took them out because I can't focus on anything, only the war inside my head.

My face whips to the side to my mom, who's smiling and crying, but I'm screaming on the inside.

Why is this happening? *Someone make it stop. Make it go away.* He has to be him. He couldn't have lied to me all this time. I can't believe that. But I know it's true.

Sobs wrack my body, and I can't move. I'm frozen in place, even if it feels like the ground doesn't exist underneath me because I have no anchor, no home . . . no Noah.

He takes a step back as he lowers himself down to one knee, and I almost buckle.

"Noah," I cry, but he takes my hand and kisses the top.

My chest burns with agony and truth—Noah isn't Noah. And that means my entire world has imploded.

My hands shoot to cover my mouth to try and stop the pain from spilling out. I want to beg, to hit him and demand it all to be untrue. But deep down I know it is. With every ounce of my being, I know he's a stranger.

But I beg anyway. To any god who will listen. My eyes close.

*Please . . . please. I love him . . . Don't take him from me.*

But like vignettes in a movie, moments flash in my mind to prove our love has been a lie, to wake me the fuck up and see. And I do.

I see all the times I asked him a question, but instead of getting answers I was kissed.

*I thought he was romantic.*

I see the moments we unpacked, and I realize now that he didn't have any pictures of his family or childhood.

*I assumed the memories were too hard.*

I see the way he's always kept secret the meaning of his tattoos, and the way he bristled at the cameras when we went to the fair that one time. And how he lost it on the guy he thought was following me. I see all the locks and how I never even knew his mother's name until I pressed.

I see the way he put a mask in place with the police and lied to me with such ease, as if it was second nature.

I don't know where he went to high school, or how he got that small scar on his back, or anything. I don't know him. I've never known him.

And just like that, the war inside stops being a war, leaving only pieces of me in its wake. It's stolen everything I've ever held true—ripping Noah from me and leaving me desecrated.

"Baby," he says, forcing my eyes open.

I stare down at him as he holds up a ring.

It's everything I've ever wanted. *He's* everything I've ever wanted.

But he's no one I've ever met . . . or loved. I feel myself going numb, maybe into shock as my pulse lowers and my shuttered breaths grow quiet. I hang on to the last moments of his voice because it's all I'll have left of him.

"Killer, I think I've loved you my whole life. First it was the hope of you, but then I found the real you, and that version was even better. I can't picture another day of my life without you. You see me for the man I am and push me to be the best version of myself."

The tears start again, blurring his face. And despite knowing the truth down to my bones, I still want to deny it because I love Noah more than anyone I've ever loved in my whole life. He's the only man I've ever wanted.

"You've given me purpose, Goldie. And I want to spend the rest of my life repaying that gift. If you let me, I'll spend Saturday afternoons trying to beat you at checkers and rainy days being your human coloring book. I'll never watch past the last episode of any show we binge. And I'll make it a point to kiss you silly every day of our lives. I want to grow old with you and laugh about how I met you shoplifting blood."

My shaky hands come to his face, cradling it as I fall to my knees in front of him, almost face-to-face as he asks me the one question I've wanted to hear since the moment I fell in love with him.

"Goldie Monroe, will you marry me?"

My chin's quivering so hard that I can't make out my words past a whisper, so with shaky hands I pull him close, my lips at his ear.

"Only if you tell me whether I'm marrying Noah Adler or Davis Keller . . ."

Noah sucks in a harsh breath, his hands clamping down over my wrist tightly, and I can feel him start to shake. My stomach caves as I pull away.

Because he doesn't have to say a thing. He just finally told the truth. I'm trying to tug my hands away, but he won't let me go.

The crowd around us cheers because we look like two people in love, so ecstatic about our future we can't let go of each other. But really, we're glued to each other because maybe he knows like I do how big a scar this will make once we rip apart.

"Please . . . I can't lose you," he begs quietly.

All I hear is the tremble in Noah's voice, along with my heart shattering.

I draw my face back and look him dead in the eyes, keeping my words between us. I want them to hurt him, because I will never recover.

"I will never forgive you. And I will forever hate, Noah."

The absolute fear on his face burns into my mind, wrecking me. My bottom falls back to my feet, but he won't let me go. We're staring at each other, the truth finally between us, as I open my mouth with a silent scream, my face morphing with the devastation I feel.

"You broke my heart."

I'm shaking my head as he holds on to me, repeating "Please" over and over. But I want to get away from him. Away from everything.

I wish I were dead. I think it would hurt less.

Murmurs begin around us as I have to force my hands from Noah. He finally lets me go, and I scramble back over the ground, digging my heels into the dirt.

My eyes frantically search the crowd for my sister.

"Get me out of here," I yell to her before her hands are on me. "Get me out of here!"

Noah doesn't make a move, his palm hitting the ground as if he's been knocked sideways. But I don't stick around to see if he's okay. I fucking run. I run as fast as I can with my family on my heels straight to my sister's car and all but rip the door open before slamming it behind me.

"Goldie, what happened?" rings out around me, but I can't answer because losing Noah is a death. I'm empty.

Even if I never really had him.

# Chapter Twenty-One

***Camp Weonoke—years prior***

Sonny had never seen Davis so mad, but then again, she'd never seen him in a lot of different ways.

"Who would do this?" He paced back and forth in front of the tree he'd carved for them.

The names had been slashed out. She told herself to keep her eyes on Davis, but she couldn't help but look around and wonder if Billy was watching.

He was always watching now.

She'd met him in secret for two weeks now, in between teaching kids to swim and mediating arguments between the girls in her cabin.

What she knew for certain was that Billy liked when she moaned almost as much as when she cried because he'd grown crueler since the storage room. Even taken to whispering "Slut" once when she passed him on the way to the lake.

She'd been naive to think he wouldn't hurt her, because the longer she refused to break up with Davis, the meaner Billy became.

"Are you listening to me, Sonny?" Davis said.

She nodded, but she wasn't. Her mind was on the boy it shouldn't have been on. This time, not out of curiosity but worry.

The truth of it all was that Billy represented the rebel inside her desperate to break out. *Mom and Dad would hate him,* she thought. *They'd be so embarrassed.*

And when she met him, that idea made her happy. She was sure all kids thought their parents were awful, but hers were truly the worst.

She'd never be that way. Not that she could have children. She'd read that having mumps makes you infertile, and she'd gotten sick when she was twelve.

"I'm going to carve it for us again. I swear," Davis said, taking her hand.

She looked into his eyes, wondering why he was going to such lengths, especially since it was almost time for the campers to leave. The summer was almost over, and that meant they were too.

She decided on a whim to say just that to him, but she never anticipated his response.

Davis cradled her face, looking deeply into her eyes.

"I love you. This is real for me. We're forever, Sonny. Don't you feel that way too?"

She didn't know. She hadn't let herself consider the possibility, but she liked hearing it from him even more than she'd thought she would.

"People say you do this every summer. How am I any different?"

"That's true. But you are, and you made me different. I know you sneak around and see someone else. And that's who probably scratched out our names, but I want you to be all mine. Because I really do love you, and I'll prove it if you let me."

She knew she could believe him because she'd already let him go all the way two days ago. And again last night, when she snuck out to the boathouse.

"Okay," she said as déjà vu hit hard. "I'm yours."

~~Sonny + Davis, Sonny + Davis, Sonny + Davis, Sonny + Davis, Sonny + Davis, Sonny + Davis, Sonny +~~

~~Davis, Sonny + Davis, Sonny + Davis, Sonny + Davis, Sonny + Davis, Sonny + Davis, Sonny + Davis, Sonny + Davis, Sonny + Davis, Sonny + Davis, Sonny + Davis, Sonny + Davis, Sonny + Davis, Sonny + Davis~~
YOU ARE MINE.

I own everything inside of you. Including your beating heart.

—Billy

# Chapter Twenty-Two

## Noah

"Noah, come on. You gotta get off the ground."

I recognize Chase's voice, but I barely hear it because I'm fucking numb. But then if that's true, why does everything still hurt?

My head hangs, eyes on the dirt.

*I hate me too, Goldie.*

"Noah," Chase presses, urging my shoulder back, but I dig my fingers deeper into the cold hard ground, feeling the hurt underneath my nails as they jam into the earth.

I want to hurt, to feel all the pain I've caused. I've ruined us. I've broken her heart with my lies and selfish cowardice.

And now she sees me for who I truly am.

So, I'm not going to move. I won't. I'll stay here until I stop hearing her call me by my name or seeing her look at me like a god-damn stranger.

"Dude," Chase calls to me again, but I shake my head.

"No," I bark, not making any sense to anyone but myself. "I never lied about how much I loved her . . . I never . . ." My voice falls off, the rest said only in my head: *I wanted this life. For her and Noah.*

I hate myself. I wish I could kill Davis. Make it so his fucked-up life never existed.

"Fuck you," I say between gritted teeth as my fist hits the ground. Then again until it grows faster and in force, pounding the ground so hard that I feel my skin pop before blood starts to spill over the grass beneath me.

"I hate you," I roar, spittle falling from my mouth. "I fucking hate you."

I hit the goddamn ground until I can't lift my arm anymore, but that doesn't stop me. I throw my other arm down, trying to demolish the spot where she told me she'd never forgive me. That she hated me.

A place like that can't exist. It just can't.

I hurl my arms down, but Chase grabs my wrists, stopping me. "Dude, stop. Noah . . . fuck. You're bleeding."

My head falls between my arms as he holds them together. I look like I'm praying. I wish there was a god to help me. I'd give anything for her forgiveness.

"I lost her," I whisper. "She's gone . . . I fucking lost her."

"Shit." I feel Chase's hands cup my armpits before he tries to drag me up to standing, but I push him off.

"Just fucking leave me. Get outta here," I groan. "Without her I'm dead anyway, so who fucking cares how it happens."

But Chase keeps fighting with me. He pulls me up until I'm on my feet and standing in front of him.

I can't even look at him. Everything fucking hurts too much. My chest jerks with the emotions I've kept at bay for so long. The self-hatred, the desperation, all of it. Everything bubbles to the surface, making my shoulders shake as I cry.

He grips my face to make me look at him, and his eyes connect with my red-rimmed ones. My hand lifts as I speak through the sadness.

"I love her. I fucking love her so much."

He nods and pats my face.

"I know . . . but she's gone. Noah, everyone's gone. And it's just me and you." My head drops as I almost buckle to the ground, but he forces it up again. "I care about keeping you around, motherfucker. So you gotta put one foot in front of the other and help me do that, because I'm not leaving my best friend out here alone. If you stay, I stay. And then we both get hypothermia."

I give no reaction to the words he's saying other than closing my eyes and nodding. Because I can't. She took my heart, ripped it out of my chest, and ran away with it. I've got nothing left.

There is no recovery from the loss of her. My Goldie.

"Put your arm over my shoulder," he breathes out. "Help me get you home. Let's start there."

He drags my arm over him, urging me to walk, so I do, but I'm on autopilot, reliving my last moment with her on a loop.

*"Only if you tell me whether I'm marrying Noah Adler or Davis Keller . . ."*

*"Please . . . I can't lose you."*

*"I will never forgive you. And I will forever hate, Noah."*

The cold slices over my face as we walk, and my eyes stay trained to the cobblestone street. I don't know how far we've gone when Chase breaks the silence.

"What the fuck happened, Noah?"

I'm watching my feet, concentrating on putting one in front of the other like he asked, hyperaware of the ache in the center of my chest as I answer.

"I happened."

I drag my arm away from him as we near the house . . . my house now. But I can't seem to get my foot up the first step. I stare down at the stoop, holding the rail, dreading having to walk inside. She'll never be inside to smile at me ever again.

"Dude, you can't stop here." He pushes me gently. "We need to get you inside—you're fucking freezing."

I drag my foot up the stair, slowly, only lifting my head to look at the door when I land on the last step.

It takes me a minute, but my heart jump-starts, beating a mile a minute, as I pull from Chase's hold and blurt out, "Is she here?" because the door's cracked open.

I slap it with the palm of my hand, letting it bounce off the doorstop as I tear inside, calling for her.

"Killer!"

My voice echoes around the emptiness, but I still scan every room, looking only for her face. Nothing around me registers as I run toward our room, desperate to see her. Praying she's had a change of heart, that I'll be able to explain and tell her the whole fucking truth.

*Just one more chance to do this shit right. Please.*

The moment I make it through our bedroom door, I grind to a stop, and cold washes over me as my mouth goes dry. The room is in disarray, shit everywhere.

But she's not here.

I feel like the wind's been knocked out of me.

"Dude, your place is destroyed," Chase bellows from the other room. "They didn't even steal anything."

I reach for the wall and use it to help me back up three steps before I turn and walk into the living room. My eyes land on all I missed—glass has been shattered into infinitesimal shards all over the kitchen floor, and the chairs have been crushed. It's as if someone beat them onto the counter over and over in a full rage, leaving splintered wood scattered across the floor.

Books have been ripped apart, pictures thrown from the walls; even the television is cracked.

There's nothing left untouched. It's all been demolished.

"This wasn't her, right?" he says cautiously. My eyes land on thick slash marks across the couch, the stuffing billowed out. "What did she use, a machete?"

I circle the room, taking it all in as he keeps talking, and all my panic and fear begin to morph into rage. I can't speak, but I can feel myself trembling as my eyes land on the front door.

"No . . ." he draws out, then under his breath adds, "this isn't G . . . maybe her sister, though."

I shake my head, my eyes fixed on the object behind him—the one stabbed into the front door. I'm breathing fast enough to have a goddamn heart attack because the fear I've spent the last thirty-two years of my life either hiding or running from closes in like a vise around my throat.

The newspaper articles, along with the four yellowed letters I discarded months ago, are pierced, stabbed into the dark oak door with the tip of a butcher knife.

"How the fuck?" I breathe out. "That's impossible—"

But it's not. Everything I walked away from that day in my office has been resurrected. Crucified on my door.

My entire focus is devoured into a cylinder of sight.

"Why would someone do that?" Chase breathes, but I already know the answer—to expose me in the way someone can do only if they also know the truth.

"He's back," I say, making Chase frown in confusion.

"What are you talking about? Who's back?"

Chase follows me toward the now-closed front door, but I walk slowly before I stop, feeling my chest rising faster and faster. I yank the letters down one by one, moving quicker and quicker as I do, discarding them all onto the floor as Chase picks them up.

My whole life, I've run from this moment. Scared to be found. Hungry to be free. I just wanted to be Noah . . . But he has to die now, because Davis has been found.

Until I tug on the last letter, and my chest feels like it caves in.

Because staring back at me is an old photo of my mother. She's smiling as she stands with her arms spread in front of a sign that reads **Camp Weonoke, 1994** in red digital print at the bottom.

But it's what's scratched in thick angry slashes that's made my pulse slow to the calmest of rage and ready for Noah to die because Davis has been found—"MINE."

"Chase," I breathe out, finally finding my voice as I look over my shoulder at him. "There's something I have to tell you."

He lowers the article he's reading before he holds up one of the letters.

"What do these have to do with you?"

I swallow hard as I understand there's no more room for lies.

"Thirty-two years ago, my mother was attacked at a camp along with the other counselors—she survived by stabbing the guy in the chest. His body was never found . . ."

Chase looks down at one of the headlines, all the dots seeming to connect in his head before he blinks up at me, ashen and shocked.

"It was this Billy guy?"

Our eyes lock as I finally tell the goddamned truth.

"Billy's my father. And he's back to finish the job."

# Chapter Twenty-Three

## Goldie

"Golds, do you want to wake up? Mom made some food."

I open my eyes as Evie sits next to where I'm lying on the couch, making the cushion depress. But I close them again just as fast because they're immediately flooded with tears. My heart is so broken that being awake hurts.

I shake my head, unable to speak.

"Oh, babe," my sister hushes. She lays herself over me and wraps me in her arms as I cover my face to try and stop the crying.

They say time heals all wounds, but what happens if the cuts are so deep that there could never be enough days or weeks to make it go away?

Noah Adler—or Davis Keller—has shattered me, and I'm not sure I'll ever recover.

"It hurts so much," I eke out as she snuggles in closer, shifting her body to lie with me.

"I know," she says gently as she just holds me, as if I'm the most fragile object she's ever touched.

But I suppose I am. This isn't just heartache. This is grief. Sorrow over a life I once dreamed of lost.

I don't know how long I cry, but eventually I fall back to sleep, dreaming of the only thing I desperately want to forget—Noah, on one knee, asking me to marry him.

I'm awake. I don't know if it's day or night, but I hear hushed voices. This time I don't risk opening my eyes, because I already know what happens when I do.

"You should call the adoption people, those detectives, and see if they can look into him," my mom whispers.

"I don't know if that's what they do," my dad responds.

"Stephen, this is your daughter," she rushes out a little louder. "You saw the apartment."

"That's not what I'm saying, Camilla. I am just as mad as you are. He's clearly fucked up and someone none of us truly knew. Jesus, I gave him my damn blessing and he—"

Evie shushes them, and my heart begins to pick up pace. *What happened at the apartment?*

My chest begins to tremble because as ridiculous as it sounds, I don't think I want to know any more information. I'm not sure I could handle it.

Still, somewhere back in the recesses of my mind, that headline pulses like a neon light. But if the universe allows me any kindness, it'll be to leave me in the goddamn dark and let me believe I loved someone who'd only lied about his name. And not force me to admit I missed every red flag and fell for someone who . . .

I can't even think it. I immediately push the thought away before it gets its claws in.

*Fuck that article—it's enough that I know we were a lie.*

"Why do we need to find out more information about him?" Evie whispers. "We know enough. He lied about who he is for a year . . . I don't care if he's running from the law or wanted in several countries."

"That's exactly why we *should* dig. We'll keep it between us," my mom insists. "She could be in danger."

My dad huffs. "Let's not get ahead of ourselves. He's probably just a grifter or a con man. I saw a documentary about this kind of stuff."

"Oh my god, Dad," Evie groans. "Regardless, I agree with Mom. Let's keep this between the three of us. We can all agree she's been through enough. And trust me, Mom, he's not getting near her. It'll be over my dead body. Or his."

"Evie," our mom admonishes.

"What? She's destroyed, and that's on him. So, RIP."

"Agreed," my father whispers too loudly again.

The thing I hate most about this conversation is the innate need I feel to defend Noah. *Not Noah, Davis.*

He lied, yet I still love him. I love him down to the depths of my bones, which makes me hate myself because I'm a traitor to my own self. That's actually the worst part about his deceit. I've been left with nobody to trust, not even my own self.

I roll over and pull the blanket over my face. I gradually hear the conversation die before sleep takes me again.

*"If you let me, I'll spend Saturday afternoons trying to beat you at checkers and rainy days being your human coloring book. I'll never watch past the last episode of any show we binge. And I'll make it a point to kiss you silly every day of our lives."*

It's two in the morning.

The only reason I know is because the first thing I did was check my phone when I woke up. I wish it hadn't been to see if Noah had texted me or called, but it was. And he didn't.

I sit up in bed, not remembering how I got here as I swallow hard because my throat's so dry. My face shifts right to see my sister sleeping beside me, then to my left, where I see a bottle of water on the nightstand.

With a quiet exhale I pick it up. As I turn the cap, the crack feels louder than it is because of the silence, so I stop and try to twist it slower as I look over at Evie.

"I'm not sleeping," she murmurs next to me.

"Sorry," I whisper back.

Her eyes open as the blanket rustles. "Hi."

"Hi," I say back, trying to smile but only managing a momentary uptick of my lips.

Her brows lift as she eyes my water. "How about something stronger?"

I take a swig to revitalize my throat before I nod. "Yes, please."

We both slip off the bed with her arm over my shoulders as we walk side by side, making our way through the bedroom and into the kitchen.

"Mom and Dad?" I ask. She leaves me to turn on the lights.

"Back at the hotel. You've been knocked out since we came back Monday."

I pull a stool out from under her island. "What do you mean Monday? Isn't that today . . . Or is it Tuesday now?" I almost start to look at my phone, but I left it back in the bedroom.

"Go-Go, we're two a.m. on a Wednesday." I stare back as the bottle of vodka clanks as she pulls it from her freezer.

"Fuck," I breathe out as I realize the self-induced coma I put myself in.

She nods. "Yeah. I told them I'd take the night shifts because I figured when you came back to life, it might get a little messy."

She pulls two short glasses out of her cabinet and pours two large shots. I reach out, slide my drink across the granite, and wrap both my hands around it. Exactly what I'm thinking tumbles out of my mouth because there's no point in hiding anything from my sister. She's the one person who can see me for exactly who I am.

"How did I get here?"

She picks up her glass and takes a sip before saying, "Not because of anything you did."

I'm staring at the dark swirls in the counter, feeling the ache in my chest that may never leave.

"Do you think he ever really loved me?"

"Yes," she says without hesitation.

I look up at her instantly, staring into her eyes to see if she's lying. She isn't.

"I do," she presses. "I also think he lied because he felt he had to . . . But that doesn't change the fact that he lied. And that makes him dangerous, Golds."

I already know where she's going with this, so I stop the hard sell.

"I heard the conversation earlier . . . between all of you. What happened at the apartment?"

She sips her drink again, looking away from me for a split second as if she doesn't want to tell me.

"Evie . . ."

She lets out a harsh breath. "It was destroyed, like completely demolished. He broke all the furniture, ruined all your books. Just fucking wrecked it and left."

I inhale a shaky breath before I bring the drink to my lips, instantly feeling the burn bleed over my chest.

"I'm sorry . . . Are you okay?" she pivots.

I nod and take another drink, clearing my throat. "So that's why Mom and Dad were so adamant about looking into him . . . Because he lost it."

"Yeah," she breathes out. "And I think it's a good idea . . . I mean, what do we really know about him? All we're operating on is your revelation from the police, and the apartment . . . I don't know, I think Mom's right, he could be—"

I lift a hand to stop her. "Stop. Please. I can't . . ."

My eyes start to well, which effectively quiets her. I should tell her about the article, but I can't. I just can't handle all the questions and the conversations right now.

"I don't want to know any more about him, Eves." My voice breaks. "It's already too much . . . I just . . . not right now."

Her hand covers mine as our eyes connect. "It's okay, Golds . . . I got you. It's on a need to know. I swear."

I nod before taking a longer swig of my drink. I wish time would pause so I could get my feet under me because I don't know how I'm supposed to keep standing against all the waves trying to pull me under.

"Listen," she says, tapping the counter with her nail twice before her lips part. "Mom's gonna try and convince you to come home with them tomorrow. She told me not to tell you."

My head draws back as I scowl. "No. Absolutely not. I do not want to go and be treated like some broken child who needs more soup. I'm a grown woman . . ." I stand, making the chair scrape the floor, before I down the rest of the Grey Goose. "Dude, no. Why can't I stay here with you?"

Her brows raise as her smile gets tight. "So, there's a tiny problem with that . . . I have that work thing. I leave today—"

"Oh god." My eyes spring open wider. "The scary sleepaway camp thing, right?"

"Yeah." She nods, and my stomach turns.

No. I love my mother, but I can't go through all of this in my old bedroom with posters of the Backstreet Boys on the wall. I can't do it.

"Wait . . ." I blurt out. "Who cares? I'll just stay and watch your place. What am I thinking? I can rot and cry alone while you're gone."

She shakes her head. "Dad made me promise not to leave you alone . . ."

"Lie. You do it all the time."

She downs her drink before she looks at me. "Goldie, Noah's—"

"Davis," I say, cutting her off with caustic exaction.

She frowns, keeping her voice steady and gentle. "He knows where I live. I'm not leaving you alone here, vulnerable."

I swallow hard because I get it. What she's saying is true. I don't know what he's capable of. I didn't ask, I ran. And now I'm left with every possibility. Then again, I'd be left with those anyway because everyone knows once a liar, always a liar.

"You have to choose, Golds. It's either a blast to the past back at the parentals' place or come with me to your worst nightmare."

I groan as I sit back down, then drop my head down against my arms on the counter.

"I hate my life."

Evie pets my head. "Look at it this way, there's nothing really scarier than your real life, so my shit should be a walk in the park."

"Okay," I mumble, looking up before sliding my glass toward her so she can pour me another. "You realize I was going to be engaged by now, and instead I'm plotting how not to shit my pants for the next week."

"Well." She smirks, but it's kind. "Then it's already working, because you're not thinking about him."

God, I wish that were true.

# Chapter Twenty-Four

## Goldie

"Remind me why this was a good idea?" I say, staring out the window from the passenger seat.

We've been driving for about an hour, and I've watched burnt orange and red leaves streak by, with the occasional burst of yellow peeking out among the tableau.

Evie's eyes stay on the windy road as she drives, the sound of her tires whipping over the wet asphalt. I slowly shift my head to look at my sister, immediately hating the solemness in her expression.

"Never mind, don't remind me. There's no joke that can make it funny."

A smile begins to bloom on her face before she glances at me. "You know what will be funny? Watching you look for a guy in a hockey mask tonight at our welcome bonfire."

My face scrunches up as droplets of rain begin to softly hit the window.

"Eww . . . who's the guy putting this on? It's so creepy. Maybe we should be more scared of him than my ex."

Evie's mouth pops open as the swishing of her windshield wipers starts up.

"Look at you, turning trauma lemons into funny lemonade. Your life is making you a full-fledged comedian." I roll my eyes and cross my arms, but she shrugs. "I say lean in. This can be a new era for you."

"Shut up," I chuckle. I can't help it. It took her a minute, but she found the funny.

Honestly, I'm glad she did. It's a nice reprieve from what I've been feeling. Still, I have no doubt I'll go right back to being numb again in no time. I reach out to adjust the heater because the car's gotten colder.

I change the subject. "Okay, so there's a bonfire . . . What else is happening?"

"Well, from what I've been told, because everything's really hush-hush . . . First, we're driving to a special location for pickup . . ."

"Pickup?" I interrupt, sitting up straighter. "Why is this starting to feel like an actual horror movie?"

She nods, but the smile on her face is disconcerting, to say the least.

"No . . . like, this guy, the one who hired us, really wants everything to feel immersive. He describes himself as an 'experience purist.'"

"What? What the hell is that . . ."

"I don't know. Rich people are weird. He wants everything to feel as real as possible, so that means we need to feel it too. Get this, we're taking a school bus up to the camp, just like the first part of the team did who left Monday."

I blink a hundred miles an hour as she continues. Somewhere between finding out we're turning in our phones for privacy and that we're sleeping in cabins, I break.

"Oh my god. Why didn't you tell me any of this before? Please say 'Psych!' right now."

She winces as she holds the wheel tighter. "I didn't really think about it. I found out months ago, and I mean, there were other pressing matters . . ."

I let out a breath. *Fuck.* My brows raise as another empty chuckle pops out. "Well, I guess you're right about one thing . . . I am, in fact, not thinking about my real life. So I suppose a win's a win."

She laughs quietly. "See, funnier by the minute."

I turn my face back to the window, my own reflection staring back at me for a second. "Yeah, maybe after this weekend, I'll be able to take my one-woman show on the road."

The soft sounds of music begin to play as raindrops dance along the window in slashes, gathering and rolling over each other. And because I can't stop myself, I reach into my pocket, pull out my phone, and look at the messages. There's nothing.

I've checked his name more times than I can count since Monday.

A part of me keeps telling myself to be grateful he's disappeared because I shouldn't have any contact with someone who might be dangerous and is definitely a liar.

But another part of me—a voice that's just a little bit louder—wants to see Noah. Because I hate that I didn't let him explain. I'll never really know why he lied, or how deep it all runs. Then again, that's really the sickest part—the desire for an explanation isn't really me wanting closure. It's my heart wishing I could forgive him and run right back into his arms.

God, it would only take the flimsiest of excuses, and that makes me hate myself.

I close my eyes, trying to block out my thoughts and listen to the music. But between the setting sun and the driving rain, my body grows heavy, and my eyes refuse to open as I fall asleep.

"Goldie . . ." my sister whispers, and I feel the car slowing.

She rubs my arm, and I take a deep breath, denying my eyes the instinct to flutter open. Shit, I must've fallen asleep.

I yawn and say, "Are we there yet?" but I'm met with her gasping and the sound of brakes screeching as my body's thrown forward.

*Holy shit.*

Darkness and brake lights fill my vision as my hands smack the dash because I've instantly woken up to see logs—huge fucking tree logs—coming straight out of a truck in front of us and at our window.

I scream a bloodcurdling amount of fear as my eyes squeeze closed, and I brace for death with one hand on Evie, the other in front of me.

My heart's in my throat, my pulse is going faster than it's ever gone, and the veins in my neck are about to explode, but nothing happens.

No shattering glass, or impact. And definitely no logs.

My lungs are still trying to commit to the screaming, except it's died out into something reminiscent of a Chewbacca impersonation because I've run out of breath.

I open one eye and see the logs hanging in the air just in front of our window. My face whips to Evie's, then back to the window.

My mind races to catch up as all the outside sounds begin to filter in, now louder than the sound of my heart. But my mouth's still hanging open and my eyes are still bugging out as I stare at the logs being retracted into the bed of the truck . . . pulled by a chain . . . connected to some kind of motor.

*Oh my god.*

"Evie!" I shriek as soon as I refill my lungs.

She's laughing, her hands in a defensive position in front of her. Not for the logs but for me . . . Because she knows I'm about to kill her. I look around and see a bunch of her FX nerds watching and laughing, too, along with the dreaded bus she mentioned before.

We're in a damn parking lot. She faked it. The diabolical witch faked it.

My heart's pounding out of my chest as I turn back to her and smack her arms in a flurry. "I hate you. I thought we were dying!"

A slew of curses falls from my lips as my car door is opened and I recognize her boss, Scott.

"I'm sorry . . ." Evie laughs, pointing at him. "He made me. We needed a test dummy, and well . . ."

I smack her arms again before I lay back in my seat and press a hand to my chest, ensuring my heart's still thrumming. My hair falls in my face, but I don't care.

"My life flashed before my eyes, Scott." I narrow them as I watch a bunch of guys she works with jump onto the fake death logs to secure the lines. "You two are the worst people on earth . . ." I whip my head to hers. "That movie is awful. Awful. I remember when we were kids and you made me watch it, and it literally made me scared of everything."

She's laughing too hard for me to ever forgive her, but it also makes me smile. *Oh, I hate her.*

I point a shaky finger at her. "If you do that to me again, this weekend will be *your Final Destination*. You got me?"

She makes an X over her heart.

"Cross my heart and hope you die. I mean, to die . . ." She laughs. "You know what I mean. I promise, no more scares . . ."

I don't miss the "from me" she whispers while looking away. I look up at Scott's smiling face, raising my brows, but he shrugs. Not at all apologetic for what he's about to say.

"We're all really excited you're here, Goldie. You're the kind of market research that makes us geek out."

I lift a leg from the car and drop my foot down outside with a thud. "Well, Scott, I hope you got paid royally because I'm sending you my therapy bill."

He laughs, then gives the top of the car a tap before walking away and leaving me to truly regret this damn plan.

"Hey, Golds," my sister says as she opens her car door. "Just send it to me, I'll expense it."

Fuck my life. There's kicking a dog while it's down and then there's this—running it over.

"You know," I tease as I grab my bag from the car, "we could just call it even and you hand over your credit card. Because I'm sure all the way up here in the mountains, I could find a decent spa to grieve and wellness at."

She laughs, shaking her head. "I'm sure you could, but then I'd worry the whole time . . ."

I frown as I look at her before she closes the distance and puts her arm over my shoulder. "Look at it this way, we never got to go to summer camp as kids. Now's our chance."

With a groan, I follow beside her as we walk toward the big yellow bus. There's a man standing outside the doors built like a house wearing a Thrills-n-Kills T-shirt. He holds out a black case, almost the size of a carry-on. It has about a dozen phones inside.

"Aww, you shouldn't have," Evie says sarcastically, smiling up at the Thor replica. "Do I just pick the one that goes with my eyes?"

He laughs and his cheeks turn red. Jesus, leave it to my sister to turn someone three times her size into a puddle.

He clears his throat. "The host requires top secret level discretion. It was in your contract."

She sticks out her bottom lip as she pulls her phone from her pocket. But I shake my head. "I didn't sign . . ."

"Yes, you did," she blurts out, whipping her head to mine and glaring at me. "Everyone in the office did. Remember?"

It doesn't take a genius to pick up what she's putting down—I've been snuck into this weekend of hell. So I nod and roll my eyes. "Oh yeah, my mistake. Sorry."

He shrugs, putting my theory to bed, clearly not having picked up anything, including the clue.

"Just turn them off and put them in," he says, holding the case closer to us. "We'll meet you back here once you return . . . *if* you return."

He lifts his brows, trying to emphasize the last part, really nailing his attempt at terrible acting, which makes Evie look at me with that shit-eating grin she gets when her thoughts play out on her face.

But she does as she's told and puts her phone in.

I stand there for a long second, looking down at my screen. She steps in closer to me, speaking quietly so only I hear her.

"You'll never be strong enough to deal with what happened if you don't walk away. Give yourself a fighting chance, Golds."

My eyes well because she's right: I need to walk away from even the possibility of Noah. *But what if . . .*

Dammit.

Before I can think twice, I turn my phone off and watch the screen go black before I carefully place it in the case, not looking back as I take the bus's steps.

Evie rubs my back as we make our way down the tight aisle with our bags, one of my hands touching the leather seats as we go. She taps me once we're in the middle before pointing to the right side.

We sit and stuff our bags under the seats as I let out a steadying breath, trying to process.

Three days ago, I was getting engaged, then breaking up with the love of my life, before now finding myself on a bus heading to my worst fucking nightmare, because I may or may not be safe from a man I never really knew.

*I couldn't write this. It's wilder than fiction.*

I don't know what the expression on my face is, but my sister touches my shoulder.

"You're not going to suddenly jump out of the window and fight the Viking for your phone, are you?"

I shake my head. "No. His wingspan is unconquerable . . . But I might sleep for another three days, if you don't mind."

She chuckles before her name is called and the engine rumbles to a start. I tap her leg and motion with my head for her to go talk with her colleagues, but she stares at me for another beat.

"Go. Have fun with the other horror weirdos. Don't worry, I have my thoughts to keep me company."

"If they get to be too much . . ." she starts, but I knock her shoulder gently with mine.

"I'm okay. No jumping out of windows to spar with the god of thunder, promise."

She smiles, then stands and makes her way up a couple of rows, where she falls into conversation easily with her work buddies as I stare out a new window with all the same old thoughts.

It doesn't take long for it to all hit me hard.

I blink a few times, the tears already perched on my lashes, before I discreetly wipe them away and keep staring outside, even though I'm not really looking at anything. It's just my cover for ignoring the conversations flowing around me as I go over and over the same bullshit like an emotional sadist.

I'm not sure how long we've been driving, maybe twenty minutes, before my sister comes back and sits down.

"Hey," she says excitedly, my face meeting hers. "So, here's some interesting info I just got out of the driver. We're in New Hampshire."

My brows furrow. "I thought we were going up north?"

Maybe it's the mention of New Hampshire that's making the sinking sensation brew in my gut. Or maybe it's the tall heavy oaks in the forest that are so dense they're impossible to see through. Either way, I'm already shaking my head.

She grins. "Apparently, we're heading to some abandoned summer camp not too far over the border. How cool is that?"

As she says it, we turn onto a desolate dirt road fairly hidden by a bank of trees. If I weren't so scared, the fleeting thought that I'm supposed to be running away from Noah instead of closer to his memory might find root, but it can't because my heart's starting to beat too fast.

"No . . . not cool . . . Evie . . . Are you telling me that we are being delivered to the most popular scene out of every eighties horror movie, minus any cell phones . . . to a man who refers to himself as an 'experience purist'? And don't tell me there's a landline because I bet you don't even know how to use one."

She chuckles. It's the maniacal kind.

"Evie . . ." I press, feeling like I might actually be losing my mind. "We're going to be hunted or . . . or . . . This is like that movie you love. The one where all the people kill each other."

She shrugs, smiling. "That's like every movie I watch. Specificity is the key to communication, Golds."

My eyes fix to the window again, straining to see out because it almost seems darker out here, as if the stars can't even shine down. I look back at her.

"We're gonna die. And the headline will be, 'A bunch of dumbass bitches got on a bus.'"

Her lips press together actively trying to hide her smile as she stares back at me before she says, "Language." She's enjoying my panic. "Relax, Golds. There's a paper trail . . . tickets sold, and event employees everywhere. Masterminding killers don't do that."

I pull the sleeves of my hoodie down over my hands as I hear someone in the front of the bus do a drumroll on the leather seats. The bus bounces over the dirt road, and the sound gathers before everyone starts to celebrate, erupting in howls and clapping just as an arched sign comes into view.

Evie cranes her neck, trying to see, as I tilt my own. I cup my hands around my eyes so I can see out the window better before I miss it.

A giant branded wood sign with carved eagles on totem poles stands tall as we pass underneath. It reads **Camp Weonoke**, with the tagline **Adventure Awaits** below it.

I turn my face to Evie, who smiles back.

"'Adventure awaits,'" she says, wagging her brows.

But something about it makes me shiver. Damn, I think I'd like to sit this one out, but something tells me I won't get a choice.

As soon as we were ushered off the bus, we were led directly to the bonfire, but not before being handed our camp T-shirts.

"Counselor," I whisper to Evie as she mouths "Purist" back to me, making me roll my eyes.

I can't help but keep some part of my body semi-attached to hers as we walk through the darkness toward ten or so logs fashioned as benches and placed in a circle around a firepit that's already raging.

"Welcome, campers," a voice bellows, drawing everyone's attention.

There's a guy standing on top of one of the makeshift log benches, wearing a red sweat suit with the camp's name on the shirt. He even has a whistle around his neck.

*What the fuck have I agreed to?*

Evie starts giggling under her breath as if she's heard my thoughts.

She takes my hand, grinning at me. "Look, it's one of your people."

It's then I notice that the guy bears a striking resemblance to Ed Sheeran . . . only in hair color.

"My people?" I chuckle.

She smiles wider. "Maybe you guys are related. From the same four-leaf clover bush. He could be your long-lost brother."

"Well, if he is," I snark quietly as he begins giving directions, "I will happily trade him for being your sister because I bet he would have rented me a hotel room with his pot of gold."

She narrows her eyes at me as we stand off in front of our bench, the fire feeling divine.

"Take it back."

"Nope," I shoot out, making her raise her brows.

"Okay," she says with a shrug. "Then I won't tell you what's behind you right now."

My eyes squeeze closed as my shoulders raise. "Evie," I rush out, too scared to turn around because I know one of her cronies is waiting to make me soil myself. "I swear to god. I'm gonna tell Mom."

She dusts off invisible dirt from her jeans before slowly sitting down on the log.

"I take it back. I take it back. I take it back," I squeal, making her laugh as she looks up at me.

"Air," she says matter-of-factly. "Just air, nerd."

I let out a huge sigh of relief before I turn over my shoulder, only to jump out of my damn skin because my assumed Irish brethren is standing directly behind me. His green eyes are locked to mine.

"Jesus Christ," I gasp.

Evie laughs as the Eddie Redmayne look-alike grins while holding out his hand. "Nope, not him. I'm Remus, assistant to the host."

I take a deep breath and shake his hand. "Goldie Monroe."

He frowns. "I don't remember seeing your name on the list. There's an Evie Monroe . . . What department are you with?"

I grin because I'm lying and that's not something I'm good at. "Research and development."

He stares into my eyes, still holding my hand, before I have to tug it gently away as he tilts his head and smirks.

"Welcome to Camp Weonoke, Goldie. I hope it's a weekend you'll never forget."

# Chapter Twenty-Five

## Noah

The smell of eggs infiltrates my senses as I open my eyes, yawning and stretching from where I've been sleeping the last few days—Chase's couch.

Princess is purring on my chest, content to stay there, before I move her off.

"You up?" he calls from his kitchen.

He's letting me crash at his place until I find a new one, but all I've really been able to think about is the old one. Especially since we went back there yesterday to clean up the mess. I noticed her clothes were gone, and I couldn't breathe. I just had to get the fuck out of there, so I locked up and left.

And I'm not going back.

It's wild, because I'm glad she's left. It's exactly what I want. But it still makes every single moment of the day completely unbearable. With the exception of the three seconds or so when I first wake up—in that fleeting moment of time, I still think I'm going to open my eyes and see her smiling back at me.

"Omelet's up," Chase's voice booms again. "And I think I found something."

I sit up and run my hand through my hair before I pull my T-shirt over my head and make my way to the kitchen with my phone in hand, immediately taking the fork he's offered to me.

We're standing around the island eating as he speaks.

"Okay, so I was poking around the dark web . . ."

I scowl, mid-chew, then grab the top of his laptop and spin the screen around toward me.

"Chase, this is Safari on private browsing mode."

He scoffs. "Regardless, I found something written about that camp from like the 2000s. At some college newspaper. They did a whole piece called 'The Hidden Secrets of Camp Weonoke.' It was a solid piece of exposé journalism."

I swallow my food, gathering more on my fork. "How does that help us find him?"

"It mentioned a relative . . . a grandmother. Maybe we could find her and see if she's heard from him or has any info."

I never knew my grandmother. The thought of relatives is so foreign. I wasn't just an only child. I was alone. This unwanted enigma who people hated and looked at like one day I'd be another headline.

I look down again reading the article before I shake my head. "This says she was in her eighties. She's gone by now, dude."

It's weird, I'm not relieved or sad. Just right where I left off.

"Shit," he says, stealing back his laptop, spinning it back toward him, and looks over it again before snapping it closed. "Everything's a dead end. How the fuck are we going to find this guy?"

It was clear the other night that I wasn't getting rid of him, so I agreed to let him help me, but that doesn't mean I won't try and change his mind every day until . . . The thought makes my stomach turn.

"Not we . . . me."

I put my fork down, having already cleared my plate. Not because I'm hungry but because my inclination is to not eat, like some lovesick Romeo who wants to waste away.

He shakes his head and crosses his arms. "Are we doing this again? I thought we cleared this up the other night. How many times do I have to tell you that I'm just a boy, standing in front of another boy, asking him to let me commit possible vigilante murder with him?"

Both my hands point at the counter as my frustration rises. "Chase. This is serious . . . My father will eventually find me again, and he's fucking crazy. He'll gut you to get to me. You can't be the Julia to my Hugh."

He holds up a hand. "I know this is serious. And I know the risks. And I'm willing to take them." Then he grins. "I'd also just like to add that I love that I'm the better-looking one in this scenario . . . Just as an aside. Continue."

I shrug, following him off track. "I mean, she is the one who delivered the line, so it's kind of by default."

He nods. "Delivered? What an impactful moment . . . so raw and vulnerable. Visually beautiful. I may have gotten teary eyed."

My hands wipe down my face as I'm jolted back to reality. "Jesus Christ. Can you focus? Can I?" I pivot before turning back again, having too much energy in my body. "This is serious shit about to go down. And I would rather do it alone."

Chase's palms press to the counter as he leans forward, his eyes locked to mine.

"That's not how 'would you rather' works. Here's one: Would you rather find out your best friend died because you left him alone and he's incapable of butting out, or almost die fighting together?"

I blink back, a deadpan expression on my face. "Are you fucking kidding? Why won't you listen to reason?"

Chase grins back at me, knowing he's game, set, matched me. "Because what you want is unreasonable."

Bullshit. He knows everything. I listed out the risks and the consequences of knowing me. All the tiny little nothings over the last year that weren't nothing—his motorcycle accident, the friend of Evie's who was attacked out front of Goldie's a year ago, even the dude she told me about months after we'd moved who'd scared the shit out of her. None of that was coincidence.

My father was getting closer and closer. My mind drifts to the night I kissed her in the alley, remembering the figure across the street.

He's been watching me, waiting for his moment. I run a hand through my hair. "I keep saying this, but you aren't hearing me. Billy's here to finish the job."

Chase crosses his arms, undeterred. I groan, throwing my hands up.

"This fucking stubborn loyalty to me is annoying. Quit."

"Nah, and leave my brother out here with only his good looks and no common sense? That's the point of the smart, funny sidekick—I save your ass. You can't be a hero without me."

A hero? I'm as much of a villain. Nobody would be in this mess if it wasn't for me. But I don't say any of that, just stare back at him as he keeps going.

"Now back to business. I was thinking about this last night. I think we should go—"

I cut him off, suspecting he's going to say "to the cops."

"No. I can't do that. They're just gonna say I'm wrong because they ruled him dead thirty years ago. Nobody's helping us . . . or me, rather. You shouldn't be helping me either."

He scowls, then rubs his chin thoughtfully, and I shake my head.

"We need to bait him," he rushes out like the idea just sprang to life.

I frown. "You really don't have any regard for your own safety, do you?"

Chase looks back at me, and for the first time, I truly see it in his eyes—the belief he has in the words I've been saying. But for reasons I'll never be able to accept or explain, he's not scared away. He shrugs.

"I'm not looking to die young, Noah. But I'm also unwilling to let my best friend handle this shit alone. We're family. We don't quit on each other. So get on board, and let's figure out a plan." The sharp sound of a knife unsheathed from its holder slices through the room before he twists it around his fingers. "Your mom wasn't the only person good with a knife."

He's serious.

I chuckle. I can't believe it, but I do. God, I hate him for giving me this feeling of hope and for forgiving me when I can't even do that for myself.

"I'm pretty sure Billy's gonna be harder to stick than a rack of lamb."

Maybe it's the fact that I've mentally given up changing Chase's mind or that we're casually talking about murder, but I'm tired again. A deep exhale sags my shoulders as I run a hand over my jaw.

I just need a minute.

"Honestly," I say on an empty laugh, "I don't know what the plan is. I'll get back to you. All I know is I need a shower . . . And if you don't mind, I'd like to do *that* alone."

Chase picks up what I'm putting down because he nods, not saying anything back. I push away from the counter, pocket my phone, and turn around. I hear him pick up his fork to gently cut another piece of the omelet before he talks through a mouthful. "You know, you might feel a little less dirty if you told her."

I freeze in place, my back to him. My jaw tenses, but I stand in silence long enough to remember how to breathe. Jesus, he doesn't even have to say her name to level me.

"Heroes are supposed to save the girl," I say over my shoulder, turning my head but not looking at him. "Right? They sacrifice themselves." My hand grips the back of my neck as I finally meet his eyes. He gives me a nod. "I'll never be able to make it right, Chase. And she'll never forgive me. But I can keep her safe . . ." I turn back this time as I walk, saying the rest loud enough for him to hear. "Don't bring her up again."

The moment I close the bathroom door, my ass hits the counter as I lean back and grip the edge, breathing too fast and too hard. My knuckles rub the middle of my chest, feeling the tightness. This feels like a panic attack, but it's grief.

Fuck, I miss her. I think about her, I dream about her. She's still all over me.

The past few days have felt like a lifetime.

My eyes close, and I hate and love the ache in the center of my chest because at least it's something that still connects me to her. The memories come slowly, as if they're testing the waters . . . making sure I don't break.

I see her laughing. The way her hair swishes when she walks. I remember the night we lay in bed and I counted her freckles, stopping at 642. And that morning she burned the quiche, then FaceTimed Chase to make him teach her how to make me a new one.

All the happiest moments of my life run through my mind until they crash down around the last picture in my mind—the look on her face as I begged her not to leave.

The fear on it . . . She was looking at a stranger.

I am no one to her now. *I love you, don't hate me.*

I blink my eyes open, clear the lump in my throat, slowly pull out my phone, and stare down at the message I received last night. The one I didn't want to tell Chase about because I'm still unsure how I want to handle it.

**617-999-5757:**
Hello, this is Mat-
thew Wright from
Origins Investi-
gative Services. I
would like to clarify
some information
obtained by the
Monroes. They've
asked me to con-
tact you privately,
and they request
you don't contact
their daughter.
Please call or text

back as soon as possible.

My head begins warring with itself again because she deserves the truth. But what if when she finds out, she gets as pigheaded as Chase? Then again, maybe if I tell this guy, he could help her understand that she's better off without me.

I shake my head as I stare down at the screen, realizing that in all my scenarios, Goldie wants me back, but no matter what subconscious thoughts I have, we're done. She'll never be able to look at me the same. I ruined us.

The truth is the least I can give her back. Her parents will know the right time to share it with her. I know that in my bones. Her heart's protected by her family. Thinking it makes me close the message and go to the one that's been burning a hole in my gut ever since Monday at one a.m. when I received it.

**Evie:** Saw the apartment. Stay the fuck away from my sister and my family or I'll kill you myself. Don't contact her either. My parents are taking her home, away from you. What you did . . . who you are. You fucking broke her, and I hope you burn in hell.

An easier breath leaves me as I start to calm. Evie's message should feel like a knife to the heart, but all I can think is *At least she's safe.*

I switch back to the message with Matthew again before my fingers fly over the keys. I toss my phone on the bathroom counter and strip, then get into the hot shower to try and wash the last seventy-two hours away.

**Me:** Tell me when
and where

The water splashes down over my face as I hear the ding, but I still get out and drip water on the floor to check it.

**617-999-5757:**
Tomorrow, Friday,
1pm, Baker's coffee
downtown

# Chapter Twenty-Six

## Goldie

"Good morning, sunshine. Happy Thursday." My sister's sipping her coffee, already fully dressed, as she smiles down at me.

"What time is it?" I groan, pulling the pillow over my head.

"I don't know, but the sun just came up, so I'm guessing early."

I roll over in my twin-size bunk to look at the clock with one eye open, groaning because the bed's hard and lumpy. People hate children if this is where they sleep. *Huh,* I think as I get a good look at the time, *the time's wrong.*

"This one's broken," I say, picking it up to show her before smashing the pillow back over my face again. "It says 11:59."

Evie laughs, "That's a *Shining* reference." She smacks my bottom. "I gotta go. I only have today to set up, and what's a scary camp without dead bodies? Time to work my magic. Whenever you're up, come find me. I'll put you to work."

"Pass," I gripe before closing my eyes again.

But I only half fall asleep, never truly reaching the coveted REMs before I give up and toss the blanket off, sitting up in the quiet cabin. It's small, almost too small for two people.

"Overrated," I say to myself, thinking about what Evie said about us never going to camp as kids.

My bare feet touch the cold ground before I yank them back up and wiggle my toes as I search under my blanket for the socks I discarded last night.

Truth is, when the bonfire ended, we made our way to the assigned cabin. Of course ours was number thirteen. I was too exhausted to shower, so I wrapped myself up in my uncomfortable bunk and passed out, smoky clothes and all.

I take a whiff of my hair and turn my nose up before I dig deeper under the covers and find my socks. I drag them over my cold toes before padding to the bathroom so I can take a shower. I'm still blinking my eyes open and yawning as I reach past the white shower curtain to twist the handle for the hot water.

But as I do, our cabin door bangs open, making my head whip toward it as my sister yells, "Goldie, wait!" But it's too late, because the fucking screeching sound from *Psycho* plays, scaring the living hell out of me.

I scream, startled almost to death as I just barely miss falling into the tub. My arms flail as they get entangled with the white curtains, and I shriek, "For fuck's sake."

"Sorry . . . sorry. I forgot to warn you," my sister laughs, trying to help set me free, but I slip on the water that's now making its way outside the shower and land squarely on my ass, the wet shower curtain covering my head.

Silence fills the small space, with only the sound of running water grating my nerves.

"Evie," I say, extremely calm. "Get out."

I hear her footsteps retreating before the door closes behind her.

*Son of a bitch.*

My eyes shut as I feel the water hitting the back of my head. I take a deep breath, forgetting about the shower curtain, and instantly almost kill myself by sucking the cheap plastic into my mouth, cutting off my airway.

I scramble to rip it off, half suffocated and panting but free to live another day as I shake my damn head.

"This is why Norman Bates's mother went crazy," I rant to myself. "Day in and day out with this kind of shit will make anyone batshit. Wait for me, Mrs. Bates . . . I'm coming."

"Actually . . ." Evie pokes her head back inside from eavesdropping. "He killed his mom and was dressing up as her."

I don't know what I grab, I think an extra toilet paper roll, but I launch it through the air. It hits her before she shuts the front door again, saying, "Ow."

"Heard you had quite the morning with the showers." A kind-faced man smiles next to me in line at the cafeteria. I recognize him.

Last year at the party, his wife was Pennywise, and he was the balloon. It was hilarious. I just can't remember his name.

"Hi . . . yeah, it was terrifying," I chuckle, trying to seem friendly, even though I'm not really in the mood to people. So much so, I came straight to the cafeteria after taking a shower . . . with the curtain open.

"I feel like I should apologize," he presses, accepting a roll on his tray.

"Ah," I say, half smiling. "You must be part of the team that arrived Monday."

"Guilty." He winces.

I nod as the cafeteria lady holds up a spoon with some kind of hash-looking stuff. *Man, I miss Chase* . . . Fuck, I can't even escape Noah-adjacent thoughts.

"Well," I breathe out as I turn my face to my new friend. "As the head of research and development, I can say if you're aiming for people to have a heart attack before showering, you're on your way."

He chuckles, and I take a scoop of the weird runny potato-like substance. "Are they feeding us the same stuff they give the kids? Because I think that's child abuse. We should call someone."

"What do you mean?" he says, taking his turn with the same future food poisoning.

I motion with my head as I hold my tray. "You know, because the guy throwing this wants a whole realistic experience for everyone. Like this is what the kids would've had."

"Oh yeah," he chuckles. "I thought that you meant this camp was still active. Like you thought kids had just been here."

I start to say something, but he keeps talking.

"From what I've heard, Weonoke was a real camp. But it closed down. Some of the locals said it was the site of a massacre back in the mid-nineties."

I suddenly realize I'm just standing there listening, but it looks like I'm waiting for him, so I turn to leave, but he follows. Still talking.

"Yeah, I guess some local kid who was a janitor went full slasher on the counselors at the end of the year, and it's been closed ever since."

*What the fuck?* I know this was the alternative to a heady situation back home, but I'm feeling like we jumped the gun.

I swallow hard. "I've never heard anything about that . . . I feel like if this was true, Evie would've been salivating over it. She's . . . morbid."

He smiles as if I've given her the greatest compliment as we put our trays down and sit.

"You know how it is with news that happened pre-internet." I watch him dig into the potato massacre in current times, trying not to dry heave. "There's probably a thousand and twelve things we'll never hear about."

I laugh nervously, hating every word he's saying. "So many . . . wow . . . yeah, that's a lot to think about. Especially since it's such a specific number . . . I don't . . ." *Love that.*

My sister's voice bleeds in behind me, saving me from trying to hijack the death-log truck so I can escape.

"Russ, are you telling my sister that freaking urban legend nonsense? You're really trying to make that happen, aren't you? Gretchen Wieners, you gotta let *fetch* die."

She sits down next to me, and I look at her, wide eyed, as Russ ruminates on who Gretchen Wieners is.

"It's not true," she dismisses.

But Russ disagrees as he takes another bite of that gross shit. "All urban legends are based on some truth."

I look down at the mush on my plate, then back at my sister. "I hate it here."

She laughs. "I mean, if it was true, then we'd probably be in the cabin of a dead person . . . You know, because we're in the staff quarters. Ooo, who here has a Ouija board?"

Russ perks up as I shake my head. *Yep. I absolutely hate it here.* Before I can say anything, a voice invades the moment: "I do, but only if I can join in on the fun."

I look up and see Remus, the enthusiastic camp guy from last night, holding a brown paper bag. "May I join you?"

He's smiling directly at me, although he's standing next to Russ. My sister nods happily. She says "Absolutely" and gestures for him to sit.

I smile tightly.

Actually, he's probably a super-nice guy who likely gives to children's charities, but everyone here is an enemy to my state of mind.

Remus smiles, then pulls an apple out of his lunch bag, making my mouth water. God, it's so shiny and plump. I stare down at my food again, moving it around with my fork, before I look back up.

"Hey, where'd you steal the meal?" I shoot out, grinning.

Evie laughs. "Dino nuggets aren't for her."

She's being nice. I would 100 percent demolish nuggets over the slop I have.

His eyes lower before he slides his lunch over to me. "Peanut butter and jelly with the crusts."

"No," I say, half laughing, and slide it back. "You don't have to do that. I was just holding out hope there was another option. No offense."

"None taken."

Remus leans over the table, beckoning us with his hand so we can hear a secret. Like a bunch of little kids, we follow his lead.

He keeps his voice low. "I think the cafeteria lady is acting suspicious . . . Yesterday, I saw her making tonight's chili with rat poison on the counter, talking to herself about her sister."

My eyes pop open, but Evie and Russ laugh as they sit back up. But I'm still leaning in. What the hell is happening?

Evie pats my arm with the back of her hand. "It's from a movie, Golds, called *Cobweb*."

Remus winks at me. "Gotcha."

I grin, feeling tricked as I sit back up. He holds his hands up in case I'm mad. "Sorry, you make it so easy."

Yeah, I don't like him. Evie pipes up, maybe feeling my vibe. "What do you know about the camp? Like its history and stuff."

He grins. "I take it you've heard the lore."

Evie's fork hangs midair as her eyes widen. "Wait, so it's true?" She looks at Russ, who seems just as riveted.

Remus shrugs. "Who knows, but it was good marketing either way."

Russ chuckles, and so does Evie, but not me. I shiver.

"You don't agree?" he says, opening his paper bag.

All the eyes at the table land on me. Shit. I clear my throat, ignoring how my sister is discreetly shaking her head, trying to tell me to be quiet.

"I think Stephen King's shown us the dangers of messing around in burial grounds. And if what everyone thinks happened actually did happen, then it's kind of creepy to be here. Movies are fun because they're fiction. Real life is full of consequences that hurt people. So no, I don't agree."

The table is silent, and I know I'm probably going to get a lecture from my sister about my loyalty to her and my fake role in research and development, but I don't care. If people died, that's not marketing for a spooky Coachella.

He tilts his head, our green eyes locked. "Well, you know what they say about art imitating life . . . The inspiration has to come from somewhere."

Goose bumps blaze a trail over my arms under the long-sleeve camp shirt I was give upon arrival.

But before too much silence passes, he chuckles and says, "Gotcha . . . again."

Everyone breathes at the same time, all the smiles tainted by how freaked out we all were.

*I'm truly starting to hate this game.*

# Chapter Twenty-Seven

## Goldie

***Halloween***

I read the note in my hand one more time from my sister, narrowing my eyes as I do.

> Golds,
> I had to do a couple of fixes on some bodies before we head out today, so I left you a present. Enjoy!
> PS—make sure you pack up because the bus leaves at 3:00 p.m. sharp.
> xx, Evie

"This is suspicious," I say to myself while staring at the TV.

I'd be irrational not to second-guess her intentions, since my heart's been getting a full cardiac workout from the time we pulled into the parking lot, pre-fucking-camp.

I scoot off the bed before standing and inspecting the vintage TV. It's one of those old tube ones from like the eighties. I didn't even think they made them anymore, but I can see the guy who's throwing this weird retreat being all in.

The polish on my thumbnail chips as I nervously scratch it. I'm looking for a clue as to whether this thing's been rigged by Evie and her minions so that, once I turn it on, a child who looks like she's half dead will actually crawl out and scare me to death.

The thought actually makes me shiver, and my fingers curl into a ball as I whisper, "Hello . . . come out if you're in there."

I reach out slowly, very slowly, trying to internally prepare myself for any and every possibility, even being shocked. I literally wouldn't put anything past these freak-ass horror geniuses.

"Please just be a real TV," I exhale shakily, drawing my hand back right before I almost touch the knob that turns it on.

*Is this how I make it work?* Shit. I don't even know how to get rid of my read receipts on my phone, and I'm supposed to figure this out?

But to my surprise, when I pull the knob, not only does nothing happen to me, but the television just powers on.

"Huh," I let out, surprised, my eyes big.

I stand there for a second, watching the news, still skeptical—as one would be, seeing as I've felt like a war's been waged on me. Finally I back away before turning around to the bed, only glancing over my shoulder a few more times as I crawl back in.

An audible sigh of relief (or maybe leftover disbelief) releases as I give in and fluff my lumpy damn pillow before I grab the remote off the bed.

It's the size of a brick, but whatever—it works. I press one of the buttons, changing the channel to a morning show, and smile. The picture isn't 4D, but it'll do.

Two hours later, I've snuck out to the cafeteria to grab some snacks and brought them back like a little squirrel. I've been watching a show that I remember my mother watching when I was a child.

God, Evie and I used to make so much fun of the fact that she watched soap operas. They were so dramatic and full of toxic relationships, but baby, I am hooked. This is so much better than watching those gross scary movies Evie loves.

I stuff some chips in my mouth as I point at the screen, talking to it like the people can hear me.

"She's cheating on you, dum-dum. With your brother. God . . . how do you not see the chemistry between them?"

The brunette vixen who everyone seems to be obsessed with begins giving her big monologue, and I'm riveted. But suddenly the picture goes out, turning to snow, before it pops back to normal just as fast.

"Shit." I frown while shoving more chips in my mouth as the TV does it again. "Uh-uh. No, no, no . . . what is happening?"

I sit up and stare as lines start to populate over the show, like the television's about to take a shit.

"Dammit. Noooo . . . I need to know who she picks."

I scooch off the bed quickly, not knowing what to do other than to channel my father. So, I hit the side of the box a couple of times.

"Work . . . if evil Hannah chooses Rick, Paul might go feral and marry good Hannah."

I squeal when it starts working again, but it only lasts for a second before the sound transforms into my favorite sleep track—white noise—and the picture stays a grainy black and white.

"Come on. How did people live like this?"

A sigh spills out, my soap opera disappointment heavily apparent, before I turn back to the bed to grab the giant remote, hoping a button on there can fix this problem.

But as I do, the faintest sound of a whimper—no, not a whimper, but like a distant cry—fills the room. It stops me in my tracks, my brows drawn together as I immediately look around, wondering what the hell it is.

No sooner do I wonder than I hear it again.

Is it coming from outside? I walk toward the cabin wall and press my ear to it, feeling as sketched out as I probably look, but that's when I hear the voice.

"Now I lay me down to sleep, I pray the Lord my soul to keep . . ."

"What the fuck." I turn my head in slow motion over my shoulder to the fucking television as my heart starts beating out of my chest. "Ohhh, no, no, no, no, no. We are not doing this."

I'm already grabbing my shoes, hopping as I put them on my feet, when I hear, "Mommy, can you hear me? It's Carol Anne. I'm scared," before a demonic screeching bursts from the TV speakers.

I was never a runner in high school; in fact, I never had any aspirations to become athletic. But today I'm winning an Olympic gold for fastest sprint away from a haunted fucking television.

I'm yelling incoherent words as I burst from the room, chills running down my spine, only to skid to a stop because my sister and her colleagues are standing out in front of me with smiles plastered to their faces.

*Someone's dying today.*

I reach down and take off my shoe, watching everyone scatter as I chuck it directly at my sister.

She scream-laughs as I jump up and down, shaking out my arms, before I stab my finger toward the open door of my cabin.

"Someone get that goddamn television out of my room. Now . . . right now."

Evie's boss is almost doubled over as he hands her a hundred-dollar bill. She winks at me. "I told you she's never seen *Poltergeist*."

"I am officially trading you in for a better model when we get home," I yell at her before storming back toward the room, only jumping out of the way as they roll the television by me before I slam the door behind me.

I am so glad we are leaving today.

## Noah

"Why are you dressed like that?"

Chase is walking down his stoop, looking like a contract killer trying to blend into a crowd.

He stops in his place and holds open the jacket like he's modeling it. "Dude, I'm incognito."

I scoff. "Not even a little. You look wildly suspicious."

He looks behind him as if I'm speaking to someone else. "What are you talking about? No, I don't. The hat . . . the black trench and glasses are making it so I'm not suspicious. And also so that nobody recognizes me."

Why did I tell him about the text? What was I thinking? I should've left him here. I cross my arms, staring at him.

"Do you get that a lot . . . people finding you unforgettable? Or maybe unable to place how they know you?" I wave my hand aggressively in front of his white work van that has the name of his restaurant on the side. "Just get in."

He drags his sunglasses down his face as he walks toward the passenger door. "Jesus. Okay. A girl breaks your heart and someone tries to kill you, but all you want to do is hurt *my* feelings? Weird choice, but I forgive you."

I can't with him today. "We deserve to die," I grit out as I walk around to the driver's side.

I don't care if it's his van, no way was I letting him get us to where we need to be. He'd have us re-creating some fucking movie scene to deflect from the seriousness of what's going on. I know that's why he's acting like this. It's what Chase excels at—making a shit situation seem tolerable—but I'm in no mood.

I slide inside the van and turn it on.

"So, what's the plan?" he breathes out. "Should we stake out the coffee shop before going in?"

With one hand on the wheel, I back up, then pull out onto the street.

"The plan is to sit down and tell Matthew Wright the truth, in the hopes it brings her parents some peace. It's the least I can do for them."

Chase drops the bullshit for a minute. "Do you think maybe they could help you find out some information about your dad? This guy's a private investigator after all."

"Working in line with someone else's interest."

We stop at a red light as he looks at me. "But he's a professional. His interest is his bottom line. I don't think it would be far-fetched to ask."

I hit the gas as the light turns green. "You got a point. Okay, I'll ask."

Chase taps the dash like he's playing the drums. "This is good. Last thought. Don't be mad . . . Do you think we should have code names?"

"Shut up until we get there. Just no talking."

The car goes quiet, but I still hear him whisper "So, that's a no" under his breath. We drive deeper into the city before I turn onto the street where we're meeting the investigator. Parking is impossible, but we find a spot half a block away.

As we're getting out of the car, I glance at Chase.

"You're really going in with the whole getup?"

"I've committed, Noah," he answers back.

"You should *be* committed," I whisper, but he ignores me.

We walk the block as the muscles in my jaw start doing more work than they should. I'm nervous and I don't know if I'm making a mistake. Before we walk inside, my hand comes to Chase's chest.

"Am I fucking up? Should I risk the information getting back to her?"

I know she's in Portland, and I'm committed to keeping her safe. But a piece of me is still scared to death that if she called and told me to come get her . . . I would.

Like a selfish, irresponsible asshole, I would run both of us away and try to never look back, because it's starting to feel like I'll never know how to live without her.

Chase pulls his glasses off and stares back at me. "Not telling her is another lie . . . I know I'm not supposed to say this, but you have to decide if one day when all this shit is finally over for you . . . Do you want to win her back?"

He didn't even have to finish that sentence before I thought of the answer. *Yes. It's always going to be yes. Even if it's a pipe dream.*

"As an aside," I say, using his phrasing from earlier today and grinning in the face of my nerves, "I really like how I'm still alive in all your scenarios."

He smirks and puts his glasses back in place as he opens the door. "Manifestation, baby. I learned it from this girl who used to only say Brad Pitt's name when we fucked."

We walk inside and grab the nearest table before he goes to the counter and orders himself coffee. I can't even think about drinking anything. When he comes back, we sit in silence, just waiting.

And waiting.

I check my phone after another fifteen minutes pass, but no messages have come through, so I send him one.

**Me:** I'm here. With a friend in the front.

"Dude, what time were you supposed to meet?"

Chase is playing with the stir stick from his coffee as he looks around. I flip my phone down, already knowing the answer.

"His text said one p.m."

Something doesn't feel right, but then again, I could just be seriously paranoid, considering my whole life is like a fucking crime docuseries.

Chase blows out a harsh exhale. "He's like thirty minutes late already." He takes his glasses off and tosses them onto the table. "Do you think the Monroes changed their minds?"

Some people walk in, drawing both our eyes, before I answer. "No. I mean, they asked me. Why would they change their minds? Her parents are scared of what I might do to her . . ."

He looks confused. "Why the fuck would they be scared of you? I mean, I get wondering why you lied . . . but scared? What do they think . . ." He chuckles like the thought is ludicrous. "That you're gonna lose it and . . ." He trails off, finally piecing it together. "Did they see the apartment?"

I nod and swipe open Evie's message, then turn my phone toward him.

He takes off his hat, swipes his hair back, secures it again, and looks at me.

"Fuck. If I wasn't obligated by best friendship to hate that girl, I'd kinda be turned on right now."

My forehead wrinkles as I stare at him. He shrugs. "Well, at least you can rest easier, knowing she's out of Dodge," he says. "Dude, why do you think your dad is back now? After all this time . . ."

"I dunno," I say honestly. "There are a million reasons, but only he really knows the truth."

"Hmm," Chase says, thinking aloud. "You know, if I were a serial killer looking for a cover to wreak havoc, I'd do my worst on Halloween, when everyone's pretending to be the same as me."

The door opens again, and we look as a man walks in dressed in a suit and holding a briefcase.

"Is that him?" Chase whispers.

I shake my head, half shrugging. "I don't know. I've never met him before."

But in answer to our question, he walks past us, joining a table full of people. I let out an audible exhale as I sit back in my chair and interlace my fingers behind my head in frustration, my nerves already on edge.

"Fuck, what is taking so long? Something's off, man. I know it, and I don't care if that sounds paranoid."

"It doesn't. This is weird. You're right. Why would he ask you and not show?"

A thought hits me. "Earlier, before we left today, he pinged me his location. I just already knew where the coffee shop was, so I didn't use it."

Chase sits up straighter. "Maybe we got the wrong place?"

I nod, smiling. "Maybe we got the wrong place."

In the back of my mind, I hear the thought—*Strange that he hasn't texted, wondering where I am*—but I need to focus on one thing at a time.

I swipe his message open on my phone, see the tiny map icon, and tap on it. A dot shows up with a blue circle around it, growing wider then smaller as it searches to pinpoint his location. Chase and I stare down intently as it homes in on him and finally stops moving.

"Oh shit," Chase blurts out, then looks around to make sure nobody heard.

We look at each other at the same time that I say, "He's a block away from here."

Chase chuckles and crosses his arms, looking way too smug. "See, I'm not the only one that thought a stakeout was a good idea."

I push up from the table and stand, grabbing my jacket off the back of the chair.

"I don't know about you, but I'm tired of waiting. Grab your shit, Inspector Gadget—we're going to him."

Chase says, "Hell yeah," like we're heading out on a secret mission. He scrambles to put his sunglasses back on before he grabs his coffee.

I walk out of the shop and pocket my cell as he catches up, grinning at me. "Can we have code names now?"

"I'm gonna make you go back inside . . ." My face shoots to his. "I'll *make you* go back inside."

He looks forward and straightens his trench coat. "Sorry, sorry. It wasn't the right time. Got it."

## Goldie

I'm standing at the top of the mountain I just hiked, in a clearing, staring out at the most breathtaking view.

The trees aren't just beautiful. This is a whole Bob Ross painting.

What's not beautiful, however, is how out of breath I am. Even after acknowledging this morning that I am not and have never been a natural athlete, I still thought it was a good idea to hike up this mountain.

Although the alternative was staying at the camp, to be further traumatized. I heard this podcast once that said, "If you don't change it, you choose it." And I don't choose scare camp.

I spread my arms, trying to take in nature, as I close my eyes and let the breeze cleanse me.

"Fuck that place," I whisper to myself with a chuckle, but the longer I stay like that, the more my mood begins to feel heavier.

I know why. It's been brewing since early this morning. It's Halloween. I met Noah a year ago today.

I drop my arms, looking out at the peaks and what feels like a million trees. And so many emotions happen all at once and hit me like a ton of bricks, fueled by all the regret I'm carrying, the denial I'm still clutching, and the truth.

It all finally settles into my bones.

My chest rises and falls, not too fast or too slow, but I'm still hyperaware of my breathing, just like the way I can count my blinks right now, because I'm waiting for the ache and the tears.

So instead of holding it in, I say it all to the damn trees.

"I love you . . . and I hate you. But I need to think that there was a reason bigger than the both of us for why you did what you did. If anyone asks, though, I'll tell people we were cursed in this lifetime, so maybe we'll find each other in a new one."

I run my hands through my hair as I take a deep breath and try to release everything. But instead of staying calm, I scream. It's loud and guttural and full of my pain. But it feels good to let it out.

I let it all out until there's nothing left and I'm laughing at myself. *Fuck.* I shake out my arms, feeling a little lighter and maybe crazier, but I'll take this to my grave, so nobody will ever be the wiser.

"Whoo," I say aloud again before the wind blows harder like it hears me, giving me a chill through my long-sleeve camp T-shirt.

This time I shiver, instinctively patting my pocket for my phone and wondering how late it's gotten.

*Damn, Thor.* If I had a watch, I'd check it, but who has one of those anymore.

I left well before noon, so I had plenty of time to do the mile up and back. Still, I don't want to risk not making it back in time for the bus, so I walk backward a couple of steps, committing this view to memory, before I turn around and head back the way I came, putting an extra pep in my step.

I'm humming to myself, walking quickly past a group of large birch trees, when unexpectedly I slip on some rocks.

"Oh shit," I gasp, shooting my hand out against a tree to stop me from rolling my ankle or breaking my tailbone.

It stings from the bark, but thankfully I don't fall. I still for a moment to make sure I'm all good before I whistle as I look down at my feet.

"Sneakers and hiking do not mix."

But the moment I lift my eyes, my brows draw together.

There's another tree in front of me, about two feet away, and it's been carved. Like back in the day when people used to want to preserve their love, and men did big romantic gestures instead of lying.

*Looks like I've gotten to the bitter part of breaking up.*

I walk to it and lift my fingers to trace the heart. God, it must've been done ages ago because it's so smooth. The names inside the heart aren't legible anymore, but it does kind of look like they've been scratched out.

*A woman scorned? The plot thickens.*

I lean in closer, trying to make out what it says. I whisper, "Love never lasts, sister," before I draw my head back and shake it. "You're a better woman than I. If he hurt me after doing this, I'd vote to cut the damn thing down."

As I'm marveling and quite possibly projecting onto a random tree in the middle of the forest, my eyes catch a burst of light off in the distance. Like when the sun reflects off some shiny metal.

I squint, unmoving, my gaze turned in the direction the flash came from as I lock on a man about thirty yards away.

*Who the hell?*

He's standing and facing me like a statue.

I can't make out his face because his hat's pulled down too low, but he's wearing the standard-issue work clothes for a scary-movie villain: navy blue jacket and dark work pants with black boots.

Neither of us makes a move; then a new emotion hits.

*Okay . . . this is honestly disappointing.*

I smile because for the first time, I'm recognizing the perk of being stuck for days at Horror U. I've finally become imperviable to Evie's shit. The television set the bar too high, and this guy isn't doing a damn thing.

"Ha," I yell, cupping my hands around my mouth to megaphone my message. "You're going to have to go back and tell them to try again. You aren't scaring me. And you can quote me as someone who fully backs the bear in the woods theory."

I roll my eyes and turn around, keeping on my path, not even looking behind me as I make my way back down to the camp, truly unfazed and ready to rub my win in my sister's face.

Even if the current score is set at something more like her 100 and me 1.

The moment I'm back in camp, I don't even know what to focus on first because there are people everywhere.

A girl pretends to slash her friend's throat as she makes a fake gurgling sound, and someone yells from their cabin for everyone to check out the shower.

*Been there, done that.*

Someone screams, making me almost break my neck as I look at them, but it's just a guy wearing a plastic baby mask running by me while holding a fake knife as his girlfriend laughs as she runs from him.

*What the fuck.*

I could've sworn my sister said the bus left at 3:00 p.m. But if that's true, then why am I suddenly in an eighties horror film with people dressed the part? As I think it, a guy walks by with hairy legs and very short shorts. He's going to catch pneumonia or a chainsaw to the forehead.

*I have to get out of here.*

I hustle to our cabin, weaving in and out of people dressed as various psycho killers who recite infamous lines that I've never heard before but hate all the same.

Jesus, the camp is pandemonium. Horror enthusiasts are everywhere, and I'm supposed to be heading home, away from scary things, even if it is Halloween.

"Kill, kill, kill," comes from my left, making my shoulders jump, and any cool I'd thought I'd banked from my time here completely vanishes. I snap my head to the side to see . . . *Wait, is that . . . ?*

Jesus, there's a grown man dressed as that killer doll in overalls.

Who are these people? Community is overrated. More people should isolate. *Bring back shame, bring back shame* chants in my head as I keep my eyes on the ground, moving quickly.

My feet literally can't move fast enough to get to my cabin, but I'm not going to actually run because who knows what would happen around this bunch. I could be chased down and hog-tied in the name of a cult classic.

Absolutely not.

The moment I get to the cabin, I barrel through our cabin door before closing it behind me, my back falling against it as I lock eyes with Evie.

"Why are there people here? I thought we were leaving before the people got here."

I'm breathless and my nerves are already on edge, but she's just staring at me.

"Evie. What is wrong with you?"

She frowns before she points to her ears and then removes her AirPods. *Oh my god.*

The music that's playing is so loud I can hear every word, all the way over by the door. The room might be small, but she's actively destroying her hearing.

"Sorry," she says with a grin. "I couldn't hear—" but that's all she gets out before her head shifts to the window; then she looks back at me. "Are there people here?"

I'm nodding, thankful she's finally caught up. "Yeah, that's what I'm saying. I thought we were supposed to leave before people got here."

She shoots to her feet. "We are. Grab your shit."

Thankfully, like she instructed earlier, I already had my bag packed, so I grab it and follow her quickly as we speed walk out of the cabin and back into the mayhem.

She looks back over her shoulder, giving me a look like *Wow* before she laughs.

"What are you looking at me like that for?" I say to her back. "These are your people."

She's a little bit faster than me, so when I see her stop and spread her arms wide as she looks around, my heart drops into my stomach.

*No. Nope. This is not happening.*

"Hell no, I have plans tonight, Goldie," she hisses as she spins around and walks past me, headed toward where I presume Remus's office is located.

I'm hot on her trail as she takes the two steps and lets herself in, not bothering to knock, her voice already raised.

"Remus. Where's my team?"

He looks up from his desk, his eyes volleying between us, the shock on his face evident. Remus was not expecting to see us.

"Oh no. What are you doing here?"

I blink five hundred times a minute as my sister's palms smack down on the desk. "What do you mean, 'What are we doing here?'"

I swear I see the slightest sheen of sweat begin to break out on his forehead before he swallows hard. "Well . . . well . . . I mean, you're on the bus, and it's already left."

The bag in my hand drops with a thud to the cabin floor. "You have got to be kidding me."

My sister echoes my thought as we both stare at him. "Yeah, say you're joking. Say this is a prank."

Remus holds his hands up from his leather chair like he's trying to calm us down. It immediately irritates me.

We have every right to be upset. We were told—rather, Evie was told—that the bus would leave promptly at 3:00 p.m. But now here we are standing in Remus's dusty-ass office while hordes of people run around the grounds with fake retractable butcher knives, wearing masks from some serial killer movie where a bunch of teenagers die.

"Okay," he starts, sounding sheepish, "I want to preface by saying this truly is management's fault. And we take full responsibility for the mishandling."

I interject quickly, "You mean your fault, Remus . . . Because *you* are management."

He nods and at least has the decency to look apologetic, but expressing his admission isn't fixing our problem.

Evie's pacing now. "How did everyone else from Mass FX make it on the bus except for us? Explain that to me . . . We're the only women here. And she's a giant tree of a redhead, and I'm the only Black girl. We're not exactly wallpaper."

He shrugs and then winces, looking around for help, but unless he has a spirit guide, he's fucked.

"I'm sorry. I thought I counted you. I even went down the line counting heads, and I could have sworn I marked you off on my list. Or maybe someone said you were coming, so I counted that. There was a lot of revelry when everyone left, and I was stressed about the incoming buses."

"Remus," I bark. "This isn't *Home Alone*, and I am not Macaulay Culkin." My voice keeps rising, and the vein on my neck pulses. "So why am I still here after my whole family left?"

He motions to Evie, looking confused. "I thought you guys were sisters."

"Ahhh," Evie yells, throwing her arms in the air. "I have a date tonight with a guy I have been pining over for three months. And now I can't even call him to tell him I'm stuck at camp. He's never going to speak to me again, and I'm blaming you."

She's pointing at Remus, whose forehead wrinkles with fear.

I close my eyes and take a deep breath in an effort to center myself so that I don't strangle him in the woods because that would be too clichéd for a place like this.

"Okay," I say in a much calmer voice. "Let's all take a beat; we can fix this. We're capable, smart adults that don't need to overreact. We just need to problem-solve."

Remus nods as Evie stares at me, her arms crossed.

"So . . ." I smile at Remus. "How long before we can get another bus up here to take us back?"

He itches his forehead and swallows hard again. Almost acting like he doesn't understand the words coming out of my mouth.

"Remus . . ." I offer, feeling my pulse quicken again, because I can already read the disappointment I'm going to have in the answer that's all over his face.

He clears his throat. "So, the . . . umm." He clears it again. "The problem is . . ." He pinches the front of his shirt, using it to cool himself.

My sister snaps. "Speak."

He word-vomits. "The problem is that we can't actually get any new buses back until the next pickup on Sunday. I have no way to authorize them."

"Call the guy throwing this," Evie presses. "The host."

His mouth hangs open as he tilts his head back and forth and then says, "He's on an expedition . . . middle of the ocean."

My face meets Evie's as we gawk at each other. I don't even know what to say. All I know is that she's in as much disbelief as I am.

"This is ludicrous."

Here I thought being stuck setting up the scariest place on earth with twenty or so nerdy special effects people was awful. Now I'm stuck at a camp for the weekend full of horror enthusiasts, kicking off the festivities on fucking Halloween.

I don't know what karmic retribution I'm paying, but I just want to go home and be miserable like a regular girl going through a breakup.

Evie shrugs like she's just had a conversation in her head before she says, "Fine, but we're not moving out of our cabin . . . And we get to participate in all the fun without paying for anything. That includes alcohol."

My eyes almost bug out of my head. "Are you serious? That's your negotiation?"

Remus nods enthusiastically. "Absolutely. Yeah. Anything you want."

I point my finger at him, doing that *lemons into lemonade* thing too. "And I want a better bed . . . If I'm stuck here for the foreseeable future, I'm not sleeping on a mattress that feels like it's filled with popcorn."

He smiles, the tension in his shoulders finally relaxing. "I'll even throw in a sweetener to make up for my grave mistake."

He leans sideways, reaches inside a desk drawer, and pulls out what looks like a very expensive bottle of scotch.

Evie chuckles. I'm not there yet.

"Who's up for an early happy hour?" He's looking directly at me. "I think you might need it . . . Seeing as how much you love all the scary stuff, I regret to inform you that the kickoff party tonight is a *Carrie* reenactment."

I'm shaking my head in confusion because I don't know what that means until I look at my sister, who's biting her bottom lip, trying to hide her smile.

She takes my hands and kisses the tops before she holds them under her chin and says, "That's the one about the prom queen who gets covered in pigs' blood and then runs berserk and kills everyone with her mind."

I steal my hands back and take the bottle from Remus before twisting the top and taking a swig. The burn slices down my chest as I let out a huffy breath.

"You know what? The old me would hate this . . . But the new me just feels like kindred spirits."

## Noah

I look down at the little map on my phone and back up again, my brow drawing together.

"What the hell. It's a brick wall," Chase blurts out, speaking my thoughts.

My eyes narrow as I look around. "We know he hasn't been masoned in, so I guess he could be across the street?"

We both look, but that's just a yarn store.

Chase taps the dot on my phone. "These things can be off, though, right?"

I nod, turning around and looking toward the only car with someone inside, but it's a woman and her small dog.

Chase starts walking again, and without a thought I follow his lead as he says, "If he's not a part of the building, maybe he's inside and sitting all the way in the back?" He points toward the alley. "We can cut through here."

He turns the corner, but as I do the same, I almost run into the back of him.

"What are you doing?"

Chase turns sideways, motioning with his head to a car about ten feet away and speaking under his breath. "Look."

A beat-up brown Camry sits idle, humming but not moving. I don't like this. My gut's already saying this is a bad idea. I hit his shoulder with the back of my hand. "Let's just get out of here . . ."

He shakes his head. "No, dude. Besides you wanting to be a hero for Goldie . . ." He stops himself and adjusts his hat. "Sorry, I forgot, no names . . . Besides all your good intentions, he could help you. So if he's in his car tugging one out, he's just gonna have to table it."

Chase takes off before I can stop him, closing the distance between us and the car. He lifts his hand to rap on the passenger-side window.

"What are you doing?" I grit out and yank his arm away, making him face me as my pulse races. I hectically look around, my mind a mush of paranoia. It has been, ever since I realized Billy was back. "This is what I meant by signing your own death warrant. You don't even know who's in the car . . . Anything could happen."

Chase leans back, his eyes narrowed as he looks through the window.

"I do know what could happen . . ." He turns toward the car, ignoring what I've just said, and barks "Hey" as he knocks hard on the window. "We could wake him up."

"Fuck," I breathe out, but Chase looks up at me.

"Relax."

I bend to look inside and see that the driver's side seat is slightly reclined. It does look like the guy's sleeping—his face is turned away from us—but there's just something . . . I don't know.

"Wakey, wakey," Chase sings as he knocks more insistently, but a frown's growing on my face.

"Do you think he's okay?" he adds as I put my hand on the door before pushing past him and hurrying around the hood.

"I don't know."

Chase looks over his shoulder and pulls down his sunglasses to see better.

"Leave it to us to find some dude who's passed out or on drugs while we're looking for a fucking psycho."

"Try the door," I shoot out as I see how close he's parked to the wall.

I can get to the window, but I won't be able to completely open the door. I narrow my eyes as I try to see past the tint of the front window, and hear the passenger-side door open.

"Hey, man . . . you good?" Chase says just as I take two steps closer. The reflection clears, and a business card on the dash comes into view.

*Origins Investigative Services.*

Chills rocket down my spine because I already know what's coming before I see it.

Chase leans inside, then nudges the guy and says "Oh fuck" at the same time my body jerks to a stop.

"Noah . . . oh fuck."

I'm breathing a mile a minute, my heart pounding out of my chest as fear courses through me. Chase scrambles out of the car, his hand covering his mouth as he begins to dry heave, but I take a step closer.

I need to see.

Bile rises in my throat because he's not just dead. His eyes have been gouged out, the sockets left empty with only spiny bits of macerated tissue dried to his skin. And his mouth's been left opened, his tongue cut out, the half left thick and swollen in the cavity.

I can almost hear him choking on his own blood in my mind. That's when it all hits me fast as I use the brick wall to help me back the fuck up and away from the car.

"Holy shit," I breathe out, repeating it a few more times.

"Dude." Chase is breathless as he turns in circles. "He's not new dead . . . He's not fucking new dead." He stabs a finger at the door. "That guy's cold, Noah."

My mind is running fast, a thousand warring thoughts pleading to be heard. I glance at both entrances to the alley, then back at the guy.

Chase dry heaves again, then takes his hat off to put it in front of his mouth. "Oh fuck, that's evidence . . . I'm gonna go to prison."

"Why would Billy kill him?" I say to myself, but Chase is full-on panicking.

"I touched someone old dead . . . oh god . . ." His hands hit his knees as he breathes hard. "Noah, I'm an LA six, but a prison twelve . . ."

I'm only half listening because, *Why would Billy kill him . . . other than to send me a message.*

Goldie. That's the only reason.

My phone's already burning a hole in my pocket as I start back toward Chase. "I need to call killer."

But he isn't listening, still mumbling about the guy being "old dead" and what's going to happen to him in prison. I grab him by the jacket and bring his face to mine.

"Get it together. We need to get the fuck out of here and find Goldie. Right now, Chase."

He lets out a steadying breath. "Yep. Got it."

I let him go and look around again as he rushes back over to the car.

"What the fuck are you doing?"

He's talking while rubbing his ass all over the door handle of the car. "Listen, this is serious shit. Your fucking dad gutted some dude's eyeballs . . . I don't even know what you'd use for that . . . an ice cream scooper? He's fucking deranged. We gotta call the cops."

I shake my head as I pull out my phone because the only thing I'm doing is calling Goldie. "No, we need to get the fuck out of here before someone sees us."

The call goes straight to voicemail, so I try again. Voicemail.

Chase groans. "Am I the only one who watches crime shows? Our fucking fingerprints are all over this car."

I look down at my phone, quickly scrolling to Evie's number. Fuck. Voicemail.

He leans sideways and uses his shoulder to try and rub where my hand was. "They hate you, remember. She probably lied about where Goldie would be too . . . That's what I would do if I wanted you to stay away. Throw you off the scent."

I run my hands through my hair before trying her mom . . . voicemail. Then her dad. The same.

"Fuck," I grind out, feeling my body going numb. If something happens to her . . . I look up at Chase, who's still wiping the car using his hands from inside the trench coat pockets. "Chase, if Billy did this, then he knows where Goldie is. None of this other shit matters until we find him. But it starts with finding her first."

Chase stills, his eyes locked with mine. "How the fuck are we supposed to do that?"

My phone dings.

I drop my eyes quickly as he closes the distance between us, and we both stare at the photo populating the text.

Goldie's standing next to a tree, her fingers touching the bark as she stares directly into the camera.

"Who sent that?" Chase whispers just as the message populates again.

**Unknown:** I don't
think Mommy
would approve.

Our eyes meet and I blink. "My father."

# Chapter Twenty-Eight

## Goldie

"See?" Evie smiles at me from across the long picnic table. "This isn't so bad, admit it."

I roll my eyes with a grin as I gather some more beads for the friendship bracelet I've been working on for the last ten minutes. She's right, in that this camp is not at all what I expected. Who would've ever dreamed up that I'd be stringing little beads that look like teeth onto red elastic so I could commemorate my time with jewelry that'll look like it's eating my wrist.

"I'm not sure what your definition of 'so bad' is," I say, holding up my chomplette, as I've decided to call it. "But yeah, this isn't great." She laughs, and I chuckle too. "But let me guess, this has something to do with a scary movie about a dentist?"

She taps her nose as she says, "Ding, ding, ding."

The girl next to her, wearing makeup like a porcelain doll, gets excited and joins our conversation, rambling off a list of her favorites.

"So obviously we start with *Little Shop of Horrors* . . ."

I zone out immediately, or the hopes of my teeth ever being cleaned again would be useless. But my sister falls into the conversation effortlessly, which makes me smile. I place my chomplette on the table and push it her way because I don't really want it.

A guy walks by as I'm looking around, wondering if it's too soon to diss my sister and go back to the cabin, which makes me do a double take.

My eyes pop open because he's wearing a Thrills-n-Kills T-shirt. I reach out and touch his forearm.

"Hey, you wouldn't happen to know a guy who works for them"—I point to his shirt—"who took all the cell phones when we came here, would you?"

He shakes his head. "We never confiscated phones."

My eyes narrow before I realize he's talking about for the guests. "No, I mean for the special effects team that was here earlier during the week. We missed the bus back, and I was hoping he sent our phones up? Or you can get them."

"Ohhh, you're talking about Jerry."

I smile, my hope blooming, only for it to be snuffed out.

"No, he stays back. This stuff spooks him too much. Sorry, but you can use mine if you need to make a call. Or there's a landline in the office."

I smile, shaking my head. "No, thank you. I appreciate it."

Fuck. Even if I wanted to call someone, I haven't memorized a phone number since I was in first grade and had to remember my parents' number.

"Hey," I breathe out, interrupting my sister's conversation. "I'm gonna grab something to eat."

She nods as I throw a leg over the bench and walk toward the cafeteria, but when I get there, the doors are closed. I pull on the handle, but it doesn't budge.

"What the heck?" I whisper as I step in closer to the window adjacent to the door and shield my eyes so I can see better through the glass.

It looks empty, but as I strain to see, I suddenly hear, "Whatcha doing?"

My whole body jerks as I half turn around and throw my hands out like I'm an old-timey boxer. Jesus.

"Whoa there, I come in peace," he teases.

I laugh, lowering my arms as Remus smiles back at me.

I dust off my pants as a method of calming down before I hitch a finger over my shoulder.

"I was just looking for a snack."

He nods, shoving his hands into his pockets at the same time as I do.

"Yeah, it's closed between lunch and dinner, unfortunately."

I shrug. "Oh well, I guess I'll have to find something to do other than eat my feelings."

"Well, I don't know. Ice cream always seems like a good idea. I could go for some cherry vanilla."

"Same . . ." I'm basically salivating.

He smirks. "Then I guess it's a good thing I'm management."

We both chuckle as he motions with his head for me to follow him. My eyes grow wide with excitement as he walks backward, then turns around and sneaks around the side of the building.

I glance over my shoulder before I follow, only briefly thinking that I should tell my sister what I'm doing, but my stomach's growling too loud, so I split.

When I round the corner, he's disappeared into the shadows. *Where did he go so fast?*

"Remus," I whisper, feeling cautious but still walking away from the crowds of people, before I hear my name, which makes me jump again.

"You have got to stop doing that."

He chuckles and waves me into a side door before I slip inside the darkened room, which I now realize is the side entrance to the kitchen.

The door closes behind me, taking with it the sound from outside, as I follow him deeper into the kitchen, all the way to the back, where the freezers are.

I shrug against the chill as he walks inside the large silver doors, where rows of large tubs sit on metal racks. He's eyeing the labels, going from one to the other, before he stops and looks up at me with a smirk.

"You know for someone so scared of everything, you're awfully trusting."

My brows draw together and my head turns over my shoulder as the door shuts on its own behind me.

"Don't worry," he adds. "I'm harmless."

"Does that open from the inside?" I rush out, hearing him chuckle again.

"Yeah . . . getting locked in is a myth. Which is great because if you did get locked in and screamed, nobody would hear you."

I smile, but I can't lie: I'm suddenly not so sure this was a good idea.

"Here we go," he says with gusto, then pulls out a tub and takes the lid off. "Grab that scoop."

My eyes follow to where he's pointing. I walk over, grab the ice cream scooper, and bring it back to him. He scoops two bowlfuls into ones he brought in with him, before he hands me mine with a smile.

"How about we enjoy these with a better view?"

I nod, my hand already on the spoon, ready to stuff my face. "I'm in."

Remus leads me back through the dark cafeteria and out the other side to the rear of the camp, where a lake sits. There's another picnic table, so we set up shop and dive into our unsanctioned treats.

"Mmm," I hum after the first bite. "This is exactly what I needed."

He has the same response as we sit and stare at the water, just eating. Strangely enough, it's comfortable.

The view is incredible, much like the one I saw earlier when I went for my hike.

"It's pretty out here," he remarks.

I'm staring out when I notice a small cabin in the distance. "Hey, what's that? Do people live out here?"

He shakes his head. "No, that's an old cabin for more staff . . . I'm pretty sure it was for the groundskeeper, or a janitor of sorts. It was usually a person from town."

"Creepy," I say, and we both smile.

"Speaking of . . . I actually looked into that urban legend Russ was telling you the other day. I asked around, and apparently there's some truth to it."

"No way." I slurp my ice cream because I'm talking with my mouth full.

"Yeah, I guess some years ago, a kid here was hired on as a groundskeeper, and he was tortured by some of the counselors . . . It's real scary-movie stuff. Rumor has it that it was over a girl."

"That's a twist I wasn't expecting . . ."

He lifts an eyebrow. "In my experience, love tends to bring the worst out of people."

I lift my spoon, then set it down as my stomach turns over. I'm feeling the same kind of déjà vu I felt when I found out about Noah.

Remus looks back out at the lake, seemingly deep in thought, before he speaks.

"The story goes that he was sneaking around with some slut—"

I blink, staring at his profile. The way he punctuates "slut" unnerves me. It's so crude in a way he's never been before, but he doesn't seem to notice my reaction as he casually eats his ice cream.

"—and when the boyfriend found out, he and his friends tortured the kid. Really messed him up and left him for dead. Guys like that always think they own everything, ya know? They tried to put him down like a fucking animal, all because they thought he was beneath them . . . just a townie, garbage to them."

I blink, feeling colder than before. I'm shivering on the inside as I keep staring at Remus. He takes another bite, the faintest hint of a smirk playing cruelly on his face.

"But the kid didn't die." His face finally turns to mine. "Instead, he came back to the camp and gutted them. Five in total."

*Five* . . . I draw my bottom lip between my teeth, biting at a piece of dry skin before I swallow.

"That's awful."

He's still staring at me. "For who?"

*What the hell?* His jaw clenches, and I don't know why I'm feeling so uncomfortable, but I am. It could be how casually he's speaking about a massacre. Or maybe how he seems to sympathize with the violence. Either way, I'm suddenly hyperaware of how close we're sitting and how he told me no one would hear me scream earlier.

And we're still far away from the other campers. I don't like this.

"You're not condoning five murders, are you?"

The expression on his face is unreadable. And it lasts for too long before he eases back into a smile, except it doesn't reach his eyes.

"No," he says nonchalantly. "I'm just relaying what I heard." He turns away, taking another bite of his ice cream. "It's a tragedy all around is all I'm saying."

I nod before clearing my throat and trying for an easier mood. "I think this ice cream would've been a better idea on a warmer day." I force a chuckle as I set my bowl down on the table. "I'm gonna head back and find my sister—she's probably wondering where I am by now."

He smiles and shrugs. "Suit yourself . . ."

*Oh, I will, you freaking weirdo.* I slide off the table and give him a small wave before I head back around the building. I only look back once, to see him emptying my bowl onto the grass.

Evie's putting the final touches on her fangs for tonight's costume party as I sit on my bunk and watch her. The new friend she met making bracelets apparently had an extra pair, so Evie is all set to be a creepy vampire.

"Are you sure you won't come?" she whines, holding up the fake butcher knife she brought me to makeshift a costume. "I promise you I'll run block from Remus the weirdo."

The minute I left him by the lake, I ran straight back to Evie and told her everything. She laughed and told me I was overreacting and living in paranoia because of the camp, but it's still bothering me.

He was weird, and that story was way too unsettling. I haven't stopped thinking about the damn article I read and still remember the part about the five people being massacred. There can't be a correlation, though.

I didn't share that part with Evie, but I wish I could look up how close we are to Darkwater Bay.

I grin as I pull myself from my thoughts. "No, I'm good. I'm better off here with locks on the door."

She points to the nonhaunted television that was delivered along with my new bunk. "And with all the reality TV I know you're going to watch."

I shrug because she's correct. I may even try and find some cheesy Christmas movies to counteract all the terror I've been inundated with.

She laughs, then trades out her red lipstick for black eyeliner. "I'm telling you, he's harmless. I think he likes you is all."

Harmless. He said the same, but I've learned that my gut is smarter than me, and this time I'm listening with both ears. Not that I could ever be some kind of monster who would ever "out-of-sight, out-of-mind" someone I was in love with a week after breaking up.

I may technically be back on the market, but I'm also not, because there isn't a guy on this planet, in any respite of time, who could make me want to give up even my grief to live without Noah.

I'd literally rather be miserable with his memory than be happy in his absence. That's how incurable the disease of heartache is.

But I'm not admitting that to anyone, including my sister.

I fluff my pillow. "Well, if he does like me, let me make it clear: (a) It's a hard pass from me. The hardest. And (b): Creeping women out is a weird way to flirt, so again, pass, forever."

"Agreed," she chuckles as she turns around for my approval, so I clap.

"Thank you . . ." She grins. "It was difficult to make my skin look translucent with only cheap drugstore powder, but in the end, I'm not like other artists; I'm a cool artist."

I giggle and snuggle under my blanket, hating the mention of a drugstore, because yet again my mind is wandering to where it shouldn't.

"Hey, not to beat a dead horse, but look on the bright side." She grabs a name badge off the console table and scribbles something on it. "Even if you're not shopping, you can say you still got it."

I scowl, then use the remote to turn on the TV. "Gross. Take it back—I don't want it."

Evie walks across the room and sits on my bed. "Hey, I know we didn't talk about it all day, and we're joking about guys who like you, but I know today is hard. I love you, so if you want me to stay and watch shitty shows and eat junk food, I will."

I smile genuinely but shake my head. "No. Go be with your people. This is the best day of your life . . . We both know that."

She laughs and shoves my body before she stands and talks like a vampire from old movies. "Thank you, I promise to have a fang-tastic time."

"Booo," I yell as she walks toward the door. "Terrible pun. Awful."

I pretend not to notice the way she second-guesses herself, giving me one last look before leaving, and then I'm alone. But truthfully, I'm not fit for consumption, so this is exactly where I should be for the night.

A heavy breath leaves my chest as I adjust my pillow again before I remember that I didn't lock the damn door. And I learned my lesson with that, so I throw off my blanket and start toward it, catching my sister's forgotten name badge out of the corner of my eye. The one she scribbled something on. It makes me grin because they must've told everyone to write down their favorite scary movie. She's written two: **THE BIRDS + MY SISTER'S LIFE.**

I laugh, swiping it up as I make my way to the front door and swing it open. I'm going to try and catch her. She couldn't have gotten too far.

But the moment it opens, a hand covers my mouth, and I'm pushed back inside.

# Chapter Twenty-Nine

***Camp Weonoke—thirty-two years prior***

> To Mine,
> We're 'til fucking death.
> —Billy

Sonny stormed into Billy's room. She was angry and yelling. "Stop writing these. Stop giving them to me."

Billy stood in the middle of the room in those familiar navy work pants while rubbing a towel over his head to dry his inky-black hair from the shower.

"You made a promise," he said, not looking at her.

Sonny's voice felt shrill to her, but she wasn't just angry; she was scared too.

"I said something stupid in the moment. It meant nothing. I love Davis and he loves me. Me and you . . . We aren't anything, Billy."

His voice was steady, and unwavering. "You made a promise."

"Billy, I ended things with you." She was pushing her point, but she still sounded like she was begging. "I told Davis about us. So you have to stop this, or he's going to hurt you."

"You. Made. A promise."

"Stop saying that," she yelled.

Sonny could feel her anger overflowing and spilling into her veins.

Billy looked up for the first time, and it made her breath halt because the hate in his eyes wasn't fleeting; it was real and palpable. He walked toward her in the small cabin, backing her into a wall.

"I told you we meant forever. Are you saying you lied to me when you said you were mine?" His two fingers forced her face up to his. "Look at me when you say it."

"Billy." Sonny's voice was shaky. "I'm sorry. I never wanted any of this. I didn't mean to hurt you."

His hand hit the wall next to her face, making her shoulders jump as she squeezed her eyes closed.

"I watched you, ya know." His deep voice sank over her, close to her ear, leaving goose bumps. "You let him fuck you."

Her heartbeat picked up an impossible pace. She hadn't realized he knew.

"Were you thinking about me?"

She wouldn't answer. Billy was fueled by cruelty. It was quiet and deep, and it always hid the rage he felt underneath.

"Say it," he snapped, making her cringe and her eyes stay shut.

She couldn't say that. She'd betrayed Davis in the past, but she wouldn't do that now.

"Billy, please . . ." she whispered.

"Say it," he gritted out as he grabbed her jaw, and it hurt. "Open your eyes. Look at me."

She did, but he brought his fingers to her lips, forcing them to move as he made his voice higher pitched.

"'I want you to fuck me, Billy. I love you, Billy.'"

Tears had sprung to her eyes now. And even though she fought him, swatting at his hands in an attempt to make him stop, he wouldn't.

He continued speaking for her, saying disgusting, crude things, until he gripped her cheeks between his fingers so violently a sob ripped from her chest.

"You made a promise," he threatened. "And that meant forever."

With his free hand, he began unbuckling her jeans. He was going to hurt her, and unlike the other times he'd been mean, this would leave a lasting mark.

"You want to be a whore? I'll treat you like one."

She tried to shake her head, but he was staring into her eyes as he held her in place against the cabin wall. There was no escape, and each button that popped on her jeans was like a countdown to hell.

"Say it . . ." he whispered as he licked her bottom lip, making her squeal in disgust. "Tell me you want me to fuck you."

He would take her no matter what she said, so he would never get the satisfaction.

"Say it."

She refused. He slapped her.

The stings ignited across her face before he kissed it, speaking softly against her skin and making the bile rise in her throat.

"I'm sorry. I'm sorry," he said. His fingers felt rough against her skin, and it made her sick. "I just wanted you to say it because you hurt me with everything you did. And I love you too. Not just him."

He knew nothing of love, only manipulation.

Billy's eyes met hers. "But if you tell me you love me, I won't touch you. I won't be angry anymore."

She didn't want him to touch her, so she swallowed her pride and her loyalty to Davis in exchange for survival.

But her voice was barely her own. Her eyes looked away as she said it. "I love you."

He shook his head and hit the wall again. "Say my name."

More tears fell from her eyes. "I love you . . . Billy."

He grinned, then flattened his tongue against her cheek and licked her tears.

"Get on the bed."

Fear shot through her, but as he tossed her on the mattress, the cabin door flew open, and Davis stepped inside.

"Get the fuck off my girlfriend."

Sonny screamed because Davis was on Billy in an instant, hitting him in the face with his fists. Blood splattered her cheek before Davis called for his friends.

More boys crowded the small room, but for some reason all she could focus on was the loose nail that had popped up on a floorboard.

"Are you okay?" she finally heard as her face met Davis's.

He was breathing hard as his friends held Billy by the arms.

Billy's beaten body sagged, and his face was turned toward the ground. She stared at him but couldn't find any sympathy to give him. He was going to hurt her, in the worst way.

Davis reached for Sonny, but she recoiled, her fear still fresh.

"It's okay. Your face is bruised."

This time she let him touch her, then pull her into his arms. Davis walked her past Billy, giving orders to the other boys.

"He put marks on her—make sure we repay the favor, then take him to the boathouse. I'll meet you there."

She didn't know what any of that meant, but as they walked out the front door, with her snuggled in Davis's arms, she looked back to see them pressing Billy's face into that loose nail just before he screamed.

# Chapter Thirty

## Noah

Goldie's eyes are like saucers as she stares back at me before she starts swinging.

"Fuck," I yelp, holding my arms in front of my face as she slaps them before trying and succeeding to kick me.

She steps away quickly, creating space between us, as I hold out my hand, a finger up.

"Shh. Don't scream . . ."

Her eyes are wild as she searches the room. She's definitely looking for a weapon, and I'm beginning to wonder if maybe she's going to be the one who does the job and puts me in the ground. I see her eyebrows raise before she swipes up a fake knife off a console table.

My brows start to draw together because it's one of those plastic ones that have fake blood dripping on the inside, but then I still my expression because I'm not trying to make her any angrier.

"What the fuck are you doing?" she shrieks, making me wince. I put my fingers to my lips to shush her again, because I need her to calm down and be quiet.

"Killer . . ." I say calmly, but she stabs the knife at me, making her hair bounce with the way her body jerks ragefully.

"Don't call me that . . . Why are you here?"

My hands are out in front of me as I try to urge her to be calm, but it's not working.

"You need to listen to me . . ."

She scoffs, drawing her head back. "Fuck you. I need to listen to you? Who do you think you are, coming in here and ordering me around? Because I know who you're not—my boyfriend, my fiancé, a guy who refrains from lying . . . Should I keep going?"

Jesus Christ. I'm going to have to pick her up and throw her over my shoulder, while she literally tries to stab me in the back, to get her the hell out of here.

She growls, making my eyes pop open wider.

"And how did you even know I was here?"

Shit. I take a step forward, wanting to explain, but she scowls at me, so I step back. "Okay . . . I'm not going to hurt you. I just need to talk, but I'd preferably like to do that *away* from this camp."

She laughs, but it's a mix between panic and a callout of what she clearly thinks is my audacity.

"You're not going to hurt me?" The face she makes is half smile, half *I hate you.* Oh shit. "Says the fucking guy who just had his hand over my mouth." Her voice raises way too loud. "And broke my fucking heart!"

"Baby, I didn't want you to scream," I rush out, instinctually closing the distance between us.

Her eyes pop out of her head as she hurries backward, and I see it in her eyes.

She's going to scream for help.

Goldie's mouth opens, and I know it's coming, so I pounce, sealing my palm over her mouth again and wrapping my other hand around her body. Our eyes are locked, both pleading with the other.

She's trembling and I hate it, but I need her to listen. But then her eyes move down, and I realize in the moment that she's fake stabbed me.

Damn. My girl actually stabbed me.

"Okay . . ." I breathe out as I look back at her. "If you're done fake murdering me, I'd like to talk." I swallow. "I promise I am not here to hurt you, Goldie. But you're in danger, and I need to get you and your sister out of here."

Her brows draw together, and I can feel her chest slowing as she stares up at me. Seconds tick by as we just stare at each other. And I know that holding her like this isn't ideal, but it's really nice to be close to her again.

I let out a breath and take advantage of the silence.

"There's a lot to say, but this isn't what you think . . . I'm not the bad guy, killer. But someone dangerous *is* here, and I think he wants to hurt you, and maybe Evie too. So we have to get the fuck out of here, okay?"

I hear and feel the fake knife retract from my gut.

But when she doesn't say anything, I realize my hand is still in place over her mouth.

"I'm gonna take my hand away now. No more screaming . . . Nod if you understand."

She hesitates, then nods.

I take a deep breath and slowly remove my hand as we never break eye contact. You could cut the tension with a knife. Her lips part as she breathes steadier and then slowly lifts her hand, making me tense before she brushes her hair from her face.

Her voice is quiet as she stares up at me. "How am I supposed to trust you?"

I frown because what I want to say is, *Because you know me.* But that's not true anymore. So I go with reason.

"Why would I come all the way out here just to lie to you? How do I gain in that?"

She only blinks once before this time she cuts me with her words. "I don't know . . . Why would you lie about who you are for a whole fucking year?"

My tongue darts out as I lick my bottom lip. "Killer . . ." She raises an eyebrow. I drop the nickname. "Goldie, I promise I'll tell you everything if you just come with me. Time is actually of the essence."

She shakes her head and crosses her arms, and it's a look I know all too well. It's the equivalent of *You're fucked.*

"No," she levels. "Tell me everything right now, and then I'll decide whether I'm leaving with you or we're fighting to the death."

"Jesus," I breathe out as I run my hands through my hair, my cool breaking. "This is not the time to be stubborn."

A scream from outside quickly draws my head over my shoulder. And that means like an amateur, I take my eyes off her. The next thing I know, the sound of the bathroom door shutting and locking echoes through the small space.

"Goddammit," I grit through clenched teeth before banging on the door. "Goldie, I'm not fucking playing. We need to get out of here."

"You're a criminal," she yells. "You stalked me, and now you're trying to kidnap me."

I bang on the door again. "No. I'm not. Will you please use your head? This is fucking ridiculous. I'll knock the door down."

I step back as I eye it up . . . *Jesus, are those real logs?*

She doesn't just yell back at me; fury oozes off each word.

"Are you calling me stupid? Fuck you, Noah! You don't even know how to spell 'convenient.'"

I throw my arms in the air. "Nobody spells that correctly. Would you please just come out of the goddamn bathroom."

I'm met with silence, which makes my fucking jaw clench.

"Goldie!" I take in a deep breath, letting it whoosh out before I drop my forehead against the door. "Baby, please . . ."

She's giving me the silent treatment, and unless I can put on another hundred or so pounds, there's no way I'm getting past this door and keeping the use of my shoulder.

Something's got to give. *Fuck it.*

"You want the truth . . . fine. I'm scared to death. There are truly fucked-up things in my past that are putting you in harm's way. And I couldn't ever tell you because I was afraid of losing you. Joke's on me, though, right, because that's exactly what happened anyway. I fucking love you, killer. I haven't been able to eat or think clearly without you. This week's been torture, but I swear I stayed away to try and keep you safe. So please just let me get you out of here, and I'll explain everything with all the finest detail you want."

My palm presses to the door as I wait for her to say something. To say anything. She doesn't understand what this feels like, for her to look at me the way she does. It's hell.

"Baby . . ." I say again, waiting, but the front door swings open, and I spin around, meeting Chase's face.

"What are you doing? You're supposed to be the lookout."

His forehead wrinkles. "Well, your girl just ran by in her pajamas, flipping me the bird, so look out."

"Fuck," I groan, and run past him, out the front door.

"She's faster than I thought," he yells at my back. "The chances someone picks her off are slim."

I bark back, "Get to the party and get Evie . . ."

If we don't die tonight, Goldie's going to be the death of me.

My feet carry me quickly as I weave through the crowd, getting glimpses of her red hair as she walks quickly ahead of me.

She glances back at me as I call out her name. "Goldie, wait."

My heart is beating a mile a minute because everywhere I look, someone poses a threat. This place is fucking unreal. Chase wasn't wrong when he said Halloween was the perfect night for a serial killer to hide out in the open.

Everywhere I look, I see ten new versions of Billy.

There are just too many knives, masks, and hammers. Someone's even carrying a chainsaw. I can't tell what's real or fake. And that makes my pulse speed up even faster.

I swear to god, this is just my luck. Imminent death is everywhere, and my girlfriend won't stop fucking running away.

"Killer," I yell louder, pushing past a guy in a Ghostface mask, but the crowd goes wild around me, chanting her nickname and yelling out as if it's a joke.

"Yeah, killer" . . . "I'm a killer" . . . "Kill me."

She looks over her shoulder one last time before disappearing around the corner of a building, so I shove through two people, hearing them gripe "Hey!" before I cut through the rest of the crowd to where she went.

As soon as I get into the shadows between the two buildings, I catch only a glimpse of her, because she closes a door behind her. Instead of running, I glance over my shoulder ensuring nobody's following me before heading in her direction, because I don't know what I'm about to walk in on. I think I saw the word "Cafeteria" on the front . . . So this time there could be real knives.

I get to the door, pulling it open slowly before sliding inside, then quietly close it behind me. I'm in a kitchen.

The room's dark but not pitch black. So I stand for a moment and let my eyes adjust before I look around for her.

"Goldie," I whisper cautiously, putting one foot in front of the other as I walk deeper into the space. "I swear to god, I am not here to hurt you."

I reach carefully into my back pocket and pull out my phone, but as I bring it to my face, the light gives away my exact location. I hear a grunt from my left side before something hard nails me right in the shoulder.

"Fuck." I drop my phone as I grab my shoulder, immediately tensing both of them. "What the hell are you doing?"

Another can whizzes by me, making me jump out of the way.

"I know what you did to the apartment," she yells before hitting me in the thigh, making me yell again. "You lied about who you are. You destroyed everything I own. You tracked me down to the middle of nowhere. And you think that I'm going to go without a fight? Clearly, neither of us knew the other."

This time a can narrowly misses my face.

"Jesus Christ," I bellow. "You're the one throwing shit at me, and I'm the dangerous one?" I'm rubbing my shoulder and partially limping from the charley horse I now have as I notice my phone is close by her feet. "Just open my phone and look at the top message. It's proof I'm here for what I say I'm here for."

She's still holding a can up by her head, aimed right at me. "Why would I do that? I'm not listening to anything you tell me."

I huff a laugh as I make my way a foot and a half over to a chair, flinching when she cocks the can back more.

"Easy, killer. I haven't actively avoided dying for most of my life to have my headstone read, 'Killed by creamed corn.'" I sit and wave a hand at the damn phone. "Would you please just look at the text?"

Goldie keeps her eyes on me as she slowly bends down and swipes my phone up quickly.

"Fine, but don't move a muscle, because I've got a whole fucking stack of cans over here."

I hold up my hands in surrender before I let out a breath and begin rubbing the knot out of my thigh.

Her eyes volley between me and the screen as she swipes it open, and I watch her thumb hit the message icon.

I chuckle at the irony . . . I'm the secretive one, but I don't have a password on my phone. She looks at me, confused.

"Why am I looking at a picture of myself, Noah?" I don't miss the way she winces when she says my name. "Did you take this this morning? That was you in the woods?"

I shake my head, relaxing back in my chair. "No. Look at the time stamp, Golds. I got that this afternoon after I found that PI who's been looking into your birth parents. He was murdered in his car."

She gasps, her eyes opening wider as her mouth stays agape.

"Before you get ahead of yourself . . ." My words are tinged with anger masking the hurt, because the way she's looking at me with so much fear makes me sick to my stomach. "Chase was with me when I found Matthew Wright. You can see in another text that he invited me there . . . Go on, look. So, if I did it, I'm really bad at crime. Plus, Chase has been with me every day for the last week, so . . ."

If I hated the way she looked at me before, I hate the look she's giving me now even more. The one where she isn't even ashamed that she thought I could've done something like that in the first place.

I jerk my chin toward the phone. "Whoever sent that to me was letting me know that they could get to you. I made it my mission to get here first."

She frowns like she's going to say something, so I lift my hand to stop her. "And before you ask me how I found you, that was also Chase. He recognized the fucking logo on the front of the shirt you had on." I let out an exhale. "He recognized it from a picture of my mother that was left stabbed to our front door after the apartment had been destroyed . . ."

Goldie cuts in, narrowing her eyes at me. "Your mother? Why would she have a Camp Weonoke shirt on?"

I lock eyes with her. "Because she was here around thirty years ago."

Goldie shakes her head and looks down. I can see her thoughts playing out on her face, and they seem to be contradicting each other because she looks confused. Like she doesn't know what to believe. Until her eyes lift and lock to mine.

"Five people were killed . . . in the massacre here."

My head draws back slightly, confused how she knows. "My mom was the only survivor."

Goldie's chest moves up and down faster. "Was it the groundskeeper? Someone from Darkwater Bay?"

I run my hand through my hair as I stand up again, but take a step away from her so she knows she's safe.

Our eyes are still connected, never leaving.

"How do you know that?" I don't give her time to answer because I shouldn't be asking anything of her. She deserves the truth.

I hold up my hand to stop her. "I'm sorry I lied to you. I can pretend it was for your own good, but lying is about being a coward. I was too afraid to lose you, to trust that you would stay. The groundskeeper was named William Bromley. He's my father. And he's alive."

Even in the dim room, I can see her eyes shining with the intrusion of her tears.

"I never knew myself as Davis. That version of me lived behind so many locks. So when I invented Noah, it didn't feel like a lie. I just wanted to start again. To become who I wanted to be on my terms without the baggage of my past."

I run a hand through my hair, hating how even though she's placed the can she was holding on a counter next to her, she's still protecting herself by crossing her arms.

"Goldie . . ." My eyes don't leave hers because I need her to really look at me. "I grew up watching my mother always looking over her shoulder. My boogeyman was my dad. I thought I was protecting us, and I ruined us instead. And I put you in danger. You should never forgive me, but please let me get you out of here. It's not safe. He's here."

Silence stretches out between us as her eyes search mine and words keep tumbling from my lips. "He'll kill you just because I love you. And Goldie, I do love you. With every goddamn fiber of my being. Even when I lied. When I hid. I don't exist without you. But that's okay because I can let Noah die if I know you'll be able to walk away and live the life you deserve." My eyes drop to the floor before I clear my throat, hoping my voice doesn't break. "You deserve it all. You deserve the fucking world . . ."

I take a step toward her on instinct, because she's my comfort and I feel like I'll never recover from this. From letting her go.

But her brows draw together, and her eyes go to my feet. She's still scared of me.

"Please trust me." The shakiness of my voice makes me clear it again. "I'm not my father. I would never hurt you."

The lump in my throat grows with the realization that she may not believe that. I've made the girl I would die for unable to see me anymore. She was always the only one. That's my real penance for these crimes.

Her arms fall to her side, my phone still in her hand, before she shakes her head and rushes toward me.

"I know you wouldn't." She breathes, "Noah, I'll always know that."

Before I can speak, her arms are around my neck and mine are wrapped around her waist as I lift her off the ground. It almost buckles me to my knees. My hands spread across her back, holding her tightly and inhaling her scent.

She shifts her head, bringing her lips to mine. We're hungry and joyous, savoring the seconds because the distance has felt like a lifetime.

"I love you," I whisper between our kisses. "I'm sorry. I'm so sorry."

She pulls away, her palms pressed to my cheeks. "You can make it up to me later with your life story . . . Let's get Evie and get out of here because you're right—he's here. And I think he has help."

*Holy fuck.*

A heavy breath leaves my body as I place her back on the ground. She turns her back to me as she heads toward the door she snuck in before looking back and holding out her hand. "Are you coming?"

I'm right behind her. Our fingers weave together as we head toward the party, the only thought in my mind cocked and loaded.

Tonight, I'm going to kill my father.

# Chapter Thirty-One

## Goldie

My hand in Noah's feels like a homecoming.

Yes, I know he lied, and I know there are still a thousand questions to be answered, but what I also know is he had a reason for lying.

A reason that ran so deep and scared him so much that he betrayed my trust and was still willing to risk his own life to come here and get me.

"Over there," I say breathlessly, pointing to another set of doors besides the main entrance to the hall the party is being held in because the line is too long.

Too long for us to wait. Like he said, time is of the essence.

Noah's leading me, walking quickly, making me almost jog to keep up. As we near the door, he looks around to make sure nobody is watching before he grabs the door, pulls it open, and leads me through first.

*That was slick.*

The moment we're inside, the music's blaring and there are people everywhere dressed in all manner of costumes. They're dancing, drinking, partying—enjoying Halloween.

But, Jesus, they have no idea that there's something heinous lurking.

"What is she dressed as?" Noah says, leaning in so I can hear him better.

I shake my head, looking out around the crowd. "A vampire."

"Great," he levels sarcastically. "That should be easy enough."

As he says it, a group of women with fangs and red contacts walk by us. I give an empty kind of desperate laugh as I squeeze his hand tighter, feeling my fear grow by the second.

"Do you think whoever is after us would try something here . . . and now?" I question, hoping for an answer that will make my blood pressure lower.

"Yeah. Especially tonight. Look around . . ."

I frown because people are pretending to kill each other in all the corners of the room. There's enough fake blood to hide any of the real kind. Fuck.

*So much for lower blood pressure.*

We're making our way through the crowd with more urgency as I whip my head around, desperately looking for Evie. There are just too many people packed in here.

"Evie," I yell, but the music's too loud for her to ever hear me.

But Noah leans down to my ear again. "Baby, don't yell. If they're close, you'll bring attention to us."

I'm suddenly rocked with a wave of fear as I look around. Noah's hand on the small of my back is the only anchor I have keeping me from getting swept away. I swear to god, all I want to do is turn around, wrap my arms around him, and hide my face in his chest. Surely then all of this would go away.

A shaky breath leaves me before Noah stops me, pulling me into a giant hug. It's like he's read my thoughts. My chin quivers, but I inhale him.

Fuck. I'm feeling too much—fear, relief, happiness, and terror all at once.

He kisses the top of my head before I turn my chin up toward him.

"Killer, I promise we're going to be okay." His hands gently rub my shoulders as he pushes me away just enough to really take me in. "Believe me?"

*Damn me to hell, but I do.*

I nod, but another thought has my hands sliding up his chest and hooking around his neck before pulling him down to me.

*If we do die, I'm kissing him one more time.*

Noah's lips seal over mine, and I swear, we both sigh into each other as he wraps his arms around me, and we kiss. Faintly, because all my senses are stolen by Noah, I hear our song play: "These Dreams," by Heart.

He pulls away, half a smile crooking his mouth. "I think it's a sign."

I smile too.

His hand slides back into mine before we turn, looking back out to the crowd and pulling strength from each other.

Out of the corner of my eye, I notice someone onstage tapping a mic. They must be getting ready to start the scene from that damn movie my sister was talking about.

A light bulb goes off.

"Noah." I tap his arm to gain his attention and point to the stage, but he shakes his head.

"It's going to take too long to find her this way," I press, but he's not listening, so I tug my hand from him and dart away, zipping through the crowd before he can stop me.

I don't care if it brings attention to us. It'll help me find my sister, and then we can get the hell out of here. But the moment I make it to the stairs up to the stage, Noah grabs my waist, having followed behind closely.

"Noah, we could find her quicker."

He urges me back down. "It'll put a fucking spotlight on you."

But I refuse to listen. I shove his hands off me and run up onto the stage anyway before looking back at him.

"Get to her faster than he does," I rush out, but he looks panicked as he takes the stairs too.

I rush to the microphone and push past the guy standing there before I grip it with my hands. The guy tries to pull it back, cursing me for being onstage, but I ignore him and hold on to it for dear life.

"Evie." My voice is louder than I expect as it echoes through the room, which makes me blanch, but I say it again as I struggle to keep the microphone in hand. "Evie Monroe."

The crowd begins to stare at me, and the music that was playing fades out. All their eyes are focused directly on me. *Fuck.* Noah was right. I may as well have an arrow over my head, but from up on the stage, I can see the whole crowd.

The crew guy manhandles the mic away and walks the setup offstage as I head toward Noah. I'm searching and so is he until my gasp gets his attention.

I see my sister in the back of the room. She's waving at me.

"Noah, she's there," I say, pointing in her direction.

His face whips away from mine, and he cups his hands around his mouth as he bellows, "Chase!"

My eyes search frantically, then see my favorite chef give us a thumbs-up as he hauls ass her way.

"Oh god," I rush out as my shoulders sag, because it finally feels like everything's going to be okay.

But as I step toward Noah, I hear my name. I turn and lock eyes with a familiar face. The man of the hour.

Remus walks toward me, but Noah's already onstage next to me. The kindness that's usually on Remus's face is gone, replaced with animosity as he stares directly at Noah.

Noah's arm moves in front of me protectively, guiding me back just behind him.

"What are you doing, Goldie? You're not supposed to be up here," Remus says as his eyes go to mine before returning to Noah's.

I look up at Noah's profile and see his jaw tensing before I whisper my words out on a very shaky breath. "That's him. That's the guy who I think sent you the picture."

Noah's face darts to mine. A frown forms before he ever so slightly shakes his head like I'm wrong.

Remus asks Noah how he got to the camp, since he doesn't recognize him, but I'm lost in my thoughts.

*I don't understand. Remus is who told me this story. Remus is who seemed too attached . . . too callous about the deaths. He gave me the shirt and knew I was taking a hike.*

My lips part to say as much to Noah, but he looks away toward the sound of heavy footsteps joining us. I follow his gaze to another man coming in behind Remus, who is looking down at his phone.

Ice-cold chills slice through my veins because I've seen him before too.

This man was standing in my doorway the day I forgot to lock it.

"Oh my god . . ." I rush out.

Noah's chest is heaving, and his muscles feel like stone as he stares past Remus at the man who still occasionally visits my nightmares. My eyes volley between the transient and Remus before finally landing on Noah.

"Do you know him?"

Noah nods. "That's my father."

Everything happens in slow motion. Remus looks up and smiles at me before the man steps in behind him and takes him by the chin. And the knife slices straight across his throat.

# Chapter Thirty-Two

## Noah

Goldie's screaming, her hands gripping my shirt and digging into my back. But I'm unmoving as I watch the man she thought I was here for stumble a few steps. He gasps for air, but it's only a gurgle as blood pours from his neck before he drops to his knees and falls dead.

There's not a sound in the room as people look at each other, trying to figure reality from fiction.

Goldie's crying, her face pressed to my side, making my body sway, as Billy wipes the blood on his knife over his sleeve before smiling.

My eyes bore into his, all my rage circling and gathering into a storm. He tried to kill my mother. He tried to kill me. And he came here to kill my girl . . . I'm going to make him truly hurt for that.

A girl from the crowd close to the stage lifts to her tiptoes and stares closer at the dead body, then reaches out and touches the puddle of blood that's pooled.

She rubs her fingers together before the horror of reality sets in, and she lets out a bloodcurdling scream.

People scatter.

They're running and pushing each other out of the way, desperate to get to the exit, as Goldie and I stand on the stage. Five feet away from my father.

He tilts his head, his eyes landing on Goldie.

"The lovers," he says, like it's some kind of inside joke. "Aren't you going to ask how I found you?"

I press my palm against Goldie's hip, trying to get her to move back behind me, but her feet barely move. She's frozen with fear as she clutches my arm, but I want her away from him and the blood on the ground, slowly creeping closer.

My eyes narrow as I watch the way Billy's staring at her, taking her all in like he's curious.

"Don't fucking look at her," I bark. "And I don't give a shit how you found me."

His eyes instantly meet mine as he points the tip of the knife at me, wagging it. "You know I'd almost like you if I didn't wonder so much about what your fucking insides looked like."

Goldie finally follows my silent instruction and moves behind me, burying her face into the back of my arm.

Billy takes a step forward, and I match it backward, moving her too.

"She has nothing to do with this. It's between me and you . . . father to son. So why don't you just let her go? And we can battle it out right here."

I glance at the room and see it clear out, and an ache begins inside me. I want to kill him, and that's exactly what I'm going to do.

Billy laughs with his head tilted back, his face to the ceiling. "Is that what you think? That I'm here for you?" His head drops back down. "Is that what your slut mother told you?"

My hands ball into fists as I press my lips together, breathing heavily through my nose.

"It's what I know," I growl back. "She told me you'd never share her."

He pats the butcher knife against his leg. "Your mother was a used-up whore who spread her legs for rich boys . . ."

I bristle, which seems to please him.

"Oh, this is a gift to me," he hisses, whiplashing into a new emotion. I look away, but only for a second to gauge how close we are to the stairs, but he moves his head to maintain our eye contact. "You've gone your whole life thinking of yourself as some kind of prodigal son . . . waiting for my return."

I'm silent as I stand straight, my spine like steel, because he can try and drag her name through the mud, but he knows I know the truth.

He grins before scraping his teeth over his bottom lip.

"This is going to feel almost as good as when I gut you, groin to sternum." He drags the knife up his body to his neck in demonstration as his eyes bore into mine. "Emerson was never my whore. You're named after your daddy, boy." He points the knife at me, then slowly moves it toward Goldie. "I'm not your father. I'm hers."

What the fuck.

I can't move. My mouth has fallen open, and I'm unsure if my heart is even beating. I'm frozen, but I can still feel Goldie's chest moving up and down quickly against my arm.

She's not crying anymore. She's silent.

My face slowly turns to hers, seeing shock and fear etched over her features.

"No . . ." She shakes her head and looks at me before facing him. "That's a lie."

He tsks, grinning evilly. "Now don't go being disrespectful to your papa, or I won't let you watch as I spill his insides all over the fucking floor."

I reach back to try and stop her from moving, but she does anyway, coming to stand next to me.

"You can't be my father. You're lying. You just know I was adopted, and you're trying to hurt Noah."

He snaps, stabbing the knife into the air as he barks, "I don't lie." Then he smiles again. "That's your little Prince Charming."

I frown as he starts to pace small steps back and forth, not taking his eyes off us. "I tried . . ." He lifts his hands, shrugging. "I tried to get over her. But when the woman you love leaves you with this"—he tugs his shirt down, exposing a treacherous-looking scar on his chest—"you can't ever really forget her."

The tip of the knife in his hand is beginning to cut a hole in his pants as he keeps sticking it more and more aggressively.

"His dad"—Billy points at me, then stops in place again—"he tried to kill me. He beat me until all I could taste was my own blood; then he held me underwater until I pretended to stop breathing. But I got away . . ."

His voice trails off and his eyes grow hooded like he's in the memory, reliving the way he killed everyone, before he blinks a few times and picks up where he left off.

"I got away and went north. Even met a girl, but she was just like all the others before her. She never stopped crying. Always saying, 'Please don't. Stop, it hurts.'"

Goldie's hand shoots to cover her mouth, disgusted by what he's saying and maybe understanding that he's talking about torturing her biological mother.

Billy's head tilts. "She's not with us anymore." He locks eyes with Goldie. "But that's the price you pay when you abandon your child to pigs."

Goldie gasps, and I know she believes him like I do. Where she was left isn't in the public record. He takes another step forward, into the blood on the floor.

But Goldie stands there, shaking her head.

"Don't you get it, sunshine? I did this for you . . ." Goldie scowls as she stares at him. "For my girl. I did all of this for you so we can be together."

"You're a fucking psycho," she snaps.

He growls violently before dropping down into a squat by the body on the floor. He stabs it quickly in succession before he lets out a deep breath and pants, almost singing his words. "Don't disrespect your father, Goldie."

"You're not my father," she counters, but in all the time she's been pushing back, I've been moving us back toward the stairs.

Billy smiles wide and turns his head just enough that we both see the sun birthmark behind his ear. Just like hers.

"Then explain this."

He's not looking at us, so I take the opportunity to whisper "Go" to Goldie as I turn her around and push her toward the stairs. Without hesitation, she listens, tearing away from me and running.

"Bitch," he thunders, lunging past the body and straight for her, but I've already anticipated him and throw my body between them.

The feeling of hot iron seers my skin directly across my left bicep. I groan but swing a right hook, hearing the crack against his fucking jaw before I cover my hand over the already-bleeding wound.

"Fuck," he yells as his body twists and the knife goes flying, skidding across the floor.

I turn and run, flying down the stairs as I hear her yell my name.

"Noah. Over here."

Goldie's waiting by the doors as I make it to her. I glance back and see Billy standing on the stage with his knife back in his hand before we run out into the night.

I am going to kill him tonight, but first I'm getting her the fuck out of here.

Everything's happening quickly. I'm barking directions, telling her how to get to the van as she rushes out, "Oh my god, Noah. You're bleeding."

Chase's van comes into view just as he and Evie come running toward us.

"She wouldn't leave until she found G," Chase yells as an explanation for why the van hasn't already been started.

"What is happening?" Evie yells, grabbing her sister by the shoulders to ensure she's unharmed.

"Holy fuck, Noah," Chase thunders. "You're fucking cut." He looks at Evie and points to the Dracula cape she's wearing. "Gimme that thing."

She takes it off, but I'm trying to talk over them, saying we need to get the fuck out of here, but nobody is listening. Chase rips the material before wrapping it around my arm and tying it, making me groan deeply.

"Did Billy do this?" he whispers, and I nod.

"We have to go. Now."

Evie points at me. "Fuck you and your daddy issues. This is your fault. You should stay."

Goldie shakes her head, but I ignore Evie's words because Billy may not be my daddy issue anymore, but I absolutely plan to stay.

I'm ushering Goldie toward the van as Chase winces. "Sorry, I told her. She's kinda scary when she wants info."

I look around to try to see if Billy's coming as we get to the van doors, but Goldie makes everyone stop in their place. "Billy's my dad . . . my biological one."

Evie's eyes grow wide. "What the heck are you talking about, Golds?"

I shake my head. "We can talk about it in the van. Let's go. Come on."

Chase bursts into action by pulling the handle and sliding open the door, but the girls are just staring at each other.

"Get in," Chase presses, pushing Evie, but she pushes him back. "Okay . . . I'm trying to keep you alive. Work with me?"

"I'll explain later," Goldie reassures her. "But none of this is Noah's fault."

We all hurry into the van and lock the doors before Chase looks at me and nods in acknowledgment of the plan. I nod back as he throws it into reverse.

A loud succession of thuds accompanies the bouncing of the van.

*Fuck,* I think as Chase says it aloud. He looks at me. "He cut the tires. The fucking tires are flat."

"Shit." I smack the dash as Evie begins to cry. Goldie's rubbing her back, telling her everything's going to be okay, but I'm not so sure anymore.

"What are we supposed to do?" Chase breathes out too quickly.

I'm trying to think, but we're in the middle of the woods with a guy hell-bent on killing us.

Goldie touches my shoulder. "Everyone here has their phones, so I'm positive the police have been called. We just need to hide long enough for them to get here."

Chase turns in his seat. "You guys have been here for days—what are some places he wouldn't find us?"

"He knows this camp like the back of his hand," I level, feeling the stinging in my arm again.

Evie's mumbling to herself, rocking in her seat, fear taking over. "We're gonna die. Golds, we're gonna die."

Goldie's looking down as she thinks before her face snaps up. "There's a boathouse. I know he knows it . . . But I heard the setup crew talking about wanting to take the boat out. They just couldn't find the keys."

"We're gonna die," Evie continues to mumble, crying a little more.

"Hey," Chase barks as he looks in the rearview mirror. "You're not fucking dying tonight, you hear me? Stop crying and get mean because the only thing that's gonna fucking kill you is my charm."

She swallows and nods, then wipes her tears as they hold eyes for another long second.

I let out a breath. "Well, if that's gonna be true, then we need to get the fuck out of here because we're sitting ducks. Anyone know how to hot-wire a boat? Let's make the motherfucker have to swim to us if he wants us dead."

Chase chuckles, raising his hand. "It's literally in the rich kid handbook: 'How to steal your dad's boat to get girls.'"

Goldie grabs Evie's hand before I open my door quietly and look around. I go to the side of the van and open it for the girls, who pile out quickly. I take Goldie's hand, and Chase grabs Evie's.

I motion my head toward the camp, where the main path forks—one leads to the boathouse, and the other leads to the entrance. We run quietly, not trying to make any noise as we stick to all the shadows.

The grounds that were filled with people a half hour earlier are now desolate. Every light is off in every cabin. People are hiding. I press my back to one of the cabins, and everyone else does the same before I hesitantly poke my head out to the open area and peer up and down.

"It's clear," I whisper.

But I can hear whoever's inside the cabin crying, and for a fleeting moment, I wonder if they would let us in. Maybe we should just hide.

Except I know better. They won't, because I wouldn't either.

Our steps start off slow as we stay in single file, until we're too exposed out in the middle, so I pick up the pace to run past a large tree stump and lead us to the boathouse, but Goldie screams.

We all skid to a stop at the edge of the forked paths. In the distance, about thirty yards away, blocking our salvation, is Billy.

He's standing and waiting, this time wearing a fucking hockey mask. The glint of the knife by his side gives it away.

"Go . . ." I say over stuttered breaths as I guide Goldie sideways. "Go to the cabin."

My head's the last to turn, but as it does, I see Goldie's hands shoot over her mouth, capturing her gasp. "He's there too."

Billy's standing by the girls' cabin. Same fucking mask, same knife.

"Oh my god. Someone's working with him," Goldie rushes out.

"Or he's a fucking gremlin, and someone threw water on him," Chase throws out. He turns around and adds, "What about the offi—"

But he doesn't finish what he's saying because he lifts a hand, pointing in the direction he's looking, as his chest rises and falls too quickly.

Our collective heads whip right and . . . *Billy*.

Panic is taking over. We're all shifting around between the three paths, fear compounding because we're surrounded. He's everywhere.

"Noah . . . how . . ." Goldie whispers.

I shake my head. "I don't know."

"What are we gonna do?" Chase presses.

But Evie walks out in front of us. She points and wags her finger as she looks from side to side and then in front of us.

"Oh my god . . . oh my god," she blurts out. "Only one of these is real. I made him." We all look at her in confusion, so she shakes her head and clarifies. "I made these two dummies to look like Michael Myers. They were meant to be in the woods and scare people. I put one by the bonfire"—she points toward where the offices are—"and one out by the boathouse."

We all look in that direction.

The moon shines down as we stand there for what feels like minutes. But it's only seconds as we deliberate silently, because two roads lead to freedom and one leads to death.

"Can you tell which ones are fake?" Goldie whispers.

Evie shakes her head with both hands on the sides of her face as she looks to the men. She blows out a harsh breath.

"Do you have a designer tell? Look for that?"

"No," she draws out. "I can't tell. Fuck."

"Come on, there's gotta be something," Chase adds.

But she starts to cry again. "I don't . . . oh my god." Her breathing starts picking up pace as she keeps looking between the paths. She's panicking. "I can't tell. Oh my god. I just don't . . . I just don't know."

Chase pulls her into his arms and whispers down to her. I can't hear what he says, but she lets him hold her while she repeats "I'm sorry," over and over.

"Fuck this," I rush out and turn to Goldie, cradling her face. "You're going to go back to your cabin and lock the door. Do you hear me?" She's shaking her head, already saying no, but I keep talking. "Take your sister back . . ."

"Noah . . . no."

I nod reassuringly. "Take her back. Chase will go with you to protect you."

Tears begin to stream down her face. "No . . . I'm not doing that." She slaps her hands against my chest. "You're not gonna be the fucking hero, Noah. We save each other tonight."

I stare into her eyes, rubbing my thumb over her wet cheek. "It's okay, baby. I'll be fine. This has to end, and I'm the one who needs to do it."

She grips my wrists and repeats herself, just a little quieter. "We save each other, do you hear me? I love you, and I don't want to live without you."

A heavy breath leaves me because I feel the same, but also I can't live knowing I've put her in harm's way. If something happens to her, it would only be because I'd let it. That'll never be her story.

But before I can say any more, Evie pipes up.

"And I'm not living without my sister, so if she stays, you're stuck with me too."

I scoff, shaking my head as the girls look at Chase. He shrugs.

"I feel like I've made my position clear on this." Chase locks eyes with me. "We ride, we die together. You're the Martin to my Will. Also, in case anyone's interested, I vote we head to the boathouse. It's four against one, and I think we can take him."

Both girls raise their hands, saying, "Me too."

"You're all nuts."

"We're all family," Goldie counters.

I don't have the emotional bandwidth to let that sit for too long, but we need to live so I can show her how grateful I am for those three little words.

My head turns to look out at the miserable motherfucker waiting for us as I say, "Boathouse it is." My face swings back to Chase. "And for the record, you're the Martin to my Will."

"Code names." He grins.

"Here we go . . . Girls, watch our backs," I say to Goldie, feeling her turn around, her back to mine as Chase and Evie do the same, before we walk directly toward what could be our deaths.

The closer we come, the more the adrenaline builds, but it's still not enough to counteract the visceral fucking fear.

We're whispering among each other as we go through a hundred different plans, trying to strategize how we're going to fend off an attack.

Billy managed to kill five people after almost being killed, so I'm wishing we had a few more of us going in.

"I love you. It's still all clear back here," Goldie says quietly, and Evie agrees.

"I love you too," I whisper back.

"You make the best steak I've ever had," Evie offers to Chase, since we're doing endearments.

"Yes, I'll marry you," he answers back.

"Noah," Chase says, looking over at me, but he doesn't have to say anything else.

I can see it in his eyes—he's as afraid as I am but still willing to risk his life for me. I nod and then turn my face back to Billy.

Fuck, this is unnerving, walking step by step toward the thing you've had nightmares about your whole life. He still hasn't moved. And a part of me just wishes he'd fucking give himself away already.

"I'm done playing games, Billy. You wanted us here, so here we are, you motherfucker."

Silence bleeds out, and none of us move because there's no turning back. We've come as close as we can before the only way to the boathouse is through him.

Evie's voice is quiet, so only we can hear: "Maybe he's a fake one. Switch with me so I can get a closer look."

"No. Stay there," Chase orders, like when he's in the kitchen.

But I'm barely listening because the longer I stare at that hockey mask, the more I can feel it—the rage.

It's just like that night when I kissed Goldie in the alleyway. The rage is palpable, drawing me in toward him. I feel his hate, and his disgust. His disregard for life. I can feel him staring at us through that mask.

We're standing in front of the real Billy.

We picked the wrong path.

Goldie's hand tightens around my arm, and I know she's turned around.

That's when I see the knife.

Evie gasps, and slowly, as if he's trying to draw out the terror, Billy reaches up and removes his mask, then drops it to the floor.

"Gotcha."

He lunges forward, knife raised, but Chase and I are already running toward him. Billy spins, the knife slashing the air in front of him, making both of us jump back a few feet.

We stand off, staring at him as he glares back.

"Who wants to die first?" he asks.

Chase and I glance at each other, but Billy looks past us at Goldie.

"Here, kitty, kitty, kitty, kitty, kitty, kitty." He smiles at her. "Don't worry, sunshine. I'm only gonna kill these pussies."

I channel all the rage I've felt during a lifetime, looking back at him. "I'd like to see you fucking try."

Billy waves his knife between Chase and me, his evil smile ever apparent.

"Yeah, you fucking loser . . ." Chase antagonizes, drawing Billy's eyes. "Why don't you try and kill us? Or are you scared we'll kick your townie ass?"

That's all it takes. Billy charges, but I move forward and duck as the knife slices overhead. I ram my shoulder into his stomach, taking us both down to the ground.

We fall with a thud, and I yell to Chase to get the knife, but as he moves in, Billy rolls away from me onto one knee, then brings the shiny blade straight down into Chase's thigh.

He howls as Billy twists the blade in. I scramble toward them, then wrap my arm around Billy's neck, not feeling any pain. I dig my heels into the ground as I try to pull him away from Chase. He falls to the ground, crying out.

"Fuck . . . fuck!"

Evie runs to him and presses her hand down over the wound as Billy tries to stab me over his shoulder, but I grab his wrist with my free hand as he tries to slice the blade through the air.

"Fuck you, you piece of shit," I growl and then headbutt him. "That's for my best friend, you motherfucker."

"There's too much blood," Evie screams, and I see Goldie run to them.

Billy uses the moment to knock the back of his head into my nose. I fall back, hearing the crack of the broken bones as blood gushes out.

"Noah," Goldie screams and then starts toward me, but I reach up and grab Billy's wrist again, struggling with it and flailing in the air as we both fight to stand to get the upper hand.

"Get Chase to the boat," I tell her as Billy stands up first, using his weight to turn the knife toward my face.

Goldie screams my name again as she runs toward me, and I'm begging her to get out of here when Evie shows up out of nowhere and jumps on his back.

He rips himself away from me, turning with her on his back, before she bites down on his ear.

"Bitch," he screams, then throws her to the ground and kicks her. I push to my feet, but Goldie grabs my arm, and as I look back at her, I feel it.

The knife cuts like butter into my lower back. My mouth falls open as Goldie's hands cover her mouth and tears fill her eyes.

I drop my eyes to the front of my stomach, half expecting to see the knife tip come out the front of me.

"Run," I breathe out, looking at her face.

But Billy pushes me aside and steps in front of her. He grabs her by the throat and squeezes, and I watch as all the life goes out of her.

*If she's hurt, it's because I let it happen.*

"You had your chance to be with me. To be my daughter, but you chose him. You're no better than his mother. So now I'm gonna kill you like I should've done to her the first time. Now let's let him watch."

He spins her around, her back to him, as he holds my baby by her throat. Her beautiful green eyes are half blinking as he chokes the life out of her before raising his knife in the air.

"Now she's mine."

With all that's left in me I spring forward as Billy stabs the air, aiming right for her chest, and I knock her from his grip. She plummets sideways as my body thrusts into his, and we both fall to the ground.

Billy's on his back, his eyes wide, as I lie on top of him and stare down at him. Because he's stabbed himself directly in the chest.

His breaths shudder as he stares up at me. My palm hits the ground to steady myself as I hear Goldie choking in air. I straddle Billy and wrap my hand around his fucking butcher knife before I pull it out slowly.

"She'll never be yours."

I raise the silverish metal above my head and lock eyes with him, seeing fear.

"Over my dead body."

I hammer the knife down, driving it through his heart with every ounce of strength I have left. He sucks in a loud breath before a long soft exhale finally exorcises him from my fucking life.

He's dead.

I fall beside him, staring up at the sky as I pant. Goldie scrambles over to me and kisses my face as I cough and look back at her.

"It's over, baby. It's all over."

She's kissing me as I lie there before we hear, "Cue the credits."

Chase's voice is weak but he's fucking alive, and so is Evie, because she says "Shut the fuck up" from where she's lying, which makes me laugh, then groan.

Goldie kisses my lips as the sound of sirens grows louder and louder.

"If this were a movie, you'd be the hero," she says quietly.

"Oh yeah," I say back. "I'd much rather be your husband."

"Deal." She helps me up as Evie does the same for Chase, and we hobble toward help like a band of busted-up vigilantes.

A long time ago, I learned from my favorite girl that once you find your family, you'll do anything to keep them.

And these three are mine, so I killed for them.

# Chapter Thirty-Three

***Camp Weonoke, present day***

An ambulance burned up the road before screeching to a stop on the grass next to some fire trucks sitting idle. First responders jumped into action, kicking up clouds of dust around the flashing red lights that streaked through the night sky.

The scene was pandemonium.

The four of them stood watching. Goldie squeezed Noah's hand as Evie supported Chase's weight.

They watched the scene like it was a movie.

A single female reporter in a navy blazer stared into the lens of a camera like a Gale Weathers impersonator.

"We're live on the scene here at Camp Weonoke, where over thirty years ago an unbelievable tragedy befell this vibrant summer camp. In a place where children gleefully spent their summers, six camp counselors fought for their lives, ultimately ending with only one survivor. Today, a few heroes decided to paint a different picture . . ."

The camera panned right, directly on the four as they stared back. Noah turned his head to Goldie's and looked down at her.

"Can we get out of here and into an ambulance?" she whispered.

"Yes, please," Chase said in agreement. "I'd like to stop bleeding to death."

"And I don't think you're supposed to lift heavy things with a concussion," Evie threw in.

Noah took a deep breath and looked around before he nodded. "Yeah, there's nothing here for me anymore."

He didn't only mean the camp. His old life was finally dead and buried.

Noah stretched his arm over Goldie's shoulder and pulled her close as they walked back down the path, past the cameras and the questions, not stopping until they reached the medics.

"Are we going to be okay?" Goldie asked, blinking her green eyes at him.

Noah's brows drew together as he cradled her face. "Killer . . ."

She wrinkled her forehead because the nickname felt a bit too on the nose, considering her DNA.

Noah smirked and corrected himself. "Rexy, we're gonna be just fine, because we've always got each other."

# Chapter Thirty-Four

## Goldie

"Call in."

Noah's voice is full of gravel, the way it always is in the morning when he first wakes up. And it's seductive. I grin, holding the phone between my ear and shoulder as I put my boot on, picturing him rubbing his chest.

"I can't. You know that. Plus, I don't think you're seeing this through the correct fiscal lenses. For those of us who are still aspiring to greatness but living in 'assistant to' floral positions, it's great. Work helps with those little things like eating and buying new furniture for our new apartment."

He laughs. And I love the sound.

The thought makes me smile—even though these last two weeks have been hell. We were almost killed. There were too many interviews with detectives that led to conversations about his legal name change to Noah Adler, which I supported. But it was all stressful. He also got the job in LA, which meant we'd had to separate again.

But that bump in the road is only temporary because today is my last day at work, and then I'm boarding a plane and landing just in time to watch the sunrise with my man.

"Trust me," I tease, "the wait will be worth it . . . I have see-through lingerie."

He groans, and this time I laugh, which makes me drop my purse while trying to gather all my stuff like a hot mess hoarder.

I sit on a chair by my sister's entryway as I plop everything in my hands onto my lap, then put on my jacket and gloves. It's colder than usual for November. But really, I just want to soak him up a little bit longer.

"I miss you," I breathe out.

He sighs, and I can almost feel it.

"Rexy, trust me. I miss you more." A meow in the background makes a smile peek out as I pick at the broken polish on my nails. "And I'm not the only one," he groans. "I've been waiting for her to shit in my shoe again, but I think she's too sad for spite."

Leave it to me to reconcile a broken home.

"Her love is justified. I feed her the good stuff. But I'm glad everyone's sad because it's me that can barely eat," I tease. "I'm wasting away over here. That's how much I miss the two of you. It's honestly worrisome. I might have to call someone soon, like Domino's."

He chuckles. "Funny, because I haven't slept in two weeks. I've been a zombie. Bloodshot eyes and all. I bet I get fired soon."

I kick my feet out, crossing them at the ankle. I love this game.

"Well, at least you can sue for discrimination. Yesterday, I cried all day. The neighbors called the cops. Thought I was unwell, in need of—"

"Sweet lovin'?" he tosses out, cutting me off and making me smile.

"Mmm. Yeah, I think that *was* the professional diagnosis. One glass of wine and a hefty injection of—"

"Protein? I hear a balanced diet can really improve your mood."

As his voice wafts through the phone again like pheromones, I giggle and hear him yawn, so I close my eyes, trying to picture exactly where he is in our new bedroom and what that looks like.

"All that's sad for you. But honestly, I win because I've been contemplating entering one of those slapping contests . . . just so I can feel again."

I laugh loudly. "You're stupid."

"I'm at rock bottom," he whines in the most boyish way, and it melts me. "I'm two seconds away from calling your job and begging them to give me my baby." He groans. "Call out . . . call out, call out. Quit and leave right now. I promise I'll spend all night eating whipped cream off your body."

I fake cry but mean it, stomping both feet on my hardwood floors.

"You're the worst," I gripe, gathering all my crap off my lap and fumbling before shoving it in my purse. With a smile, I add, "I thought you were a feminist. You're a terrible boyfriend not to support my dreams of money and respect."

He laughs like a villain while I head to my front door, then lock it behind me as I leave.

"Joke's on you, Rexy. I am supporting your dreams. I'll give you plenty to write about. Something I would've thought my writer girlfriend would appreciate. Then again, we've been apart for two weeks, and not even one poem for me?"

I laugh again. He's ridiculous. "Are you accusing me of not being a romantic? How dare you, sir."

I walk to my car through the slushy, half-melted snow before clicking it open and tossing my purse inside, then put my phone on speaker. He's still talking shit as I slide inside and start the car, pulling my glove off with my teeth and holding it there while I type. If he could see me, the look on my face would give away what's about to come.

The swishing sound of my message makes my brows rise in anticipation. He chuckles.

"Hold, please. I suddenly have a very important text to read."

I see the bubbles populate on our text chain. Noah must put me on speaker because he recites it aloud.

"Roses are red. Violets are blue. Stop giving me shit, or I'll get a pew-pew."

The laughter from his end of the phone bursts through the speaker, making me do the same before I speak over it.

"Now, say goodbye to me," I tell him. "And say that you'll be miserable until tomorrow, when we worship each other on a blanket in front of the fireplace. I'm bringing snacks."

I bite my lip. "You are the snack, but fine," he says, giving in, and it's way too attractive. "Goodbye . . ." He mumbles the rest like one big run-on sentence. "See you tomorrow, when we worship each other on a blanket in front of the ocean."

"'Kay, bye."

A long beat of silence hangs there, neither of us hanging up. The way I love him tugs at my whole body, trying to get out.

But then Noah says, "Bye, Rexy."

I have to let out a long breath before checking myself in the mirror. *This time tomorrow, your life starts all over again,* I think to myself with a smile before I pull onto the street, working on autopilot.

The drive is fast, mostly because I'm still stuck in my thoughts, until I park and finally zap back into the present.

It's bittersweet to say goodbye to work. I'm determined to write in Los Angeles, but I'll miss this place and the people inside it.

I stay inside my head the whole way in, over the gravel from my space in the back of the brick building to the moment I touch the brass door handle. I don't even look up until it's swinging open.

The smell almost knocks me off my feet first. "Fragrant" isn't the correct word. This is an assault on my senses. Like when little kids get into their mom's perfume and put every bottle on.

Every kind of arrangement, big and small, from roses to lilies, litters the floor and most of the counter space. The entire back stockroom is vases and boxes of chocolates with little stuffed animal bears adorned with sweaters that say *I love you beary much.*

"Oh my god," I let out, shock hitting me hard as I lock eyes with Lee, who's nodding in agreement with my shock.

I point to the contemporary Garden of Eden, rubbing my glossy lips together.

"Are all these deliveries for today? Were you guys trying to make it so I'd never want to come back?"

"Yep." Lee laughs. "We don't even have many flowers left. We're down to only what's left in the front room cases to sell."

My eyes are bugging out. It's way more than I anticipated delivering today. I really will be here until I leave for the airport.

"Wow. Okay," I breathe out. "Let me put my purse and coat away, and I'll start loading the van. Yay, love, I guess. It's not even Valentine's Day."

He gives me a thumbs-up as he looks away. "The good thing is, they're pretty much all going to the same place. You're just going to have to do multiple runs there."

I slide my purse under a counter, having to teeter over two dozen roses. "No way. All of these are for the same person?" I look around again. "That's so romantic. God, can you imagine being that girl?"

Lee smirks. "Bet she's really good with her hands."

"Eww," I counter, trading my coat for my work apron from the hooks on the back wall. "Don't ruin it. It's so romantic."

"Or a good apology."

"I said don't ruin it." I laugh.

I wrap the long strings around my waist before tying them in a bow, all while picturing some random woman's joy.

"Lucky girl," I say to myself.

But as I lean down to grab the first vaseful of gorgeous violets, Lee looks up from some daffodils he's wrapping. "Hold up. Start with the ones in the front room."

My head snaps up. "The front room? That's full too. Stop it . . ."

I start walking that way, making my way through the floral maze. Out of habit, I put my hands in the front pocket of the apron before my shoulder connects with the swinging door. I say, "Jesus, what is this guy trying to prove?"

But the moment I'm through, I freeze. All the air in my body is sucked out. Because what . . . What is happening? Noah's standing in the middle of the room, vases and vases of baby's breath packed in around him.

*My favorites.*

He smiles at me. "I'd say he's trying to prove he loves you."

"What?" My fingers instantly cover my mouth as I stare back at him, still unable to speak. Because . . . oh my god. I can feel myself blink too many times. And my heart's thumping at an irregular rate.

He lets out a nervous breath.

"Goldie, I've been looking for the right moment to do this again, and I swear, everything kept making it impossible. So I decided it couldn't wait any longer."

He starts walking toward me, and goose bumps explode over my arms.

I keep glancing at the bushel of wildflowers mixed with my favorites in his hand and back to his eyes as he speaks.

"I figured if all the orders were for you, they'd have to give you the day off."

*Genius.* I shake my head as I bite my bottom lip, still feeling like I can't process what's happening. My head swings over my shoulder, then back to him, before I repeat what he's just said.

"The ones in the back are for me too? Wait . . ." My voice is shaky. "You told me to call in . . . How are you here? What's happening?"

*He bought me all the flowers. All of them.*

Noah grins, then stops in front of me and forces me to look up at his face.

"It's called skillful distraction. Although I did get worried for a minute I was too convincing and would have to think of a plan B."

The flowers in his hand make it into mine. Not that I realize it because I feel like I'm having an out-of-body experience. And none of the three million thoughts whirling around in my head seem to stay in one place long enough for me to grab hold.

But then he looks at me. Really looks at me. And instead of feeling like I'm floating, I feel tethered to him, like I always do.

"I don't know if this is the perfect moment . . ." Noah rubs the back of his neck, because that's what he does when he's nervous, and his eyes drop to my lips before locking on my eyes. "But I hope so because you have my heart . . . You always have. I asked you to marry me in this city once. And I'm gonna do it again because I love you, Goldie Monroe."

*Am I blinking? Am I breathing?*

His knuckles brush my jaw. "Baby . . . did you hear me?"

My chest feels tight, and I know my hands are starting to shake. Butterflies cyclone in my stomach as I look up at him.

"I already said 'deal'; what more do you want from me?" I whisper with a grin.

Noah bends down, our faces so close we're sharing all the air as he grins back.

"Good, because everyone's waiting at the courthouse—I'm asking you to marry me today."

"Say it again," I add as his fingers tickle along my jaw.

"Marry me today," he breathes, our foreheads touching. "I am so fucking in love with you."

Pure joy washes over me as I throw my arms around his neck and seal our lips, saying yes to him over and over between kisses.

"I love you too. I love you. Love you. Love you. Love you. Yes. Yes. Yes."

Noah holds me tight, his arms wrapped around my rib cage as he lifts me off the ground. And we kiss for what feels like an eternity until I pull away, a hazy glimmer in my eyes like I'm coming out of the best dream.

And I am.

"Mr. and Mrs. Noah Adler," he whispers.

"I like the way that sounds, me plus you, forever."

# Epilogue

***Eighteen months later***

The theater's dark, and everyone's silent. Not even the sound of popcorn is interrupting the hero's monologue. While the music builds, I squeeze Noah's hand, not even blinking as I watch the movie . . . my movie.

"Honeysuckle, we're gonna be just fine because we've always got each other."

The camera pans to the sunset as the two actors kiss passionately before fading out. Applause erupts, and I smile as I turn my head toward Noah.

He smiles back. "Okay . . . 'honeysuckle,' though?"

I chuckle playfully and smack his shoulder. "I had to pick my battles."

Over a year ago, as therapy, I wrote our real life into a screenplay. It was this weird kind of empowering idea I had one night as I colored Noah's tattoos. The journey to find my birth parents and stop shaming myself for wanting a deeper self-discovery had definitely turned left when I'd turned right, but in the end, it made me realize that I decide who I am and what that means. Nobody else. I guess I had to go through it all to finally find me.

I suppose it was relatable because, atypically of Hollywood, not only was it picked up immediately, but the movie was made in record time.

So today Noah and I invited those closest to us to a private screening before the release date.

The lights come up as my mom leans forward from the seats behind us.

"Baby, I loved it. But I also hate it because when I think back to what could've happened . . ."

She's crying again. I stand from my seat and turn to hug her. "Mom, I'm okay and alive."

She hugs me back before releasing me to rub Noah's shoulder.

"I know, and I have my favorite son-in-law to thank for that."

He gives her a wink. Telling my parents all the gruesome details was awful, but for Noah it was worse because he still felt responsible. However, in true Camilla and Stephen glory, not only did they understand, but they also welcomed him into our family without ever second-guessing their decision.

Chase leans over him, looking at me with his brows raised.

"I personally would like to say thank you for the accurate representation of my character. Because I think we can all agree he's a bit of a scene stealer. And a hunk."

"Oh my god. Why did you invite him?" Evie groans as my dad taps her leg, giving her a subtle hint to be nicer.

She won't be. It doesn't matter that Chase saved her life. I laugh and wrap my arms around Noah's neck as he stands up.

He looks down at me, adoringly, as I say, "Hey, thanks for being such a sexy muse."

"You're welcome, Mrs. Adler."

I smile wider.

Noah pats my ass. "I'm gonna go talk to my friends for a minute. I'll be right back, okay?"

I nod. "'Kay, I'm gonna head to the bathroom anyway. Meet me out in the lobby?"

I start to leave, then look back over my shoulder, "Grab some of those chocolate-covered raisins for me, too, please."

"Done, Rexy."

My smile never leaves as I leave the theater. I glance back at him, loving watching him just being a normal guy with his friends. I run my hands through my hair and get lost in my happy thoughts as I walk to the ladies' room.

The theater is empty and quiet, a small neighborhood one in the Southern California town we now split our time living in as we shuttle between Los Angeles and Boston. Since Noah's new design job came with the luxury of working from home, we're now bicoastal. He can still peek his head into the Los Angeles office without having to move from our beloved Beacon Hill.

My palm hits the bathroom door as I push it open. The quiet hits me again, with only the sound of my footsteps echoing over the tile.

I push against the first stall door, but it's locked, which makes me frown and bend to look underneath—no feet.

"Huh," I say to myself, thinking it's probably out of order.

I look over at the mirrors and check out my hair as I walk a few more doors down and push one open.

It gives, so I walk inside and lock the door. I pull a seat cover out, place it over the porcelain, and shimmy my jeans and panties down. I'm humming to myself as I sit and relieve my bladder, but as I reach for the paper, a loud bang interrupts my thoughts.

The paper sits idle in my hand. "Hello?"

Nothing. No answer, no sound. I bend forward between my legs to look, but I don't see anything or anyone.

I wipe quickly before I stand, and my hand hangs in the air in front of the lock as panic sets in.

*I'm fine. I'm fine. There are no monsters, just the here and now.*

But I take a deep, shaky breath, open the stall, and step out quickly.

The room's empty. I shift as I look around with a frown. My eyes go from mirror to mirror, peering through them to each stall, before I land on the farthest one away.

Seconds feel like minutes, and my body feels chilled as if my veins are on ice.

The door is slightly ajar, but none of them were when I came in.

Slowly I bend down again and look under the stalls, seeing nothing, so I put one foot in front of the other as I walk toward the cracked bathroom stall door.

The sound of my pulse throbs in my ears as I get closer. My fingers twitch because my hand is shaking as I reach out. Just my fingertips lead the way as I push it open slowly, trembling on the inside.

*Go. Look. Do it.*

I step quickly into view, just as the bathroom door swings open, hitting the wall with a bang. "Goldie."

I scream, hand over my heart, as I jump what feels like ten feet in the air.

"Oh my god. What is wrong with you?" I rush out.

My sister's standing in the entrance of the bathroom, looking at me like I'm insane. But that's fair, because I'm breathless and scared shitless as I glare at her.

"Sorry . . . I have to pee. What are you doing?"

I tuck my hair behind my ears. "I was . . . nothing."

She shrugs as she walks toward the stall that's out of order. "Wait for me . . . Mom's trying to make a love connection with me and Chase again. I swear she'd force an arranged marriage just because he was stabbed in the leg."

I chuckle as I point to where she's walking. "That's out of—"

Before I can finish, the door squeaks open, making me frown, but as she turns her head, Evie lets out a bloodcurdling scream.

My heart stops and drops into my stomach as I run to her, and we both stare inside, clutching each other as fear takes control.

A human heart has been staked to the wall, blood dripping down to the floor.

My eyes lift to the wall. Two words smeared above.

**She's mine.**

# Acknowledgments

Writing these acknowledgments makes me smile because it's been a wild and insanely fun ride. I hoped for so long to be here, writing a book like this, with a team like this, and it's finally all real. It feels magical, and I need to say thank you.

So, in no particular order other than being all the loves of my life, here goes:

Maria Gomez and Lindsey Faber at Montlake—Thank you for being the most amazing editor duo. And for allowing me to be as creative as I wanted to be. For always making me feel seen, heard, and uplifted. You're the best at what you do, and I'm so thankful for you.

My agent Stacey Graham—You're always right. Which is why you're the very best agent. I don't deserve you, but I'm never letting go.

Caroline Teagle Johnson—The ultimate cover, and it rocks my world.

Sarah Pierce—I almost can't remember a time when we didn't know each other. The way you always cheer me on and believe in me is a gift I will never take for granted. You are the best assistant, friend, hype girl, and comic relief I could ask for.

Serena McDonald—You keep me sane. And that is not an easy task. Thank you for always being levelheaded and ready for a challenge. I appreciate you more than you know.

Gretchen Eddy—May we always have long conversations about plots I will inevitably change three hundred times.

Sandy—You deserve a medal for cleaning up what I say so that it's readable. One day I'll remember to put the commas in all the correct places, but until then I'm stuck to you like glue.

To my betas and sensitivity readers—your feedback was an immeasurable gift.

To my readers—You read, hype, review, and support me like I didn't know was possible. I love you so much, and I appreciate you every day for wanting to read the stories I write.

Last but not least, my friends and family—I'm so lucky to have people around me who always cheer me on and irrationally believe that I will be the largest success in history. You guys make me think I can do anything. And I love you for that. But the truth is, I'm only cool because you love me.

## About the Author

Trilina Pucci, a #1 Amazon and *USA Today* bestselling author, is a connoisseur of pop culture and Sanpellegrino, but her true passion lies in crafting tantalizing romantic novels that delve into the depths of desire, emotion, and hearty belly laughs.

When she's not penning steamy love stories, you'll find her indulging in Netflix marathons and Korean dramas. To connect with the author and learn more about her work, visit her on Instagram (@authortrilinapucci), Facebook (https://facebook.com/trilinapuccibooks), TikTok (@authortrilinapucci), and BookBub (www.bookbub.com/authors/trilina-pucci).